PRAISE FOR

CIJI WARE'S

HISTORICAL FICTION

"A mesmerizing blend of sizzling romance, history, love, and honor… Ciji Ware has written an unforgettable tale."

—The Burton Review

"A fascinating portrayal… with characters convincingly drawn from history. Ware again proves she can intertwine fact and fiction to create an entertaining and harmonious whole."

—*Publishers Weekly*

"A deliciously wonderful novel of fiction and history culminating into a rich historical romance filled with tender affection and wrenching heartache… absolutely brilliant."

—Rundpinne

"With its intriguing characters, exciting dialogue, and a highly interesting woman at the center of it all, *Island of the Swans* is a must read."

—Night Owl Romance, Reviewer Top Pick

"A great historical fiction author… Ciji Ware certainly knows how to touch hearts."

—Reading Extravaganza

"Ciji Ware is a master storyteller."

—Libby's Library News

"Quite an ambitious work of historical fiction. I so appreciated the depth and complexity of it and the historical picture that Ciji Ware creates."

—Medieval Bookworm

"A masterpiece read; an epic on its own."

—Enchanted by Josephine

"A historical novel so lively and intriguing, you don't realize you've learned anything till after you close the book. Exciting, entertaining, and enlightening."

—*Literary Times*

"A well-researched and entertaining novel... excellent."

—*Library Journal*

A RACE TO SPLENDOR

CIJI WARE

sourcebooks
landmark

Published by Sourcebooks Landmark, an imprint of Sourcebooks, Inc.
P.O. Box 4410, Naperville, Illinois 60567-4410
(630) 961-3900
FAX: (630) 961-2168
www.sourcebooks.com

Library of Congress Cataloging-in-Publication Data

Ware, Ciji.
  A race to splendor / by Ciji Ware.
    p. cm.
  1. Women architects—California—Fiction. 2. Architects—California—Fiction.
3. San Francisco Earthquake and Fire, Calif., 1906—Fiction. 4. San Francisco
(Calif.)—History—20th century—Fiction. I. Title.
  PS3573.A7435R33 2011
  813'.54—dc22
                                2010049267

Printed and bound in the United States of America
VP 10 9 8 7 6 5 4 3 2 1

This novel is dedicated to:
JOY McCULLOUGH WARE, my loving sister
with whom I share a California childhood and
a passion for writing;

LOY, our great-grandmother's Chinese houseboy
whom Elfie McCullough treated like a slave and
whose last name we never knew;

my husband, TONY COOK, whose refined sensibilities,
generosity of spirit, and ability to make me laugh
create a journey worth taking;

JENNIFER JAHNER, whose sure eye
dug me out of the rubble;

and the nameless Chinese forced into prostitution
who perished in the devastating 1906 San Francisco
earthquake and fire—and whose numbers weren't
included in the official death toll.

Author's Note

SOMETIMES THE SEEDS OF an historical novel sprout many decades after they're sown.

And so it is with great pleasure that *A Race to Splendor,* published by Sourcebooks Landmark in April 2011, commemorates not only the 105th anniversary of the 1906 San Francisco earthquake and firestorm, but also a germ of an idea that probably began to gestate when I was sixteen years old.

A figure not necessarily heralded nationally in telling the story of San Francisco's remarkable recovery from utter devastation is Julia Morgan, the first licensed woman architect in California who accepted the task of restoring the fabled but deeply scarred Fairmont Hotel atop Nob Hill.

I first heard Morgan's name as a teenager when I stood with a gaggle of "grown-ups" in the forecourt of Hearst Castle, the fantastical Shangri-la built during the years 1919 through 1947 in Central California by the newspaper baron, William Randolph Hearst. The guide drew our attention to the massive structure's wedding-cake towers and, later, the incredibly ornate wood-paneled interiors. During a pause, I timidly raised my hand.

"Who designed this place?" I asked, awed by its over-the-top magnificence.

"Julia Morgan," the guide said, and in the next breath announced, "Ladies and gentlemen, shall we step into the reception hall?"

I remember thinking, "Wow! A *woman* designed and built this?" but in those pre-feminist days, I posed no follow-up questions for the taciturn tour guide who obviously felt it was more important to keep to the schedule than waste time elaborating on some "lady that old man Hearst had hired back then." (These days Morgan merits her own, full page on the Hearst Castle-California State Park website.)

In the late 1990s, I "re-encountered" California's preeminent woman architect when my husband and I moved from Los Angeles to San Francisco and rented a flat in an early twentieth-century apartment building on Nob Hill, designed by none other than... Julia Morgan.

Remembering that moment of wonder at Hearst Castle so long ago, I pressed our building manager for more details and learned that Morgan was also the architect who won the post-quake commission to restore the *beaux arts*-styled Fairmont Hotel on Mason and California streets, located only a few blocks from our second-floor apartment at Taylor and Jackson.

The speculation was that the female doctor who hired Morgan in 1906 to replace her home and infirmary neighboring the Fairmont after her original buildings were destroyed by the 8.25 temblor was either the architect's personal physician, a sorority sister, or classmate at UC Berkeley where Julia Morgan had received a degree in engineering in 1894—the only woman student in the entire department. Talk about your Old Girls Network!

After graduating from Berkeley, Morgan had gone on to L'Ecole des Beaux Arts in Paris and received her diploma in architecture, the first woman in the world to gain that honor.

As my husband and I settled into our Northern California environment, I was curious to learn more about my new city and the cataclysmic 1906 event. I soon stumbled across more material relating to Julia Morgan's restoration of the Fairmont, including insurance pictures of the hotel's interior destruction and the absolute obliteration of the surrounding area, including harrowing images of the corner at Taylor and Jackson, the exact spot where we were then living!

What historical novelist could resist such a call to her computer?

Added to this was discovering that Morgan, who was only thirty-four when she signed on to restore the Fairmont, had a nearly morbid abhorrence of my former profession, journalism. She rarely gave interviews and despised notoriety. Anyone who worked for her and ran afoul of her edict to "let my buildings speak for themselves" suffered harsh reprimands.

I also found it curious that there wasn't much evidence that Julia Morgan made a practice of mentoring *other* women architects coming along behind her—and from that observation sprang the plot of this book.

I have chosen to cast the "real" Julia Morgan as a secondary character, and tell the story of San Francisco's initial recovery from the devastating quake and fire, along with its subsequent "race to splendor," through the lens of a composite heroine drawn from the lives of the people who worked for or knew this extraordinarily talented trailblazer.

After Julia Morgan, no other woman would graduate in architecture from L'Ecole des Beaux Arts for years to come. However, in this novel, I pit the fictional Amelia Hunter Bradshaw, determined to follow in Morgan's footsteps, against J.D. Thayer, a tall, dark, and dangerous young entrepreneur who vows *his* hotel will open before the Fairmont, even if he has to resort to some less-than-aboveboard tactics to accomplish this feat.

As with other heroines I've created in my historical novels, I wanted Amelia's story, based on the facts that are known about this era, to illustrate how a few, feisty women overcame unimaginable obstacles to forge careers in formerly all-male realms—in this instance, that of designing and constructing buildings. What makes these women even more noteworthy is that, despite tumultuous times in post-quake San Francisco, some also fought hard to achieve that elusive balance between work, love, personal relationships, and everyday life.

Given the fact that the San Francisco earthquake rendered some four hundred city blocks a pile of cinders and left 250,000 of its citizens homeless for up to two-and-a-half years, the novel focuses on the whirlwind competition between several legendary hotels vying to re-open their doors *before* the first anniversary of the quake in April 1907—putting to lie the dire predictions that the City by the Bay was "Pompeii, never to rise again."

Remember when Bette Davis declared in the classic film, *All About Eve*, "You'd better fasten your seat belts?" As with all earthquakes, what follows is likely to be a bumpy ride...

Ciji Ware
Sausalito, California

Ciji Ware enjoys hearing from readers at www.cijiware.com

California 1906

A grave danger lurked below the placid crust,
beneath the cypress trees clinging to cliffs,
under eucalyptus and sea grass and soil and sand,
lulled by pulsing tides sweeping in and out of San Francisco Bay
and along the coast of western North America.
For eons, this capricious natural force tiptoed
along tectonic sheets of layered rock,
shifting, settling, sending coded warnings of its impending wrath.
Poised like a predator,
the unspent power waited, silent and sinister,
for the uncharted moment when it would explode
from its compacted lair to confront each soul who crossed its path
—and teach humility to all who survived its brutal assault.

—Anonymous

PROLOGUE

16 February 1906
No. 7 Rue de Lille, Paris

By post to:
Miss Julia Morgan, Architect
456 Montgomery Street
San Francisco, California
United States of America

My dear Julia:

I write to you both in sorrow and elation—the sorrow, as you can well imagine, occasioned by the news last month of the passing of my adored grandfather, Charles McQuinty Hunter.

I am sure you have read by now in some vile publication of our most recent family disgrace involving my father and our beloved Bay View. The unhappy news of my grandfather's death and the loss of our family's hotel due to my father's misdeeds arrived in the person of Mother herself, standing at my very door on the Rue de Lille, surrounded by a clutch of massive trunks. Presently, she refuses to return home, despite my own pending departure from Paris for the City by the Bay.

Needless to say, the elation I felt over finishing my architecture degree now hardly seems anything to celebrate.

Even so, I wish you to be the first to know that I have, indeed, passed my final examinations at L'École des Beaux Arts—and, as you did, on the first try!

According to the French, at least, I am now a full-fledged architect "comme Mlle. Julia Morgan"—although I still must pass the California State Licensing Exam and be judged a bona fide American practitioner of the "building arts" in a region long known for its terra infirma.

When I look back at these years of hard work, I am humbled to recall how you bravely forged the way. Of course, like yourself, I have had to withstand the slings and arrows of disgruntled professors and fellow students at L'École who do not wish a female in their midst, but I have survived by smiling sweetly—and silently counting to ten.

I will be forever grateful to you for your benevolence and enduring support dating as far back as my entry into the engineering program at the University of California at Berkeley. Your letters of encouragement to me here in Paris spurred me forward when I seriously thought many times of quitting the entire enterprise.

I am very impressed to learn that you have founded your own practice on Montgomery Street. You once said that you might offer me a drafting table in your San Francisco office, "but only on condition that you earn your certificate." Well, now that I have officially done so, I lay claim to your proposal to work for you—if the offer still stands.

I will get in touch with you immediately upon my arrival. It would appear that I am very much in need of becoming instantly self-supporting, especially if I am to legally challenge my father's right to hazard my legacy as he has—and to contest the "new" owner of the Bay View Hotel, James Diaz Thayer, whose complicity in that all-night game of chance has the markings of a man of predatory temperament, utterly without honor.

And so, with an anxious, heavy heart, I now pack my trunk and portmanteau. On Friday, I sail on the City of Paris for New York, and thence by train to California. I yearn to see the fairest city of all—San Francisco—and to once again greet fast friends like you, dear Julia.

I pray this letter arrives home before I do, so you will know I am

Most Sincerely Yours,
Amelia Hunter Bradshaw

CHAPTER 1

J AMES DIAZ THAYER SCOOPED the deck of cards bearing his initials into a pile on top of the late Charlie Hunter's desk in the bowels of Nob Hill's celebrated Bay View Hotel.

"You lose again, my friend," J.D. announced to Henry Bradshaw, the deceased Hunter's son-in-law. "I not only now own this hotel, but virtually the clothes on your back."

The losing poker player's bloodshot eyes bulged below his perspiring brow in an alarming fashion. Bradshaw was so drunk by now, his words were barely intelligible.

"I wan' a rematch... for the hotel, theesh time. *And* the gamblin' club. The whole damnable lot!"

J.D. ignored these slurred demands and shifted his gaze to his other business associate, Ezra Kemp, who repeatedly stroked his mutton-chop whiskers from ear to chin, as if the recurring motion might offer solace for his own recent losses to J.D.

Fatigue strained Thayer's usually rigid self-control and he slapped a fist on his desktop. "Now, get out of here! The both of you! For God sake, we've been here all night. I've had no sleep and I have a mountain of things to do to get this place ready for the gambling club's opening next week."

At that same moment, the office door slammed against the wall and a slender young woman stood ramrod straight at the threshold. Thayer and Kemp jerked their heads in surprise while Henry Bradshaw took one look at the visitor and slumped in his chair.

The intruder gazed directly at the disheveled creature grasping the chair's arms for support as she addressed all three.

"Gentlemen, if this is a meeting about the future of the Bay View Hotel and that shoddy, disgraceful gambling club you've erected next door, you had better include *me*."

J.D. reckoned the young woman was dressed too conservatively to be a potential barkeep or disgruntled upstairs maid seeking back wages. She was slim and held herself erect as if she'd been born with a book on her head. She had appealing wisps of dark brown hair escaping her upswept hairstyle, and from her well-formed earlobes, black marcasite fobs sparkled fetchingly against her graceful neck. Though hidden beneath a beautifully tailored jacket and a gored skirt brushing the tips of expensive kid boots, he considered her fine figure, which had little need of a corset to render a waist as trim as hers.

Nor did she appear wanting in confidence. In fact, her self-assured demeanor indicated that she had dealt with difficult men before and wasn't in the slightest intimidated by them.

"And just who might you be?" J.D. asked, intrigued by this sudden and rather welcomed interruption.

"A-Amelia…" stuttered Henry Bradshaw, slumping lower after an unsuccessful attempt to heave himself out of his chair. "Your train… the ferry… I-I'm sorry, daughter," he slurred. "Business prevented me—"

"Ah, yes, business." She advanced into the room a few feet. "Mr. Thayer has the right idea, though." Her glance in his direction bordered on contemptuous. "There'll be no more rounds of poker because, as of this minute, gambling is strictly prohibited at the Bay View. I also demand you immediately cease additional construction of that ill-built edifice out there, and that you, Mr. Thayer, remove yourself and that concubine of yours from the Hunter family suite upstairs."

So their fiery visitor had met Ling Lee on her way down to the basement office, thought J.D.

Amelia's voice wavered only slightly as she continued her tirade.

"There will be no gambling or other illicit activities at this hotel," she declared. "This was my grandfather's *home*, as well as his business—and it is now mine. I intend to take full possession of it. *Now*."

Her sweeping gaze indicated all three men were being addressed. "If you have any questions about the ownership and operation of this hotel, you can take them up with my grandfather's lawyer. He assures me that my father had no right to wager my newly inherited legacy while I was studying in France, and therefore the transference of this property to Mr. Thayer by virtue of a poker game was entirely illegal."

Aha, J.D. thought. So the daughter has returned from Paris, even as the mother had fled to the same city. Well, he could deal with this. He'd even half expected it, given what he'd already learned about a woman he'd known when he was in knee britches and she but a child, but hadn't seen in years.

So this is the celebrated Amelia Hunter Bradshaw, newly minted architect.

J.D. summoned a welcoming smile. "Please, Miss Bradshaw, do come in."

"Yes, indeed," Kemp said, hastily gesturing for her to be seated. "Perhaps you'd like a cup of tea?"

Ignoring the offer, she snapped, "And you, I presume, are Ezra Kemp."

"I am," Kemp said, eyeing her warily.

She hadn't asked J.D.'s name, so he assumed she remembered they'd once attended elementary school together and that, for a time, their mothers had been social friends. However, Miss Bradshaw was currently ignoring him completely, which allowed for enough time to conclude she'd grown into a comely enough creature—if one's tastes ran to attractive, lecturing schoolmarms.

"Well, Mr. Kemp, rather than tea, I'd ask *you*—and Mr. Thayer—to remove yourselves from the premises, forthwith."

Before Kemp could express his consternation, J.D. intervened. "As difficult as this may be for you to accept, Miss Bradshaw, the fact is, I *own* the Bay View now, fair and square. Our club—which Mr. Kemp, here, and I financed and annexed to the hotel—is due to open in a week."

She threw him an imperious glance. "I gather that is your *claim*, Mr. Thayer. However, you've built it illegally on *my* property, and thus the opening will be canceled. That new building appears to have been thrown together in a week," she added with disdain. "Trust me, sir, it will *never* be used as a gaming parlor."

"Miss Bradshaw," J.D. said with the politesse of a man who understood the rules of society, even if he didn't obey them, "please do sit down and let us discuss this."

"No, thank you, I prefer standing."

"Well, now. At least tell us why you believe you have the authority to issue orders regarding the Bay View Hotel."

J.D. was amused as well as annoyed. She had sass, all right. Her complexion was stained with color now, and her hands were planted firmly on slender hips clothed by the latest Paris fashion. He had never met an attractive woman for whom flattery was not catnip and therefore he softened his tone.

"According to the newspaper, I understand congratulations are in order on your earning your degree in architecture. Quite an unusual and praiseworthy accomplishment for a young woman, I'd say."

Bradshaw's daughter ignored the compliment and took her time removing her soft kid gloves. J.D. suspected that she was stalling to formulate her next line of attack. She clutched her handbag and lifted her square chin, one feature of her physiognomy not nearly as feminine as her perfect skin and lovely bosom. For the first time she gave him her complete attention.

"I am fully authorized to put an end to the unfair advantage you three took of my grandfather during his last illness, and that especially applies to *you*, Mr. Thayer."

J.D. snapped to attention, scuttling any contemplation of Amelia Hunter Bradshaw as easily biddable.

"*Authorized? By whom?*"

Her accusations were serious and could produce unhappy consequences if they traveled beyond the four walls of her grandfather's former office.

"I have been informed that I am Charles Hunter's sole heir, and as such, the Bay View is under my control. This hotel and its assets were *never* my father's property to hazard in a poker match. Surely you've had a look at my grandfather's updated will and testament?"

Charlie Hunter had signed a new will?

J.D. marveled at how cool and collected she sounded. Yet, how angry. Amelia caught his glance and held it.

"Therefore, Mr. Thayer, the outcome of any boyish games that took place in my absence is meaningless, and whatever business matters you may have conducted here are null and void."

But J.D wasn't really listening. The daughter was now the late Charlie Hunter's *sole* heir? What about the mother—his partner Henry Bradshaw's wife? She had been holy hell to deal with too, with her hysterics and fainting fits, but fortunately for all concerned, she'd simply taken flight while they'd completed their transactions.

Ezra Kemp's startled reaction mirrored J.D.'s own. They both glared at Amelia's father, who stared at his boot tips as if he were about to be ill. Amelia noticed their shifted attention and pointed a well-manicured finger at her father.

"My grandfather never did—and never would—put a known drunkard in charge of the Bay View, and *all* of you know that," Amelia said sharply. "Apparently, when he saw what was happening after his first stroke, he was well enough, thank the Lord, to call in his lawyer, change his will to make me his sole heir, and had it witnessed and notarized, as well."

"Amelia!" Bradshaw exclaimed. "How dare you! I want you to cease this—"

Amelia didn't even take a breath, let alone acknowledge her father's admonishments. "Frankly, I think you so-called partners of Father's knew my grandfather's last wishes very well, but proceeded with this scheme nevertheless."

"Well, well, Henry," J.D. said quietly. He drew a narrowing glance on Bradshaw Sr. "Did you know about this new will your daughter says Charlie Hunter drew up?"

Ignoring the question, Henry pounded the desk with his fist. "Everybody knows that after Charlie got sick, I was perfectly within my legal rights as his son-in-law to take charge of this place! His second stroke made him a babbling idiot!"

"No one ever put *you* in charge of anything, Father," Amelia cut in.

J.D. was frankly caught off guard by this news of Charlie Hunter's revised will. Bradshaw had assured him his wife was the heir, and therefore her property was legally her husband's to manage and control, even if it meant wagering it in an all-night poker match six weeks ago and gambling away the rest of his assets last night.

"What you must understand, Miss Bradshaw," J.D. said in as calm a tone as he could muster, "is that our lawyers have told us that heads-of-households have legal authority over wives and—it is also assumed—over unmarried female relatives to decide all financial matters as they see fit. I'm afraid substituting you for your mother as heir to Charles Hunter's estate makes no substantive change, as it might if the new heir were an emancipated son or grandson. Therefore your father, as your and your mother's guardian, has operated squarely within the law—"

Before he could finish his sentence, Amelia Bradshaw whirled in place and unleashed her pent-up wrath.

"This is a *perversion* of the law and it's utter nonsense—and you know it, Mr. Thayer. I am thirty years old and in no need of a guardian! And there is one more thing you may not know about. Very soon, this hotel property will be *outside* the purview of my parents' marriage—and therefore your assertions just now will be moot."

J.D. had riled her, and for some reason he didn't find as much satisfaction in the deed as he would have thought. For the briefest moment, he considered his own mother's legal predicaments and then pushed such contemplations aside.

Meanwhile, Amelia's father had been emboldened by J.D.'s show of support.

"Lord knows Victoria couldn't run this place, Amelia," Henry Bradshaw protested to his daughter. "Who *else* was there to take over the reins with you being gone? Charlie changing his will from your ma to you means nothing. I'm the head of this family now and the steward of this place!" Only his garbled speech came out "Ah'm su'ward o' thesh playsh," which considerably lessened its impact.

"That's right, Miss Bradshaw," echoed Ezra Kemp. "Before I invested a dime, I checked with *my* attorney. The law is mighty clear on husbands' and fathers' rights over their womenfolk."

After all, thought J.D., possession was nine tenths of the law, and their lawyers had said that if they picked the right judge, there was little likelihood the radical 1872 California Civil Code provision—giving wives the power to manage their separate property—would be enforced. A bit worrisome, however, was that the revised law said little about the separate or inherited property of unmarried females past the age of twenty-one whose fathers were habitually blind drunk.

Then, J.D. felt his stomach unclench a few degrees. With Victoria and Amelia Bradshaw abroad while Charles Hunter lay paralyzed in Room 12, any judge would surely find that Henry, as Hunter's son-in-law and only male relative, was legitimately in charge of operations at the Bay View Hotel. Therefore J.D.'s prize, won from Bradshaw just before Charlie Hunter went to His Maker, would likely remain intact.

If it came to it, he'd *buy* the damn hotel furniture from the chit, though from the way Amelia Bradshaw tilted her chin with a look of iron determination, he suddenly doubted if much would dissuade her from challenging his claims of ownership. Nothing, it would seem—not even her father's bluster—appeared to daunt her.

"May I remind you gentlemen I have written proof on my side. Besides the will, which I have just been shown by

Grandfather's—and now *my*—lawyer, I also possess a number of letters written to me while I was in France by Charles Hunter that relate how, in front of witnesses here at the hotel, my grandfather declared that he wanted *me* to oversee all operations as soon as I returned from abroad." She turned to face J.D. once again. "After all, I am a grown woman with a degree in architecture, as you so kindly pointed out, Mr. Thayer, and perfectly able to take on these responsibilities. Let us not forget, gentlemen, times are changing—and so are our laws. It's 1906, for pity's sake!"

"Things haven't changed to the degree where females rule the roost, eh, J.D.?" Kemp retorted. "Especially *unmarried* females like Miss Bradshaw here."

She shot back, "Four western states have already granted women the vote."

"Not yet California, thank the good Lord!" J.D. replied mildly.

He assumed his rejoinder would get a rise out of her and was not disappointed. Her eyes flashed with incandescent fervor and no small degree of irritation. She strode over to the desk looking anything but a naïve spinster longing for compliments.

"It's a new century, Mr. Thayer, and we 'females,' as you put it, are quite capable of seeing to our own affairs. My grandfather understood this perfectly. Why can't you?"

J.D. paused to consider his next words carefully. "I've nothing but respect for you and your grandfather, Miss Bradshaw, but Charles was mortally ill and—"

"As inconvenient as it may be for you three," she interrupted, "I presently speak and act as the true owner of this hotel." She turned toward Bradshaw. "I'm home now, Father, and you'd best start adjusting to the fact that *I'm* in charge from here on out."

"*You* in charge?" bellowed Bradshaw. "We'll just see about this!"

Following this outburst, he clapped a hand to his mouth and lurched from the room, apparently to be sick in the water closet down the hall.

"Miss Bradshaw," J.D. began, "surely we can come to some understanding—"

"The understanding you all must come to is that when my mother's divorce from Father becomes final—"

"*Divorce?*"

Thayer and his partner had pronounced the word simultaneously.

"Ah, more bad news for you, I fear," she said. "As my mother tearfully explained before I left Paris, she filed for divorce from my father on the basis of desertion by reason of habitual drunkenness here in San Francisco prior to departing for Europe. One day very soon, she will legally be beyond the reach of my father's schemes. Or yours. And therefore, so am *I*. Meanwhile, your gambling club is closed before it opens. You don't own one joist or crossbeam of this hotel."

"But what about the twenty thousand dollars still owed me on that new building out there?" Kemp protested.

Amelia smiled sweetly, but J.D. saw the steel in her jaw. "Perhaps you should consult with that lawyer of yours, Mr. Kemp. I'm sure he'd be happy to advise you."

J.D. dug into his vest pocket and swiftly laid out several small strips of paper. "Is this your father's handwriting?" Amelia drew closer to the desk and peered down.

"Those may be his IOUs, but as I said before, Mr. Thayer, the Bay View Hotel and its assets were never his to wager. They aren't worth the paper they're written on."

"You can't just ignore—"

Amelia held up a hand. "Ah... but I have a plan to reconfigure that space you built so shoddily, shore it up properly, and then turn it into additional hotel rooms. Thus, as our profits increase, I'm sure we can come to some equitable arrangement to pay you back for the cost of your materials."

She was a clever woman, he'd allow her that, but the only compensation he'd accept was clear title to the Bay View Hotel. J.D. Thayer had dreamed, schemed, and even scammed a bit to gain the upper hand with his two unreliable partners. No one hundred-ten-pound female, however talented, attractive, and self-possessed, was going to wrest *this* particular prize from his grasp.

CHAPTER 2

TEN DAYS LATER, AMELIA sat quietly in a courtroom with John Damler, an attorney specializing in real estate law who had been hastily recommended over the telephone by Julia Morgan, her college friend from the engineering department at the University of California at Berkeley. Amelia and her lawyer awaited Judge Haggerty's pronouncements at a preliminary hearing into the matter of Charles Hunter's will and the ownership of the Bay View Hotel.

Damler had done his level best to get the preliminary hearing to show cause before another judge of his own choosing, but had been out-maneuvered by Thayer and Kemp's cronies in city government.

She cast a quick glance over her shoulder. During the entire proceedings, J.D. Thayer lounged in a chair at a table to her left, positioned in front of the wooden railing that separated the two combatants from the rest of the courtroom. From the corner of her eye, she saw he appeared the ever-so-reputable businessman and had the air of a person without a care in the world. Today on his six-foot frame, he sported a dark, three-quarter-length coat and matching trousers, gray vest, and pointed-toe boots. He was perfectly groomed from his trim black mustache to the lustrous shine on his footwear. His tanned skin looked even darker against his starched white shirtfront and winged collar. Tall, dark, and handsome, to be sure.

Tall, dark, and dangerous, you mean... a voice echoed in her head.

Despite Thayer's clever legal maneuvering, Amelia was pleased that her attorney had been impressed by the raft of letters she submitted in evidence to the court. They'd been posted to Paris by her late grandfather and bolstered her case rather well, she thought—especially the last one sent immediately prior to his second stroke. Charlie Hunter had penned:

> *As we both know, your father has the Irish disease and your mother has neither the temperament nor a head for business. Your da's been drinking more than ever while you've been gone and I have now determined that the Bay View will only be safe in your hands. But never fear, Melly. You and I will see to it that poor Victoria will always be cared for, wherever that wastrel son-in-law of mine ends his days.*

The missives, as well as her grandfather's newly drawn and duly witnessed Last Will and Testament, seemed irrefutable evidence, Amelia thought. The judge was bound to see that Charles Hunter's wishes had been utterly thwarted by her father and his smarmy partners, and their recent machinations were therefore invalid.

Even so, a voice of warning rang in her head. J.D. Thayer was unscrupulous, perhaps, but she had to admit that the man was impeccably attired and carried himself like a gentleman, which is more than could be said for Judge Haggerty.

In Amelia's opinion, the judge they'd been assigned was a glib, overbearing blowhard whose pronouncements in the courtroom, thus far, sounded like nothing so much as the declarations of a snake-oil salesman. What worried her the most—in addition to the fact Haggerty was obviously a political appointee—were the legal issues of female separate property and the archaic tradition of male guardianship under California law—and its interpretation from the bench.

Just as Amelia stole another glance in Thayer's direction, her adversary shifted his weight, turned his head, and stared at her with a faint smile creasing his lips. He inclined his head in a polite gesture of recognition, an action that only served to infuriate Amelia even more.

During the lengthy hiatus waiting for the judge to appear, Thayer hadn't deigned even to look at her, and here he was, making a grand show of manners!

Playing the victor was more likely, fumed Amelia. It disturbed her that the fellow appeared so cocksure of himself. His glance might even have been construed flirtatious, if she hadn't been painfully schooled in the ways a man might appear to be showing a lady deference when, in fact, he only used that ploy to secure something *else* he desired.

Yes, J.D. Thayer was a handsome devil, in the same way Etienne had been a vastly attractive creature. Amelia certainly knew enough by now not to trust that either one of them had her best interests at heart.

Curiously, J.D.'s portly partner, Ezra Kemp, had not come to court at all, and her father's whereabouts remained a mystery. After their confrontation at the Bay View on the day of her homecoming, Henry Bradshaw had bolted out the door and had not been heard of since, taking refuge at some dive on the Barbary Coast, no doubt.

Blast them all to Hades!

Amelia twisted in her chair to see if the bailiff had returned to the courtroom. When would Judge Haggerty get off his derrière and do what was expected of him? Her pulse quickened at the sight of the court officer who burst through a side door and strode to the front of the chamber.

"All rise," barked the bailiff as the judge entered through a paneled opening behind the bench. The black-robed justice took his place while the bailiff intoned, "Be seated."

Judge Haggerty cleared his throat and gestured to the documents spread before him.

"The court finds the letters in Miss Bradshaw's possession merely to be the expression of a loving grandfather's vague sentiments toward his only grandchild." The jurist picked up an official-looking document. "This purported Last Will and Testament of Charles Hunter was signed with an 'X,' which might, under certain circumstances, be considered accept-able by this court. However," he continued, scowling in Amelia's direction, "it was made immediately prior to death and attested to by a Miss Edith Pratt—his private nurse and Miss Bradshaw's longtime school friend—and by one Grady O'Neill, a hotel employee who owes his livelihood to Miss Bradshaw's continuing good will."

Amelia shot a look of outrage at Thayer and bent to her right to whisper to her attorney. "I knew *nothing* of the new will before I returned to San Francisco! It was made while I was still abroad. How could I have influenced its outcome or told anyone else to do such a thing?"

Damler swiftly patted her hand as if he feared she would violate courtroom decorum with an angry outburst. He nodded toward the judge, indicating they should give him their full attention.

"And even if it *were* Charles McQuinty Hunter's intent to leave his estate solely to the petitioner," intoned Judge Haggerty, "her father, Henry Bradshaw, had a perfect right to guide female family members as to the management and control of their property. This he did when his wife was sole heir, and in my opinion," he added with a grimace from the bench, "the role of fathers' inalienable rights to guide their unmarried children are still valid under California law, despite any newfangled pronouncements by the State Legislature."

So much for the new California Code affecting the rights of women!

Amelia turned to look at her lawyer, unable to mask her ire at these pronouncements from the bench. The judge's words proved too much even for the staid John Damler. Her attorney rose to his feet with a forefinger raised to the ceiling.

"A point of order, your Honor. Mrs. Henry Bradshaw is *divorcing* her husband on grounds of habitual drunkenness and mismanagement of her funds. Furthermore, Miss Bradshaw is not a child, but a mature woman of thirty and therefore in no need of guardianship, especially by a known drunkard. Mr. Bradshaw has, as these letters reveal, shown no steady guidance whatsoever. Rather, he constantly indulged in strong spirits while sacrificing the Bay View Hotel in an all-night poker match with Mr. Thayer when Charles Hunter's true heir—my client sitting here—was en route from abroad where she'd been studying architecture."

Haggerty's frown deepened, but her lawyer drew a deep breath and continued stating his client's case.

"Since by virtue of Miss Bradshaw's traveling on the high seas from Europe and across the country by train during the period Charles Hunter changed his will, my client could not possibly have exerted undue influence on her grandfather to change his will in her favor, and thus it would seem, your honor, that Mr. Bradshaw's actions are therefore invalid and—"

"Are you proposing to take my place on this bench, Mr. Damler?" Haggerty asked, slamming the palm of his hand on top of Charlie Hunter's disputed will. "For you certainly appear to be offering the court your own, misguided legal conclusions."

The judge turned his sour expression on Amelia. "It is not this court's business regarding the Bradshaws' divorce proceedings, of which any decent Christian court takes a dim view, by the way. Nor is it the court's purview how well Mr. Bradshaw does or doesn't hold his liquor. The new Civil Code," he added with undisguised disdain for the recent laws defining a female's separate property, "would perhaps apply to Miss Bradshaw *if* the new will was witnessed by disinterested parties—but it was not."

Damler brazenly interrupted. "But, Your Honor, Miss Bradshaw hadn't spoken to or conducted written correspondence with the witnesses to the new will and could not, therefore, have exerted any undue influence over them, despite her acquaintance with them in years past. And if you are ruling out the new will, what of the mother's separate property rights as the *former heir*, under the new code? Is Victoria Bradshaw not, *de facto*, now entitled under current California law, the management and control of her separate property, nullifying her husband's reckless actions?"

The judge looked startled and J.D. shifted in his seat.

Haggerty's eyes had become slits and his bushy brows drew together as he declared, "Mrs. Henry Bradshaw is not a plaintiff before this court. If you will look around you, Mr. Damler, Victoria Bradshaw isn't even *in* these chambers." He smiled faintly in Thayer's direction. "In my opinion, Mrs. Bradshaw has deserted her husband and fled our beloved land, forfeiting her rights under the laws of this state and nation. Therefore, it is clear to me that Mr. Bradshaw's legal rights as a father and guardian of an *unmarried* female allow him to proceed any way he wishes—his recklessness notwithstanding."

"May I say, your Honor," Damler countered, "that in this new century, I had hoped to have the court affirm, under the new Civil Code, that an intelligent, highly educated woman architect like Miss Bradshaw would be deemed as far more capable than a man known in the community to be a hopeless drunkard, hazarding the Hunter family legacy in an imprudent game of *chance*!"

Judge Haggerty was rumored to be an officer of the court installed by the notoriously corrupt Mayor Schmitz, along with Schmitz's enforcer, Abe Reuf, and their political circle downtown—which included Ezra Kemp. Even so, the jurist appeared mildly discomforted by Damler's impassioned declarations. Haggerty shuffled the documents for a few moments and cleared his throat a second time.

"Nevertheless, counselor, I find that these letters—notarized and attested to by no one—are *not* the legal equivalent of a Last Will and Testament. Secondly, in *my* judgment, this document purported to be Mr. Hunter's new will meets the test of 'undue influence' since it was drawn up when Mr. Hunter could barely move or speak clearly, and signed by witnesses who are obviously partisan to the sole beneficiary, Miss Bradshaw. Furthermore," Judge Haggerty declared with a glare in Amelia's direction, "legal *precedence* in this state confirms what this court deems is the *proper* guardianship roles of fathers and husbands. Notwithstanding the new Civil Code, society would fall into chaos if the court didn't adhere to this hallowed principal of hearth and home! Case dismissed."

Amelia ducked her head, her cheeks hot with indignation as she strove to control her emotions. She couldn't bear to look across the courtroom at J.D. Thayer or imagine the relief that must have washed over him. He had bested her this day and unquestioningly was glad of it. No matter that her parents and his had once been friends. No matter that she had lost her grandfather, the dearest person in her life, and had been robbed of a precious legacy by such outrageous double-dealing. She doubted anything pulled on the man's conscience.

Outside the courthouse, her attorney appeared as upset as she by the outcome of the hearing.

"It's simply wrong-headed," John Damler fumed as they walked down the courthouse steps. "We could appeal, Miss Bradshaw, but I fear Thayer and especially Kemp, with his political connections, will put this case before the same political hacks with the same hidebound views, wherever we might file in this state."

"You're probably right. And besides, I can ill afford any more California justice."

Her words were tinged with defiance when, in fact, she yearned to simply weep as a child. Once she paid her legal fees, she was virtually out of funds except for the pittance she had remaining from her trip home from France. All she wanted at the moment was to get as far away as possible from Judge Haggerty's courtroom so she could rage to the heavens or pound a fist against a wall. Indeed, suppressed fury was the only emotion she would allow herself, for if she accepted the truth that the Bay View Hotel no longer belonged to her family, she feared she would behave like a madwoman.

She blindly handed her lawyer an envelope containing what was owing—which he refused.

Yet she insisted. "No, please, Mr. Damler. You put on an excellent case. I appreciate your efforts."

Just then, J.D. Thayer strode down the courthouse steps.

As he passed, he offered attorney Damler and Amelia a civil nod, hurrying in the direction of a large, open-air vehicle parked at the base of the granite stairs. Amelia endured the final indignity of watching Thayer turn the crank and then climb into the driver's seat of her late grandfather's pride-and-joy, a gleaming, midnight blue Winton motorcar.

She turned back to Damler and nearly shoved the envelope into the lawyer's hands. "You must take this. Perhaps it will further your work in Chinatown."

Amelia knew from her brief telephone conversation with Julia Morgan that John Damler also represented Julia's friend, Donaldina Cameron, the Methodist missionary who ran a shelter for young Chinese women desperate to escape the brothels flourishing mere blocks from Nob Hill. The irony was not lost on Amelia that Miss Cameron was the same person whom both her own mother and the mother of J.D. Thayer had once supported in her efforts to help the city's poorest women flee forced prostitution.

And now, Thayer had apparently taken the comely Ling Lee as his mistress and recruited similar young Chinese women to serve in the gambling club—or worse. How *could* he have become such a blackguard? What would drive a man who had good looks, breeding, and intelligence to use these gifts to such ill purposes?

Damler clutched the envelop Amelia had forced upon him and flashed her a smile that transformed his earnest expression. "I will use the money to fight for *justice* for those poor beleaguered women, kidnapped from their homelands and brought here to do the Devil's work. You've made me feel better already, Miss Bradshaw. And you? What will you do now?"

Amelia turned to watch Thayer, outfitted in goggles and

duster coat, shift the motorcar into gear and swiftly pull away from the curb. She knew it was childish, but she felt like throwing rocks at his windshield. Her chest felt hollow, her heart empty of all emotion but a sense of far-flung blackness like the bay on a moonless night. She stared vacantly as her grandfather's magnificent machine turned the corner and disappeared.

"What will I do?" she repeated faintly. "I will try to accept the unacceptable, Mr. Damler, and begin to earn my own keep."

CHAPTER 3

THE DAY FOLLOWING THE hearing, Amelia sat gazing out the Bay View's Turret Suite window at the persistent fog that was as leaden as her mood. She longed to fling herself upon the silk coverlet gracing the handsome bed in the next room and cry until she had emptied herself of all feeling—but she couldn't even do that. She supposed she was numb, barely able to summon the energy to look at the gray moisture curling over the bay.

It was hard to countenance that she and J.D. Thayer were still housed under the same roof. To her amazement, she had returned to the hotel prepared to pack her belongings, only to find a polite note in her room from the hotel's now-legal proprietor urging her to stay as his guest as long as she needed before moving to her aunt's home across the bay in Oakland.

What's worse? Thayer's charity or his double-dealing…

The Ferry Building's new clock tower at the foot of Market and California streets was partially obscured by this shifting blanket of gray. The structure's cloaked spire had been the subject of several letters to Paris from her grandfather who was justly proud of San Francisco's emergence as an important seaport, opening to the vast Pacific.

Amelia ached with the sense that the loss of Charlie Hunter was now a raw wound that simply would not scab over. When she hadn't slept following yesterday's court hearing, she poured over her grandfather's missives, running her fingers over his spiky penmanship to try to recapture his presence and gain some intuition of the actions he would want her to take next.

From Thayer's point of view, she supposed she could understand why he hadn't given an inch or proposed any sort of compromise—because neither had she. She felt like the proverbial immovable object that had slammed into an irresistible force.

By early the next morning, the fog finally lifted. Amelia forced herself to face facts. She had no choice but to be the one to give way. She couldn't impose on Thayer's pragmatic hospitality forever. Too many loyal hotel retainers of her grandfather's providing for her comfort at the Bay View would probably pay the price at Thayer's hand if she stayed much longer.

And besides, she had a profession to ply and a burning desire to make use of all that she had learned these last, arduous years. In the end, she had to admit that her own ambition got the best of her, not J.D. Thayer's possession of her lost legacy. It was time to move beyond grief and resentment and begin her life over again.

She swiftly packed her trunk and portmanteau and ordered Grady O'Neill at the front desk to have it sent to her aunt's bungalow on Thirteenth Street in Oakland, on the east side of the bay. Then she dressed and took the elevator to the lobby, vowing to make no public farewells, lest she embarrass herself or the staff by dissolving in tears.

Long before most guests were awake, Amelia marched through the lobby, seeing her profile reflected in the glittering succession of gold-framed mirrors that lined the walls. An unpleasant scent of sauerkraut permeated the hallway, the hallmark of the new chef that had replaced the wonderful Mrs. O'Neill, Grady's wife and long-time hotel cook.

Amelia was dismayed to spot J.D. Thayer talking to Grady himself, along with a slender Chinese woman whom Amelia already knew was Ling Lee, Thayer's Chinese concubine.

"Miss Bradshaw!" he hailed her across the lobby. "I see you're—"

"Leaving," she abruptly finished his sentence, continuing her pace.

"Can we call you a driver to—"

"The cable car stops at the corner," she said between clenched teeth. "Grady has kindly seen to my luggage—which I hope will not jeopardize his future in any way," she added, and realized how peevish her words rang.

"Of course not," J.D. replied shortly. "He's a good man, Grady."

"The best... as are all my grandfather's employees. I hope you'll remember that, Mr. Thayer."

And before her despised adversary could respond or defend the changes already wrought at the Bay View, she marched through the swinging brass-framed doors with a brief, stricken nod to Joseph, the hotel's longtime doorman. Barbary, her grandfather's faithful hound, stood sentinel beside the hotel's majordomo, and when he wagged his tail at her passing, she nearly burst into tears.

Amelia virtually sprinted down Taylor Street, hardly glancing at the Bay View's newest competitor, the spanking new Fairmont Hotel crowning the hill and due to open its doors to the public soon. She boarded a cable car poised on the summit of Nob Hill and blindly sat down on the hard, wooden bench, her chin on her chest so no one would see the moisture streaming down her cheeks.

Nothing in this world or the next could make her turn around to watch the Bay View Hotel receding from view.

❦

Number One cable car squeaked and creaked down California Street past the quiet world of Nob Hill in early morning, toward the Ferry Building at the foot of the steep incline. The few people out at this hour went about their business in the usual fashion, yet to Amelia, everything was changed.

As far as she'd heard from Grady, no one—including Thayer or Kemp—had caught even a glimpse of Henry Bradshaw since the day of Amelia's fiery arrival at the basement office of the Bay View. Brushing the moisture from her cheeks with her gloved hand, she finally raised her head to look out at the sapphire and green water at the foot of California Street, trying to convince herself that she hoped the father whose drunken behavior had caused her mother and her so much heartache had drowned himself in San Francisco Bay.

By quarter to eight, she had trudged from Market Street to the office building on Montgomery where Julia Morgan had established her fledgling architectural firm barely two years earlier. Nothing prepared her, however, for the small room on the ninth floor where slanted drafting boards were crammed into a space that could barely accommodate three normal-sized desks. The place had nothing in common with the airy ateliers she and Julia enjoyed while studying at L'École. Those featured large, open spaces and floor-to-ceiling windows to allow for natural light and a glimpse of the rooftops of Paris.

The glass door to Julia's minuscule inner office was guarded by a table where a secretary pounded the keys of her typewriting machine.

"Well, my stars!" the young woman exclaimed, scrambling to her feet. "Amelia Bradshaw, you are a sight for sore eyes!" Blonde and pretty as a milkmaid, Amelia's former college classmate Lacy Fiske rushed to embrace her. "Dear, dear Amelia," the young woman added with burbling sympathy, "I cannot tell you how sorry I am about the loss of your grandfather and what's happened at your family's hotel."

Amelia gazed with surprise at the buoyant Miss Fiske. Lacy had been the person least likely of all the women she'd known at Berkeley to end up as an office mate. Lacy had changed her field of studies so often during college, Amelia didn't actually know which department at Berkeley had ultimately granted her friend a degree. She was pleased, however, to see that the younger woman had finally settled on office administration.

Lacy reached out and gently patted Amelia on the shoulder.

"Your grandfather was such a dear man. I have so many happy memories of parties at the Bay View when we were in school."

As usual, Amelia found herself fighting tears whenever someone spoke kindly of Charlie Hunter, the only person in the world that had stood between herself as a little girl and the utter chaos of her parents' disastrous marriage. Lacy sensed Amelia's distress and immediately changed the subject.

"I can't believe it. Since we saw each other last, *I've* finally learned to type—can you fancy?—and you've become an architect!" She eyed the empty desks. "I suppose you're accustomed to being around men all day, but I must admit, it still takes getting used to." She lowered her voice a notch. "I'd better be quiet. The thundering hordes'll be here any minute."

Amelia glanced over Lacy's shoulder at Julia, hunched over her desk in the inner office. "How long have you worked here?"

"Since the day the firm opened," Lacy said proudly. "Julia was terribly long-suffering in the beginning while I was taking my typing course, but here we all are. Isn't it grand?" she enthused. Then her face fell. "How thoughtless of me. I can only imagine how hard everything's been for you since you came home."

"It's been quite a saga, but thank you, Lacy. Your sympathy means a lot."

"Oh yes," Lacy said with an earnest expression clouding her eyes, and Amelia sensed an odd shyness had crept into her voice. "Julia and I both felt ever so sad for your circumstances."

Amelia felt awkward in the face of Lacy's sober compassion. There was something else in her tone that she couldn't quite identify. She swiftly glanced toward the inner office. "Is it all right if I go in to speak to Julia?"

Lacy bent forward as if imparting a secret. "I suppose so, but I'm warning you, she isn't in the best of humors this morning. She prepared the monthly billing yesterday. Lately, that exercise puts her terribly out of sorts, so approach at your peril."

Amelia hung her cloak on a peg where Lacy directed and knocked softly on the office's glass door. Julia frowned, looked up, and, when she recognized her visitor, beckoned her inside.

Amelia hesitated, surprised by a sudden sense of playing the petitioning acolyte to Julia's master status—a reminder of their unequal relationship that had originated during college days. It had been a long time since she'd felt she must kneel at someone else's feet, but the tiny, intense woman was, at times, a force of nature and certainly deserved Amelia's respect.

"Julia, if this isn't a good time, I can come back later."

"Nonsense. Come in, come in. Finally I can officially bid you welcome home and congratulate you on earning your certificate."

"Well, we did speak briefly on the telephone, but thank you. I would have come to see you long before this, but—"

"I completely understand. No need to apologize. Edith Pratt filled me in a bit."

Of course Julia would have talked at some point to Nurse Pratt, Charlie Hunter's private caretaker who'd also been their classmate at Berkeley.

The Old Girls Society, for certain, Amelia reminded herself wryly. After all, how many young women of their set eschewed marriage for continuing academic or business pursuits?

Very few, Amelia silently answered her own question.

Julia pointed to a chair opposite her desk. "Please sit down. And I'm so deeply sorry about your grandfather. Everyone is. I was distressed, also, to learn the results of the hearing. Did John Damler not—"

"John Damler did an excellent job," Amelia hastened to assure her. "Thank you so much for recommending him. The problem was that awful Judge Haggerty—who is obviously one of Schmitz's crooked cronies—and the controversy that still swirls around the control of a woman's separate property."

"I thought that issue had been resolved," Julia said, frowning. "At least the suffragists claim it has."

"Apparently it depends on what judge sits on the bench *interpreting* the new laws. At the moment, I don't have the funds to take it to a higher court and can't chance I'd get another Judge Haggerty deciding the matter."

"I only wish you'd both had more success."

A minuscule figure of less than five feet, Julia Morgan stood up from her drafting board. This mild April morning, the architect was dressed in a mannish, olive-green double-breasted jacket, matching skirt, and a silk blouse of exquisite softness complimented by a silk tie that Amelia guessed she'd purchased at a lovely shop they both had patronized on the Rue de la Paix. Julia's hair was neatly piled on top of her head and her round glasses sat halfway down her nose, giving her a highly studious appearance.

"I so appreciate everything you've done on my behalf, Julia. Without people like you and Edith, I don't know how I would have managed. It's been just ghastly." She felt a catch rise in her throat. "I miss Grandfather so much, and you can't imagine what it's been like to lose his hotel as well."

"Your grandfather was a wonderful, generous-spirited man. We all miss him." Julia resumed her chair facing her drafting table. "Actually, I'm rather surprised to see you so soon. I should have thought there were many loose ends for you to deal with."

"Not many, now, unfortunately, since J.D. Thayer took over complete control of the Bay View. Though I haven't given up," Amelia added quickly. She hesitated. It was so humiliating to reveal, even to Julia, her family's current state of personal and financial chaos. "I still intend to fight for the hotel, though I'm not quite sure how yet—or with what funds. With Mother in Paris and the hotel now in other hands, my aunt and I barely have a sou between us. Besides wanting to express my thanks for your support, Julia, I'm here to see about employment. Can you take me on, as you said you might? *Immediately?*" she added with deliberate emphasis.

Julia glanced down at her desk. "I feel absolutely horrid about this, Amelia, but I can barely pay my employees' wages as it is." She shook her head. "I don't need to tell *you*, it's an uphill battle, being the only female in a male profession.

I'm terribly sorry to disappoint us both, but with the limited number of commissions I have presently, I'm afraid I can't put you on as a full-time architect as I'd hoped."

"You *can't*? But then who in the world will hire me?"

Stunned, she sank back into the chair and stared at the woman she had hoped would serve as a professional mentor. All her hopes, all her *assumptions* of at least six years came crashing down to earth. Flashing through her mind were endless late-night sessions at the atelier and a host of arduous design projects at L'École des Beaux Arts. For years now, her principal goal had been to gain a place in Julia's firm, even when she thought she didn't have to make her own living.

Now, she *needed* to earn her keep and support her aunt and mother, especially since Victoria had already written from France complaining that "the price of caviar and suitable lodging here are *so* dear." Mrs. Hunter Bradshaw had been a coddled woman all her life and would expect to continue that privilege.

Yet, Julia Morgan had just said there was no room for another desk and no funds to pay Amelia's wages.

"You can't imagine how sorry I am," Julia continued, but Amelia's mind could only echo the architect's earlier pronouncement that she wouldn't be hiring her.

Julia's troubled gaze did little to soften the blow. Amelia warded off a sudden sense of panic that could easily bring on tears of frustration.

"There isn't another firm in all of San Francisco likely to hire a woman architect," she murmured, ashamed of the flood of self-pity that threatened to drown her.

"I know. Believe me."

Julia had worked briefly for John Galen Howard, the haughty master architect at the University of California at

Berkeley, and had parted company fairly quickly, founding her own firm as a result, with the enthusiastic support of her well-to-do family in Oakland. She gestured toward the adjacent room with its drafting boards squeezed into a tiny space.

"Our friends from college do what they can to give me commissions. A residence here, a garage for a new motorcar there. If it were just me, I'd probably be doing reasonably well, but with my rent here in the city, and the draftsmen on my ledgers—"

"But what about Mills College?" Amelia interrupted, referring to the women's institution of higher learning in the East Bay. "You wrote me about designing the bell tower. Any chance of further commissions there?"

Julia grew silent, apparently mulling something over. "It's true… I am being considered as the architect for the Mills College library and I could use some help with my presentation."

Amelia's dashed hopes fluttered into the tiniest flame.

"Part of the problem is that I just don't have the physical space for you to work in this office."

Amelia recalled the jumble of desks in the outer office and her spirits sank even lower.

Julia paused again then asked, "Would you be willing to work here at night?"

"At *night*? You mean after everyone else has gone home for the day?"

Julia nodded. "You could use Ira Hoover's desk."

Amelia supposed Ira Hoover was Julia's second-in-command. Working at night alone in this office at someone else's desk sounded grim, but it was better than the alternative.

"So the ladies didn't hate your concrete bell tower, after all?" Amelia asked, a glimmer of hope fanning marginally brighter. Julia gave her a startled look. "I had heard from Grandfather that there was considerable public debate in the press that some Mills College alumnae took issue with the campanile's 'unorthodox' construction."

Amelia meant it as a jibe at Julia's critics, but the architect obviously saw no humor in the situation and pursed her lips with distaste.

"Concrete is by far the strongest and newest innovation, but the uninformed often prefer wooden geegaws and such. I detest the newspapers and the way they write about subjects with both arrogance and ignorance!" she exclaimed. She wagged a forefinger at Amelia. "And by the way, if I do employ you, *never* speak to reporters. I was upset when the *Call* wrote that you were going to work for me. I never confirmed that."

"I know, Julia," Amelia said apologetically. "I never spoke to anyone from the newspaper. Someone at the hotel was contacted by the society page when they got wind I was coming home from Paris, and whoever it was at the Bay View repeated assumption as fact, hoping to get a mention of the hotel in the paper. I'm terribly sorry about that."

Julia's frown furrowed the bridge of her nose where her wire-rimmed glasses magnified her eyes to owlish proportions.

"My point exactly! You give those news people an inch, they take a mile. Well, at any rate," Julia continued, "my thought is that if you will come here evenings at six p.m., when everyone else leaves, you can transfer to proper scale the drawings and designs I'm doing for the Mills College library. No one working for me has the skill and training you do, but as I've already hired employees, I can't decently let them go without cause. I can't guarantee anything, Amelia, but perhaps if we get this big library commission, we'll find a way to put you on full time," adding, "in the daytime, of course."

Amelia was deeply grateful for this reprieve—and hugely relieved.

"That's *so* kind of you, Julia. I accept your offer with pleasure," she added almost gaily, and to make it official, thrust out her hand. "Thank you so, *so* much."

Julia shook hands with an even gaze and suddenly switched subjects.

"Are you certain, Amelia, you can perform your duties in this office if you are to continue to pursue your struggle proving J.D. Thayer obtained the Bay View Hotel from you through underhanded methods? He's become a very prominent figure in San Francisco, you know. Such actions on your part are bound to attract notice of the very people with the means to employ architects."

Amelia tried not to show her dismay. Of all the reactions she'd anticipated from Julia Morgan, barely masked self-interest had not been among them.

"N-Naturally, the ultimate fate of the Bay View Hotel is of utmost importance to me." She attempted to steady her voice, hoping she didn't sound as desperate as she felt. "And to that end, I will have to devote a bit of time and energy to see if there are any further remedies. But I give you my word, Julia, that I will keep as low a profile on this as I can and I will complete every assignment, on time and within the budget you deem appropriate."

"That is good to hear. There are rumors that J.D. Thayer plans to build another hotel downtown to rival the Palace from the profits of his gambling club. I have a business to run, Amelia, and can't afford to antagonize the mighty, if you understand my meaning. And I need every hand here to pull equally on her oar, regardless of any personal issues." She straightened the papers on her desk. "One more thing. I'm afraid in an office environment like this, you will have to address me as 'Miss Morgan' in front of other staff. As Lacy does."

"Of course," Amelia murmured. "I completely understand."

But, of course, she didn't at all. Lacy Fiske was a secretary, but peers and colleagues, if they were friends, routinely addressed each other by their Christian names. Julia's edict felt like a demotion before Amelia had even begun to work for her firm.

But Julia just offered you employment! Show some gratitude...

Amelia *was* deeply grateful, but it was plain to see that Julia Morgan, architect, was a far different person from Julia, classmate.

Amelia rose from her chair. "I'll let you get back to your work. Shall I start tomorrow night?"

The founder of the Morgan firm merely nodded and bent over her desk while Amelia quietly let herself out the door.

CHAPTER 4

J.D. THAYER ENTERED CHARLIE Hunter's owner's suite, walked swiftly to a side table laden with old man Hunter's handsome cut crystal glasses and a bottle of whiskey, and poured himself a stiff drink.

He avoided the horsehair sofa in favor of a well-worn leather chair that had belonged to the former owner of the Bay View and sank into its comforting girth, staring moodily out the window at the fog curling across the bay.

God, what a day dealing with those damnable partners of his!

Partners?

Swindlers and cheats was a more accurate description. Henry Bradshaw only made the occasional appearance at the Bay View to steal spirits from the bar, and Ezra Kemp blatantly filched money from the till in the wee hours when he thought no one was watching. Thieves and liars, the both of them!

And what do you suppose Charlie's granddaughter thinks you are, my man?

J.D. often found himself thinking about the starchy Miss Bradshaw when surrounded by the very walls that had sheltered her as a girl.

Well, now she was a woman, and a formidable adversary at that, though he'd checked around and discovered she'd virtually no funds with which to challenge him again in court.

He pictured Judge Haggerty pontificating all that legal nonsense from the bench, but it didn't make him smile as it had that day. Amelia and that lawyer she'd hired through Julia Morgan had done an excellent job making their case. J.D. had put up a confident front during the hearing, but in point of fact, he'd been worried. Very worried.

Luckily, though, he'd won, thanks to a few markers he'd called at City Hall.

Then why did this victory disappoint? Why did the memory of that young woman standing forlornly on the courthouse steps fill him with an all too familiar sense of self-loathing? It had clung to him these last days like the fog on the cypress trees hugging the hills outside his window.

The Mood was upon him, he realized, a sense of melancholy that occasionally overcame him when he slowed down long enough to consider the unconventional path his life had taken since Grandfather Reims had died. He found himself wondering how Amelia Bradshaw was coping with her own loss of Charlie Hunter.

J.D. gazed into his untouched glass of whiskey. Finding no answer in its amber depths, he set it aside and headed for bed.

❦

In the late afternoon two weeks into her new job, Amelia dragged herself from the narrow cot wedged into the tiny space that had been serving as Aunt Margaret's enclosed back service porch attached to her bungalow on Oakland's Thirteenth Street. All day long she had been attempting without success to sleep while the rest of the world went about its normal business. She began to dress for work, shivering in the dank air that seeped under the screen door as soon as the sun went down. She wondered if she could spare the cash to install some insulation to keep from freezing when April showers tattooed on the metal roof above her head.

"I've got your supper all ready, dear," Aunt Margaret called from the kitchen of her modest one-story cottage where a row of similar abodes lined the narrow street.

Amelia had been startled to learn that Aunt Margaret's new home, leased while Amelia was in Paris, was less than a mile from the large, shingle-style house belonging to Julia Morgan and her family. Margaret's bungalow, however, was only big enough to provide bedrooms for herself and her brother—should they ever find Amelia's father. Meanwhile, Amelia made do in makeshift quarters off the kitchen.

"Thank you, Aunt Margaret" she called through the half-opened door. "I'll be right there."

Amelia had been faithfully turning over her weekly pay packet and, in return, Margaret paid their rent and produced hearty meals to appease her robust appetite and Amelia's modest one. Her elderly aunt had had a suite at the Bay View for some twenty years, courtesy of Margaret's wayward brother's father-in-law, Charlie Hunter. Following her benefactor's death, the bombastic Ezra Kemp had been rude to the kindly woman one time too often and she'd relocated across the bay. Amelia greatly admired how her aunt had adjusted to her reduced circumstances. In fact, the older woman almost seemed to relish shopping for and cooking her own meals after years of eating gratis, in the hotel's excellent dining room.

True to form, Aunt Margaret presented Amelia with a mounded plate of fried pork chops and thick slabs of corn bread slathered in butter. Not only had Margaret endured the loss of her husband in a mining accident when she was just a bride, but as a child, along with Amelia's father, she lived through an unimaginable tragedy in an ice cave in the High Sierras that even today she refused to describe—or discuss.

Her portly aunt plopped a fourth chop on her own plate. Amelia sensed that the woman, who, at the tender age of seven back in 1864, had survived the legendary horrors of Donner Pass, never wanted to go hungry again.

At five p.m., Amelia boarded a ferry bound for San Francisco and another night as a very junior member of Julia Morgan's architectural firm. She paid her fare to the purser, Harold Jasper, whom she knew slightly from her college years going to and from her undergraduate classes at Berkeley. She immediately pulled a sketchbook from her portmanteau, signaling to the renowned busybody that she was in no mood for a chat.

But Purser Jasper was oblivious to her signals.

"Living with your aunt now, are you?" he said, cranking out her receipt from the metal machine strapped around his waist. "Just goes to show, don't it, that in the end, life is just about paperwork? Such a shame the court said your grandfather was so weak that he couldn't do more than sign an X. Anybody could've done it and said it was his, so they say. Pity."

Amelia resorted to her familiar habit of calculating the multiplication tables backwards to try to calm her nerves. How in the world did Jasper know the particulars on a legal case with the ink barely dry?

The purser's expression grew dour. "I 'spose you've heard the private gambling club's opened on schedule up at the Bay View. Those fellas stand to make a fortune, they say."

Now that she had moved to her aunt's, she didn't want to hear anymore about J.D. Thayer and his damnable gambling enterprise. Fortunately, she was spared any more conversation as the *Berkeley*'s horn sounded and the boat pulled away from the dock. However, ten minutes later, Harold Jasper reappeared by her side.

"I 'spose you know your father was seen bummin' drinks on the Barbary Coast a few days back." Amelia suppressed her dismay and merely shook her head. Harold Jasper shrugged at her silence, adding, "Don't it just prove that even fancy folk like you'un have skeletons in the closet like your da?" and ambled down the deck while she busied herself by sketching neat rows of bookshelves that might be suitable for the second floor of the Mills College library.

During the rest of the trip across the bay, she tried unsuccessfully to avoid either thinking about her father—who was probably lying in a gutter—or replaying in her head the purser's cutting remarks or the courtroom scene and memories of the disintegration of her family that preceded it. Deep into her unhappy reverie, she hardly noticed when the ferry docked in San Francisco and the passengers began departing the gangway.

"Better step lively, Miss Bradshaw," chided Jasper, baldly peering over her shoulder at her notebook, "or you'll be finding yourself on your way back to Oakland."

❧

A cable car clanged and clattered nearby as Amelia walked a block up Market Street and turned right to reach California Street, heading for Julia's office farther down on Montgomery. As anxious as she was to get to work, it was hard to ignore the staccato rhythm of hammers and the hiss of welders' torches at so many construction sites in the downtown district. Most of the new buildings were standing on "made land" that skirted San Francisco's hills. The shifting mudflats had been filled in along the shoreline with the residue of rotting ships abandoned by gold-fevered crews during "The Rush" fifty years earlier, along with decades of garbage buried by the ebb and flow of tidal sands. Now a thriving new city was thrusting up, proud and tall, on its marshy banks.

San Francisco, she thought with a glow of pride. Beautiful... bawdy... brand new San Francisco. And she would now be part of it becoming a great metropolis!

She lowered her rooftop gaze and came face-to-face with a tall figure in a smart black cape, gloves, and top hat.

"Why good evening, Miss Bradshaw."

J.D. Thayer was obviously headed into Tadich's Grill at 240 California Street.

The restaurant had been a coffee stand for incipient gold miners about to head off for Sutter's Fort in 1849, but for decades now, Tadich's had been a staple of fine San Francisco dining.

"Hello," Amelia answered, her abbreviated greeting just short of rudeness. Thayer was alone, she noted, but then Chinese concubines were not welcome at such establishments as this culinary landmark.

The new owner of the Bay View Hotel was dressed impeccably, as usual, and appeared to her poised to meet someone for supper. He had seen her first. Even so, he looked as surprised to encounter her on the street corner as she was to nearly bump into him. He glanced at the large sketchbook under her arm.

"I heard you are now employed by Julia Morgan," he commented with a quizzical look. "Aren't your day's labors at an end? Why are you trudging up the street, rather than heading towards the Ferry Building at this hour?"

Did the man know *every* detail about her life? But, of course, the Bay View's staff would have told him her trunks were sent to her aunt's in Oakland.

Well, she wouldn't give him the satisfaction of knowing that she worked at night.

"I spend time in the city for reasons and at hours for which I have no need of accounting to you, sir. Now, if you'll just excuse—"

J.D. rested his hand on her forearm, halting her forward progress, and she suddenly felt the fool for sounding so churlish.

"Miss Bradshaw, I…"

Amelia felt herself stiffen. She glanced at her arm encased loosely in his grasp. He released her but remained silent, his expression unreadable.

"What is it, Mr. Thayer?"

"I was wondering how you were faring in your… in your new…"

"Circumstances?" she filled in. "I'm working hard. I'm looking after my aunt who used to live with us at the Bay View. And I'm worried about my father. Have you seen him?"

"I? No, not I. The barman sees him in the storeroom occasionally."

"Oh."

An intense awkwardness bloomed between them.

"Miss Bradshaw…"

J.D. took her gloved hand in his, and the familiarity of the gesture, coupled with his having seized her forearm to halt her in her tracks a few minutes earlier, somehow infuriated her.

"I must be on my way, Mr. Thayer," she announced abruptly, pulling her hand away.

"The ferry to Oakland won't leave for another hour.

Won't you to allow me to buy you dinner after such a long day of toil?"

She was flabbergasted by his invitation. She studied his face and detected the faintest curve of his lips beneath his jet-black mustache.

"You are mocking me, Mr. Thayer, and such an approach is unlikely to persuade me to take anything you say to me seriously."

"But I *am* serious, Miss Bradshaw," he replied. "I would very much like to have supper with you. There are a few loose ends concerning the Bay View we need to discuss."

"Loose ends? Such as what?"

"Well, for one thing, you mentioned on that day you burst into my office—"

"My *grandfather's* office!" she interrupted.

"—that day you noted that part of the gambling annex needs to be shored up for safety's sake. Perhaps you, Miss Morgan, and I could discuss ways to ameliorate—"

"Ah… so your conscience *is* pricking you ever so slightly and you intend, by throwing me a bone, I'll just quietly accept the fact that you propositioned a known drunk into an all-night poker contest and thus swindled the Bay View away from my mother and me."

J.D. paused a moment and Amelia guessed she'd managed to challenge his scruples—that is, if he had any.

"My intentions are rather more mundane," he replied at last. "I agree with you that the construction work was shoddy. I'd like to remedy the problems if I can. And besides, I think I'd enjoy your company of an evening."

He had ignored her insult and appeared, instead, actually to be flirting with her!

"And Miss Lee?" Amelia asked, gazing at him steadily. "Would she be joining us?'

Thayer's eyes narrowed, but he did not reply.

"I think not, Mr. Thayer," Amelia said, securing her sketchbook more tightly under her arm. "I'm not interested in assisting you with your structural problems at your club, and I won't have supper with you at Tadich's this evening. Good night, sir."

And without further exchange, she hurried on her way, praying Julia wouldn't notice she was five minutes late—or ever find out that she'd turned down a potential commission.

❧

In the waning hours of the fogless spring night, a sharp vibration rippled beneath the redwood planking on the ninth floor of 456 Montgomery Street.

Startled, Amelia lifted her head from her arms, which were braced against the slanted drawing board, and tried to remember, in her just-wakened stupor, where she was. To gain her bearings, she focused on the large sketch of a floor plan she'd been working on for hours, its precise, black outlines vivid against the ivory-colored vellum.

It's my drawing of the library. I'm still at the office…

After a few more seconds of soothing quiet, she pushed her wire-rimmed drafting spectacles lower on her nose and peered through the windows across the room. The sky was a pale gray wash. It would soon be dawn.

A few blocks away, the Ferry Building stood rooted at the edge of the congested shoreline. Ships' masts bobbed on both sides of the clock tower whose alabaster face registered a few minutes past five. The faint tremor that had just rippled through the room was like so many other small jolts she'd experienced as a native San Franciscan. Not like the earthquake in April of 1898, that had broken windows in the women's residence hall adjacent to the Berkeley campus, frightening some of her fellow sorority sisters half to death.

"Mornin', Miz Bradshaw."

She peered across the room at a bewhiskered man in a dark blue cap who'd poked his head through the open office door.

"Zack! Goodness! You gave me quite a turn." She paused and then asked, "Did you feel anything just now? The shaking?"

"What, miss?" the night watchman replied, furrowing his brow.

She glanced around the room and shrugged. "I thought I felt a little earthquake a few minutes ago, but maybe not. I think you caught me cat-napping."

"The charwomen will be comin' soon."

"I know. It's after five. You must think me daft."

Zachary Webb cocked a disapproving eyebrow in so fatherly a fashion that Amelia laughed. "You've worked long enough, it seems to me," he said. "It's just comin' on daybreak. You'd best enjoy a cup of coffee with me in the basement and have yourself a bit of a rest while the ladies be at their cleanin'."

"Yes, of course. That's a lovely offer." The watchman had been extraordinarily kind to her from her first day entering the building just as everyone else was leaving. There was kinship in the night shift, she concluded, happy to have his company. She pointed at her drawing. "Just give me five more minutes."

Webb shook his head in another show of friendly censure. "I'll just be makin' one more round of the building, miss, and be back for you in my elevator when the chars arrive."

"You're very kind," she murmured, absorbed in her handiwork. After a few minutes, Amelia sighed, absently tucking her shirtwaist more securely into her skirt. "*Voilà!*" she exclaimed, pronouncing the project complete. With a flourish, she stashed her drawing implement in a tin cup atop her drafting table.

As if that triumphant flick of her wrist had set a giant machine in motion, the clutch of sharpened pencils rattled an alarming tattoo inside their metal container.

Amelia would remember that staccato sound the rest of her life.

In the next second, a vicious tremor struck beneath the soles of her sturdy shoes. She grasped the edge of her drafting table to steady herself and hung on tight as a large photograph of Julia Morgan's controversial Mills College bell tower swung in a wide arc along the paneled wall. Then a second gigantic jolt of primordial energy shot through the room.

"Oh!" she cried as the four walls began a terrifying dance. "Oh *God, no!*"

A loud rumbling in the distance, deep and powerful as a hundred locomotives, gathered strength, and in seconds roared beneath her feet. The black-framed photograph of the campanile catapulted off the wall and crashed onto the desk normally occupied by Lacy Fiske. Lacy's desk, her typewriting machine, and the smashed picture then toppled to the floor, overturning the drafting boards like a row of dominoes.

Amelia clutched her own desk for support. Church bells from a few blocks away sounded, joined by peals from the tower of old St. Mary's on upper California Street by Chinatown. Then, bells all over the city began a dissonant clanging, as if heralding doomsday.

It is *an earthquake!* she thought, stunned. *And it's a big one!*

By this time, the entire ninth floor was undulating like a deadly carpet. Rolls of blueprints flew out of their storage bins as bottles of ink exploded off the shelves in the supply room. Agonizing seconds ticked by while the noise grew even more deafening—the unforgettable roar of the earth splitting open and nearby buildings collapsing in lethal piles of debris.

Amelia's stool pitched out from under her, hurtling her to the floor. Behind her, a waterfall of bricks and mortar erupted through a paneled wall from a stairwell leading to the roof.

Chunks of concrete and heavy ceiling moldings crumbled, filling her mouth with the chalky taste of plaster dust. The drawing she'd painstakingly completed slid to the floor, which was blanketed with gravel-sized chunks of rubble.

Amelia's worries of material loss were soon replaced by the gut-wrenching fear that she was about to lose her life. Her world kept shaking as terror gripped her insides and left her gasping for breath.

What of Father? Did he finally go home? And Aunt Margaret… all alone in Oakland. Will I ever see Mother again?

She heard herself scream with fright as a water main burst through a baseboard like a broken bone puncturing skin. On her next breath, she inhaled a foul-smelling stench as the nine-story office building's principal sewage pipe fractured and hemorrhaged its rank contents in all directions.

I'll never have a child! I'll never see the Bay View again.

Then, years of training suddenly drew her fragmented thoughts to the inside stairwell spiraling to the lobby.

The center core of the building's the strongest… get away from the windows… get to the center!

Blindly, she inched along a floor pitching as violently as the deck of a boat in a midwinter storm. Her hands touched the threshold opening onto the ninth floor foyer at the instant the glass transom over her head exploded into a thousand pieces. Reflexively, Amelia cast her right arm in front of her face, but not before blood spurted from her scalp and ran down her checks. She crumpled beneath the doorframe, curling into a ball.

Amelia screamed again as a twenty-five-foot expanse of wood paneling and masonry pitched outward and plunged nine stories to Montgomery Street below. She knew that no structure on landfill, no matter how well built, could withstand much more shaking without collapsing.

Then, just as suddenly, the convulsions subsided.

For several long minutes, Amelia clung to the doorjamb, her mind drifting like a seabird's flight. She gazed beyond the missing wall on the ninth floor at several buildings now visible across the street. Their facades too had disintegrated into heaps of rubble. Desks where accountants once sat were exposed to the elements. Bathroom urinals were immodestly revealed, and entire office floors were twisted into a jumble of metal girders.

The gray sky in the east had deepened to a rosy pink interspersed with streaks of palest blue. Incredibly, though, the Ferry Building's clock tower was still standing above the roiling salt water below, hands frozen at 5:14.

Amelia's entire body had started to tremble uncontrollably as if she, like her father, had been trapped in an ice cave in the Sierras. Her gaze skittered from crumbled cornice to buckled ceilings to the flag still flying from the top of the Ferry Building as she tried to absorb the chaos of her surroundings. Miraculously, she was still alive, but what of the rest of the city? What of her father and Aunt Margaret? Julia and the colleagues she hardly knew? What of people across San Francisco asleep in their beds?

She struggled to her knees and then fell once more against

the doorjamb. A light breeze blowing gently through the missing wall lifted a few strands of hair from her bleeding forehead. She stared vacantly at the sky beyond the line of wounded buildings ringing the shore.

April 18, 1906, had dawned eerily clear and mild in the City by the Bay.

CHAPTER 5

AMELIA HAD NO IDEA how long she remained crouched in the doorway with her back to the open gash that had been the ninth floor's east wall. Bruised, bleeding, and coated with plaster dust, she willed herself to stop trembling as she listened to the unnatural quiet, wondering if she were the last person alive in San Francisco.

Fine plaster particles still hung suspended in the air, making it painful even to breathe. Somewhere within the shell of the building she heard bricks break loose and cascade for several long seconds until they hit bottom—wherever bottom now was.

Without a plan or promise of reaching safety in a building in its death throes, she began crawling across the littered floor toward the elevator. The brass arrow above the door indicated that the car had halted one-and-a-half floors above the basement.

Zack! Oh God... the poor night watchman...

Zachary Webb had made a final trip down to the basement and had been on his way back to get her when the quake struck. What if she hadn't remained in the office to put the finishing touches on her drawing?

Don't think about that... not that.

Finally, she found the strength to limp toward the center stairwell and creep down an endless series of steps—many missing or warped by the tumultuous upheaval. Her ankle-length skirt and petticoat were now as potentially lethal as the jagged spikes of wood and chunks of brick that impeded her way.

At length, she arrived at the mezzanine where a broad staircase had once descended into the building's resplendent marble lobby—now an enormous open pit. Gone were the tall brass torchieres. Gone were the bronze and amber glass chandeliers hanging from the ceiling—for now, there was no ceiling. The elevator shaft on the lobby and mezzanine levels was a tortured mass of steel and plaster. The car itself had been flattened to half its size, probably with Zack's body inside. The enormity of the damage was so devastating that Amelia stared in disbelief at the destruction of one of the city's grandest office buildings.

Like a diver poised on the edge of a cliff, she took a deep breath, counted to three, and then stepped backwards onto a jagged peak of the lobby's remains. She clung to the sharp edges of the wreckage above her head and, step by step, slowly eased herself down the pile of rubble until she reached the buckled sidewalk.

By this time, she was trembling uncontrollably, her frightened state made worse when she caught sight of a woman's hand clasping a crumpled tin wash bucket nestled among the debris.

The poor soul... it could have been me... the poor soul... rang in her head like a hideous nursery rhyme.

Amelia quickly turned away from the mangled corpse and limped to the Montgomery Street side of the shattered structure. She knew from her engineering studies that the force of the shaking had turned solid mortar into grains of sand and transformed the building's foundation into liquefied earth. That, and the simple Law of Gravity, caused huge chunks of the building's facade to crash into the street, leaving a twisted superstructure that now resembled a rusted, empty birdcage. In the distance, Amelia heard the clanging bells of fire brigades and the occasional muffled explosion. She knew there would be gas pipes erupting, coal stoves overturned.

She sank onto a pile of debris as a tremendous well of fear and grief filled her chest. Like a water main rupturing, the pressure reached the bursting point and she covered her face with her hands. She cried for Zachary Webb and his daughter Josie, whom she'd never even met. She cried for the woman who'd died with a wash bucket in her hand, for a father who never came home at night—and for a mother who'd never come home at all. And for her elderly aunt, haunted by her own, long-ago traumas, across the water in Oakland.

Finally, she cried for San Francisco.

❧

At length, Amelia rose to her feet to stagger uncertainly toward the bay. Lurching onwards, she was continually overtaken by scores of battered San Franciscans fleeing their homes. Women and small children, many swathed in bandages, struggled with all manner of household items: quilts and cook pots, family portraits and sewing machines. Men wielded wheelbarrows piled high with clothing and books, even a wicker cat-carrier or two, and carts overflowed with everything from bedsteads to teakettles.

"I left a note tacked to Lotta's Fountain," she heard one fellow say who was pushing a pram with an ornate mantel clock where a baby normally reclined. "Maybe someone in the family'll see it and know we're alive."

"If *they're* alive, maybe they will," his companion replied.

At the waterfront Amelia witnessed a sickening spectacle as anxious crowds pressed toward a lone approaching vessel. Then, without warning, the earth roiled beneath her feet once again and a wail rose in unison from the crowds waiting in long lines at the wharves, people and property pitched against each other.

"Aftershock!" someone cried, a word tragically familiar to San Franciscans after the recurrent temblors of 1898.

Amelia imitated seasoned veterans crouching and covering their heads. The jolt lasted only a second or two but seemed much longer. It felt to Amelia as if the Apocalypse was at hand.

The ferry hooted a warning to alert deckhands and stevedores to prepare for docking. The instant the *Berkeley* bumped against its mooring, the desperate throng surged forward as one body, ladies elbowing children out of their path, men casting women aside—all scrambling to be first when the gangplank was lowered.

Slowly, Amelia rose to her feet and joined the swelling tide of humanity.

"I hear Oakland's not hit too bad," a woman confided to her companion in a low voice. "Heard it from a deckhand on the first boat over this mornin'. Think that no good brother of yours'll take us in?"

Just then, Amelia was shoved aside by a gentleman in black evening clothes sheeted with white dust. Amelia seized his filthy sleeve and angrily pushed back. "For heaven's sake, sir! Could you please—?"

Their eyes locked in a startled look of recognition. "Mr. Kemp! Are you all right?" Amelia exclaimed, gazing at her father's erstwhile poker partner.

Ezra Kemp's barrel chest and broad shoulders loomed over Amelia as he regarded her shocking dishevelment. He noted the blood and bruises. "And you, Miss Bradshaw?"

"I'm alive," she replied, taking in his tattered sleeves and dirty face. "Where were you when it hit? I was at the top of 456 Montgomery."

"At five a.m.?"

"I work at night and had a deadline for a design project for Julia Morgan. Most of the building collapsed."

Kemp gestured toward a scene reminiscent of a Matthew Brady Civil War daguerreotype. Rubble was scattered everywhere, and the acrid smell of smoke from Market Street intensified by the minute.

Kemp jabbed a stubby finger at the prevailing chaos. "All the water mains burst, so there's no means to fight the fires. A member of the brigade told me that the fire chief fell two stories and is probably dead by now. The city's doomed, Miss Bradshaw. Get yourself across the bay and stay there," he ordered gruffly.

"That is exactly what I am attempting to do," she retorted. "I'm terribly worried about my aunt in Oakland and—" She hesitated and then asked a hopeless question. "By chance, have you seen my father?"

Kemp didn't answer as he forced his considerable bulk past anyone standing between him and the gangway.

"Mr. Kemp!" she cried, attempting to follow him. He turned at the sound of her voice. "This ferry is going to Oakland. Don't you live in Mill Valley? Won't you step aside and let me—"

Ezra Kemp ignored her desperate plea and turned toward the docks. Furious at his indifference, she shouted, "At least have the decency to tell me if you've see my father?"

To her surprise, Kemp looked back, calling out over his shoulder, "He's probably still at the Bay View."

"At the hotel? Have you actually *seen* him?"

"Yes," Kemp yelled over the heads of the surging throng. "At about five a.m. this morning, wagering his very last penny."

Without another word, he thrust aside a young boy clinging to his mother's hand and climbed on board the *Berkeley* seconds before a harried deckhand pulled up the gangway. Ezra Kemp might reside to the north, but the lumber magnate was obviously hell bent on fleeing the city any way he could—and saving his own hide.

❧

The ferry set off east across the bay while Amelia headed west, back into the grim remains of the city, weaving her way past chunks of masonry and twisted trolley tracks and setting out for the Bay View atop Nob Hill. Despite the devastation surrounding her, she was buoyed by the hope that her father was alive. She hurried onward, the crowds flowing in the opposite direction like a raging river toward the bay.

Soon she began the arduous climb up California Street. The higher she scaled the incline, the less quake damage she witnessed. Several open-air horseless carriages, packed with sightseers, whizzed by. She was amazed, in fact, by the carnival atmosphere prevailing in San Francisco's upper-class district, some of whose residents were heading downhill to enjoy firsthand observations of the collapsed docks and shattered structures along the waterfront.

A boy interrupted his game of hopscotch and pointed at her bloodstained shirtwaist. "Hey, lady, what's it like downtown? Musta been pretty bad down there, huh? Seen any dead bodies? Did ya know your hair's all white? Those are some mighty nasty cuts on yer forehead."

Amelia ignored him and sped toward the top of the hill. Panting by the time she finally reached the summit, she turned right onto Taylor Street and paused to catch her breath.

"Oh, thank goodness…" she murmured.

Her favorite cluster of Victorian-style mansions belonging to the Big Four railroad barons, Crocker, Huntington, Stanford, and Hopkins, along with the new Fairmont Hotel— all built on the hill's foundation of bedrock—appeared relatively unharmed. Alarmingly, though, bells on the fire trucks were clanging a quarter-mile away in Chinatown.

Four blocks farther down the crest of Nob Hill, she caught a comforting glimpse of one of the Bay View's turrets. Just the sight of the place was reassuring, but, as she drew nearer, her hope soon turned to horror.

In contrast to other buildings on Taylor Street, every chimney of her grandfather's hotel had crumbled, leaving jagged holes along the massive shingled roof and shattering windows and walls on the Jackson Street side. Why had Charlie Hunter's pride and joy suffered such terrible damage and not other buildings in this neighborhood rooted in Nob Hill's sheet of basalt and serpentine? Why was the grand old lady listing treacherously to the east, appearing as if it might tumble down the hill toward the bay?

And then the truth hit her full force.

"Oh God! *No!*" screamed Amelia, limping faster down the incline of Jackson Street.

The recent addition of the gambling club built by Ezra Kemp and J.D. Thayer on the downhill side of the property had completely collapsed, taking with it some of the older sections of the original building and severely damaging its roof. As she'd learned from Lacy Fiske, the designer hired by Thayer and Kemp to build the annex to the hotel was a mere dandy in spats that barely knew his architectural ABC's, let alone how to calculate the load-bearing requirements of a structure built on a hill. Surveying the extensive wreckage, Amelia felt sick to her stomach.

Bruised and battered hotel guests wandered aimlessly in the street or sat on paving stones, looking like lost children as they watched her pass by. At the bottom of the hill, the nine blocks of Chinatown had been reduced by the upheaval into piles of oversized kindling. Orange pockmarks of flame dotted the landscape below.

Amelia lifted her skirts and hobbled down a narrow slate path toward the remains of the newer building, her aching muscles protesting each step. She searched for safe entry into the annex that had suffered such terrible damage, peering through a yawning hole in a wall that had—for the few weeks of its existence—kept prying eyes from well-heeled nobs hazarding thousands of dollars on a single hand of cards.

Now the interior was merely a jumble of fallen gas lighting fixtures, piles of bricks and mortar, heaps of wood, and a long, elaborate cherry wood bar toppled onto its face. Two-thirds of the roof lay open to the sky. Amelia leaned forward and squinted into the gloom, steadying herself against an exposed four-by-four whose splintered surface pressed painfully into her lacerated palm.

"Father!" she shouted. "Henry Bradshaw, are you *in* here?"

Her cries were greeted by ghostly silence. An act of God had changed J.D. Thayer's glittering gambling den into a pile of rubbish. Against the only interior wall of the club left standing, Amelia could barely distinguish the outline of several upholstered sofas piled high with debris. On one, beneath five-foot mounds of plaster and wood, a length of crimson silk and the slender arm of a woman lay limply amidst the rubble. Amelia had overheard scuttlebutt that female Chinese "hostesses" were employed here for the enjoyment of a select clientele at the new club. Here was the gruesome proof.

And Father? Please, God, don't let my father be—

Weak from her own ordeal and dismayed by everything in view, Amelia cast one last frightened glance around the shattered room and saw no other signs of life. Maybe her father had the sense to call it a night before the quake struck. Perhaps, for once, Henry Bradshaw had done the sensible thing and joined the chaotic throng jockeying to board the first boat to Oakland, even beating Ezra Kemp in his ignoble retreat.

By now, huge clouds of black smoke downtown tarred the sky, tendrils belching a mile high. *Could an entire city burn to the ground,* Amelia wondered.

Just then, a ragged voice called out, weak and rasping.

"Help… *Please* help."

She gazed down into the club's devastation from the street's higher elevation, barely able to make out the shadowy figure of a man slumped against a doorjamb with a small dog curled up at his side. It was difficult to determine that the man's hair, sprinkled with plaster dust, was nearly as dark as his fashionable evening clothes. Dried blood crusted his battered face.

Amelia immediately recognized her grandfather's dog, Barbary, who normally slept in the basement and had somehow survived the cataclysmic events upstairs. Then she saw that J.D. Thayer was painfully pulling himself to a standing position. He clung to the threshold with one arm and stretched the other toward her in a gesture of abject supplication. His face contorted in agony and he paused as if he were gathering his very last ounce of strength.

"Please… I beg of you. Help us! The roof's caved in on—"

Thayer's voice broke as he gazed toward the couch where the woman's arm, partially cloaked in red Chinese silk, protruded from a pile of debris. He pulled his eyes from the corpse and turned his head to stare at Amelia through the gloom, recognition dawning.

"Please… I know I have no right… but in God's name… can you *help* me?"

CHAPTER 6

AMELIA GAZED PAST THE ruins at the new owner of
the Bay View Hotel, now a pathetic-looking creature
huddling less than fifteen feet away, his gaze pleading. The
cuts on his head looked deep and his voice sounded reedy.
How could she ignore the suffering of a fellow human at a
time like this, even if he'd wreaked havoc on her life? But
who could come to his aid?

"Of course I'll try to help you, Mr. Thayer," she assured
him across the wreckage, "but you must tell me whom I can
summon for you here."

Thayer looked at her strangely as if some discomforting
thought just occurred to him. "Oh God…" he said and then
fell silent.

Amelia, the last person he'd expected as a potential
rescuer, stood at the edge of the broken wall that overlooked the devastation below. It was impossible to envision how posh this establishment had appeared only a few
hours earlier. The *San Francisco Call* had been rhapsodic in
its description of the club's elegant gaming tables, expensive
mahogany paneling, rich Persian carpets, and discreet nooks
where all manner of business was transacted. What wasn't
reported was the inadequate foundations or the private rooms
in the adjacent hotel reserved for romantic assignations—or
so went the rumors.

As of five fifteen that morning, the entire place looked as if a barrage of cannon fire ripped through all four walls and pummeled the occupants, including Thayer. Amelia found her gaze once more drifting toward the pale arm of a woman buried beneath a pile of plaster and bricks. She quickly looked away, remembering her own near brush with death.

"Don't risk coming down here," Thayer called out, wincing at his effort to speak. "Just send help. The rest of the roof may cave in. I can barely breathe. I think I've broken my ribs. Ling Lee... has been crushed."

"Oh *no*! That's your... friend? I'm so terribly sorry."

Thayer, having spoken the woman's name, closed his eyes and fell silent, as if incapable of saying more. He slipped to his knees once again, head bowed as Barbary pressed closer to him. The only other man Amelia had ever witnessed weep was her drunken father, begging to gain admittance at the door of the Hunter Family suite after a particularly extended binge of drinking when she was nine years old.

Unlike Henry Bradshaw's harsh sobs, Thayer made no sound now, but remained mute, shoulders heaving. His former air of confidence and command had vanished, and in its place was the raw vulnerability of a man who had faced forces he could not possibly control. Like she, he'd been laid waste by the earthquake's stark, vicious impartiality and Amelia felt a sudden, irrational kinship with a fellow survivor.

Despite Thayer's warnings, she cautiously made her way deeper into the pit of rubble and knelt by his side, lightly placing a hand on his dust-covered shoulder, her fingertips leaving an impression where she touched his dark dinner jacket. Barbary gazed up at her, his terrier tail giving a few, desultory wags. The animal appeared to have transferred his allegiance to the hotel's new owner, for he licked Thayer's dust covered hand and then rested his furry head on his thigh.

"Hello, Barbary," she murmured, and then turned her attention to Thayer. "We must get you medical attention right away."

"You shouldn't be down here," he muttered. "It's too dangerous." He raised one arm across his chest and encased her hand that was resting on his shoulder with his own, a joining of two wounded souls. His palm felt cold and Amelia guessed that by now, he was probably suffering from shock.

"You're very kind," he murmured, closing his eyes. "More than I deserve. I can hardly move and—"

"Then you must rest here awhile and I'll see if I can find someone to help. Things are rather desperate downtown," she confessed reluctantly. She peered past a shattered wall in the direction of the street, wondering if any hotel guests were wandering about that could lend a hand. "The fires appear to be spreading downtown something fierce. Perhaps someone on Taylor Street could—"

Thayer's lids fluttered open and he stared at her. His brows suddenly knit together and then he murmured, "I'm sorry… I'm so sorry…"

To Amelia, the man again seemed amazingly close to tears. Thayer's chin sank to his chest and he shook his head in little motions of despair. "I think… he's over there," he said, barely above a whisper. "Near Ling Lee."

A stab of dread, sudden and real, clutched at her. "Who?"

"Your father."

"*What?* Where?" She scanned the wreckage in disbelief that anyone else could have survived the collapse of the building.

Thayer nodded in the direction of a gaming table that was minus its legs.

"The table and chandelier fell on him… right after he dove for cover."

A gigantic brass gasolier that once hung overhead had made a bull's-eye landing on the top of its green baize surface.

"Dear God!" Amelia searched for a path to make her way across the shattered room where the city's high rollers had entertained themselves, and where her father apparently lay entombed.

"Don't go over there!" Thayer grimaced each time he spoke. "There's nothing you can do… on your own."

Amelia ignored his directive and, instead, worked her way on all fours until she reached the middle of what was left of the room.

"This table?"

Battling panic, she didn't hear Thayer's response for she had caught sight of a gentleman's dress shoe and spats covered with a layer of white powder.

"Father! Oh my *God*…"

How in the world had Ezra Kemp been sitting in the same spot and walked away from this disaster? She had no idea where she found the strength to yank the brass gasolier to one side and push the heavy wooden table off her father's body. Henry Bradshaw lay face down in the wreckage. His left cheek was black and blue and blood had congealed over nearly every inch of visible skin.

"Is he breathing?" Thayer called out hoarsely.

"I don't know," Amelia mumbled. "I can't tell." She moved several chunks of plaster to kneel by her father's side. "He's badly injured. His face—"

A low moan interrupted this exchange.

"He's alive! *Father!*" She bent close to his ear. "It's me, Amelia. I'm here. Please, Father—"

"I… need… a whissss-key," slurred the injured man.

Amelia raised her head and stared across the expanse of debris at Thayer.

"Your father was… shall we say… in his cups at five a.m. Perhaps he's—"

"Still drunk!" she finished, pulling more debris off her father's back.

Just then, Henry's eyes opened wide. "Whiss-key! A cele-bray-shun izin order!"

Amelia's relief turned to despair, then to anger. "Oh, Father!"

"Pour me a glass, daughter," he growled, "and be quick about it!" Then, he slipped back into unconsciousness.

Amelia closed her eyes. Her father had survived after all. But as always, Henry Bradshaw—when intoxicated—had turned belligerent. He was a regular Dr. Jekyll and Mr. Hyde. Everybody said so. Where was the laughing young man who had built castles in the sand at the rim of San Francisco Bay and joyfully lifted his little daughter high in the air? After everything that had happened, here he was, behaving appallingly, even after the world had collapsed on top of him.

Amelia sank deeper among the debris, wrapped her arms around her knees, pressed her forehead into the folds of her filthy skirt, and, like J.D. Thayer had a few moments earlier, began silently to weep.

❦

J.D. never knew how he managed to push away from the doorjamb and stumble toward the two figures in the center of the little that remained of the club, but when he got there, he placed a hand gently on top of Amelia's head, brunette wisps of her upswept hairstyle cascading about her shoulders.

"Who can judge why bricks fall on some heads and not others?" he said.

Barbary had managed to follow him and stood between them, as if he were waiting to hear their next plan of action. Amelia raised her head from her knees. "I've taken my father home from scores of saloons, but this… *this*…" Her words drifted off.

"This isn't like anything we've ever known."

"No, it's not." She nodded toward her father's prone figure. "Perhaps it's just as well he passed out again."

She made no protest when J.D. gingerly knelt beside her and wrapped his right arm around her shoulders, but she soon pulled away. He winced and put the palm of his hand against his rib cage. For a moment, he thought he might faint with pain.

"I'm sorry if I hurt you," she said in a rush, "but my father wouldn't even *be* in the Bay View Gentlemen's Gambling Club right now if you and Kemp hadn't goaded him into wagering—again!"

Yes and no, J.D. thought, too weary and sick at heart to explain the origins of the previous night's insane contest. Or its outcome.

Amelia leaned toward her injured parent. "Father, I'm going to try to find someone to help us. Do you hear me? I'll be back as soon as I can."

Henry's eyes suddenly opened wide.

"Can't move…" he mumbled. "Can't… move… anything…"

"Not *anything*?" she asked. "Not even your fingers?"

"It's likely he's broken his back," J.D. said under his breath, each word sending a stab of pain through his chest. "The Winton is garaged on the Taylor Street side of the hotel. I know an army doctor. A friend who lives at the

Presidio. If we can get to it and the engine will start, can you drive?"

"No." She stared down at her father for a long moment. "But I'll try."

They could hear the persistent clanging of fire bells coming from many directions. J.D. felt sweat beading his forehead and feared he might keel over before they'd even taken a step. "Allow me to lean on you and we'll see if I can get the motorcar running," he said.

Just then a slight tremor shook the room, followed by a crash of plaster somewhere in the hotel itself. Barbary gave a yelp while Amelia crouched near her father's prone figure, her arms held over both their heads for protection.

After several seconds of quiet, she pulled herself to a standing position beside J.D., who hadn't had the strength to move an inch. "I can't *stand* these aftershocks," she confessed on a shaky breath. "Put your arm around my shoulder and let's try to get the Winton started. You'll have to tell me every single thing to do, but we must hurry. The fires look as if they're spreading rapidly."

J.D. could barely make the effort to nod in agreement. "We'll bring Dr. McClure here," he murmured.

He could tell that she was loath to leave her father alone with the neighborhood ablaze, but what choice did either of them have? He was forced to lean heavily on her for support while they struggled out of the club's wreckage and up the steep Jackson Street slope with Barbary following along behind. When they turned the corner, they discovered to their surprise that, with the exception of its collapsed chimneys, the Taylor Street section of the building was relatively undamaged.

Likewise, the enormous six-seater Winton, parked in the

subterranean former stable at the north end of the old hotel, had come through the earthquake amazingly unscathed. J.D. marveled at the good condition of its polished, midnight blue fenders, tufted black leather upholstered seats, and steering wheel so formidable it threatened to impinge on his damaged chest. Amelia located the crank under the driver's seat while Barbary jumped into the back seat in the normal fashion he'd adopted as J.D.'s shadow since Charlie Hunter's death. It was strange that the dog had taken such a liking to him, considering how J.D. had succeeded his original master at the Bay View.

"If you can... get the crank to turn," he proposed to Amelia, each breath an effort, " I think I'll... be able to... drive."

Appearing vastly relieved to hear this, Amelia followed his step-by-step instructions and started the automobile's engine after only a few rotations of the crank. A small crowd of hotel guests gathered as J.D. backed the touring car onto the street. A number of injured scrambled for seats when Amelia revealed that they were off to find a doctor.

"Get in! Get in!" he called to her urgently as nearly all the places were quickly claimed.

Amelia remained where she was, apparently torn by indecision. "I can't leave Father alone. I just can't! What if he should die while I'm gone?"

J.D. glanced at the smoke from downtown that billowed in their direction. The odds that Nob Hill would be next to burn were fast increasing. The sooner he left, the sooner he or McClure could come back for her and her father.

"Then I'll return as fast as I can." He was wheezing now and had difficulty putting the car in gear. The effort to extricate himself from the basement annex and climb into the car had only aggravated his rib injury. Pain pulsed throughout his rib cage, making it hard to focus his thoughts. "Blankets are… in the hotel…" he directed hoarsely.

"I know," she said. "In the housekeeper's pantry."

Of course she'd know, he reminded himself. She grew up there.

By now, he was practically speaking to her in code. "Careful… more ceiling… collapse… other… shocks. Watch out."

"I will," she assured him. "Now go!"

"I'll come back."

"Good! Hurry!"

She was holding her left forearm as if it pained her. Blood had dried on her pale skin and soiled the sleeves and front of her shirtwaist. Additional strands of her dark chestnut hair had escaped her topknot and hung limply against her flushed cheeks. She gave a brief nod to indicate that she would be all right, despite his leaving her in the midst of such terrifying chaos.

He wondered suddenly if he would ever see her again. Would this courageous woman survive the terrible Act of God that had befallen San Francisco?

Or would he?

Should he tell her about last night, he wondered suddenly.

Tell her what? said a voice in his head. He wasn't completely sure, himself, what happened. Exactly. It was all such a jumble.

"Please!" he said, infused with a sudden surge of energy. "Get in the car. At least save your own life if we can't save your father's!"

Amelia glanced at the darkening skies. Flames and funnels of smoke dotted the landscape at scores of locations near the waterfront. In the distance, a series of loud concussions punctuated the air.

"Explosions," she murmured. "Gas boilers, do you suppose?"

"Dynamite. Army work. Creates firebreaks."

"It looks as if it also starts fires." She pointed to a puff of smoke rising in the area of the latest explosion. "I *have* to stay with my father," she said, holding his glance. "Send us help if you can." And they both knew how slim the chances of that would be.

Then she added, "Godspeed, Mr. Thayer."

For a split second, as he stared into the depths of her brown eyes, J.D. suddenly felt a kind of intimacy more potent than anything he had ever experienced. It was as if they'd been lovers and he'd never played her father for the fool while her admirable grandfather lay upstairs in the resplendent Bay View Hotel, dying of a thrombosis.

Then the moment shifted back to the harsh reality bearing down on Nob Hill. "I'll bring the doctor," he wheezed, barely able to speak for the pain in his chest.

"Or just send him to us. You need to lie still as soon as possible."

Grimacing again, he shifted gears, applied the gas, and the Winton sputtered away.

CHAPTER 7

A MELIA STARED AT THE cloud of dust kicked up by the retreating automobile. Then she turned toward the phalanx of flames converging from several directions at the bottom of the hill and advancing northwest. Where were the fire brigades? Surely Mayor Schmitz and his City Hall cronies would mount a defense of Nob Hill.

By now, she began to wonder what she would do if she were J.D. Thayer. Wouldn't she simply drive that fancy automobile as far away from San Francisco as the fuel in the tank would take it? The question was: would *he*?

By the time she returned to her father's side, he was groaning in agony. The numbing affects of the alcohol from the previous night were fast wearing off.

"My hand…" he moaned. "My hand…"

"Your hand pains you, yes?" She gently covered him with a blanket that she'd found in the housekeeper's closet in the main part of the hotel.

"My *hand*!" he grunted. "A flush…"

"It's been crushed by the table. It's bound to hurt quite a lot and turn red."

"Noooo!" He pursed his lips in frustration. "A *royal* flush. I won! I won it back! Look at my hand!"

Startled, Amelia lifted a corner of the blanket and gently slipped three playing cards from between his palm and thumb. On the backs of each card, the words "Bay View Hotel" were etched in bold script. The initials "JDT" were also stamped in a corner.

"There are three cards here, Father." She turned them face up. "An ace, queen, and ten. All diamonds. J.D. Thayer's initials are on the backs."

"Jack... king too..." he murmured. "Had all five of 'em. I won the Bay View back. Fair and square. Just as I lay down the last card... hot damn! All hell broke loose."

"You mean the quake hit? Where are the other two cards?"

"I grabbed all of 'em when I dove for cover," Henry said with sudden strength. "Look around, damn you!"

Amelia scanned the chaos and shrugged helplessly. "We'll never find two playing cards in this rubble, Father."

"I bet it all... and won it all back! *Find* them!"

"Oh, Father..." She shook her head in disgust. "Mr. Kemp wasn't exaggerating. You wagered your last *sou* last night... and for *what*!?"

"For you! And I won! Everything's ours again! You tell that J.D. your pappy's a rich man again."

So Thayer and Kemp had once again competed to divest their favorite pigeon of his last cent in another winner-take-all poker fest. And she had just helped Thayer escape from the fate that was certain to overtake her father and her in the next few hours if the fire lines didn't hold.

She scanned the jumble of debris where Ling Lee's lifeless arm made her wonder if there were other women buried in the rubble piled on top of several additional sofas and chairs.

"Mr. Thayer isn't here anymore," she said dully. "Neither are the two cards."

"You don't believe me?" her father demanded.

Amelia had reached beyond her ability to cope with her belligerent parent.

What difference does it make now? she wanted to scream, but closed her eyes instead and whispered "Seven times four… seven times three…"

Amelia could not count the number of times her father had sworn that he would have nothing more to do with gambling, spirits, or whores. Neither could she, her mother, nor her aunt tally the occasions when Henry Bradshaw claimed he'd triumphed in some great endeavor—save for an untoward event that was never his responsibility. And each time, her father's excuses proved to be an endless series of lies and self-deceptions. No wonder Mother had finally fled to Europe, filing for divorce before she left. At least she'd saved herself, which was a great deal more than Amelia could say for her own plight.

Again, she searched in the immediate vicinity for the two other cards, but to no avail. Once again, her father had lied to excuse his outrageous behavior. Numb with exhaustion, she tucked the three crumpled cards into the pocket of her skirt and curled up in the rubble near her father. Under a second hotel blanket, she wrapped her arms around her torso to keep warm as overwhelming fatigue pulled her into unconsciousness, oblivious to the distant sound of clanging fire bells and the acrid smell of smoke.

⁓

Sometime later, Amelia was shaken awake by the rapid, jolting motion of another aftershock. The temblor rattled the debris beneath her, forcing her to her feet, her heart racing. Forgetting even her father, sheer instinct for survival propelled her up a mountain of bricks and onto the sidewalk on Jackson Street. By the time she found herself in the road, the tremors had stopped. She gulped for air and tried to calm her racing pulse.

In the lot adjacent to the wrecked gambling club, a gray-haired woman stood beside a pit dug in her back garden. She clung to a shovel while howling an unearthly series of cries. Grandfather Hunter had written Amelia in Paris that a fabulously wealthy, reclusive widow had purchased the three-story house next door and made it abundantly clear to everyone in the neighborhood that she wished to be left alone. Even so, her emotional outburst cried out for attention, and Amelia stepped over a gate toppled by the latest tremor.

At that moment, a Chinese man clad in black, pajama-like attire came around the corner of the house in a dead run. When the old woman saw that he was carrying a lifeless small dog in his arms, she began to shriek with despair. She pitched down her shovel and threw her arms around both the dog and the servant, clinging to them fiercely.

Amelia drew near, exchanging looks with the Chinese servant.

"I'm so sorry," she began. "Is there anything I can—?"

She hesitated at a look of warning that flashed in the servant's eye. Before she could say anything further, the old woman reared her head and screeched, "Get away! Off with you! Chung, make her *leave*!"

The distraught woman bore down on Amelia, wailing like a banshee. From the a pocket in her skirt she withdrew a revolver and pointed it at her would-be savior.

"I told you to leave us alone!" the woman shrieked.

"But the fire is—" Amelia protested.

"Get away, missy!" the Chinese house servant cried. "She no like—"

At the sound of the pistol being cocked, Amelia flattened herself on the sidewalk. A split second later, a bullet smashed into the crumbled fence near where she'd been standing.

"Come, Missy Lolly... come, come," the servant demanded with surprising authority. "I take care... I take care of everything. No worries... come."

Amelia's heartbeat thundered in her ears while the crunch of steps receded toward the center of the woman's garden. On hands and knees, she crawled thirty feet uphill, reaching the gaping hole where she had initially discovered J.D. Thayer. Sticking out of the rubble, Ling Lee's lifeless limb was now the color of slate.

"Please..." Amelia called weakly, her knees beginning to fold, "somebody help me!" Her lungs strained against the smoke-filled air and in her ears, the incessant clanging of the fire brigades' bells began to fade. For the first time in Amelia's life, the world went gray as she collapsed on the buckled sidewalk in a heap of cotton petticoats and a stained serge skirt.

"Someone just tried to kill me," she muttered to the corpse buried under five feet of debris, "and I don't even know why."

෴

Amelia awoke to find herself slung over the bony shoulder of a redheaded man struggling up the steep incline of Jackson Street en route to Taylor. He deposited her unceremoniously on the Winton's running board, propping her against the driver's side door. About the same age as J.D. Thayer, he leaned close and squinted at her, his russet whiskers practically brushing her face.

"Let's see what's wrong with you now." He pulled down one of her lower eyelids and then the other. Then he extracted an amber vial from his medical bag and gave her a whiff of smelling salts that made her cough and sputter.

"The woman next door… tried to kill me," Amelia choked. Her terror came back in a rush and she reached for the man's arm to steady her. "I was just trying to—"

"It took awhile to find you after we pulled up. I'm Dr. Angus McClure."

Amelia clung tighter to the physician's arm as he waved the bottle under her nose a second time, soothed somewhat by his Scottish accent that reminded her of her grandfather's burr.

"The old woman next door shot a pistol at me when I offered to help her."

"The veneer of civilization gets mighty thin when disasters strike," he said.

"Why was that old crone shooting?" wheezed J.D. from the passenger seat.

Amelia was startled to hear his voice, for in the hours she dozed fitfully next to her father in the ruins of J.D.'s gambling club, she came to the conclusion that, like Kemp, he'd save his own skin.

"When I first found your lady friend, J.D., I saw that the old woman next door and her Chinese houseboy were burying a trunk," McClure reported. "Must've had something in it she considered valuable."

Amelia shook her head, her eyes still watering from the contents of McClure's vial. "No. The woman was very upset because her dog was killed in the quake. Her houseboy was about to put the poor beast in the trunk for burial. When I urged them to escape the fire and come with me, she grew hysterical, pointed her pistol, and shot right at me."

"And how are you feeling now?" the doctor asked.

"Better." She sat up abruptly. "My father! Oh, thank God you're here!"

"I'm here because this maniac forced me to come," McClure said, meaning J.D. "I told him to stay put, but he wouldna lie on his cot."

Amelia rose unsteadily to her feet, peered across the open-air motorcar, and judged her rescuer in worse shape than before. "Thank you for returning," she said, "but anyone who stays here much longer will be burned alive." She pointed down the street at flames marching up the hill-side. "My father's in the back annex with rubble everywhere. I have no idea how we're going to move him."

"J.D., you stay right where you are," ordered Dr. McClure, "and don't budge, or you'll make matters worse." He groped in the backseat for two poles rolled in a length of canvas—an army stretcher, guessed Amelia. "If you're feeling up to it, come with me," ordered McClure. "We'll try to recruit some of these hotel guests to help us." He leaned forward and peered closely at her forehead. "Those cuts have scabbed over but they look nasty, miss. I'll attend to them once we see what we can do about your father."

McClure collared two men wandering dazedly down the deserted street and ordered them "under martial law," he barked, to assist in the removal of Amelia's father from the debris.

Henry Bradshaw's eyes were closed when they found him, his dress woolen trousers covered with a new layer of rubble from the recent aftershock.

The doctor pulled a smaller mirror out of his pocket and held it within an inch of the injured man's lip.

"Barely breathing," he muttered. He glanced at Amelia. "He won't last the night, you know. He'll be taking a place in that car out there that might better be—"

"Take him or leave *me*!" Amelia cried, her voice rising shrilly.

McClure hesitated for an instant, and then ordered the two men he'd commandeered on the street to put Henry Bradshaw on the stretcher and removed him to the backseat of the Winton.

Meanwhile, Thayer lifted his head from the passenger seat's backrest and said in a weak voice, "Look... the fire." Amelia spotted Barbary curled up on the Winton's floor.

The others turned to gaze at flames that were now consuming the shanties and lean-tos and collapsed brick hovels along the waterfront and racing uphill toward them, burning large sections of Chinatown to the ground in the process.

"Oh my God!" Amelia cried, pointing south. "The Fairmont!"

The beautiful *beaux-arts* hotel that had survived the quake admirably and was three days away from opening its doors to the public was about to be enveloped by flames advancing in a wall of orange and black. Even where buildings still remained, the heat had grown more intense and Amelia and the others began coughing convulsively as the smoke began to fill the air near them.

"We've got to get out of here," McClure said. "Climb onto the running board, lassie, and hold on tight."

He vaulted into the driver's seat as J.D. suddenly struggled to sit up. "My safe! I just thought of it, Angus! The property deeds... some gold... everything I have—"

The doctor glanced over his shoulder. Behind him, the growing conflagration had devoured upper Chinatown, just below where their motorcar stood on Taylor Street. Another explosion rattled the windows of the Bay View and showered the sidewalk with glass shards.

"Sorry, laddie. There's no time. The tires on this automobile will be exploding in a moment. We're *going!*"

Amelia turned to Thayer. "About an hour after you left, an aftershock dumped tons of debris on top of the safe behind the stairwell. You'd never get near it now." She felt sorry for the man but was relieved there would be no more delays in getting her father to the field hospital McClure said had been set up at the Army Presidio.

As the Winton pulled away from the roadside, Amelia detected that Henry Bradshaw's chest was moving, but his battered face looked like a death mask. She squinted at a sky turning peach and black as smoke surged skyward in huge funnels. *Dante's Inferno and the end of the world, all rolled into one*, she thought, picturing fire engulfing the Bay View and the spanking new Fairmont Hotel in the next hours. She was grateful Grandfather Hunter wasn't alive to witness such devastation.

What did it matter what was in the safe or who had won the blasted card game the previous night? After today, the only future that seemed clear for the entire populace of San Francisco—J.D. Thayer and herself included—was a choice between misery and destitution... or death.

∽

Angus McClure piloted the Winton toward the U.S. Army's base at the Presidio as the conflagration raged in their dusty wake. Along the road, Amelia saw humans transformed into draft animals, men as well as women pushing baby carriages, wagons, box carts, and even wheeled toys in a desperate effort to move possessions to safety. One wild-eyed man wheeled an upright piano through the chaos.

The Winton slowed to a snail's pace when it approached

a group of fifty or so Chinese women struggling along Van Ness Avenue in two columns. Amelia could hear high-pitched chatter among the throng clad in colorful silk and cotton dresses, carrying their worldly goods in fat bundles balanced on the ends of broom handles.

"Good God, J.D.!" Angus exclaimed. "There's Donaldina Cameron! She's even got the children marching."

The Winton drew up beside a tall, imposing woman with rust-colored hair akin to Dr. McClure's. This was the famous, perhaps notorious, Miss Cameron, noted for scaling walls and climbing down skylights in Chinatown in her ongoing effort to rescue victims of the "highbinders" who kidnapped women in China to serve as unpaid domestics—or worse—in San Francisco. The noted young woman wore somber attire and hair piled neatly on top of her head. A distinctive streak of premature white waved at the crown of her forehead—*like angel's wings*, Amelia thought.

"Those are the residents of the Presbyterian Mission Home, on Sacramento Street," McClure called to Amelia as she clutched the rear passenger door in order to steady herself on the motorcar's running board.

"I know of Miss Cameron's efforts," Amelia shouted against the wind. "She tries to help girls like the one killed in the gambling club."

Thayer suddenly returned to life. "No. Not like her. Ling Lee was no willing—"

"Ling Lee was an unusual woman," Angus volunteered over his shoulder. "She was one of the lucky few who escaped from China Alley and was brought to the Mission Home. If it hadn't been for Donaldina, Ling Lee would have died long before the earthquake got her." He watched his patient struggle to sit up. "And you, J.D.," he added ominously, "you'd better not move a muscle if you don't want to puncture a lung."

As they slowly passed by, Miss Cameron raised a hand high to halt her group and strode toward the car. McClure pulled over and waited.

"My dear Angus! And Mr. Thayer! What a blessing it is to see you both alive." Her beatific smile abruptly faded when she got a closer look at Thayer and heard the low cries of the older man sprawled on the backseat. "Can I do anything to help? We've carried some medical supplies with us and will gladly share."

"That's kind of you, Donaldina, but you should hoard every bandage you have. You're going to need them." McClure introduced Amelia and identified her father as the most gravely injured. Then he asked, "What happened to the Mission Home?"

"The brigades started dynamiting firebreaks. The soldiers ordered us to leave so I thought it best if we moved the women in broad daylight. The highbinders are vigilant about their 'property,'" she added, referring to Chinatown's brothel owners and procurers. "They'd snatch their girls back in a heartbeat if they could—never mind the quake and fire. We'll spend the night at the Presbyterian Church on Van Ness Street."

Thayer shifted in his seat and dug in his pockets, gasping in pain in the process. He extended her a gold piece. "Please take this. To help the children—and little Wing Lee."

Miss Cameron smiled faintly, nodded, and retrieved the coin. "Bless you, Mr. Thayer." Her regal bearing softened and she regarded him kindly. "And Ling Lee?"

Amelia watched as J.D. Thayer bowed his head and did not reply.

Angus cast a concerned glance in Thayer's direction. "She died in the quake," he explained cryptically. "Killed instantly, she was, when a ceiling caved in on her."

Miss Cameron put a sympathetic hand on Thayer's sleeve. "I am truly sorry to hear that. It's a tragic time for so many in our town." To Angus she said, "God bless."

And with that, she glided to the head of her "troops" and motioned for them to continue their march. By this time, Thayer had closed his eyes and appeared to lapse into semi-consciousness.

As for Henry Bradshaw, Amelia couldn't tell if her father was dead or alive.

CHAPTER 8

I T WAS LATE AFTERNOON before the Winton reached the Presidio's Lombard Gate, inching past a quake-torn crevice paralleling the crowded escape route. Once on the grounds of the army base, Amelia saw a wide field on her right already filled with rows of round, white army tents. The canvas structures were topped with conical roofs that made the encampment look like a scene out of the *Arabian Nights*. Sloping to the water's edge, the area offered a spectacular view of the bay, even as smoke from the scores of fires downtown cast a pall over the local surroundings.

The doctor drove the group directly to a large tent off to one side that had a placard reading MALE AMBULATORY. A group of uniformed orderlies greeted them as the car rolled to a stop in front of the open canvas flap.

"Easy, men… this fellow is definitely *not* ambulatory," Angus said with a physician's sense of black humor. "In fact, he's unconscious and probably broke his back, and *this* one," he added, referring to J.D., "is awake and nothing but trouble. He has a couple of broken ribs. Don't make 'em any worse if you can help it."

To Thayer he said, "Lie still on your cot in there, and don't do anything but drink water till I come back to see you. I'll look after your dog." The second set of orderlies eased Henry Bradshaw out of the car and onto a stretcher.

"Take him to Ward H and start giving him laudanum. A large dose."

Before Amelia could protest, her father was swiftly borne away. J.D. lifted his head from his stretcher and rasped, "Don't crash my car, damn you, McClure."

"Aye, laddie," the doctor replied. "And what can you do about it if I do?"

⚘

Henry Bradshaw had been assigned to a tent for those who survived the quake and fire, but for whom little could be done.

"Every ward in the hospital is already full, and we're starting to put even critical cases in some of the tents," announced Angus McClure to Amelia as they walked from sunlight into the dim interior. "Your father is housed here in Ward H on the far side of the parade ground."

"Next to the military cemetery," Amelia noted, squinting at the bright white tombstones visible through the open flaps of the tent.

"Aye, lassie," McClure answered soberly. "Now anyone can be buried at the Presidio."

It was only later, when Amelia was pressed into service as a "volunteer" nurse that she learned Ward H stood for "hopeless." On the day of the quake and fire, however, her spirits had already sunk to a new low when she realized that her father had been given so much laudanum for the pain that he had consequently taken up residence in the land of the living dead.

"He has broken his back in at least two places," McClure confided as she stood dejectedly next to her father's bedside. "Nasty business, I'm afraid."

"So he will be an invalid? In a wheeled chair?" Amelia asked.

"With the bad weather rolling in and the primitive conditions around here, pneumonia's a real danger. I'm afraid you should prepare yourself for the worst."

McClure gently took her arm and drew her away from her father's bedside to have a private word. "You're welcome to sit by his side for a bit, and then ask someone to find me so I can stitch up those cuts on your forehead. After that, report to the nurses' tent and they'll give you a cot. You'd best get some rest while you can."

At the mention of bed, Amelia experienced such a wave of fatigue she thought she might simply keel over then and there. The idea of a clean, horizontal surface to sleep on sounded like a gift from heaven.

"Thank you, Dr. McClure. I appreciate that."

Once again, his lilting Scottish accent made her think of her late grandfather. It seemed impossible now that Charlie Hunter had still been alive only six weeks ago, before her world turned upside down.

"Do call me Angus," the doctor said. "No point in maintaining such formality when we can't rely on the earth beneath our feet, eh, Amelia?"

She nodded and tried to smile. "Angus, then." She turned to study her father's immobile features. It only then occurred to her that the doctor had been trying to tell her that her father would be dead by dawn's light.

"I'll just sit here a while," she murmured.

❦

That night, Amelia refused to leave her father's side, making her bed on a nearby cot and listening to his labored breathing until she fell into an exhausted sleep. Long past midnight, she heard him call her name. Scrambling to her feet, her blanket gathered around her shoulders like an Indian squaw, she stood shivering by his bedside.

"What is it, Father?" she murmured, not wanting to wake the other patients. No one had come to administer laudanum and he sounded more like himself in sober days.

"I was dreaming about you, Melly," he whispered between gasps for breath, "and when I woke up, there you were... sleeping on the cot."

"Yes?" She was touched by the wistfulness of his tone. She knelt at his side and felt his forehead. He was feverish, which Angus warned might bring on vivid dreams. "I'm right here. Feeling any better?"

"Sand castles..." he said with a sigh. "You were building sand castles down by the bay."

She felt a stab of nostalgia at the memory of constructing fanciful turrets with a tin bucket as a child, but all she said was, "Was it Blarney Castle I was building? Remember how you'd always say that was the one we should make?"

"Well, we Bradshaws *are* Scots-Irish. We're canny people, but we'll still spend our last penny on a whiskey. And sometimes our next-to-last too." His stab at humor resulted in a fit of coughing. When the attack subsided, he seized her hand. "In the dream, you were building the castle all by yourself. You can do that now, can't you?"

"Well, maybe not castles, Father, but I can build buildings."

"I know," he whispered. "You're a clever girl." It was a rare compliment, she thought, and all the more precious since the alcohol he'd consumed the previous evening had evidentially worn off. "That's why I had to try to win back the hotel. I did it for you and your mother, Melly," he added, peering up at her. "To make up for... for all the harm I've caused."

In all her years as his daughter, she'd witnessed a sober Henry Bradshaw act charming, witty, even sometimes wise, but she'd never *ever* seen him truly repentant.

"It doesn't matter now, Father," she hushed, brushing a stray shock of hair off his forehead.

"It does, Melly! It does."

She gently patted his bandaged hand. "Of course, it matters, but what I mean is that I always knew, somehow, you were sorry when you hurt us."

Her father motioned for her to lean closer. "I think earlier tonight, I dreamt I was back in Donner Pass," he whispered, "trapped in the ice cave."

Her father had never once mentioned this unspeakable subject. Amelia had assumed he'd mercifully been spared any memory of the many days the Donner Party a half century earlier endured the snows near Lake Tahoe without proper food and supplies. He had only been three years old at the time and Aunt Margaret barely seven when their parents died en route. Little Henry wouldn't have even understood the word cannibalism.

"Maggie gave it to me," he murmured. "She chewed on a piece of cowhide and gave me the only real food she had. We were just young 'uns, but I remember that cave and people dyin', one by one, and the bitter cold. And then, there was just me, along with a cow wrangler, a farmer, and Maggie alive in that hellhole. When the cowhand died... well, the survivors reckoned we *had* to, Melly."

Amelia shuddered at the allusion to the topic that had been forbidden all her life.

"That was a long, long time ago, Father," she said softly. "You need to sleep now."

"They said it was wrong. The newspaper fellows hounded

us for years afterwards. Still do. Came sniffing around just before Christmas last year. Coming up on the anniversary, y'know. They said Maggie was bad to feed me and I was wicked to take it."

"You were a tiny little boy," she said with genuine sympathy for the horrors he and Aunt Margaret had endured. "None of it was your doing."

"The whiskey made it all disappear, Melly. That was wrong too, but the memories and pesterin' get so bad, I have to find a way to blot it out. Your mother never understood about the cave. How *cold* it was. How hungry we were…" He was shivering with the fever—or was it because of the horrible memory, she wondered.

Soon he appeared to drift to sleep. Amelia was about to return to her cot when he suddenly opened his eyes.

"Did you keep those three playing cards?" he demanded hoarsely.

She patted the pocket of her skirt. "Shhh… yes, they're right here."

"Good girl," he rasped. "Go back to the club. Find the other two."

"I'm sure the club burned in the fire," she whispered, seeing in her mind's eye flames licking at the buildings a block away from the Bay View. "I expect everything on Nob Hill's gone by now."

Continuing as if he hadn't heard, he said, "We were playing five-card stud. I had four cards up and one face down. After the call, I turned the last one over. Kemp saw me put that winning ace on the table, I know he did! He was sitting on my right side. He *had* to have seen it! J.D. was across the table, though, so I'm not sure if he—"

"*Quiet* over there!" croaked a voice from the dark.

"Shhhh," Amelia soothed her father and glanced at the rows of shrouded cots. "We're waking the others."

"But, Melly—"

"You must sleep," she insisted firmly. "We'll talk more in the morning." She bent down and kissed his forehead. He'd had no liquor for hours now and, sober, seemed much more like the man she'd adored as a girl.

Spent from the effort to talk, he soon drifted back to sleep, leaving Amelia to wonder forlornly what life might have been like if her father hadn't taken to the bottle, and if the shock that followed his injuries was the cause of his wild story about drawing a rare royal flush.

She continued to kneel in the damp grass beside her father's cot, studying his pallid cheeks. They had sunk into craters of parchment, as if death had already carried off Henry Bradshaw to an unknown land. Soon, he was barely breathing. She leaned over and kissed his forehead. "I love you, Melly…" he murmured. "Always have."

"Good-bye," she whispered in his ear, choking back tears. "I love you too. I've always loved you. God speed, darling Daddy."

After that neither of them spoke again. By morning, he was dead.

◦✦◦

On the day following the quake, Dr. McClure appeared in his office, his shoulders slumped with exhaustion. Barbary was curled up quietly in the corner, one of the luckier victims of the quake, mused Amelia. McClure greeted his patient with a sympathetic nod.

"Not a good day any way it's sliced, is it? I'm sorry about your da."

"Thank you," she murmured. What else was there to say?

"'Twas peaceful, they told me."

"Yes. At least it was that."

A kind of gentle acceptance had come over her this morning, a sense of serenity that her father had died a loved and loving man. Now if only she could learn the fates of Aunt Margaret and friends like Julia, Lacy, and her grandfather's nurse, Edith Pratt.

Meanwhile, the doctor busied himself removing a thin needle and something resembling thread from inside his black bag. He turned toward a white metal cabinet pushed against the wall and withdrew a bottle of whiskey, pouring a stiff shot into a glass and handing it to Amelia. "Drink it all, please. We'll wait a minute for the spirits to take effect and then I'll clean your wounds and stitch you up."

"What kind of doctor *are* you, anyway?" Amelia asked, eyeing the needle that he was threading with a few false starts.

"I'm just an old sawbones," McClure answered with a shrug. "I joined the U.S. Army when I got out of medical training in Edinburgh and came to this country."

"Well, that's reassuring."

"What is?"

"That you've actually had formal medical training."

McClure shot her a look and then appeared to recognize her weary attempt at humor.

"That's how I know Thayer," he explained. "In fact, ol' Jamie and me, we met in Teddy Roosevelt's Rough Riders, back in ninety-eight. The U.S. Army needed doctors and I sailed over from Scotland and signed up. After I mustered out, I came to the Presidio as a contract surgeon when they opened the hospital here. Used to be a Major."

"J.D. Thayer was in the *army* in Cuba?" She had difficulty imagining Thayer taking orders from anyone.

"Indeed we were," McClure said proudly.

The regiment that fought the Spanish-American War was famously staffed by adventurers and soldiers of fortune, joined by a smattering of blue bloods like young Teddy Roosevelt who'd made a name for himself during the conflict. While Amelia was finishing college at Berkeley and before departing for Paris and L'École des Beaux Arts, the treaty with Spain had been signed, giving the United States control over Cuba, Puerto Rico, Guam, and—after a twenty million dollar Congressional appropriation—the Philippines as well.

The defeated combatants had promptly labeled America "Imperialistic," but none of this had concerned Amelia. She had been so focused on her engineering studies, she hadn't even been aware that the Presidio of San Francisco had become an important jumping-off place for American troops going overseas and, later, a demobilizing base for those returning to U.S. soil. Hence the ample supply of tents.

"What possessed Mr. Thayer to go to Cuba? He doesn't strike me particularly as the patriotic type."

"That's what his parents wondered," Angus chuckled. "They couldn't forgive him for joinin' up… 'specially as a foot soldier."

"How old was he then? And why wasn't he an officer? Surely, his family had the money and influence."

"Wouldn't provide one cent of support for such a daft adventure. Who could blame 'em? But ol' Jamie was at odds with his family as a young lad, and was determined to show 'em they couldn't run his life when he up and enlisted. We met in the battle for San Juan Hill. At one juncture, the man saved m'life and later, I did him the favor of leaving his leg on when he took a bullet. This round, I've put his ribs to rights, so I'm up one on him."

"Not if you play cards with him, you're not," she replied, arching an eyebrow.

McClure chortled. "How right you are." Thayer might be a boon companion of Dr. McClure's, but Amelia had not forgotten his role in the loss of the hotel. Inside her skirt pocket, she fingered the three cards found in her father's hand. The physician merely shrugged. "I've learned to limit my exposure to his gamesmanship. See, Jamie's the reason I came out to San Francisco, as a matter of fact. Told me the new hospital was hiring ex-Army physicians, and so here I am, ready to stitch you up, my dear."

The whiskey had done its job. Amelia felt warm inside now and couldn't have cared less what the good doctor planned to do next.

"Now, tilt back your head, there's a good lass," he murmured. "Fortunately, this shouldn't take more than a tick."

And even more fortunately, Dr. Sawbones did quite a credible job repairing the wounds on her forehead with very little discomfort—except for a mild headache the following day.

CHAPTER 9

THE FOLLOWING DAY, THURSDAY, hundreds of individual fires across some five hundred city blocks converged into one monstrous inferno fed by super-heated winds. By Friday evening, both the sun and the moon glowed a malignant blood red. A group of injured firefighters Amelia attended confirmed that, indeed, all but a few structures on Nob Hill had virtually burned to the ground and the Bay View Hotel was part of the smoking wreckage.

Amelia clung to rumors that Oakland had largely escaped the awful fate of its sister city across the bay. She hadn't been able to gain any word of Aunt Margaret or glean news of the welfare of Miss Morgan and her colleagues because the few operating telephones and the telegraph office were reserved for emergency use only. There was simply no way of communicating with the people who mattered most.

The other unsettling reality in Amelia's world was that aftershocks continued to rattle their surroundings. She began to regard the very earth beneath her feet as unreliable and the sky a hot blanket that might soon smother them all. Her emotions careened between an aching sadness over the death of her father and utter numbness in the wake of the chaos reigning everywhere. Buried even deeper was a private, raw grief about her other losses that she kept hidden, surrounded as she was by a sea of fellow-sufferers.

Henry Bradshaw had been buried swiftly and without ceremony in an area of the Presidio designated for the post-quake victims who'd survived the natural disaster, only to succumb ultimately to disease and exposure.

Towards that evening, Angus appeared at her tent and handed her a tied-up bundle.

"These are your father's trousers and jacket that we took off him when he first arrived and needed examining," he explained. "You'll probably want to reuse the wool, given the shortages and all. And I'm sure you'd want this," he added, reaching into his own pocket. "He gave it to me for safe-keeping." He placed in her palm a small watch and a gold fob dangling from a finely wrought chain. Tiny gold nuggets the size of sand grains were encrusted on the metal cover. Angus closed a fist peppered with fine red hairs over her hand as she clutched the timepiece. "A souvenir of better days, eh, lass?"

Amelia stood frozen in place, too shaken to weep. A deep melancholy and the memories stirred by the sight of her father's pocket watch careened in her mind.

No matter how drunk or down on his luck her father had been, he never wagered his watch. To Amelia, the elegant gold timepiece represented the upstanding family man even Henry Bradshaw knew he might have been.

She wasn't even aware that Angus had backed out of her tent as she carefully placed her father's garments at the head of her cot to use as a pillow. Wool cloth was indeed in short supply, and besides, the possessions Angus had returned to her were all she had left to remember her father.

She slipped the watch into her pocket, next to the three cards Henry Bradshaw had claimed had been part of a royal flush. Then she stretched out on the cot and fell into a dreamless sleep.

❧

From the first day of the disaster, citizens of Chinatown had been segregated at a refugee camp on the western edge of the Presidio lands and already a campaign had been launched to prevent them from rebuilding within San Francisco proper. The Empress of China immediately telegraphed Washington, offering funds to help restore Chinatown on its original site, once the fires were extinguished. All the talk at camp was that President Roosevelt declined her largesse. Her outraged ambassador reminded Administration officials that the Chinese sovereign *owned* several blocks in San Francisco's Chinatown and intended to rebuild exactly where she pleased—or she would impose severe trade sanctions. Diplomats scrambled as an American disaster acquired global dimensions.

Adding to the ongoing nightmare, a few cases of typhoid and smallpox were reported in the refugee settlements. Angus alluded to suicides and mental collapses among several of the displaced populace. For Amelia herself, the mere act of recalling her narrow escape from the building on Montgomery Street was enough to make her palms moist and her mouth dry.

As for members of the state militia that had been called up, they tended to be a disorderly, undisciplined lot. Amelia had heard tales the soldiers had shot homeowners trying to salvage their own possessions and then carried off the ill-gotten booty under color of authority.

As the hours ticked by, her world as a practicing architect had taken on a dreamlike quality. Like many of the able-bodied seeking shelter at the Presidio, she was pressed into service as a volunteer nurse. Reality now consisted not of drawing buildings to scale, but of swabbing wounds and

stabilizing the broken bones of quake victims until Angus
McClure or another doctor appeared to treat the case.

In Amelia's agitated state, sleep began to elude her till far
into the early hours of the morning, and she feared life would
never seem normal again. In a perpetual state of anxiety, she
stumbled back and forth to the food tent and the open pit
latrines with the other women in camp.

"Amelia? Is that you?" asked a female voice behind her in
the breakfast line.

She turned. "Edith Pratt? Oh my goodness, of course
you'd be *here*! I should have asked Dr. McClure about you."

Nurse Pratt gave Amelia a fierce hug. Like Julia Morgan
and Lacy Fiske, she'd been a classmate at Berkeley and also
Amelia's late grandfather's caregiver in his final illness. In
fact, Amelia recalled ruefully, Edith's status as a friend in her
youth had been cited by Judge Haggerty as proof of "undue
influence" when it came to Charlie Hunter's revised will
granting his entire estate to his granddaughter.

Within minutes, the two friends of long-standing were
sitting beneath a cypress tree sipping cups of anemic coffee
and nibbling bread from the supply trains beginning to arrive
from Los Angeles and points east.

"I was on another private nursing case when the quake
hit," Edith explained. "The house I was in collapsed,
but because I was quartered with the servants, our back
bedroom built as an addition jutting out from the ground
floor was the only room left standing. Everyone in the main
house died."

"How awful!" Amelia exclaimed. "What news about
your family?"

Edith shook her head. "I hear the telephone company
workers are trying to get the phones up again in the Western

Addition, where my parents live, but so far, I can't get in touch with anyone. What about you?"

"The same." Amelia gave her friend's shoulder another squeeze. "I pray my Aunt Margaret survived in Oakland. I've not had word either about Julia or any of my colleagues at her architectural firm. What worries me most is if the flames aren't soon extinguished at Van Ness Street, the Western Addition could burn too. God help us if the fire comes all the way to the Presidio."

"Think you can swim across the bay to Sausalito?" Edith asked grimly.

Amelia offered a bitter smile. "I heard that Mayor Schmitz and his crony, Abe Reuf, are already plotting to cut down every tree in Marin County over there, and rake a profit on each one when serious rebuilding gets under way."

Amelia was sure that Ezra Kemp had found the means to parlay his lumber business in Mill Valley into City Hall's profitable schemes. Then the thought crossed her mind that perhaps her father *had* been telling the truth: what if Kemp did, in fact, see her father lay down a royal flush the instant the quake struck? And what about Thayer? How much had *he* witnessed that night?

Or had Henry Bradshaw been hallucinating on laudanum about a longed-for winning hand? Anything was possible.

A plan began to form in her mind. She would track down Kemp and J.D. Thayer and simply look them in the eye and ask them what really happened in the moments before the Bay View Hotel annex fell down around their well-tailored shoulders. The land on which the hotel stood had value, she calculated. If she could prove her father won it back and she, now, owned it, it might offer a way of starting over...

❦

Amelia's nursing assignments left her no time or opportunity to conference with J.D. Thayer. On the fourth day, the blessed rains came and the fires still smoldering all over San Francisco were finally extinguished, but not before twenty-five thousand structures were demolished within a four-hundred-square-block area. Equally devastating, more than two hundred thousand of some four hundred and fifty thousand city residents, now officially homeless, were told they would likely remain so for a year or two. Unless Amelia could find her way to her aunt's bungalow in Oakland, she too would be counted among those statistics.

Thanks to Dr. McClure's connections, Amelia finally was able to get notes delivered to Harold Jasper aboard the *Berkeley* to pass on to her aunt and Julia Morgan in Oakland—if they were still alive. Her brief communication to each explained that she was serving as a nurse under the order of martial law and would return to Oakland when the authorities gave permission.

She had barely closed her eyes that evening when she was roused by the arrival of an orderly.

"Miss Bradshaw, wake up!" The young medical assistant glanced curiously at the other volunteer nurses trying to sleep. "Doc McClure needs you in the bone tent."

Amelia walked across the fog-shrouded parade grounds and stepped into the large canvas ward marked MALE AMBULATORY. She peered at a row of a hundred or more cots stretched out on the damp grass. In the course of Amelia's nursing duties, she'd often seen J.D. Thayer sleeping for hours at a time, or observed him staring vacantly into space. Edith too had remarked that like so many quake victims, his spirits seemed to be sinking, for he barely acknowledged his surroundings, or anyone in them.

Angus had already left on his rounds at the military hospital itself, leaving instructions that she was to change all dressings that needed attention in this big tent. For several hours, she worked her way down the rows of cots inside the stuffy enclosure. Then, with more than just bandages on her mind, Amelia squared her shoulders and approached Thayer's litter.

"You're next, I'm afraid, Mr. Thayer. Let me help take off your shirt and I'll change your bandages."

By now, she'd learned to forego any embarrassment at the dishevelment of the patients—or the stench. Nor did she blanch at nudity or exposed genitals, whether male or female. Most of the injured were grateful for her ministrations, but Thayer merely muttered, "I'm fine. Go help the others."

Amelia paused and then spoke softly so his tent mates wouldn't hear. "Not to put too fine a point on things, Mr. Thayer, you and your bandages smell. Nurse Pratt told me you declined her help yesterday, so changing them is a must today, if only to spare your neighbors."

She knelt down beside J.D.'s stretcher. "Look, Mr. Thayer, I'll do my best to make this as painless as I can. Let me help you sit up, if you would, and let's get this shirt off you. I've brought you a clean one from the donation pile."

Obviously still in pain, he slowly hoisted himself upright and allowed her gently to remove his shirt.

"Take a deep breath and release it slowly as I pull your arms through the sleeves," she cautioned. Divested of his shirt, she could see the well-defined muscles of his chest wall tighten, but he made no sound as she began to unwind the tight bandages. The skin under his arms still bore the purple marks of a serious bruising, but the rest of him was burnished a healthy bronze with little body hair, except for a dusting of black on his chest.

As Angus had taught her to do, she lightly pressed her fingertips against Thayer's rib cage.

"Does this pain you?"

He shook his head slightly.

"What about this?" she asked, pressing only slightly harder.

His answer was a swift intake of breath.

"Oh, I *am* sorry!" she exclaimed. His dark eyes appeared to dilate as she swiftly pulled her hand away. "I need to do this to know how tightly to wind the new bandages, but I do apologize if I've hurt you."

"So it's not an act of revenge then?" he said on a long breath.

Amelia realized that he was attempting to make light of how much her palpating his rib cage had pained him. She fell silent then and dipped a clean cloth into a bowl of soapy water and washed a week's worth of sweat and grime from his back.

"Ah…"

His sigh was one of utter contentment, startling her with its expression of naked pleasure. "From devil to angel you are, Miss Bradshaw," he murmured.

"Turn toward me, please," she said crisply.

Angel.

He was merely teasing, of course, but she felt a jolt of… well, something she'd rather not admit to. How long it seemed since Etienne had spoken such endearments…

She continued gently to scrub Thayer's upper body from his face to a trim waistline. She hadn't been this close to a man's bare chest since the last night that she'd made love in her garret on the Rue de Lille. She imagined that the junior ship's officer was currently doing something similar with yet another American traveler he'd met aboard the *Normandie* and she wondered, briefly, if news of the

San Francisco disaster had been telegraphed to all the ships at sea.

Amelia willed herself not to color at the memory of her foolish but rather enjoyable liaison with Monsieur Etienne Lamballe, a reverie made more intense by the sheer masculinity and proximity of her handsome patient.

"Not much like your duties at Miss Morgan's, is it?"

Startled from her meandering thoughts, she handed Thayer the cloth and said briskly, "Do your best with the rest of you, please, while I organize the fresh bandages."

She battled to keep her eyes on the task of preparing clean strips of cloth while he washed his nether regions. J.D. appeared to have lapsed into moody silence and Amelia wondered suddenly if she wouldn't be in a similar depressed state if not for the endless routine of nursing duties Angus had insisted upon. After all, J.D. had lost everything in the recent disaster, just as she had. She pointed to the dirty bandages piled on the grass next to his cot.

"Having just witnessed my nursing abilities, I'm sure you'd agree that I'd be far more useful to the recovery effort at my drafting table, than inexpertly poking at the injured, but there you are. I find it most frustrating, but then, it's all rather out of my hands." She stuffed the bandages into a knapsack. "Again, please forgive my lack of skill."

Thayer didn't respond, and she was annoyed at herself for attempting to engage him in conversation to lift his spirits. Without further comment, she encircled his torso with strips of clean cloth, winding them as tightly as possible without making him wince.

"How *are* you faring, Miss Bradshaw?" he asked suddenly. "Your state of mind, I mean? Do you get down in the dumps—as I do upon occasion?"

She eyed him closely, but he merely gazed at the washrag he was holding.

"I must confess that I do feel blue lately, like everyone else, I suppose," she admitted. "It's hard to believe that San Francisco has practically disappeared."

He set the washrag aside. "I heard it confirmed yesterday that virtually all of Nob Hill was obliterated by the fire."

A vision of the Bay View's turrets aflame flashed through her mind as clearly as if she'd witnessed the final conflagration.

"Yes… I heard that too."

Her voice caught and she ached for the loss of the grandfather who had built such a magnificent hotel on the crown of the hill. The land was still there at least, she thought, and a new hotel could one day take its place, a living monument that the city would rise again from the ashes.

But who owned the land?

An overwhelming urge to ask Thayer what he had seen of her father's poker hand just before the world turned upside down grew too great to suppress. She reached into her skirt pocket and pulled out the three playing cards she'd retrieved from her father's fingers amidst the rubble of J.D.'s gambling club.

"My father gave me these on the day of the quake," she said under her breath.

She watched him intently as his eyes lowered. He stared for a long moment at the ace, queen, and ten of diamonds, the cards' white backgrounds smudged and soiled.

Thayer's gaze remained on the cards. "Did he now?" he murmured.

"My father claimed that he'd just drawn the last card in a royal flush when the quake struck. He told me he'd won back ownership of the Bay View Hotel and all it's contents, fair and square."

"He said that? Did he tell you he betted the last item in his pocket—his gold watch?"

Amelia felt as if she'd been stabbed.

"He told me he had drawn a royal flush, but he never mentioned he'd bet his watch."

"He won the watch back one round and didn't bet it again."

"Because his luck had turned?" Amelia asked, holding her breath. "He was *winning* when the quake struck?"

Thayer raised his gaze from her hand holding the three cards and winced as soon as he'd shrugged his shoulders.

"I didn't see what was in your father's hand, if that's what you're asking," Thayer replied. "I really have no clear idea of anything that happened at the moment the quake hit, Miss Bradshaw." He paused a second, looking at her steadily. "Do you?"

She recalled the instant at 5:12 a.m., April 18, when she'd tossed her drawing pencil into the tin cup that immediately began dancing along the edge of her drafting table.

Yes… I remember that moment exactly…

Silence fell between them as they locked glances, neither willing to back away from their challenging stares.

"Hey! What about *us*, little angel?" called a grizzled man from a cot nearby. His broken leg had been trussed with a spare board and wrapped in muslin that looked to be as filthy as J.D.'s discarded chest wrappings.

The other patients too, were intently watching their exchange for wont of other amusement.

Suppressing a sigh, Amelia called out, "Your turn next, sir!"

She turned back to her current patient. "There you are, Mr. Thayer," she managed briskly, reinserting the playing cards into her skirt pocket. "All clean and taped. We won't be torturing you again for at least another week."

Later that night, a jumble of thoughts disrupted Amelia's quietude as she got ready for bed. She sat on her cot in her chemise with the three playing cards placed face-up on a crate next to a kerosene lantern. On the morning of the quake, J.D. Thayer had commandeered Angus to come to her rescue, risking his own life and that of his friend. Would he have done that if he knew her father had won the last hand?

Unlikely.

Yet, here was two-thirds of a rare royal flush that her father swore he'd been dealt at the end of an all-night, high-stakes poker contest. Whose version of that fateful card game could she *believe*?

With a troubled frown, she reached to douse the lamp. In the dark, her thoughts drifted aimlessly for a time, and then she found herself thinking that both Thayer and her father initially had cheated death on the day of the earthquake and fire—all because Amelia came looking for the wayward Henry Bradshaw and saved the younger man's life in the bargain.

J.D.'s dark eyes seemed to peer at her across the gloomy tent's interior. She had a strange sense that now her path had crossed that of her father's competitor at a number of dramatic junctures, the fates of Thayer and her were somehow entwined. The clarity of this odd notion shone through the jumble of emotions unleashed by the certain knowledge that she would never see her father or grandfather again. The passing of these two men broke all links with the past, and perhaps even the present.

She sat up in bed. "Nonsense!" she whispered into the night.

She wasn't linked with anyone now, least of all J.D. Thayer. She had the power of choice and could guide her own destiny from here on out. She, and she alone, would decide the company she kept—and once the emergency was over, it was highly unlikely she'd have any reason to be involved again with the likes of J.D. Thayer.

It's finished. Finally finished. Let it go… the past… the hotel… it's impossible ever to know the truth about that night. For sanity's sake, Amelia… let it go…

CHAPTER 10

THE STEAM-DRIVEN TUG *Valiant* bobbed in the churning bay while a crew of stevedores struggled to position the last wooden coffin on the slippery deck. Amelia waited quietly as Dr. Angus McClure and J.D. Thayer completed their duties. Angus pointed to the rows of redwood boxes containing quake victims who had succumbed to everything from pneumonia to dysentery, typhoid, and even gunfight wounds.

"That's all of 'em in your charge, J.D.," Dr. McClure declared to Thayer with a nod to the ship's captain. In the four weeks since the disaster, certain signs of normal life-and-death rituals had begun to reappear, including the transport of bodies to cemeteries other than the makeshift one for civilians at the Presidio. Angus gestured again toward the coffins. "Family members have been notified to come claim 'em on the Oakland side. J.D.'ll just be sure the bodies get matched up correctly."

Amelia was glad both her father and grandfather were buried in San Francisco's soil and didn't have to be transported across the bay en masse like these poor souls.

The captain of the tug nodded. "The undertakers will also be standing by to meet the boat. Got a routine now, they have." He noted the mantle of pewter clouds hanging low in the sky. "We should make the crossing before the heavy weather rolls in. 'Til the next trip then," he added, touching his cap while heading for the pilothouse.

"Amelia? You ready?" Angus turned to his former nurse who stood with elbows braced against the boat's railing. "I'm sorry you have to travel with these silent companions, but it was the only chance to get you back to your aunt. I can't take leave right now to escort you home, and—"

"Angus, I've traveled halfway across the globe on my own. I'll be fine," she assured him.

Why did men think a woman was incapable of moving from one place to another without an armed guard?

"Are you sure?"

She forced a smile, wishing Thayer would stop eavesdropping so intently. She summoned a bright smile for the doctor's benefit.

"Completely sure. And thank you so much, Angus, for securing my travel pass and releasing me from nursing duties. It was such wonderful news to hear Miss Morgan had established her practice in Oakland for the time being. I will be ever so much more useful sitting at my drafting table there, don't you agree?" She was teasing him, but Angus took no notice.

"That's what I told the authorities to persuade 'em to grant you the pass. Glad I could help," he added, looking at her hopefully. "Well, it's good-bye for now, you two. Hope to see you again, Amelia, when things have righted themselves around here. It may be a while, though. May I write to you?"

Amelia was mildly alarmed by this proposal and, for some reason, highly embarrassed it was uttered in the presence of J.D. Thayer.

She liked Angus McClure. Admired him greatly, in fact, for all he had done to organize the care of the sick and injured.

However, there was no point in encouraging him to think that she regarded him as anything more than a "comrade in arms" as he liked to call J.D.

"Oh, I expect you'll be far too busy to write, but I'm sure we shall see each other again at some point. Be well, Angus."

She turned to regard J.D. At least his ribs had stopped aching enough for him to make himself useful around the Presidio as a de facto ambulance driver, transporting the injured in and around the encampment in the Winton motorcar whose sides now sported painted red crosses.

Today, however, Thayer had another assignment—that of making sure each body in the coffins was handed over to its rightful next of kin. She took a closer look at him, noting the gaunt slant to his cheekbones and the dark eyes that gazed somberly across the chilly bay. She hoped that the moth-eaten black woolen cape he'd found among the piles of donated clothing at the Presidio decently warded off the damp. Currently, the dashing J.D. Thayer more closely resembled a derelict than Angus's ad hoc director of a funeral cortege.

"So long, Jamie, my boy," Angus said to their companion. "Thanks for seeing this cargo arrives safely."

"Don't mention it. Thanks for my travel pass as well. I'm doing you a favor, and you're doing one for me. I need to see those insurance adjusters in Oakland, so I can determine exactly how much they're *not* going to pay me."

Angus laughed. "Well, safe journey to you both."

Amelia nodded her thanks and repaired immediately to the pilothouse where she could keep warm.

J.D. Thayer sat on the corner of one of the coffins in his charge and continued to gaze, unseeing, across the bay.

For Amelia, the next days passed in aching sadness. Aunt Margaret had not appeared dockside when the *Valiant* pulled into the Oakland pier. In fact, her aunt, sick with grief over her brother's passing and the trauma of everything that had gone before, could barely lift her head off the pillow when Amelia first arrived at her aunt's rented abode. Now that Amelia had heard from her dying father's own lips the difficult choices forced upon a seven-year-old Margaret Bradshaw— and the guilt suffered by survivors of the Donner Pass tragedy all these years—she found new compassion and patience for her elderly relative who had long tended to become upset by the slightest change of plans.

Thus, it had been Amelia who composed the telegram to her mother in Paris telling of Henry Bradshaw's death. Amelia who greeted the visitors calling at the bereft inhabitants of Margaret Bradshaw's bungalow, set out the food they brought, and wrote letters of thanks for the kindnesses shown by their friends and her new neighbors in their time of mourning.

So many other families in the Bay Area had suffered losses in the wake of the San Francisco quake and fire that Amelia suppressed any display of her own grief, especially since circumstances in Oakland were far superior to its sister city.

A few afternoons following Amelia's return to Oakland, an overseas cable was delivered with word that her mother intended to remain in Paris since time and distance had precluded returning to California for her husband's last rites. Amelia could only deduce from the final four lines of the communication that financial help was unlikely to be forthcoming from Victoria.

COSTS IN PARIS OUTRAGEOUS—STOP—ASSUME
MORGAN'S FIRM NOW THRIVING—STOP—NEED FUNDS
MYSELF FOR PAINTING CLASSES—STOP—CAN YOU
PROVIDE?—STOP—

GRATEFULLY, MOTHER

A few days later, Amelia was due to meet with Julia
Morgan about possible full-time employment. Having no
need to sleep on the drafty service porch any longer, she
lay in the same bed that Aunt Margaret had reserved for her
father, but in which he had never slept after the loss of the
Bay View. Hands behind her head, she stared at the ceiling,
fretting about several pressing problems.

It would certainly be considered unseemly for the daughter
of a deceased family member to immediately resume employment, but the harsh reality was that she and Aunt Margaret
had almost nothing to live on.

Amelia reached for her father's gold watch on the bedside
table and ran her fingers over the tiny gold nuggets on the
top of the case, wondering if she would soon be forced to sell
it just to put food on their table. The time was just after seven
a.m., so she snapped the timepiece shut and hurried to dress
and eat breakfast. Twenty minutes later, she set out on foot
for Morgan's temporary offices in the family's carriage barn
less than a mile from Aunt Margaret's bungalow.

The moment she entered the door, Lacy Fiske jumped
up from her typewriting machine. "It's Amelia! Oh look,
everyone! She's back!"

A group hunched over the drafting boards chorused
their greetings, including Ira Hoover, the young architect
whom Amelia had barely gotten to know before the quake

but found far friendlier than men at L'École des Beaux Arts. Behind the staff, a visitor rose from the small table where he apparently had been conferring with the firm's founder.

"Hello, Miss Bradshaw. I hope to find you well—or as well as can be expected, given the circumstances."

J.D. Thayer clearly had paid a visit to a barber in bustling Oakland—the East Bay city, spared by some miracle, of much of the earthquake's devastating fury. Thayer's trim black mustache and starched white shirt had done wonders to restore his former air of confidence. His bronze skin had lost its unnatural pallor and his welcoming smile quite dazzled her with what appeared to be genuine warmth.

"I *am*… as well as can be expected," she echoed him, adding lamely, "…and you?"

"Much better, thank you, now that I've spent a few days where there's hot water and something other than a canvas cot to sleep on."

For some reason his allusion to life at the Presidio conjured memories of tending to J.D.'s bare chest and the intimacy of her washing his naked back—and *that* thought had the power to flood her cheeks with warmth.

Startled by this involuntary reaction, she swiftly retreated to hang her coat on a peg in a small anteroom at the back of the remodeled barn.

What is wrong with you, Amelia Bradshaw? You are behaving like the biggest ninny in the American West! Just stop it!

She could easily guess the reasons for J.D.'s call on her employer, and that knowledge filled her with dread. The Julia Morgan firm might be asked this very morning to take on the task of rebuilding the Bay View Hotel property.

Which actually might be *her* hotel property.

Amelia was frankly surprised to see Thayer at the Morgan

firm. Given her own recent legal battle with him and her pointed conversation about the playing cards she'd found in her father's hand, she would have supposed he'd have avoided the possibility of rubbing shoulders with her at all costs and selected another firm to rebuild the hotel.

He said he didn't see what was in Father's hand, and the other two cards were lost, so he's confident the Bay View is his…

And besides, she thought with the knowledge of how difficult it was for women to succeed in business, the services of qualified architects in San Francisco had quickly been snapped up, so perhaps Thayer's last hope to reconstruct a hotel on Taylor and Jackson streets was to employ the firm in less demand than the usual male design practitioners—and therefore less expensive.

Julia pointed to a solitary drafting station devoid of the large sheets of vellum upon which Morgan's employees made drawings to their leader's precise specifications.

"Yes, Amelia, we've reserved that empty desk for you. I'll be with you in a minute after I conclude my meeting with Mr. Thayer."

Reserved for you…

Amelia's spirits rose a notch at the intimation that Julia had already determined she'd require the services of her junior architect.

Miss Morgan addressed her administrative assistant. "Lacy, show her my new set of sketches for the Mills College library. Amelia, see if you remember those ideas for shelving that you incorporated before the Montgomery Street office was ruined."

The mere mention of the library drawings and the harrowing experience that had followed her all-night efforts April 18 had a sudden, peculiar effect. Amelia's heart began to pound and her palms grew clammy.

She felt J.D.'s scrutiny. "Are you quite all right, Miss Bradshaw? You've gone quite pale."

She waved her hand in a small gesture. "Yes. Yes of course. I'm fine." To Julia she said, "Right away, Miss M. I'll do my best to recall the drawings that were lost," remembering at the last second to address Julia by her surname.

Thanks to the earthquake, it would seem she was to be hired full-time without debate—and during regular business hours, thank heavens.

"Are you *sure* you're all right?" Lacy whispered as their employer and Thayer resumed their conference at a dining table commandeered from the Morgan family home next door. "Your forehead's perspiring and you look white as a sheet. Here, I'll get you some water."

"Thank you."

Intermittent aftershocks had continued to rattle the Bay Area, and Julia's casual reference to the disaster brought the horrifying experience rushing back as if it were yesterday. Amelia clutched her glass of water and tried to speak in a normal tone of voice. "Lacy, do you think you can find me some proper drawing pencils? I haven't a single one."

"I know. We've had to purchase an unholy amount of new supplies—not to mention a new typewriting machine for me that cost a fortune." Lacy lowered her voice to a whisper so as not to disturb the others. "The firm needs every commission it can get, even if it's to build a doghouse. We've got to pay for the expenses of starting over. But *you* know Julia. She's very picky about some things and a perfectionist about everything." She brandished a fistful of drawing implements. "I sent to Chicago for these beauties."

During the next few minutes, Amelia did her best to concentrate on her work while studiously ignoring the conversation in the corner of the carriage barn—but their lively discussion made it impossible.

"I've had a look at that bell tower you built at Mills College, Miss Morgan," J.D. Thayer was saying, "and I don't mind telling you, I was impressed."

"That it's still standing?" Amelia could tell from Julia's tone that her amusement was mixed with irritation.

"That and its grand design. I was thinking that a new, strong interior structure employing some of the techniques you used in that tower, along with a handsome exterior like the hotel had before, would be just the thing. That's why I've come to see you."

"It's been a month now, since the quake," Morgan noted. "Surely, you've discussed your ideas with other architects based closer to Taylor and Jackson streets?"

"Yes, I have, but that was before I saw your bell tower."

"How kind of you to say so." Julia Morgan smiled with genuine warmth. "And you hadn't realized, I suspect, that the services of the other architects were already spoken for?"

Amelia marveled that staid Julia almost appeared to be teasing her visitor.

Thayer paused and then said, "I couldn't seek an architect's services until I had some idea whether the insurance would pay, and yes... by the time I could consult with these fellows here in Oakland, most San Francisco builders had many more commissions than they can handle."

Amelia could see that Thayer was a skilled diplomat as well as a flatterer. Much as she hated to admit it, those were precisely the attributes her grandfather had always called upon in his role as a successful hotelier.

Meanwhile, the visitor pointed to a sheaf of drawings Julia had made for another client. "The owners of the Fairmont, as you probably know, felt they had to go as far as New York City to find someone qualified to get the rebuilding under way," said J.D. "I just heard they hired the famous Stanford White, of McKim, Mead, & White, to restore my competition."

"So it seems." Julia's lips had settled into a prim line. Amelia knew that Julia had vied for that commission—and lost. "And will your insurance carrier make good on the policy?"

Thayer frowned. "I still don't know yet. Nevertheless, I've decided I mustn't wait to proceed. I want to propose a plan whereby I pay you a small retainer, starting today. Then, at some later date to be determined, I would discharge the remainder of what I will owe with the fees I will get from paying guests as soon as we reopen our doors."

"Ah... yes... that sort of scheme has been offered this office several times in the last few weeks." Julia looked narrowly at J.D. "Were you also thinking of having me order the building materials and supervise the construction, as I did the bell tower at Mills College?"

J.D. paused, and Amelia could practically read the questions in his mind: could a mere woman acquire the lumber, bricks, mortar, and cement needed for such a huge undertaking? Could this slip of a female order crews around and make them come in on budget and on time?

From the corner of her eye she also observed he'd come to the conclusion that she could.

"Miss Morgan, it's no secret. Every businessman—whether rich or merely prosperous before April eighteenth—has very little capital to work with at this time. The point is to get private enterprises going again, and I can't do that sitting on an empty lot."

"I expect not, just as I cannot operate this office without paying my people and purchasing the supplies needed to rebuild your hotel."

"I certainly understand that you have serious expenses and cash flow issues of your own," J.D. replied in a conciliatory tone. "But I would very much like you to both design the building and supervise its construction. I have applied to the Committee of Fifty and have every expectation they will see it is vastly in the city's interest to get the Bay View Hotel up and running again. Are you willing to proceed on the promise of my word that I will somehow secure the funds you require?"

Julia Morgan heaved a small sigh. "These are trying times indeed, Mr. Thayer, and it will be an important symbol to the world that San Francisco is rebuilding its most important buildings. I accept your offer, especially since you wish to recreate the hotel's exterior design as it was before, and we can work from photographs that surely exist in the Oakland newspaper files. Plus Amelia, here, knew every inch of her family home, didn't you, my dear?"

Amelia set down her pencil because her hand had begun to tremble. It certainly appeared that Julia and her staff—including Amelia—would be constructing a hotel that might actually belong to the Morgan firm's newest employee! Yet here was a chance to be part of the effort to recreate a building more precious to Amelia than all the magnificent edifices she'd studied in France. It was a tribute to her grandfather that Thayer wanted the exterior of the new building reconstructed to look exactly as it had before the quake and fire.

For a split second, she utterly ignored the fact that the project was J.D. Thayer's. All Amelia could think was that at long last, she was going to be able to satisfy her yearning to help build something *real*, a new and improved Bay View Hotel that, until this minute, resided only in her imagination.

"As Miss Bradshaw has just returned to work following her father's passing, I have not yet assigned her a new project." Morgan hesitated. "It's a bit awkward, I know, that Amelia will be working to rebuild a hotel that her grandfather created and ran for so many years, but her knowledge will be invaluable to us. Are you willing to have her part of my team?"

J.D. turned slowly and regarded Amelia sitting frozen on her drafting stool.

"Part of the team?" he said with a laconic smile pulling at the corners of his mouth.

Did he actually *wink*?

"Well, why not?" he said at length. "There are many strange aspects to this grand disaster, aren't there, Miss Bradshaw? The sooner we get the Bay View rebuilt, the better, so I'd welcome your contributions to this effort... that is, if you are willing to be part of *my* team."

Was she willing? Was that toad, Ezra Kemp, part of J.D.'s efforts? And what about rebuilding the gambling club? She certainly wanted no part of *that* project!

However, experience told her she had little to fear about having to work regularly with Thayer and his cronies. Her employer would no doubt keep her junior, untried architect on a short leash, demanding Amelia prove herself designing tool sheds and library shelving before being given the responsibility as a full colleague.

In a quiet corner of her mind, Amelia was grateful that J.D.'s building project—however much or little she had to do with it—had proved to be the guarantee that she'd have employment with the Morgan firm.

She would never admit this to a living soul, but the man was one of those infuriating creatures in the mold of Etienne Lamballe whose very presence could make her pulse quicken and color streak her cheeks. She was mortified to acknowledge this fact, but there was no denying it—even to herself. All the more reason to be thankful that she was more than likely to be designing garages, not grand hotels.

But before she could summon a suitable response to Thayer's question about being willing to be part of *his* building efforts, Julia Morgan intervened briskly.

"Excellent then! It's settled. I will commence the preliminary sketches of the Bay View based on Amelia's familiarity with the site. Come, my dear, and tell Mr. Thayer about your winning a *Prix d'Or* in Paris."

CHAPTER 11

J.D. SPED ON FOOT toward the docks, hoping he'd arrive in time to catch the next ferry back to San Francisco. Repeatedly en route, his mind ran through the scene he'd just witnessed at Julia Morgan's office in her family's converted carriage barn. It served him right if the only qualified and available architects in all of the Bay Area included the woman whose inebriated father had been persuaded to hazard the family's hotel in a series of reckless games of chance at the instigation of James Diaz Thayer.

And *why*? So that the cast-off son and black sheep of the exalted Thayer clan could acquire a prime piece of real estate that would finally garner its new owner—*what*? Respect from his father?

Highly unlikely.

What had possessed him to take advantage of Amelia's grandfather, the admirable Charlie Hunter, who had lain upstairs at the old Bay View, dying of a stroke?

The sheer desire to beat James Thayer Sr., at his own game.

Usually, J.D. didn't make it a practice to dig too deeply into the motives that launched him into business deals with the likes of Henry Bradshaw and Ezra Kemp. It was also probably wise not to dwell on the reasons he was strangely glad Miss Morgan's talented protégée would be part of the team rebuilding the hotel, or why he'd felt he *had* to possess the property atop Nob Hill in the first place.

Amelia Hunter Bradshaw would probably be astounded to know how much he looked forward to hearing her informed opinion about what should be done with the land at Taylor and Jackson streets. Or how he privately acknowledged that he certainly owed her a great deal more than merely "allowing" this feisty female to join the group that would be rebuilding the Bay View.

After all, she did save your pathetic neck a month ago.

And now, a lifetime later, all he owned was a pile of rubble, plus a mountain of debts, a dodgy business partner, and certain knowledge of the havoc he'd wrecked in the life of the fledgling architect, her aged aunt, and Amelia's mother.

And let us not forget that Ling Lee and Amelia's father died due to the poorly constructed gambling club… and whose fault was that? The chiseler, Ezra Kemp? Or the man that looked the other way while corners were cut?

There was enough on his conscience without taking on the total burden for that too, he reflected. Even so, there was no question in J.D.'s mind but that he had plenty of sins to account for.

The arriving ferry he would take back to San Francisco was just nudging its hull against the Oakland dock's pilings when J.D. realized that The Mood had descended upon him once again in full force. While he watched the travelers from across the bay trudge down the gangway, he fought a familiar mental battle to stiffen his resolve not to allow his gloom to become a paralyzing force in his life.

The Mood could easily persuade him to throw in his cards and abandon his dream. But that way led to folly and doom. He had to *do* something about this city and his own life, both of which could be said to lie in ruins. He had to take action of some sort. If he merely went back to the black pit on Nob Hill where the hotel had been and crawled onto the makeshift mattress in the shattered basement, he might never crawl out.

By the time J.D. emerged on the ferry's deck, the wind was gusting fiercely and white caps stippled the bay. The ship's horn blew, the engines vibrated beneath his feet, and the ferry backed away from the dock. The *Berkeley* turned in a froth of water and made for San Francisco.

Suddenly, J.D. wished he could simply sail off on this boat through Golden Gate Straits to the far South Pacific—and never come back.

❦

Two weeks after Amelia's encounter with Thayer at the Morgan office, she set off for work as June sunshine struggled to poke through a high morning mist. At a corner newsstand, a headline caught her eye:

ARCHITECT STANFORD WHITE SHOT BY LOVER'S HUSBAND!!!

Murdered at New York City's Roof Garden Theatre
By Enraged Henry Thaw
San Francisco's Fairmont Hotel In Search Of
A Successor To Rebuild Landmark

"Good heavens," she murmured, swiftly scanning the first paragraph reporting on the homicide involving the famous partner of McKim, Mead & White, the New York architectural firm celebrated for mansions, monuments, public buildings, and churches across the nation. White, a notorious profligate and womanizer, had apparently been shot point blank by the cuckolded Harry K. Thaw the previous evening.

"No wonder the husband plugged 'im," noted the newsboy. "That Stanford White fella was even two-timin' his mistress! Wanna paper, miss?" he asked pointedly.

"Ah... yes, thank you." Amelia swiftly handed him a few coins and set off for work again. She hadn't even hung up her coat before Lacy Fiske grabbed her sleeve.

"She's been chosen!" Lacy exalted. "Can you imagine? Julia's going to replace that awful man who got shot."

"She's joining McKim, Mead, & White?" Amelia was aghast at the notion the office might shut down if Julia moved to New York City.

"No, silly!" Lacy replied with a dismissive wave of her hand. "The owners of the Fairmont have sent for Julia this morning."

"The Law brothers want *her* to restore the hotel?"

To Amelia's way of thinking, the *beaux-arts* design of the Fairmont, sitting like a marble crown on Nob Hill, was leagues ahead of the Palace, the St. Francis, and—though it pained her to admit it—even the Bay View. Its restoration would truly be a symbol San Francisco would rise from the ashes.

Lacy kept nodding emphatically. "Yes, the Law brothers sent an emissary to escort her to San Francisco for the meeting this morning! I heard them say that she'd beaten out the competition by promising to finish the job by the first anniversary of the quake."

"You must be joking!" Amelia did a rapid calculation. That was only ten months from now! "Does she really think it can be done?"

"It must be," Lacy pronounced.

"But what about the Bay View and Mills College and all the other projects we're doing? We're over-committed as it is. Didn't Julia say just yesterday that we're too swamped with work for her to take on any more big commissions?"

"Oh, for heaven sakes, Amelia, this is the *Fairmont Hotel* we're talking about! Though she says it's in the most deplorable condition."

"*How* deplorable?" Amelia asked with a worried frown, for she'd studiously avoided passing by Nob Hill since the quake and had not been to San Francisco since returning to Oakland to resume living with her aunt.

"Apparently, the hotel's got twisted metal beams, the Tiffany glass ceiling in the lobby melted into lumps on the marble floors, and virtually everything on the interior is charred to a crisp." Lacy's cheeks were pink with excitement. "Oh, Amelia, I have not the slightest doubt that our Julia will make it the jewel of Nob Hill!"

"The Bay View was the jewel of Nob Hill, as far as its customers were concerned," Amelia said reproachfully. "The Fairmont hadn't even opened its doors by April eighteenth."

"Well, at least the shell of that building is still standing," Lacy countered. "The Fairmont had about three hundred rooms and the inside looked like an Italian palazzo, they say… that is before some of the floors collapsed seven feet. Julia says not just *any* architect could cope with the mess it's in and do this job. I'm sure it was her degree in engineering and her certificate from L'École des Beaux Arts—and your credentials, too, by the way—that ultimately prompted the offer. When we're done with it, it will be the grandest destination in California!"

A woman architect had been chosen to restore the glorious Fairmont!

The impact of this news began to sink in. "But, given our small staff, how in the world will Julia be able to rehabilitate two hotels at the same time, not to mention all the other projects she's taken on?"

Lacy smiled mischievously. "I reckon she'll head up the Fairmont operation and supervise you and Ira Hoover as lead architects on everything else, silly!"

"Oh… my… Lord," Amelia said on a long breath, as the consequences of this amazing turn of events became clear. She would probably be assigned to work for J.D. Thayer. Exclusively. Day in, day out for the next *year*!

Meanwhile, Lacy clapped her hands with excitement.

"Of course, we'll have to hire more people—if we can find them. But the point is, Amelia, the Fairmont's owners apparently have the funds to spend on restoration, so therefore *we* can afford to put on more staff. It works out well for Mr. Thayer too, don't you think? More money in Julia's coffers means she can afford to wait for her architectural and construction management fees from the Bay View until the hotel has paying guests. *Two* wonderful hotels will be brought back to life, which will show the world San Francisco *isn't* Pompeii, never again to rise from the ashes."

It was all so much to absorb, Amelia thought, feeling faintly light-headed. "We'll manage somehow, I suppose," she murmured.

However, considering her own situation, she truly wondered *how*? Julia supervised everything down to the smallest detail. Would she finally start delegating to her junior associates?

There was no question but that the Fairmont commission was a huge feather in Julia Morgan's cap, especially if she managed to get the place reopened by the first anniversary of the quake and fire.

As if echoing her thoughts, Lacy crowed, "No more having to build so many garages for our sorority sisters' motorcars!"

"Newspapers all over America are bound to write about the architect who takes over for the murdered Stanford

White," Amelia agreed, pointing to the headline on the front
page of the paper she'd brought to work. "It should give our
firm a huge boost."

"That's right!" Lacy said, grinning, and then her face fell.
"Julia will hate that, of course... the newspaper bit. She has
such a fetish about reporters poking their heads into her business." Then she brightened. "But just think of it, Amelia!
You'll likely head up the Bay View project, since you know
so much about it already, don't you imagine? And what a story
that would be: two women restoring two of San Francisco's
landmark hotels! Worth a paragraph or two, don't you think?"

Amelia nodded absently. "Well, at least this guarantees I'll
truly have a permanent position at the firm."

Lacy gave her a startled look and then began rummaging
around in a desk drawer.

"Not only are you officially on permanent staff, but
you passed your licensing exam! I was so excited about the
Fairmont commission, I totally forgot. Confirmation came in
this morning's post."

She thrust a sheet of paper into Amelia's hand. For her part,
the most junior employee in the firm admitted sheepishly she'd
nearly forgotten she'd taken the test a week before the quake.

Lacy laughed gaily. "Well, congratulations, Amelia! You
are now a bona fide architect in the Great State of California!"

❧

Julia Morgan's conference in San Francisco with Herbert and
Hartland Law, the beleaguered owners of the Fairmont Hotel,
continued for the rest of the day while her staff remained busy
at their drawing boards. Around four o'clock, the tiny woman
walked through the door, and not five minutes later, she was
followed by a familiar figure clad in a tattered opera cloak.

Amelia looked up from her drafting table, papered with the plans for the Mills College library, to see J.D. Thayer step inside the carriage barn and firmly shut the door.

"Ah, Miss Bradshaw, you're here too, I see. Well, we might as well have everything out on the table."

Lacy and Amelia exchanged looks.

Thayer advanced into the room, removed his cape, and flung it on a chair beside the conference table.

"So!" he demanded of Julia without preamble. "Are the rumors true?"

"Won't you sit down, Mr. Thayer," Julia said calmly. They each took a seat at the table.

"I heard people saying this morning that the Fairmont has found a local replacement for the architect Stanford White. Is that *you*, Miss Morgan?"

"Yes, it is."

"And is it also true the Law brothers insist that you finish the restoration in time to open the Fairmont on the first anniversary of the quake?"

Amelia watched the ensuing dialogue as if watching a tennis match.

"Why, yes, Mr. Thayer. That was our agreement."

"But that was my plan also, and I secured your services first. How do you intend that both hotels achieve the same goal?" he demanded.

Julia smiled confidently. "I don't see this as any sort of problem," she assured him calmly. "No one understands the site at Taylor and Jackson any better than Amelia Bradshaw here, and since you wish to reconstruct the Bay View as it was, you couldn't be in better hands. I, of course, will supervise both the concept, design, and actual execution of the construction each step of the way."

"And how can you be in two places at once, Miss Morgan?" J.D. eyed her steadily for a moment and then spared a brief glance for Amelia. "Miss Bradshaw is a highly intelligent and well-trained young woman, and I'm pleased she's helping you, but she's a novice. Building supplies are extremely scarce. Workers, even more so. Both hotels are vast and complicated projects, built on extremely steep sites."

Julia hesitated a moment and patted some drawings sprawled across the conference table. "After the collapse of your gambling club, Mr. Thayer, I am happy to see you *now* appreciate the potential problems of such a difficult site."

Amelia could hardly suppress a gasp at her employer's veiled insult, a practice Julia Morgan had never before been heard to employ with a client. To Amelia it appeared that her employer clearly was attempting to gain a psychological advantage over her agitated client.

"All the more reason that the Bay View requires your complete attention," J.D. snapped.

"And it will *have* my attention, Mr. Thayer," Julia said, abruptly switching tactics and now adopting a soothing tone. "Miss Bradshaw has an engineering degree *and* graduated from architectural school with the highest honors. I personally vouch for her advanced skills. And besides," Julia added brightly, "she grew up in the building you wish to replicate. The two hotels are four blocks apart. Miss Bradshaw and I will live on the sites as soon as practicable, so as to be able to supervise every detail. You will have the benefit of *two*—in your own words—highly intelligent and well-trained architects building your hotel."

What? thought Amelia. *I am to live for ten months in a soot-filled basement with J.D. Thayer? I absolutely refuse!*

She watched, dumbfounded by these rapid developments,

as Julia indicated the large sheets of paper strewn across the conference table.

"We have already produced these preliminary drawings of the Bay View's facade, which I think you will deem excellent, and will start on the final versions later today." The architect appeared to draw up her tiny form and looked her six-foot client squarely in the eye. "And I assure you, Mr. Thayer, that I will sign off on each detail of the plans before a foot of foundation has been laid."

J.D.'s expression revealed nothing, nor did he reply, a fact that didn't seem to faze Julia in the slightest.

"You, sir," she continued, "along with Miss Bradshaw, Ira Hoover, and I shall meet every other day to review the ongoing work. Together, we will rebuild your hotel to a very exacting standard."

"By the anniversary of the quake? Just like the Fairmont?" challenged Thayer.

Julia did not immediately offer an answer. Amelia could practically hear the gears grinding in her employer's head: *Two* hotels built in ten months' time in a city surrounded by four hundred blocks of rubble, plagued by a shortage of skilled labor, and infested with the worst sort of political corruption?

Impossible! Amelia wanted to shout.

Julia Morgan leaned across the conference table and gazed at J.D. through her owlish glasses. She tapped a forefinger on Amelia's drawings.

"You have my word on it, Mr. Thayer. Barring another Act of God, the doors to the Bay View Hotel will be open on or *before* April 18, 1907."

She turned toward Amelia with a smile, adding, "Won't they, my dear?

CHAPTER 12

A CHARACTERISTIC SUMMER FOG flowed in waves up from the bay. Wisps of chilly mist cloaked the ragged remnants of houses that once lined California Street, turning the landscape ghostly and forbidding. At the foot of Market, only a few cable cars were back in service, so Amelia decided her fastest route to her first day at the Bay View site was to walk up to Nob Hill.

During the ferry ride from Oakland, she'd tried to steel herself for her first private meeting with Morgan's client, J.D. Thayer, on the site of the former Bay View Hotel. She also tried to brace herself for her first full view of her former neighborhood's collapsed landmarks and blackened piles of bricks, but nothing could have prepared her for the devastation scarring the cityscape in all directions. She could see that the damage to four hundred city blocks was nothing less than cataclysmic. Little wonder that more than two hundred thousand citizens were still homeless, camped out in green wooden "earthquake shacks" lined up in long rows across the Presidio.

Even so, Amelia marveled at the extent to which the principal thoroughfares had been cleared of rubble in a few weeks' time, by an army of ordinary citizens, pressed into service by martial law. Businessmen in suits and laborers in overalls stood side-by-side throwing debris into carts that were hauled to the shoreline, its refuse dumped in the bay.

Amelia was shocked to note the way dynamite, as well as the fire, had disfigured this neighborhood reserved for the city's loftiest millionaires. It looked to her as if explosives had done a lot more damage than Army officials and the fire department had thus far admitted. She'd heard rumors that the newspapers had been ordered by the city fathers to emphasize the fire damage over the havoc wrecked by the earthquake, thus glossing over fears that recurring temblors might hurt the business community's rebuilding campaign. Would the municipal officials responsible for the recovery effort ever truly know whether the earthquake or the fire had done the most damage, she wondered. Without this intelligence, how would they reconstruct the city in the safest mode possible while planning properly for calamities that might threaten in the future?

Each block she passed revealed more shocking sights. She glanced over at Sacramento Street, one hundred yards to her right, and saw that Donaldina Cameron's Mission Home was obliterated, a solitary chimney marking its former site. The "Angel of Chinatown" and her Chinese charges had been forced by the fire to flee from their first sanctuary, the Presbyterian Church on Van Ness. Word was that they'd escaped by ferry to the seminary at San Anselmo and now had moved again, relocating in Oakland's burgeoning Chinatown. Someday, when she had more funds, Amelia vowed to donate to Donaldina's cause.

When she finally reached the summit of Nob Hill, the backs of her calves were aching from exertion. Breathing hard, she took in a scene of such ruin that she realized suddenly she was clutching her portmanteau so tightly her knuckles had turned white. A lingering acrid odor of burnt cinders stung her nose.

"Oh… dear… God," she murmured, glancing around.

A lone figure with a sack on his back trod gingerly among acres of wreckage, looking for some small souvenir of a world reduced to rubble. She'd heard scavengers were everywhere, combing the debris for anything that might be of use or value. Amelia stood, dumbstruck by the stark landscape where the Crocker, Huntington, Hopkins, and Stanford mansions of the city's railroad and banking barons had once stood. Every one of the grand structures she'd adored as a child growing up on the hill had been leveled by the fire, to the extent that the six square blocks of the once-posh district looked like a battlefield in the heart of a city. Wisps of fog swirled around the occasional blackened chimney stack, decorative column, or a set of granite front steps leading nowhere. Except for these desolate remnants, millions of dollars' worth of palatial grandeur had been reduced to powder.

Only two buildings in this part of the city were not obliterated. The Connecticut brownstone mansion that belonged to silver baron James Flood was a shell now, minus one wall and its roof.

And across the street stood the scorched granite citadel that had been the brand new Fairmont Hotel, three days shy of its grand opening, sooty eyebrows blemishing nearly every window of its six floors. The roof was gone and through the broken windows, Amelia could see that the grand lobby was littered with mountains of rubble. Given its derelict state, the notion that the Morgan architectural firm would restore this monumental edifice *and* the Bay View Hotel to their former splendor by April 18, 1907—only ten months away—seemed laughable.

Amelia didn't stop there to greet her colleagues, who were ensconced—as of the previous day—in makeshift sleeping quarters in the basement of the Fairmont, a section of the hotel that had been made marginally habitable. The office all of the Morgan team would share was a hastily constructed shed built on what had been part of the Fairmont's grand, terraced gardens.

She turned her back on the broken hotel and continued down Taylor Street, the littered roadway that ran along the spine of the hill. Methodically, she counted the streets, fearful that she wouldn't recognize her former home, the Bay View at the corner of Taylor and Jackson. On her right, she spied the broken smokestack from the collapsed brick cable car barn that stood sentry over a block strewn with mountains of shattered brick. The fog was even thicker here, uncoiling tendrils in all directions.

Further downhill on the Jackson Street side, only the ragged perimeter of the foundation gave any hint that either a hotel or a gambling club had ever existed on the site.

Amelia stared at the remnants of her former life and grieved for every lost doorway and chimney of the grand Victorian lady. Somewhere in the charred ruins were the carbon splinters of a cherry wood bar and a couch where Ling Lee had met her end. The table and the lighting fixture that had broken her father's back had since dissolved into ash. She scanned the cones of black and broken plaster, some ten feet high, which looked like extinct volcanoes. Next door, the crazy, trigger-happy old lady's three-story house and back garden fence were reduced to cinders.

Near the Taylor Street side, a few scorched, broken walls of the subterranean stables marked the spot where the Winton had been garaged. Today, the motorcar was parked in front of a slagheap of bricks. The car's doors still had painted red crosses on them, a reminder of the vehicle's brief life as an ambulance.

Unlike the Fairmont, only a partial wall and some flooring remained of the Bay View's basement. Amelia couldn't be sure but thought she recognized the hallway that led to the stairs near the hotel kitchen where her grandfather's impenetrable metal walk-in safe might still exist under all the wreckage.

"Oh my Lord…"

Her throat tightened at the sight of a barrier of bricks that had been part of the hotel's foundation. Now, the rectangles were melted, misshapen blocks of clay. And no wonder. One of the firefighters she'd treated at the Presidio told her the inferno had generated temperatures up to three thousand degrees. It was as if a giant eraser had swept the Bay View Hotel and Gentlemen's Gambling Club off the face of the earth.

Without warning, tears began to stream from Amelia eyes and spill down her cheeks. Through a blur of sadness, she saw the pitted field where her childhood home once stood and where she'd known every corridor and cupboard.

At length, she wiped her eyes with her sleeve. The game was truly over. Her father and grandfather were dead. The Bay View of her youth was no more. Three sequential cards did not a royal flush make, she considered with a sigh. It was time she got down to the business of helping to build a hotel for Julia Morgan's client.

For a few more moments she absorbed the view, then squared her shoulders and picked her way past the heaps of wreckage in front of her, stepping down a short set of ragged cement stairs.

Amelia peered through the eerie gloom. Surely, Thayer couldn't be living in what was left of the hotel's basement? Yet there had been no sign of a tent or shed on his charred property. And to Amelia's educated ear, a series of thuds echoing from somewhere below ground told her someone was at work, already clearing rubble.

She eyed the structural support holding up what remained of the garage and judged it reasonably safe to enter. After a morning of inhaling briny breezes, the odor of burnt wood and pulverized concrete inside the ruins of the Bay View stung her lungs and prompted a fit of coughing. When it subsided, she cleared her throat several times and shouted into the ash-black cavern that had comprised the old hotel's lowest floor.

"Mr. Thayer? Are you down here?" she called out. The steady reverberation was surely coming from someone with a sledgehammer or pickaxe. "Hell-ooo!"

The noise ceased.

"Who's there?" barked a voice.

And then Amelia heard another bark—that of a dog.

Amelia advanced farther down the cement stairs. "Mr. Thayer?" she called again, suddenly apprehensive that the building might collapse if the anonymous excavator didn't know what he was doing. "Is that you?"

"Who's *there*? Identify yourself at once." The dog barked again, fierce and protective.

"It's Amelia Bradshaw," she shouted. "I'm trying to find Mr. James Thayer. Is he here?" She retreated a few steps. She had a sudden thought: what if the inquisitor was some wild-eyed scavenger who might not appreciate being disturbed?

A figure in tattered black trousers and no shirt appeared with a filthy handkerchief tied around his face, bandit-style. The late Charlie Hunter's half-terrier half-unknown breed Barbary was by his side.

"What the—?" Then, "Oh, it's you," he said.

In one hand he held a pickaxe, in the other the butt of a pistol, its business end aimed straight at her. Amelia had a sudden, swift memory of the old lady next door pointing a pearl-handled revolver straight at her. Thankfully she recognized Thayer, or she probably would have let out a scream.

The upper portion of his face was blackened with soot— except for the scars on his forehead that stood out in lighter shades. His black hair was coated with plaster dust.

J.D. Thayer looked like a pirate, and a dangerous one at that, despite the fact he swiftly lowered his firearm.

"Hello, Mr. Thayer." Amelia tried to avoid staring at his bare chest. "My goodness, must you brandish a gun? Are your ribs mended enough to be wielding a pickaxe?"

J.D. lowered the heavy tool and tucked the pistol into his waistband.

"Sorry, but it's been necessary to take certain precautions around here. When I stopped by the Fairmont earlier, Miss Morgan said I might expect you today," he said, voice muffled by the handkerchief. "Do you have the final drawings?"

"Designs, yes. We still have a lot of measuring to do once the site is cleared of at least some of rubble. Then you'll get your buildable drawings."

He leaned the pickaxe against the remnants of a wall, tucked the pistol deeper into his belt, and reached for a torn dinner jacket heaped on the floor near his feet. He buttoned its front until only a triangle of his bare chest showed. Then he removed the handkerchief from his face. His black mustache contrasted sharply with his plaster-dusted hair.

Amelia lifted her portmanteau. "May I leave them with you for your review?"

"I'd like to see them *now*. Please step into my humble abode, such as it is.

Amelia followed him and Barbary around the corner, down several more concrete steps, and along a subterranean corridor to the rear of the basement. They stopped at a cluttered area that once had been part of the furnace room. Sheets of melted tin lay about in piles. Recently discarded newspapers had been stuffed into holes where Amelia recalled ventilation pipes had once been routed toward the outdoors. The only light came from a substantial hole above their heads that opened to the sky. On the dirt floor itself, a makeshift pallet took up one corner, with J.D.'s moth-eaten cloak serving as a blanket. In another corner stood an up-ended wooden box and two smaller wooden cubes that provided a table and chairs. A kerosene lantern faintly illuminated a mound of neatly stacked bricks and jagged chunks of concrete and broken plaster.

"Not much like what you remember, eh?" He gestured for her to take a seat on one of the boxes. Barbary curled up on J.D.'s borrowed cloak.

Amelia nodded her agreement, for she couldn't find the words to express the terrible sense of loss she was battling as she absorbed the devastation surrounding them. Finally she asked, "What were you excavating with such enthusiasm?"

"I decided I couldn't sit around and do nothing until your drawings were approved by Miss Morgan and me or I'd go stark mad, so today, I'm trying to get nearer to the walk-in safe on the other side of that pile." He gave a short laugh. "If I could get to it, I could make my first payment to your employer—and thus pay your salary."

Amelia stared at a mountain of rubble. "Ah, yes. My grandfather's old safe. I read in the *Call* recently about people in Chicago after the big fire there, opening their safes before they had cooled down sufficiently. Cold air rushed in and incinerated paper money and documents still hot enough to burn."

"I read the same article." He pointed to the newspapers stuffed into gaps in the walls to protect him from the elements. "But in my case, it's taking me forever to get even this close to where the safe is buried. By the time I reach it, it'll be stone cold."

"It's a big job," Amelia agreed, her mind leaping to the other subjects she'd come to discuss. She gestured toward a series of two-by-four posts shoring up the ceiling above Thayer's one-man excavation. "It's good to support what's left of the floor above like that. There're some dangerous load factors to contend with, aren't there?"

Thayer nodded as an awkward silence ensued.

"Right," Amelia said at length and dug deeper into her portmanteau. She extracted a set of furled drawings and smoothed them in opposite directions. J.D. reached for two misshapen bricks to keep them flat. Amelia also placed a note on the improvised table. "Miss Morgan wished me to inform you that she has gotten permission from the owners of the Fairmont to offer you a room in the basement over there."

J.D. was absorbed in gazing at her drawings and didn't look up as he said, "The Law brothers themselves made this offer?"

Amelia nodded. "The note's from them."

Thayer quickly scanned the short missive. "Well, that's… interesting." He looked up and smiled faintly. "And where will *you* be living?"

Ignoring his question, she replied, "The Laws told Miss Morgan that you're welcome to use the Fairmont as a base until the foundation here is laid and the framing goes up, at which time they assume you'd prefer to move back."

Thayer fingered the edges of the note from his rivals until the corners were black with soot, and set it down on the table again.

"That's amazingly decent of them. I'm not quite sure I would have done the same if our situations had been reversed." Amelia studied J.D.'s expression and decided she wasn't quite sure either. "And while I appreciate this gesture of hospitality," he continued, "it will do nothing to discourage my desire to be the first hotel open before April eighteenth next year."

"You've made no secret of that. And I believe the Laws understand that's your intention."

He regarded her steadily. "I wish to know, by the way, if you are willing to do *your* utmost to help that happen—even if you too will be a guest of the Law brothers these next few months and answerable to their architect? I'll need you available night and day while we push to get the Bay View rebuilt."

J.D.'s piercing gaze underscored the intensity of his demands.

"Miss Morgan has already made arrangements for me to move into a room in the Fairmont's basement," she replied, "along with the rest of our staff working on these two projects. Of *course* I will work my hardest in the interests of my firm."

"Even if it means besting your employer?"

"I don't think of these rebuilding efforts as a competition, Mr. Thayer. Julia Morgan, the rest of her staff, and I are simply trying to construct two hotels in the space of ten months—as we've promised you and the Law brothers—that will be both beautiful *and* safe structures. Why must you always make everything a gambling game?"

"Because I am a betting man, and this *is* a competition."

"And do you intend that a gambling club still be part

of the rebuilding plans here?" she shot back. "I've had no instructions and we've designed nothing in that regard."

"That's because I haven't even raised the funds to build the hotel itself, let alone an annex. But don't worry, I haven't given up on that score." His dark eyes had taken on a cool, speculative gaze. "And I am most hopeful that the Committee of Fifty on the Reconstruction of San Francisco—whose executive board has several bankers I know, plus Ezra Kemp—will look favorably upon my requests for government funds. Therefore, I have every expectation that within the week, I shall have what I need to begin competing handily with the generous-spirited Law brothers."

"Will you now?" It was a silly remark, but it was all she could think of.

Amelia had to admit she was rattled by the idea that Thayer could wave a magic wand and secure the money for the hotel and the gambling hall because of his contacts with the likes of Ezra Kemp. Julia had been having a devil of a time locating the materials she needed to commence reconstruction and the city's politicos had done nothing to smooth the way. Amelia wondered how in the world she could work on a daily basis with a man who could be fair-minded and supportive one minute and cold and calculating the next—to say nothing of living and sleeping near him in close basement quarters for months.

"I would think that you'd had enough of the gambling life," she ventured. "After all, thanks to the club you and Kemp built, you nearly lost your life. Why risk running such an unsavory business, dependent on the grace and favor of the scalawags in City Hall, when you can be a respectable hotel owner now?"

"But haven't you heard? I've never been respectable."

"Actually, I *have* heard that, Mr. Thayer."

He arched an eyebrow, as if to say touché. Then he asked, "Are you a prude, Miss Bradshaw, when it comes to gambling? Your having lived in Paris made me think perhaps not. Didn't you ever visit Monte Carlo?"

"Yes I did."

She was more annoyed to recall the week spent with Etienne in the south of France—soon after which they had the altercation that had ended their relationship abruptly—than being called a prude by J.D. Thayer.

She reached for the handle of her portmanteau, suddenly desperate to be free of Thayer's company. Then she met his gaze, refusing to be cowed by his veiled rudeness. "My objections to building a gambling hall as part of the restoration of the Bay View, Mr. Thayer, are rooted in my belief that allowing such activities in what is essentially a residential district is highly misguided. If we're rebuilding a city, we have a golden opportunity to think in terms of appropriate use of land, of the pressing needs of the citizenry, and—"

By the middle of her pronouncements, the corners of Thayer's mouth faintly curled.

"You're not a prude, you're a preacher!" he said, laughing. "The truth is, though, that I think you're correct in saying that the disaster gives the city the perfect chance to rethink planning as a whole."

Amelia blinked with surprise. "You do?"

"Yes, in fact, I do. And your recent assessment of my penchant for the gambling life is rather accurate. On occasion, I wagered more than was prudent and certainly overextended my credit—and look where it's left me. I'm camping out in a dark soot hole with barely a penny in my pocket or a roof over my head."

Amelia judged he wasn't whining about his fate, simply stating facts and she rather admired him for his candor. "Well, surely your family will lend a hand?" she said. She knew that Thayer's parents lived in a grand mansion in one of the few districts spared by the fire.

"Not likely," he replied with an enigmatic shrug. "You see, my father agrees with you, Miss Bradshaw, that a gambling establishment in a posh neighborhood like Nob Hill is an affront to 'decent' people, in whose company he doesn't count his only son."

Amelia noted the bitterness in his tone and wondered if J.D.'s living openly with Ling Lee and employing her cohorts in his gambling den upset the senior Thayer to the point of disowning him.

"And your mother? What's her view on… your choice of profession?"

"Mother? For years now, I've had no idea what her views are on any subject. As you may have also heard, I am considered the outcast of the Thayer clan, especially after Ling Lee came to live with me. I rarely see either of my parents."

Ah ha! J.D.'s relationship with the Chinese harlot was *the cause of the family estrangement…*

Amelia was amazed by the openness with which he spoke of his late lover. Thinking of her own living arrangements with Etienne during her final year in Paris, she could at least credit Thayer for his honesty on the subject. "So, I take it that you can't expect financial help from your family?"

"I don't know the answer to that question yet. Meanwhile, I've spent what little cash I had on life's necessities." He pointed toward the kerosene lamp, the pistol, the pickaxe, and a small store of food heaped against one wall of his burnt-out shelter. "Until I can dig out my safe, I am, to put it bluntly, stone broke."

"Most everyone is," Amelia sighed. "Isn't it disgraceful the way prices are almost as outrageous as they were in the Gold Rush? I hear the mayor and his cronies are already demanding bribes like before the quake. It's disgusting." She regarded Thayer for a moment. Why should she assume he wasn't a member of the mayor's inner circle? "What about Ezra Kemp?" she asked. "Can't he help you? I hear that he's doing a land-office business selling lumber at inflated prices."

"I'm already in debt to the man for the late, lamented gambling club and I'd prefer to avoid any further obligations if I can. Unfortunately, he appears to have nearly cornered the market on redwood. But don't waste time fretting on my account, Miss Bradshaw. As I said before, I already have applications in to the Committee of Fifty, as well as to the Department of Relief and Rehabilitation." He gestured toward the drawings sprawled on the table between them. "I'm hoping at least one of them will extend me some credit so I can cover what I need to hire a builder to implement your very fine designs."

A compliment out of the blue, and he'd only seen these few sketches and not even her final drawings!

She never knew what to expect from James Diaz Thayer.

She wondered if she and Thayer would ever truly have a meeting of minds. What if financial constraints or his burning desire to best the Law brothers at the Fairmont prompted him to order the Morgan firm to cut corners in the rebuilding of his hotel, just as he had when he threw together the Gentlemen's Gambling Club?

She could clearly see that the subject of the Bay View Hotel was bound to render her wary and distrustful of the man who, for all intents and purposes, was now her employer even more than Julia Morgan.

Amelia stood to take her leave. "I need to be going now. Tomorrow, you can tell me any design changes you might desire. Come to the small office they've set up in a shed on the Fairmont site. Once you and Miss Morgan agree we're headed in the right direction, I'll begin the renderings that Miss Morgan deems essential, and from which we can begin to build—that is, when you secure the funds to completely clear this site and pay for our preliminary building materials."

"And when do you move into the Fairmont basement?" he asked.

"I'll be sleeping there as of tonight."

"Well, then," J.D. replied with the ghost of a smile, "please tell the hospitable Law brothers to expect me this evening as well."

Amelia felt color stain her cheeks. "But you sounded as if—"

"It all seems too delightful to pass up. Rather like a house party."

"Mr. Thayer, really—"

J.D. gave her a roguish smile, "And please convey my thanks to my generous hosts. It will be good sport to see which hotel opens for business first, given the vagaries of life in San Francisco these days. I should start a betting pool."

Amelia heard herself say somewhat peevishly, "Ever the gambler, aren't we?"

I do sound like a prude…

J.D.'s expression showed he was close to smiling again. "As you are well aware," he said, "the Bay View is to be rebuilt on a smaller scale than the Fairmont, and from the ground up. Once the site is cleared of rubble—which in itself will be no easy task, I admit—I anticipate you and I will have far fewer problems than the ones Miss Morgan will face rehabilitating the inside of that burnt-out behemoth down the street. I think we're the odds-on favorite to open first, don't you?"

Amelia affected a shrug. "Well, let me leave these drawings with you so you can study them before your meeting with Miss Morgan. It's probably wise to remember, with regard to any competition between the Bay View and the Fairmont, there are always unexpected problems during construction, whatever size the project," she warned.

"Let's just hope any delays happen at the Fairmont and not here. Good day to you, Miss Bradshaw," J.D. added crisply, announcing their interview was at an end. "We'll soon begin rebuilding in earnest, yes? And I can count on your loyalty?"

Amelia briefly studied his expression. He must be goading her, she thought with irritation, reminding her of their strange predicament in order to keep her off balance and retain the upper hand. Her jaw ached from clenching her teeth, but she managed to force a polite smile to her lips. Strange as it might seem, she was disappointed that the terrors they'd shared hadn't forged a stronger bond of… comradeship, she supposed it was called, seeing each other as fellow survivors in a dangerous world.

The reality of building a new Bay View made that impossible. They were—and would remain—adversaries, despite both being on the team devoted to the goal of seeing the Bay View Hotel rise from the ruins and open its doors *first*.

"Thank you for bringing these," he said, indicating the drawings.

"You're welcome," she replied by way of a final farewell.

A few minutes later, Amelia emerged on to Taylor Street to find that the fog still had not begun to lift.

"Summer in San Francisco..." she murmured.

Fog and more fog. Sometimes it seemed as if the sun would never shine again on this City by the Bay.

CHAPTER 13

WHETHER JULIA MORGAN REALIZED it or not, Amelia knew full well that the race to restore the splendor of San Francisco's hotels on Nob Hill had begun.

To Amelia's surprise, halfway down Taylor Street, a few blocks from the charred but standing walls of the Fairmont, the increasing glare of the noonday sun suddenly made her squint and shade her eyes with her gloved hand. Shafts of silver light penetrated the low-lying clouds, and she marveled as the wispy curtain of moisture began to lift, revealing the pristine, panoramic vista of water and islands dotting the bay. A light breeze freshened the air, relieving the surrounding atmosphere of the lingering smell of smoke.

The city might be wounded, but the landscape was immutably one of the most beautiful in the world, she thought with a rush of giddy pleasure. She was gripped by an overarching love for San Francisco, piercing in its poignancy for what was lost and for what might yet be brought back to life.

Yet so much in her world depended on J.D. Thayer pulling off a financial miracle, Amelia reflected, instantly sobering. She found herself wondering to what lengths a gambler would go to secure the funds needed to rebuild the Bay View Hotel?

The Thayers' housemaid was speechless when she recognized her employer's son standing at the front door. She recovered her composure and bobbed a curtsey.

"S-Shall I announce you, sir?"

J.D. wasn't surprised the young woman was flustered to behold the not-so-heir-apparent on the doorstep of the Thayer family mansion. After all, he hadn't paid a call there in more than two years. "No need to show me in, Sophia, thank you. I'll just look for my father in his study."

"It's good to see that you're all right, sir, after the quake and all."

"That's kind of you to say. And your family? What of them?"

"Little Italy's burnt to a cinder," she reported dolefully. Then she brightened. "But so many of our people are in the building trades. They say our neighborhood will be the first section of the city to be put to rights."

"It wouldn't surprise me." He turned toward a heavy oak door off the vestibule, paused a moment, and then reached for the glass knob and turned it.

"Big Jim" Thayer was lounging in a leather chair reading a newspaper in the curve of the bay window, taking advantage of both the sunlight and the spectacular view of the Golden Gate straits. His good fortune included living on Octavia and Pacific streets to the west of Van Ness, where the fire had finally been contained. In the glare of day, the mansion's appointments of velvet-covered furniture and high-Victorian artifacts appeared all the more ostentatious, given the deprivations J.D. had endured of late.

The elder Thayer's light brown mane was in distinct contrast to his son's dark hair, as were the older man's pale, watery blue eyes to those of his namesake, which were intensely brown. Where J.D. sported a trim mustache, his father fancied luxuriant sideburns *and* mustache, the latter twisted on each end, below which was the distinctive Thayer chin with a cleft practically as large as a one-cent piece. Both men were over six feet tall, but where the son was lean and hard-muscled, James Thayer Sr.'s, waistline bespoke overindulgence in seven-course meals at the Cliff House and too many brandies at his club.

The most distinct contrast between them, certainly, was their complexions: Big Jim's pallid as paper, his son's bronze, a few shades lighter than his mother's Spanish ancestors.

It was barely three in the afternoon, but the elder Thayer held a whiskey in one hand, resting the newspaper in his lap. J.D. drew some satisfaction from the startled expression on his father's face when he recognized the unannounced visitor.

"Well, blast and damn. The Prodigal returns. And dressed in virtual rags."

J.D. ignored the sarcasm aimed at this threadbare attire. "Hello, Father."

Big Jim set his whiskey aside. "I figured you might turn up one day soon. Kemp told me you were alive and sorely in need of funds."

J.D. advanced toward a table piled high with familiar legal documents he knew detailed the particulars of his application to the Committee of Fifty to rebuild the Bay View.

"I see you've received my requests to the Committee."

"So you need my help, do you?"

Thayer Sr. had not risen from his chair to greet his son. Both were well aware that Big Jim sat on the executive board of the powerful civic group charged with overseeing the reconstruction of the city—and was among its most influential members. It galled J.D. to have to make this show of deference and grant his father the required respect, but if it could gain him the required funds, he'd do it.

"Well, I definitely need your good will, sir."

At that, the older man pointed to the last page of the document. "And you're not shy about asking for a substantial figure, are you?"

"I believe that's a realistic sum."

"And why would I be moved to extend a hand to a wayward son like you?"

Big Jim gazed at his only offspring from beneath eyebrows as bushy as the wheat-colored sideburns that framed his cheeks.

J.D. strove to maintain an attitude of studied detachment. "If I can't expect your good will, sir, then I come here to ask that you not vote *against* me."

"I won't have to. If I privately put in one negative word with the other members on the executive board, I could be the only 'aye' vote in your favor and still get my desire to withhold funds from your shameful project."

"Let others do your dirty work for you? I'm not surprised."

Idiot! J.D. cursed himself silently.

His earliest childhood memories of his lawyer father were of a man who employed an infamous brand of courtroom pugilism toward friend and foe alike in an ongoing display of adversarial banter. J.D. had learned this art at the knee of a master. Even if it hurt his case, however, he took some small solace in the fact he'd obviously landed his own verbal punch to his father's flabby jaw.

James Thayer inhaled deeply, a sign to J.D. that he was attempting to rein in his temper. "Most people would say that you're the one doing dirty work, disgracing this family by becoming a common gambler and pimp."

"So you will oppose my petition then?"

"Not if you make a few amendments to it."

J.D. was surprised to be granted this reprieve. Surprised and wary.

"Such as?"

"Do not rebuild the gambling club as part of this venture on Nob Hill," his father replied, gesturing to the sheaf of papers. "My friends there find it offensive."

"Your friends—and you—no doubt find it competition."

"Not very shrewd of you to insult someone whose vote you need, J.D."

How right you are, he thought. But goring his father's ox was nigh irresistible after all the insults the senior Thayer had dealt him over the years.

"Are you saying, Father, that you and Schmitz and Reuf can no longer be found in Chinatown these days? That you've given up silently investing in brothels and gambling halls or wagering yourselves?"

"The mayor and Reuf hold no investments there now, that I know of."

"Payoffs, protection money, and anonymous partnerships are a kind of investment, wouldn't you say?"

Ignoring the remark, Big Jim pointed again to the documents. "I have no objection to men indulging in a friendly game of chance at their private club. And there are unquestionably places in the city where certain… recreations can be indulged without offending the larger community. What I *do* find objectionable is that a member of such an esteemed family as mine should engage in running a gaming den where any riffraff can sit at the tables in an otherwise respectable neighborhood, and Chinese harlots—"

"If I request funds simply to reconstruct the hotel on Nob

Hill, will you vote yes?" interrupted J.D. It was high time he called a unilateral halt to their stupid sparring and got down to business.

His father looked at him with surprise. "You're willing to forego rebuilding the gambling club?"

"To get the loan? Yes."

"Then what I've heard must be true. The Chinese girl *did* die in the earthquake. Without her to assist you, perhaps you've soured on being a card shark and procurer—or maybe you fear you couldn't succeed in such crafty businesses without her skills in or out of the bedchamber."

J.D. had a sudden, deadly impulse to pummel his father's fleshy face with his bare fists. Instead, he managed a shrug.

"Yes, Ling Lee was crushed in the quake. What's important to me now is the financing."

Big Jim's pleased expression showed that he believed he'd finally gained the upper hand with his troublesome son. "It would please your mother no end to hear that her only child has finally come to his senses."

"Will you vote 'yes' under the terms you've just described?"

The two men stared at each other for a long moment and then the father nodded.

"Yes."

"And your cronies on the executive board?"

"I cannot speak for the boorish Mr. Kemp, but if you swear on your honor that you will no longer taint my good name by running a gaming enterprise or fancy house in the heart of Nob Hill—*or* overindulging in such winner-take-all contests as you have in the past—I will not poison the well with others on the Committee of Fifty."

"And at City Hall?"

"I'm sure His Honor and the redoubtable Mr. Reuf will

be happy to see that the rebuilding of the esteemed Bay View Hotel is proceeding apace."

"Do I have your word on this, sir?"

"More to the point, do I have yours?"

"Yes. I will not run a gambling establishment on Nob Hill where Chinese women entertain customers in their bedchambers."

He avoided promising not to gamble himself, or hire Chinese laborers, if needed, at the building site—and his father apparently overlooked that omission.

"Fine then." Triumph flickered on Big Jim's face as the elder Thayer set the loan application aside. "I will recommend that my friends on the executive board and in City Hall contribute toward the rehabilitation of my son as a decent member of society."

J.D. turned and prepared to make his departure.

"How has it been working with that Morgan woman?" his father asked suddenly.

"An improvement over that fake builder Kemp recruited for the gambling club. At least she's qualified as an engineer and is a bona fide architect, trained in France."

"And her assistant? What's the chit's name? Her father was that drunkard you hornswoggled into hazarding the deed to the hotel."

All J.D.'s senses went on high alert. His father had his spies everywhere, which obviously included Ezra Kemp.

"Amelia Bradshaw, you mean? She's equally well trained as an engineer and architect. She's greatly in need of employment—which means she'll do exactly as I say. It's an excellent arrangement in my view."

His father stroked the ends of his mustache and smiled faintly. "Knowing you, I'm sure it is. But isn't it a mite dangerous to entrust your future to a woman who may not have your best interests at heart? After all, I hear Charlie Hunter changed his will and she was to inherit—except for the poker game you played with her father that apparently put the hotel in your hands."

J.D. gazed steadily at his father for a moment. "I am quite accustomed to the reality that no one has *my* best interests at heart. Good day to you, sir."

He'd taken a few steps toward the study door when his father called after him.

"Just a moment, James. If you want these funds, I have one further condition."

J.D. slowly turned around. "And what might that be?"

"You must visit your mother. Once a month. From now on. I've grown weary of her moods and tears. I dare not allow her out in public any longer. Perhaps you can improve her humor, or at least serve as a diversion."

J.D. acquiesced with a small shrug. "You *do* drive a hard bargain, don't you?"

Since a bitter day twenty years earlier—and for his mother's sake and safety—J.D. never appeared to take her part against his father. Fortunately, Big Jim had just provided his son with an open invitation to monitor, at long last, how Connie Thayer was faring in her prison overlooking San Francisco Bay.

❧

The grand oak staircase in the Thayer mansion ended on a second floor landing, aflame this late afternoon from a golden stained-glass sunburst embedded in the wall overhead. J.D. hesitated outside a heavy door and cocked an ear toward the murmur of hushed voices. Beyond lay his mother's inner sanctum.

His father's sleeping quarters were located down a long

corridor to the left and behind an equally thick wooden door, leaving J.D. to wonder if, perhaps, the pair had not occupied the same bedroom since the night their son had been conceived, thirty-five years earlier. He knocked softly.

The male voice from beyond indicated that the intrusion was highly unwelcome.

"Who is it?"

"Mrs. Thayer's son. Here at the request of her husband."

Within seconds the door was opened by a man who looked disturbingly familiar. J.D. offered a curt nod as his official greeter held out a perfectly manicured right hand.

"Well, hello, J.D. It's been quite awhile, hasn't it?"

Dr. George Ellers, in his early fifties, was the picture of refinement. Clean-shaven, save for a fastidiously maintained blond mustache, his chiseled features were only just softening with age. He sported a tweed suit cut in the latest fashion and clasped a gold-headed cane in his left hand.

J.D. ignored his outstretched hand and turned toward the woman who reclined on a chaise lounge with a lap rug tucked about her small, fragile form. Blue-black hair hung loosely about shoulders covered by a lacy bed jacket that matched the beige upholstery. Her eyes and skin were amber—the legacy of Spanish blood—and her face was still smooth despite her fifty-three years.

Arrayed on a table beside the chaise was an impressive collection of pill bottles and jars filled with medical elixirs. The room's curtains were pulled shut to block out the glare, and only a gas lamp, its globes painted with pink cabbage roses, illuminated the shadowy chamber.

Consuela Diaz-Reims Thayer nervously fingered the edge of the velvet lap rug while she regarded her son, her black eyelashes fluttering in apparent consternation.

"Oh thank God, James, you're all right! Why didn't anyone—" She gazed beseechingly at Dr. Ellers.

"I will leave you and your son to enjoy his visit," Ellers said pleasantly. He eyed J.D.'s tattered appearance with distaste. "I have work to do in my study upstairs."

"Oh, George," Consuela pleaded, "I—I still feel rather unwell. Couldn't you—"

"I'll just be one flight up, Connie dear. That tincture I've prescribed will do its job in very short order. I'll check back on you in a little while."

"My mother has fallen ill?" J.D. asked of Ellers, knowing full well the nature of the medicines this physician dispensed so freely—and on whose orders.

"A continuing case of nerves, J.D." The doctor's expression suggested that the visitor was a prime cause of Mrs. Thayer's infirmity. "Like so many others, your mother has had a difficult time since the earthquake. She was especially upset when no one sent word of your whereabouts."

J.D. lifted a vial from her bedside table and studied the label. "Ellers, you prescribed this potion for my mother long before April eighteenth. And since when have you made your home here?"

"My infirmary and flat were destroyed in the fire. Your father was kind enough to accommodate me until I could get my practice reestablished, which is, of course, taking longer than expected."

"And you have found living as a member of this household more comfortable than expected?" J.D. countered in a tone just shy of insulting.

"J.D., really! George has been nothing but a godsend since—since—"

Clearly, he thought, the prisoner had come to feel kindly

toward her guard. J.D. ignored his mother and addressed the doctor.

"You've been meddling in my family's affairs ever since my Grandfather Reims died under such unfortunate and *unusual* circumstances. That's been nearly twenty years, Ellers. And now, here we all are, under the same roof. Amazing, really."

J.D. heard his mother's sharp intake of breath. The doctor strode toward the door and grasped the knob as if he were weighing his next action. Then he turned to address the interloper.

"Archibald Reims should be allowed to rest in peace and your mother and father spared from your brand of false and churlish accusations. Such behavior is, perhaps, excusable in a headstrong boy of fifteen, but your father and I find it rather tiresome in a man your age."

"Weren't you and Father fast friends even before my grandfather drowned in the bay?" J.D. countered. "Folks say you were such an inferior doctor back then, you'd do virtually anything to stay in Big Jim's good graces—and it would appear you still would."

Ellers returned J.D.'s stare but eventually looked away. "You haven't changed much, have you, boy? Your mother tells me that, sadly, you have developed a strong penchant for gambling like your late grandfather."

"George, please let's not—" Consuela began.

"Young James, here, should not be allowed to upset you in this manner, my dear." Ellers pursed his lips and addressed J.D. again. "I find it most disturbing you should be so like the unfortunate Mr. Reims. As your doctor, I must suggest that you watch yourself in that regard. It would break your mother's heart if you came to the same, sorry end."

"George, don't!" Consuela pleaded, appearing close to tears.

"And *you*," snapped J.D., "charlatan that you are, haven't been my doctor in decades. And I wonder if my father knows how *often* you insinuate yourself these days into the family's private quarters."

"Not that he would care," Consuela interjected with more petulance than bravado.

Without further comment, Ellers closed the door with just enough force to indicate that the son of his long-time patient had irritated him to no end.

"That was horribly rude," Consuela declared sotto voce.

"Good, the pill-pushing quack." J.D. spoke his last words directly at the door, hoping Ellers heard.

"We didn't have a *word* from you after the fire. For the longest while, I feared you were dead." Consuela took in his disreputable clothes and scuffed boots. "Are you all right? What of your hotel? Why have you come here after all this time?"

J.D. realized only too well that for years his mother had been as isolated in this soft, pink boudoir as if she'd been incarcerated in a garrison on Alcatraz Island. Little wonder she knew nothing of the fate of the Bay View Hotel. Ellers and her husband controlled whom she saw, what papers she read, what medicines were prescribed, and what withdrawals were made from her considerable bank accounts.

"My hotel burned to the ground," said J.D., taking the seat that had been vacated by Dr. Ellers and reached for her hand.

"Oh, how terrible! I am so sorry, son," replied his mother, ever his champion, and most likely unaware that he'd won the Bay View in a poker game.

"It's good to see you again, Mother. You're still beautiful as ever."

"Oh nonsense," she scoffed, but he could tell she was

pleased. She tightened her grip on his hand like a drowning sailor. "I was so worried about you. Does your father know you've come upstairs to see me?" she asked anxiously.

"He sent me. I plan to rebuild the Bay View and came to get Father's approval of the project so that the Committee of Fifty would vote me funds for it."

"Are you also rebuilding that dreadful gambling club on Nob Hill? Don't tell me he'd help you do *that*? All our friends were outraged a place like that was built in such a fine neighborhood."

J.D. could clearly see his mother was allowed only negative news about her only child. He wasn't shocked or surprised to see that she opposed the building of gambling establishments—wherever they might be. San Franciscans still joked about the way in which her grandfather, Eduardo Diaz, gambled away the sizeable acreage comprising Rancho Diaz in the Sacramento Delta—along with the hand of his daughter, Antonia, Consuela's mother. Both the original Diaz Spanish land grant *and* J.D.'s maternal grandmother had been won in an impromptu shooting contest in Nevada City between the hot-tempered, hard-drinking Eduardo and the equally boisterous Archibald Reims when both men were silver miners. Such reckless gambling had sealed the fate of the Diaz clan in California. Antonia Diaz was wed to Archibald Reims and their "honeymoon baby" Consuela Diaz-Reims—now Connie Thayer—appeared nine months to the day of Archie Reim's sharp-shooting triumph.

For a split second, J.D. allowed himself to consider the plight of Amelia and her mother, Victoria Hunter, helpless to halt the wagering of their assets by that other inebriate, Henry Bradshaw, which resulted in the loss of *their* family legacy.

Then, just as quickly, he pushed from his mind the

stark truth that heiresses like the Bradshaw women—and his mother—had virtually no freedom to decide their own matrimonial or financial fate.

Recalling now the infamous story of Archie Reim's dead-eyed destruction of five glass whiskey bottles perched atop a hitching post outside a saloon, J.D. could only remind himself that the win brought about the marriage of the youthful German immigrant and the lovely Antonia that, in turn, resulted in the birth of J.D.'s mother, Consuela.

I suppose I should be profoundly grateful for old Archie's penchant for gambling and his skill with a pistol.

The noteworthy event in the previous century also marked the beginning of his grandfather's string of good fortune in land speculation and mining in California and Nevada. Unfortunately, the lucky streak ended one foggy day aboard a San Francisco ferryboat, four decades later, when the elder Reims—said at the time to be morose over sudden financial reversals—mysteriously pitched overboard and drowned.

When tragedy struck, Archie and Antonia's only child—Consuela Diaz-Reims Thayer—was still a beauty of thirty-four and by then the wife of James Thayer, a Harvard-trained lawyer and prominent San Francisco businessman. His son, J.D., saw Grandfather Reims die in the waters of San Francisco Bay. Merely a gangly youth in his teens, Archie Reims's grieving grandson had been helpless then, to stop his father's confiscation of his mother's fortune or the subsequent campaign to portray her as a highly strung woman, emotionally unstable like her father. In an act of self-preservation, the underage J.D. eventually had joined Teddy Roosevelt's brigade as the swiftest way to escape from home.

And now, in the prolonged aftermath of so many family dramas, he watched his mother nervously pluck at the coverlet covering her legs, wishing he could abandon his shield of wry indifference to assure her of his love and concern for her welfare.

But he dared not.

Truth was, he'd learned long ago that any action he took on her behalf often resulted in devious retaliation by his father. Big Jim had married Consuela for purely mercenary reasons when the senior Thayer's own coffers were depleted at one juncture from foolhardy land speculations in San Francisco's boom-and-bust economy.

J.D. had fought this triangulated battle for more than two decades. Now it was rendered even more deadly by Consuela's increasing dependence on the tinctures dispensed so liberally by Dr. Ellers at Big Jim's direction. The methods of controlling the fairer sex could be subtle, indeed.

"Son, please," Consuela complained, interrupting his reverie. "I asked you a perfectly civil question. Are you rebuilding that awful gambling den or not?"

"Not. I'm reconstructing the hotel only, at this point. And in return, Father has promised not to set those City Hall rowdies on the rebuilding project or blackball me with the Committee of Fifty."

"He wouldn't do that!" his mother exclaimed. "Not to his own son!"

J.D. was touched by the expression of horror that flooded her still handsome features. For an instant, he saw a glimmer of the fiery temperament Consuela Diaz-Reims had once been known to exhibit against her husband's wishes.

"Surely, Mother," he replied gently, "you of all people should know by now that Big Jim Thayer will do whatever damn well suits him."

"James! Your language!"

For a moment, in the midst of her distress, J.D. detected

a trace of the Spanish accent his mother had worked so diligently to eradicate. When he was a small boy, she'd urged him privately to correct her every mispronunciation. It was part of her defensive campaign to gain acceptance from the lofty wives of her husband's friends and acquaintances. These were mostly Protestant, east coast Americans whose hatred for people of color included olive-complexioned Spanish Catholics.

Even so, as time went on, she'd desired the good opinion of the nobs as much as she'd come to yearn for the potions Dr. Ellers so freely prescribed to calm her nerves. Exterminating her Spanish heritage had taken nearly thirty years to accomplish, but James Thayer Sr.'s, exotic, dark-haired wife was known now, to friends and relations alike, as simply "Connie Thayer."

"Well, I must be off," he announced abruptly and rose from his chair.

"But you've only just arrived," she protested. "Stay for tea, won't you?"

J.D.'s saw the look of panic and pleading she cast at him. He steeled himself from offering outright succor and support. He could only help her in the long run if he kept up the fiction of playing the wayward son.

Well, it's not a complete fiction, is it, J.D.?

"It's been good to see you, Mother." He leaned down and kissed the top of her head. Then he took her hand and gave it a soft squeeze. "It's hard to believe, but I've just been ordered by Father to pay you a visit at least once a month."

"Truly? Oh, J.D., I've missed you *so*."

He'd missed her too, and her look of joy made him suddenly want to lower his head to her lap and weep like a child. Shocked by this infantile reaction, he merely bowed with exaggerated formality.

"Hasta luego, Señora."

CHAPTER 14

P ILES OF LUMBER, HEAPS of gravel and sand, and lengths of newly forged steel girders littered the grounds of the burnt-out Fairmont Hotel. As was typical for June, marine moisture poured through the straits of the Golden Gate, sucked in by another scorching day in California's Central Valley, fifty miles to the east. Amelia tried to remember the name of the wag who said, "The coldest winter I ever spent was summer in San Francisco."

He wasn't joking.

With a scarf wrapped tightly around her neck, she peered through the morning's mist at workers putting the finishing touches on seven levels of scaffolding—six stories, plus a seventh tier for access to the roof, which this day was shrouded in fog. The Fairmont's sooty granite and terra-cotta shell was nearly all that remained of the monument to the *beaux-arts* style.

For days now, Amelia, Ira Hoover, and Julia Morgan spent hours in a drafty shed erected on a corner of the property, plotting their plan of action for both hotels. They poured over the drawings created by the Fairmont's original architect, James Reid, and his businessman-brother, Merritt. Word around town was that the pair weren't interested in rebuilding a hotel they had so recently completed. The truth was, they had many other lucrative and challenging projects in post-quake San Francisco.

When the Fairmont's current owners—another set of brothers, Herbert and Hartland Law—learned that their second-choice architect, the famed Stanford White, had been murdered, they'd turned to the Morgan firm as their *third* choice for the restoration job.

Now duly anointed by her employers as both architect *and* construction site supervisor on the Fairmont job, Morgan outlined what came next.

"Thirty-seven columns in this building have buckled and a number of floors have dropped at least seven feet. As we excavate the debris, we must shore up each section of the remaining walls in turn, to prevent the building's collapse." She wagged her finger sternly at her entire staff, adding, "Safety for the workers is as important as speed. We have an enormous job ahead of us, everyone."

Amelia wondered if Dick Spitz, the construction supervisor J.D. Thayer had hired to oversee construction at the Bay View Hotel, was as conscientious about the welfare of his workers. Thayer had employed someone who generally wore a scowl, whatever the weather. Despite J.D.'s sleeping at the Fairmont most nights, the de facto owner of the smaller hotel was rarely seen. At dawn's light, he departed from his borrowed basement room, located a few doors down the corridor from Amelia's, and went straight to the Bay View construction site, exhorting the workers to speedily erect the hotel's framing. His evenings were a mystery to Amelia and he apparently returned in the wee hours to grab a few hours' sleep long after everyone else had retired.

Julia instructed Amelia to divide her time between the two projects. On a Monday, the younger architect arrived at Taylor and Jackson with a revised set of drawings for the Bay View's roofline. Immediately, something caught her attention on the ground floor of the construction site where workers appeared ready to begin pounding nails into two-by-fours to raise the framing for the second floor.

"That framing crew you hired isn't mitering the corners properly!" she announced to J.D.

She insisted that he climb the scaffolding encasing the project so she could show him the flaws first hand.

"Just look at this!" she exclaimed, a breeze ruffling her hair. "The southeast corner is dangerously out of plumb. You *must* make the site supervisor tell them to rip it out and do it correctly, or your building will pitch down Jackson Street—with or without another earthquake!"

J.D. squinted in the direction she was pointing. "Can't be off by much," he said doubtfully.

"Just wait until they reach the top floor! I promise you that you'll notice it *then*."

It disturbed her to discover that J.D. appeared willing to overlook such mistakes in order to get a task accomplished, while Amelia, an echo of her employer Miss Morgan, constantly argued that *nothing* was accomplished if it wasn't done right.

"Look, Mr. Thayer, these problems of shoddy work will only get worse as construction progresses." She pointed toward a gigantic load of redwood delivered by four horse-drawn carts marked KEMP LUMBER, MILL VALLEY. "I thought you said you wanted nothing to do with Ezra Kemp."

"Unfortunately, he's the only source in the Bay Area capable of delivering the amount of lumber I need," he said, adding, "and he knows it."

"Well, be that as it may, the people you have working for you—whom I'm probably correct in assuming you hired through Ezra Kemp—aren't following our instructions properly or watched over in the way they should be by either the site supervisor or the foreman." In an effort to staff both projects quickly, Morgan had acquiesced to her client's hiring decisions. Amelia added, "Can't you at least order that there be *no* drinking of spirits during working hours? I think that alone would help the situation."

J.D. acknowledged he'd hired his crew through Kemp, nodding wearily. "I've told Dick Spitz to tell the men I've forbidden spirits on the site—and I'll say it again—but a bigger problem is that the chaps are stealing lumber and nails from here as they leave work every day, and then reselling their booty down the street!"

Amelia stared at him, appalled. "Then, why don't you just discharge this whole lot?" she demanded. "There're scores of people whose businesses were lost who are now desperately looking for work."

J.D. arched an eyebrow. "Were there carpenters' unions in France, Miss Bradshaw? Were there bullyboys who could shut down a construction site with a wink from the mayor of Paris?"

"I was attending architecture school there, not working at construction sites," she replied.

"Ah... well, then... you may be adept at drawing pretty pictures, but I venture to say you learned little in France about the way buildings get built in America."

"And I venture to say that you and Ezra Kemp learned very little from the disaster we three barely survived last April eighteenth!" she shot back, stung by Thayer's attempt to belittle her observations of his building crew's shoddy work. "And now you blithely condone the same substandard workmanship. I just don't understand how you could allow such a thing to happen again!"

J.D.'s faintly mocking expression sobered instantly.

"I know there are problems, Miss Bradshaw, and I will try, in future—"

But Amelia was unable to rein in a sense of frustration and anger that had started to boil in her veins. "If your club had been properly built in the first place, it wouldn't have collapsed and brought the rest of the Bay View Hotel down with it. At least *then* my father and Ling Lee might not have—"

Their glances locked and Amelia's unfinished sentence ballooned between them: *they might not have died.*

J.D.'s gaze took on a closed, shuttered look.

"Oh never mind!" Amelia muttered, wishing she could risk climbing down from the rickety scaffolding without waiting for a hand from her employer. Instead, she turned her head and gazed at the panorama of the bay and continued to fume.

Obviously, Ezra Kemp was more deeply involved in the reconstruction of the Bay View than Amelia had ever suspected—which could only mean trouble ahead.

And to think that she'd been tempted to feel sorry for J.D., she thought, annoyed by her previous empathy for the man.

Thayer had indicated earlier that he intended to avoid doing business with Kemp at all costs to prevent becoming more deeply in debt to the Mill Valley lumber baron than he already was. Now it would seem they were practically partners once again! Today's exchange with her employer was a timely reminder never to believe—or sympathize with—someone who consorted with the likes of Kemp and his cronies.

J.D. had remained silent while she lowered her gaze from their vantage point atop the scaffolding encasing the Bay View. She could see that wagering establishments were springing up among the charred ruins of Chinatown and along the notorious Barbary Coast. Most likely, that was where Thayer could be found most evenings when he absented himself from the Morgan team housed at the Fairmont.

"Well, enough lecturing on my part, Mr. Thayer," she announced suddenly to J.D., steeling herself for a solo descent backwards down the ladder that led from the second floor construction to the first. "I expect you'll build this hotel however you please. I will notify my employer of these deviations from our specified plans. Could you please write a note saying you absolve Julia Morgan's firm from any and all liability that may result?"

J.D. hesitated, and then nodded. Much to her surprise, his next words even sounded conciliatory. "I understand and share your concerns, Miss Bradshaw. I'll do my best to demand corrections from Kemp's men."

Startled, Amelia looked up from the top rung of the ladder to meet Thayer's gaze.

"Well… ah… thank you," she murmured, the wind suddenly taken out of her sails.

"And certainly I'm willing to put in writing that I will not hold you or the Morgan firm responsible for any subsequent problems."

"That's good of you, Mr. Thayer. I appreciate it."

"And please let me descend the ladder ahead of you so I can give you a hand," he offered.

Amelia stepped back onto the second story platform to allow J.D. to precede her down from the scaffolding.

"Thank you, sir," she echoed faintly, baffled once again by her employer's unpredictable response to her speaking her mind.

❧

Meanwhile, over at the Fairmont, Julia Morgan's troops dutifully followed in the architect's wake, clambering through the hotel's scorched remains with the insurance adjustors to inventory the destruction in greater detail. In addition to the damaged support columns and sagging floors, many ceilings had collapsed. Plaster walls had been pulverized into heaps of powdered limestone and sand. Struts and wiring were twisted into macabre shapes.

Worst hit of all were the stained glass windows in the lobby domes that had survived the quake but had exploded during the fire that had roared through the building in the hours following the temblor. Metal framing and glass panes had melted into molten masses that puddled onto the first floor.

Julia, who also had taken to wearing a woolen scarf against the summer chill, had not let a bad cough and a persistent earache confine her to the more commodious office in her family's repurposed carriage barn in Oakland. Despite her obvious suffering, she had supervised every aspect of erecting the complicated scaffolding that now nearly encased the six-story hotel.

Pointing to the metal cage that held the colossal building in an ironclad embrace, she sighed. "I can only imagine the wreckage on the roof," she said, as Morgan's foreman, Myron Spellman, shouted from above that the scaffolding job was finally complete.

"I brought my Aunt Margaret's spyglass from home," Amelia volunteered. "I thought perhaps it would help with our exterior survey of the fifth, sixth, and roof levels. You could call off the problems that you spot through the glass, and I'll write them down."

Julia arched an eyebrow. "Amelia, there is no substitute for first hand observation. I can assure you, the men's trousers we're wearing under our skirts are far more useful than your spyglass."

Amelia scanned the expanse of the exterior walls coated

with soot. Julia was famous for fearlessly scaling scaffolds, but the building was six stories high on a windy hill!

"We're going to climb up all the way to the top on the *outside*?" She dropped the spyglass into her portmanteau with a soft thud. Standing beside J.D. Thayer two stories above the ground at the Bay View that week had been quite enough.

"You are under no obligation to join me in this expedition," Julia declared. By this time, foreman Myron Spellman had cautiously worked his way down the last ladder and stepped onto solid ground. "I am quite used to heights, but perhaps you're not," Morgan added brusquely.

Amelia surveyed the ladder and the wood-and-metal scaffolding encasing the mammoth front facade. Only the most sure-footed workers had been assigned to assemble the upper regions of the maze of latticework necessary for reconstruction.

Julia's curt nod reminded Amelia that the coolness in the air had nothing to do with the temperature. Ever since the younger architect, along with Ira Hoover, J.D. Thayer, and Julia herself, had moved into their temporary living quarters in the basement, there had been subtle shift in Morgan's behavior toward her. The woman whom Amelia had once considered an inspiration and guide repeatedly made it clear that now reconstruction was about to begin in earnest, her erstwhile acolyte had much to learn. This was especially evident when it came to the Law brothers and J.D. Thayer, all of whom tended to ask their questions of the younger architect rather than address the slightly forbidding Miss Morgan.

On several occasions, Julia made it plain to Amelia that the clients were to be *her* exclusive province. "Amelia, I wish all conversations and requests be referred directly to me. That way, there won't be any confusion or miscommunication," she added pointedly.

A few days earlier, Amelia and Ira Hoover had been alone in the work shed after Julia had given Amelia a public dressing down for informing Hartland Law directly that a friend had stopped by to see him earlier that morning.

"For pity's sake, Ira! Julia doesn't even trust us to tell the clients what size *nails* we'll be using!"

Hoover, a slender young architect with wire-rimmed glasses and dark hair, parted in the middle, grinned across his drafting table. "To tell the truth, Amelia, I was mighty lonely in this job till you turned up. Now, at least, there are *two* of us she can verbally horse-whip if we dare speak directly to her precious clients."

Now on this cold, dank day, Amelia gazed at the ladder leading to the scaffolding and mentally squared her shoulders. Julia Morgan was a genius of sorts, and nothing would alter Amelia's respect for her talent and ability. Her employer obviously had a bee in her bonnet about keeping *her* employers as her special province.

Well, so be it, thought Amelia, taking a deep breath to steady her nerves at the thought of climbing six stories. At least they all had work, thanks to Julia. She made a silent vow to rededicate herself to prove her mettle to the senior architect—and her loyalty.

"Wait!" she called out, hurrying to catch up with her employer who had one boot on the bottom rung of the ladder. "I'll go with you."

A half hour later, the two women hoisted themselves from the scaffolding onto a section of the ravaged roof that looked reasonably intact and peered down the air shaft into the shattered lobby nearly a hundred feet below.

Just as the pair of architects had reached the top of the Fairmont's charred remains, J.D. Thayer wheeled up to the site in the Winton, red crosses still painted on its doors. He stood with hands on hips, his dog by his side, gazing upward, along with many of their construction workers, apparently awestruck by the sight of two ladies dressed in men's trousers beneath their skirts, scampering up the outside of the building.

Unaware of Thayer's arrival below, Amelia surveyed with dismay the extent of the devastation to the upper floors caused by the fire that had reached some 2700 degrees.

"Oh Lord… what a mess," she murmured.

"If anyone ever doubted that heat rises, they should stand right here," Julia declared. She surveyed the other sections of the collapsed roof. "The Law brothers have finally accepted the sad truth that we must replace many of the structural beams and columns that support the upper floors. From what we've seen so far, it looks as if we'll have to start in the basement and methodically work our way to the sky with reinforcing construction."

"At least the basement's already cleared of rubble and shorn up with support posts," Amelia volunteered, putting the best face on the enormous job that lay ahead.

"My biggest task," cautioned Julia, "is to be sure that the standing walls, and the brick masonry reinforcing them, don't cave in when the workers cart away all that deformed metal and wood on the upper floors. Ira or I must be at their elbows every single instant."

In Amelia's opinion, the architect already looked worn out, and they still had miles to go before the job was complete. "Julia, I hope you'll count on me to help you in any way possible."

"That is what I pay you for," the older woman replied briskly, and Amelia marveled that the same person who had been unfailingly kind during her years of training now treated her as if she couldn't put a foot right. "And besides, you'll have your hands full seeing to it that Mr. Thayer doesn't use substandard materials and craftsmen in the execution of my plans for the Bay View."

Your plans? Amelia thought, an unexpected wave of rebellion tingling her spine.

In this rare instance, given Amelia's intimate knowledge of the site and the pressure of time, Julia had assigned her the lion's share of the design work.

A collaboration at the very least.

No wonder Ira Hoover called their employer The Czarina behind her back.

Amelia shifted her glance to avoid Julia detecting the annoyance she could hardly disguise. Six stories below she caught sight of the big, blue Winton, and couldn't resist looking to see if J.D. was in the audience observing the women's daring ascent to review the state of the Fairmont's upper floors.

One look at the ground, seven floors below, and she felt a momentary attack of dizziness. To steady herself she surveyed the astounding panorama of water, hills, and sky. Facing north, she brooded over the impressive progress at Taylor and Jackson streets, four blocks away. In spite of giving Julia J.D.'s letter holding the Morgan firm harmless, should she describe in more detail her ongoing problems at the Bay View project? Julia was so preoccupied with similar issues at the Fairmont, Amelia had wanted to spare her having to wrestle with such additional difficulties.

The younger architect had already demanded J.D. force his workers to reframe a good third of the second floor this week. Dare she relate the countless wrangles she'd had about Kemp's men cutting every corner they could get away with?

Given Julia's recent moods, she'd probably consider Amelia's independent efforts to keep bad news from her blatant insubordination. And despite Julia's recent frostiness, Amelia couldn't help but feel sorry for the poor woman, wondering how many problems could her small shoulders bear.

Meanwhile, Julia pointed to an army of carpenters swarming over the framing of the new Bay View Hotel. "So, Mr. Thayer's site supervisor and workers are toiling away, I see. I must get over there tomorrow to inspect the quality of their work."

"I'm sure Mr. Thayer will want your opinion," Amelia replied.

Let Julia see for herself, thought Amelia, feeling some of her sympathy for Julia draining away. Without truly deputizing her second-in-command to act in her stead, it *was* Julia's responsibility to monitor developments at the Bay View. If the head of the Morgan firm insisted on controlling every little detail on both building sites, then *let* her!

Site supervisor Dick Spitz had continued to arrive at the site drunk half the time and thus let his workers like foreman Kelly, who also served as head carpenter, get away with larceny. When she'd pointed this out, J.D. replied he was equally frustrated and did, indeed, dress the men down, but no changes in their behavior were evident.

"The problem remains, Miss Architect," J.D. had said during this same conversation, "that Ezra Kemp is still the only source of manpower I dare employ if the Bay View is to be completed and opened for business ahead of our rival down the street."

Amelia was startled from her reverie by the sound of Julia's boot scuffing against some charred wreckage on the Fairmont's roof.

Face it, Amelia… you can do nothing to affect the way any of these headstrong people behave…

She inhaled a deep breath and drank in her airy surroundings atop the wounded Fairmont and attempted to keep her thoughts upon the majestic view of the bay.

"It's so beautiful up here," she murmured, scanning the misty outlines of Angel Island and Marin County to the north. "Even when it's overcast like this."

"You're not bothered by the height?"

"Truthfully, I feared I might be, but I'm not very much if I don't look down." Amelia stretched her arms to encompass her new world. "In fact, now that I'm finally up here, I find it exhilarating!"

"Well, I wouldn't get carried away, and please, *do* hold on to the scaffolding."

Obeying orders, Amelia surveyed the roof. "You know, Julia, if the Fairmont Hotel can open its doors on or before the anniversary of the quake and fire, think how the entire city will take heart."

To the best of her professional ability, she would perform every task J.D. and Julia asked of her, and certainly would do nothing to retard the progress at Taylor and Jackson, but she secretly hoped that the Fairmont would beat the new owner of the Bay View Hotel at his own game. Maybe it would teach Thayer an important lesson: quality far outweighed speed, especially when it came to erecting public buildings.

"The citizens of San Francisco will take inspiration from our work," Julia agreed, "but only if we meet the deadline, our budget, and our standards of excellence. Let's hope we can do all three for both hotels." Julia gestured toward the bay. "Few women, Amelia, ever have the privilege of gaining such a rarefied view." She squinted at the western sky. "The day's drawing to a close. It will take us at least a half hour to climb down from here. We'd best be going."

Amelia again noted the Winton parked below and was now acutely conscious that J.D. Thayer was watching intently as she and Julia began their treacherous descent. Thayer was paying them a daytime call—or more likely, he was making a close inspection of progress at Mason and California streets. Vaguely uneasy, Amelia wondered if something untoward had happened at the Bay View site.

Well, she thought, gingerly putting her weight on the next rung of the ladder, Julia's sharp-eyed inspection was bound to discover what it was.

At long last, Amelia's sturdy ankle boots rested on solid ground. Before she could turn around, she heard J.D. address Julia in a tone that signaled he was highly displeased.

"Look here, Miss Morgan. I thought Miss Bradshaw was working for *me*."

CHAPTER 15

W HAT IS IT YOU require, Mr. Thayer?" Julia asked, glancing with barely veiled annoyance in Amelia's direction. "Is there something Miss Bradshaw has neglected to do?"

"No, quite the contrary," J.D. replied, pointing to the complex scaffolding embracing the Fairmont Hotel. "It's something I'd like to ask of *you*, Miss Morgan."

For once, even Julia appeared disconcerted. She pressed a forefinger against her right ear as if it continually pained her and invited Thayer to move their discussion to the office shed a few yards from where they were standing. He ordered Barbary back into his motorcar, and the dog complied reluctantly.

Ira Hoover watched their retreating backs and turned to Amelia.

"What do you suppose is going on?"

Amelia shook her head, mystified as he was.

"I have absolutely no idea," adding under her breath, "but it can't be good."

An hour later, when J.D. had driven away from the Fairmont, Julia stood at the door of the work shed and beckoned Amelia to take a seat inside at one of two drafting tables squeezed into the small space. The one-room office also featured a narrow cot and a potbellied stove, cold now in August, though Amelia wouldn't have minded a bit of warmth on this chilly foggy afternoon.

"Mr. Thayer wishes to demote his site supervisor to foreman and have you take over."

"Good heavens!"

"I explained to him your inexperience and assured him that, now the scaffolding was completed here, I would be able to adequately oversee his operation as well."

Amelia nodded, though her mind was spinning. "Yes. Yes, of course. Frankly, he's a bit mental about the notion of the Fairmont's reconstruction getting ahead of his own."

"Has he discussed this with you?" Julia asked sharply.

Amelia knew instantly they were treading in dangerous waters.

"Not in so many words," she said carefully. "I merely got that idea, just from a few remarks he's made when I delivered the drawings and various notes you'd sent over there."

"I would greatly appreciate it, Amelia, if, henceforth, you would promptly report all such 'remarks' directly to *me*. I thought I'd already made that quite clear."

Amelia sat back in her chair, quite at a loss for words. Finally, she asked, "So, I assume you told Mr. Thayer you don't think I'm qualified to be his site supervisor?"

"Regardless of what I say, he apparently prefers you in that role, and that being the case, I could only acquiesce. He says your knowledge of the former Bay View Hotel makes you invaluable when it comes to building the new hotel as quickly as possible."

"Julia, I had no idea he would…" Amelia's voice trailed off as her employer eyed her steadily.

"Nevertheless, I will expect anyone who works for me to keep me informed on the substance of all conversations they have with my clients outside my presence. And in your case, as regards to Mr. Thayer, that seems especially relevant."

"Excuse me?"

What was Julia insinuating? That she had some sort of special relationship with J.D. Thayer? The man who had taken such advantage of her father's weaknesses?

Amelia rose from her chair, acutely aware she couldn't afford to lose her place with the Morgan firm. "As you wish, Miss Morgan," she said stiffly. "I will report every word. But perhaps it would be best for all concerned if you'd assign Ira to work principally with Mr. Thayer. You may remember I sued the man in court and sometimes I fear this is putting me in a rather awkward situation."

"It is not I who has created this situation," she replied tartly. "Mr. Thayer insisted you be assigned to this task—which is why I've asked you to be forthright as to any special relationship that may exist between you two."

"What kind of 'special relationship' would I possibly have with a man whose associations with my late father have caused me so much grief, including the loss of my property and inheritance?" Amelia replied, barely keeping hold of her temper. "I am merely your agent, assigned by you to help your firm complete its commission to rebuild Thayer's damnable hotel!"

"And build it, you will—under *my* complete direction."

Julia Morgan was as tough as any man, Amelia thought. She wanted things to be her way—or no way at all.

Well, that's probably why she's succeeded where no other woman ever has…

"Yes, Miss Morgan," Amelia replied at length, utterly drained of energy from this exchange and wondering why her friend Julia had somehow become her adversary.

～

With routine safety procedures firmly in place, restoration work at the Fairmont began in earnest, as did putting the finishing touches on the framing at the Bay View. Amelia took note of the way Julia checked deliveries thoroughly to be sure they weren't receiving inferior or undercounted goods—which was a serious problem at building sites throughout the city.

One morning near the end of the summer, Amelia emerged from her basement sleeping quarters on her way to the Bay View and saw a man in an ill-fitting suit lounging at the spot where the wagons arrived on Mason Street.

"May I help you, sir?" Amelia inquired as she arrived at the site.

"Who are you?" he demanded with a faint leer.

"An architect from the Morgan firm. Are you looking for work, by chance? I'm afraid we have all the—"

"I work for the mayor," he said with undisguised insolence.

Amelia stiffened. It was no secret that His Honor and Abe Reuf often sent their minions out to constructions sites to shake down owners for money in order to avoid "labor troubles" or delays with the permit process downtown. The hapless employer would agree to pay in advance for an additional complement of workers who then never turned up. Amelia had no intention of falling for this ploy.

"Well, you can certainly report to Mayor Schmitz that we're making excellent progress here at the Fairmont."

The man scanned an enormous pile of rubble being loaded onto a flatbed wagon. "Hard to see it. Think maybe you need more people put on?"

Amelia glanced around, looking for Julia, until she remembered she'd taken the morning ferry to Oakland to catch up on some paperwork at the carriage house office.

She summoned her sunniest smile for the visitor.

"Our workforce and plans have been approved by the Committee on the Reconstruction of San Francisco. And surely, you know of Rudolph Spreckels—that admirable reformer who's done such a wonderful job recently, keeping the building trades honest—and some of the other worthy gentlemen in that group? Why, even the mayor and Abe Reuf attend the meetings, don't they?"

"Wouldn't know 'bout that."

"Well, that Committee agrees that this project has all the workers we need. But if you'll just leave your name and an address, I'll be sure to let Mr. Spreckels or the mayor's office know, should we require more help."

Without responding, he turned abruptly and walked down the hill. Amelia watched his retreat, amazed that Schmitz and Reuf had the gall to dispatch one of their heavies to try to extort payoffs from the owners of the Fairmont Hotel, of all places.

Upon Julia's return, Amelia immediately reported the exchange. Morgan quickly informed Herbert and Hartland Law, who, in turn, had a word with crusader Rudolph Spreckels—and the little man from City Hall was seen no more.

As the weeks passed, the steady banging of hammers and the sight of the Bay View's landmark turrets appearing against the sky were proof that her crew was making significant progress.

Meanwhile, Julia, dashing up and down the Fairmont's scaffolding all day to inspect the enormous amount of restoration work under way, was showing increasing signs of fatigue. A spate of dank autumn days had exacerbated Morgan's ongoing ear infection, a condition that had troubled her since her childhood.

There were other indications that the pressures exerted by J.D. Thayer and the Law brothers on their chief architect were intense. Julia was often testy not only toward Amelia, but Ira Hoover as well.

"The woman's always right," Ira muttered at the end of a long day in a rare show of irritation, "but when *I'm* right, she never acknowledges it."

Amelia understood his frustration only too well. Julia Morgan might be as close to a genius as her staff was ever likely to know, but at times, she could be hell to work for.

❧

By late October, the Morgan team commemorated the sixth-month anniversary of the quake by removing the last mountainous pile of charred rubble from the Fairmont's upper floors, while the Bay View's framing was now completely enclosed.

Soon after, most of the Fairmont's steel girders, joists, and beams were in place on floors one through five. Next, damaged sections of reinforced masonry on the interior were repaired up to the fifth floor as well. These milestones prompted everyone at the firm to breathe more easily.

Meanwhile, over at the Bay View, Thayer put all his attention on advancing the construction of the hotel while a mountain of rubble still remained on the site where the Gentlemen's Gambling Club had once stood.

"We can't just leave that mess there," Amelia complained to J.D. "It's become a definite hazard to the workers and scavengers who climb over it at night, looking for anything of value. It's also blocking access to the big underground safe and the cistern."

"Well, if you can find some laborers to remove that mess, be my guest."

"Can't your Mr. Kemp corral some Chinese workers for the job? They desperately need employment, you know."

J.D. shot her an odd look, but made no further comment.

When Amelia repeated the gist of the conversation, Julia remarked dryly, "It would seem that even Ezra Kemp dare not employ Chinese workers, or the white carpenters will walk off the job."

Following this pronouncement, a paroxysm of sneezes overtook her and Amelia hastened to brew her employer a cup of hot tea.

One chilly morning in early November when Amelia walked to the shed before departing for the Bay View, Julia was huddled in the spartan construction shed with her woolen scarf, per usual, wrapped around her throat and her feet swaddled in a blanket. She was already sipping her perpetual mug of hot tea, looking worn and drawn, her round glasses magnifying the dark circles ringing her eyes. Amelia guessed that the poor soul probably wanted nothing more than a month in her own bed.

"Ears bothering you again?" she asked sympathetically.

Before Julia could answer she was seized by another fit of sneezing. When it subsided, she heaved a sigh. "I shall be seriously ill if I don't get more sleep and have a few meals cooked by someone other than myself. I haven't done the billing in two weeks." She pressed her forefingers on the base of both her ears to ease the pain. "Amelia, would you consider taking complete charge of the Bay View for a few days while Ira oversees everything at the Fairmont? I must try to shake this infection."

Julia looked small and frail, her voice taking on the uncharacteristic tone of a supplicant. *She must be very ill indeed,* thought Amelia.

"Of course I would," she assured her with genuine concern. For her own part, her heart leapt at the idea that she would serve as de facto architect-and-builder-in-charge, since J.D. constantly depended on her to double-check the invoices with him as supplies were delivered and ride herd on his unreliable workers. Perhaps this situation offered her the perfect opportunity to show Julia her professionalism and thus earn her respect. "I'm honored you'd ask me to."

"I'm having a telephone installed in the basement here at the Fairmont and expect you to call me each evening and keep me informed about every detail. I am placing a lot of responsibility on your shoulders, Amelia," she said, sounding worried. "Are you sure you're willing to be accountable as a principal member of the firm until I return?"

"Yes, of course I am." The truth was, she was performing many of those duties already—and reporting every move she made to her exacting employer.

"I'll speak to my clients today." Julia stifled a cough with the end of her woolen scarf. "Just remember, you and Ira are to check with me whenever you have a question or a problem, understood?"

"Understood."

An hour later, Amelia was called into the shed, just as Ira was leaving.

"I've already spoken with Mr. Thayer," Julia announced. "He is amenable to putting you in full charge in my absence. I assured both the Laws and him that I will be available by telephone whenever needed." Julia regarded her steadily. "Remember, Amelia, you and Ira are merely placeholders. All decisions are to be made by *me*. Ira understands this, but are you quite clear on this point?"

"Of course. Yours is the final word on everything."

"And try not to let the charming Mr. Thayer or his friend, Dr. McClure, distract you."

Amelia attempted to mask her annoyance at Julia's line of admonishment. Rather than point out that Angus McClure had stopped by exactly twice in recent weeks and Thayer now slept under his own, drafty roof, she determined her best course was to tactfully change the subject.

"I do hope you're feeling better soon. It's obvious you need this respite."

Julia ignored Amelia's show of concern. "Just be sure you're at the Bay View site no later than 5:30 every morning to receive early morning shipments."

For weeks now, she and J.D. Thayer had been checking in the supplies each morning at dawn.

"I'm sure everything will be fine on both sites," Amelia murmured, though privately she'd begun to have her doubts.

To her would fall the responsibility of anticipating problems involving suppliers who were forever delivering their stores late, or not at all. She would have to deal with Kemp's recalcitrant workers, and Thayer's eccentricities. Her private concerns would have to be put aside, even though she owed her mother in Paris several return letters and poor Aunt Margaret in Oakland felt utterly abandoned while mourning her late brother.

The press of Amelia's duties had even forced her to refuse invitations from both Angus McClure and her attorney, John Damler, to sample two newly opened restaurants. For the foreseeable future, she might as well abandon all hope for a social life.

And in that instant, Amelia felt the enormous weight that had been on Julia Morgan's shoulders suddenly shift to her own.

❧

The next morning at five, Amelia pulled herself out of bed and went along Taylor Street in the pitch dark. She had just set foot upon the curb in front of the Bay View's half-completed front entrance when a low-pitched voice said, "Good morning, Miss Bradshaw."

Stifling a small gasp, she saw a tall, familiar figure push off the door jam and walk toward her, Barbary dutifully trailing along behind him.

"Ah... well. Good morning, Mr. Thayer." Amelia set a sheaf of drawings on top of a pile of steel girders. "I didn't see you there in the shadows."

He was holding two steaming mugs.

"Coffee?"

Surprised, all she said was, "Thank you."

Make no mistake, she thought grimly, this was no welcoming committee. J.D. Thayer wanted something.

He shot a glance at the roofline. "How's our roofing coming along?"

Amelia paused. His crew had proceeded at a snail's pace.

"As slowly as can be expected, given the workers you have in your employ."

Thayer gave her a steady look. Then he flashed her a smile. When he grinned, he was, indeed, a handsome devil, white teeth gleaming and a glint in his eye. She remembered thinking her first day back in San Francisco when she'd walked in at the end of the all-night poker game that Thayer's tanned complexion gave him the look of a common field hand. Now, his long legs encased in boots that came up to his knees, he appeared more like the Spanish conquistadors from whom she vaguely recalled he'd descended on his mother's side.

"I suppose you'd be the best judge of the roof, Miss Bradshaw, since you scamper to the top of the scaffolds each day. I hold my breath whenever I see you up there."

So he'd been keeping an eye on her activities, just as she'd warily been watching his.

"Have you been able to locate a reliable source for shingles yet?" she asked, making conversation. "Miss Morgan says they're in terribly short supply."

His smile faded. "Haven't you found nearly everything in short supply, Miss Bradshaw?"

For an instant, they shared a knowing glance. Then, Amelia became aware that Dick Spitz, J.D.'s demoted site supervisor whom she'd replaced, had suddenly come around the corner. Now merely foreman, along with his cohort Kelly, the beefy head carpenter, Spitz scowled in her direction and slunk into the shadows. The pinpoint of a cheroot glowed in the distance and served as a reminder that he too watched her every move.

"What I need to locate at the moment is a supply of strong men to help me clear that rubble at the back of the property," she said. "Please excuse me, Mr. Thayer, as I must have a word with Mr. Spitz."

"Good luck with that, Miss Bradshaw."

Amelia couldn't help but smile at J.D. for understanding, at least, the challenges that faced her every waking moment. "Thank you. I could use some good luck. But wouldn't you say that congratulations to us both are in order? Our walls are standing—and that's at least something, isn't it?"

J.D. looked amused. "Yes, the walls and roof joists in place are definitely signs of progress. And we'll make even more, now that I have you all to myself. Good day to you, Amelia."

CHAPTER 16

AMELIA'S FIRST WEEK WORKING full time at the Bay View site without the constant presence of Julia Morgan was uneventful, save for being awakened in the wee hours by the sound of a rat gnawing on something underneath her iron cot in the basement of the Fairmont.

Stifling a scream, she stood on top of the bedcovers and lit her kerosene lamp. Then she knelt on the bed and peered beneath the mattress where the creature nibbled daintily on what appeared to be a dismembered mouse. Its nose twitching furiously, the larger rodent cocked its head as if offended by Amelia's intrusion, before scurrying away into the darkness of the Fairmont's basement.

"Well!" she muttered, settling back into bed and pulling the bedcovers tightly around her neck. "I shall board up that hole in the baseboard myself. That's the last time you'll dine at *this* hotel, Mr. Rat!"

A few days later, Angus McClure stopped by the Bay View in the late afternoon to invite her to join him at another newly reopened restaurant he'd favored before the quake. She recounted her adventures with the rat and had expected him to laugh, but instead he scowled and wagged his finger.

"That rat might have bitten you in your sleep, lass, and you could've been dealing with rabies or typhus, rather than that slide rule of yours. What's more, it's not safe for you to stay in that drafty basement. All sorts of hooligans roam the streets scavenging among the ruins. How long must you remain in such a daft place?"

"As long as Julia Morgan wants me to." She didn't remind the good doctor that when J.D. wasn't out gambling—or whatever activities he might be indulging in until late into the night—Thayer was asleep in far draftier accommodations at the Bay View, now he'd moved down the street to the half-built hotel.

"Don't worry, Angus," interrupted J.D., who had overheard their conversation as he walked up to them standing near the pile of lumber delivered earlier that morning. "Miss Bradshaw tells me she'll soon have the Bay View's roof finished, which means we'll have a few habitable rooms she can stay in, rather than that dank basement at the Fairmont where she sleeps presently."

Before she could put to rest any notion she would ever agree to sleep under Thayer's roof, Angus shook his head as if he thought both of them should be confined to a mental ward. His scowl deepened when Amelia begged off his invitation.

"Thanks so much, Angus, but I've just got too much to do," she apologized. She cast a quick glance in J.D.'s direction. The fact was, without Julia able to work full time, each evening, she had mountains of paperwork to keep up with after the laborers left both sites. She hated to hurt Angus's feelings, especially in front of her employer, but there was no help for it. She smiled encouragingly at the doctor, adding, "Maybe another time."

"*I'll* keep you company, Angus," Thayer said genially. "I've been wanting to see if Tadich's is up to its former standards."

"Aye, laddie," Angus said, sounding not particularly pleased about this substitution. "Pity I can't persuade Amelia to desert her duties. She must have a difficult boss."

Two difficult bosses, Amelia said to herself.

⁓⁓

The following week, Amelia was again awakened in the middle of the night. This time she heard clanging metal and high-pitched voices in the lot where the Fairmont's terraced, formal gardens had once been laid out. She cracked open the back door and peered outside.

Outlined in the palest of moonlight were two Chinese men—or rather a boy and a man—struggling to lift the heavy lid of the newly restored cistern. The deep cavern was filled with water that would one day be available to douse any fires that might break out on the property. The lid thudded to the ground and the older of the two seized a length of linen hose that most probably had been liberated from the half-completed firehouse on Powell Street a few blocks away.

The taller figure plunged the hose into the well, and in a burst of Cantonese, gave the little boy a litany of instructions. The youngest of the pair wrestled the other end down the sloping hill toward a large metal receptacle in a battered wheelbarrow. Clearly, they were siphoning water out of the cistern, but for what purpose, Amelia hadn't a clue.

She swiftly donned her shirtwaist, skirt, and jacket. Stealthily, she emerged from the basement and crept down the hill without either of her uninvited visitors noticing her approach.

"What are you doing?" she asked sternly.

The little boy was so startled that he dropped the hose, soaking himself in the process. "Oh! Sorry!" cried his companion. "So sorry. Need water. For laundry shop. They no fix water in Chinatown."

Amelia stared at the little boy who hadn't uttered a word and, by this time, was shivering with cold. His saturated, black pajama-like garb matched that of his companion, and both wore odd little red silk pillbox hats and sported solitary pigtails down their backs. Amelia recalled the similar hairstyle worn by the Chinese houseboy who had been burying the old woman's dog on the day of the quake.

"Come," she said. "Let's get you into the work shed. The little one will catch cold. I'll give him a blanket to dry off, and you can tell me why you think I should allow you to steal my water."

Amelia had known several Chinese houseboys employed by her grandfather in the old days. During the mid-century Gold Rush and the building of the east-west railroad, Chinese immigrants had flocked to San Francisco seeking money to send home to their impoverished relatives. Few had found little more than bare subsistence, a fate hardly better than what they'd left behind in Asia. Over the years, San Francisco's Chinatown had expanded into a dozen streets that steadily crept up the steep incline toward the Bay View perched on the summit of Nob Hill. After April 18, all that was left below the hotel was a wasteland sloping toward the equally devastated shanties and saloons of the Barbary Coast.

In Amelia's youth, she was forbidden to go anywhere near Chinatown, an area infamous for gambling parlors, opium dens, and whorehouses. Despite the enclave's unsavory reputation, her personal experiences with the hardworking men from down the hill now prompted her to offer her visitors a cup of tea. She herded them inside the work shed where a low fire still burned on the hob, and set the kettle to boil.

"What are your names? Have you still no drinking water in Chinatown after all this time?" she asked, handing each a mug. They clasped the containers gratefully as if they held ambrosia—though she was certain that Chinese green tea would have been vastly preferred to her English blend.

"I am Loy Chen," announced the elder of the two. "Foo here, is my cousin. Laundry shop burn up. No water. No money. No can live."

Amelia deliberately kept her gaze steady. "And so you were siphoning *our* water. To use at your laundry? I thought everything where you live was burned to the ground."

"No one here at night, so I take water," he shrugged. "I do laundry in hole at old shop in Chinatown." He squinted at her doubtfully. "This *your* water?"

Amelia had to laugh. "No… it belongs to the owners of the hotel we're rebuilding."

"Lady rebuilding hotel?" he asked, plainly skeptical.

"Yes. Two ladies and lots of gentlemen, working very hard, and we need our water."

"Water in ground," Loy said firmly. "Belong to everyone. And more come later, when misters need it, right?"

Amelia suppressed a smile. "You have customers for your laundry?"

"Oh yes, missy! City very dirty. Everybody need clean clothes!"

Amelia thought of her own soiled garments that she transported on the ferry to Oakland so that Aunt Margaret could wash them.

"I suppose you're right," she said with a sigh. "Clean clothes are a necessity."

Loy cocked his head and inquired, "You want me wash clothes? I do that—if you give water. I wash all clothes you need, yes?" He shifted his gaze to the small iron stove and the tin of burnt bread resting on top. "I cook for you too. I be houseboy for you—if you give me water!"

Amelia could only imagine the desperate straits suffered by the thousands of Chinese who had been displaced. After the half-hearted attempt to banish the Asians to the periphery of San Francisco, a shadowy consortium of Chinese and Caucasian businessmen had sprung into action. Based on reports in the *Call*, now publishing out of Oakland, several brothels and opium dens had already reappeared, with City Hall turning a blind eye—and perhaps turning a profit, as well, Amelia thought cynically. She remembered the little man in the ill-fitting suit who had not-so-subtly suggested he could supply workmen approved by city officials. When he was rebuffed at the Fairmont, he'd probably moved on to Chinatown to extort for the mayor and his sidekicks. Amelia had witnessed how hard men like Loy were willing to work—yet were prevented from seeking "white men's jobs"—and felt a great deal of sympathy for him.

"For the time being," she said, "and until the waterworks return to Chinatown, you may take what you need. At night."

"Oh, missy, you very nice lady!" Loy crowed. He beamed triumphantly at little Foo, who, by this time, was so sleepy he was about to topple over onto Julia's daybed, where the senior architect was known to rest after a long day. "We make good dinner for this lady every night, yes, Foo? We make laundry very white!"

"For your own safety," Amelia insisted, realizing suddenly that she had made a decision without consulting Julia, "you must come *only* late at night, after everyone here is asleep, do you understand?"

Amelia noted that Loy had listened carefully to her

admonitions as to when he could come onto the property. "Oh yes, missy. We come when very dark."

She wondered what her strict employer would think of this scheme, not to mention the Law brothers. Even though Julia's health had improved, she tended to prefer returning by ferry to her own bed in Oakland each night while Amelia continued to sleep on a cot in the Fairmont's basement. The mains in Chinatown were due to open soon, so Loy's borrowing water from the Fairmont's cisterns a few times was unlikely to come under scrutiny. At least she hoped so.

"This is only temporary, you understand? Just for a few days."

"We come only when okay. Men who work here no like Chinese."

Amelia sighed and gave a brief nod of agreement. She gazed at Foo who was now dozing while sitting upright. He couldn't be more than six or seven years old. "Let him sleep, Loy. If I hold the hose for you, you can fill your buckets and transport them to—where? Is anything left of your family's laundry?"

"All gone 'cept hole on Clay Street."

"You do laundry in what's left of a basement?" she asked, thinking of J.D. Thayer, who'd had to live for weeks in what was left of his underground lair before the Law brothers offered him temporary shelter in the Fairmont's basement while the Bay View was first under construction. The disaster had certainly been a leveler of society. Many in the city were still living like moles. "What about the other members of your family?"

Loy hesitated and lowered his gaze. "Mostly gone now."

"Back to China?"

"No. Dead. In quake or in fire."

"*All* of them?"

"Most. Seven dead. Trapped in house when fire came."

"I am so sorry."

She was struck by the unbelievable loss so many had endured, yet people like Loy Chen and J.D. Thayer soldiered on, regardless. It made no difference what nationality or color or sex or class a person was. The suffering was the same.

Amelia gently removed the mug from little Foo's hand, seized by the memory of Ling Lee's arm protruding from the rubble on that fateful day. In her mind's eye, she could still see dead horses and cattle lying in the street, wheelbarrows full of injured children, and the terrible vision of her father with the gaming table and lighting fixture heaped on his shattered body.

These unwanted memories came suddenly, unpredictably, and she found herself choked with emotion over the many deaths she had witnessed, including scores as a volunteer nurse at the Presidio.

For several moments she struggled to regain her composure, then rose from her seat and gestured toward the door. "Come, Loy, we'll leave Foo here to sleep while I help you siphon some water from the cistern. Then, you must take this child home."

Home? A burnt-out room among hundreds of burnt-out basements housing the city's unwanted. It was simply *wrong* to treat the Chinese so shamefully.

And then Amelia told herself she had her own problems to attend to.

"Let's work quickly, so we can all get some rest," she said.

❧

J.D. and Amelia stood side-by-side surveying the enormous

pile of debris littering the site of the short-lived Bay View Gentlemen's Gambling Club. Hammers rang out next door as the last floor of the Bay View was about to be enclosed against the elements. J.D. had already moved into a room off the unfinished lobby and was urging Amelia to do the same in order to be on site full time from now until the hotel's completion.

"When we hook up the water, I mean," he amended.

"Well, the old cistern's probably located about... *there*," Amelia said, relieved that the issue of her sleeping quarters was postponed for a while. A mountain of the building's remains would have to be removed before the well would be uncovered.

"What about your grandfather's safe?" J.D. pressed.

Amelia eyed the debris for a moment and then pointed.

"I expect it's about twenty feet to the right, under where the bar used to be."

He heaved a disappointed sigh. "Oh."

Thayer had not allowed her access to the safe to gather her grandfather's papers after she'd lost the court hearing. "What's in the safe, anyhow?" she asked, fighting off a stab of resentment. "The deed to the place?"

She immediately regretted her arched tone and wished she had better control of her emotions when it came to ownership issues of the Bay View.

It's finished... just accept that and be grateful for what you have...

Instinctively, she slipped her right hand into her pocket and slid her fingertips across the smooth surface of three playing cards she kept close as a strange touchstone to the past.

J.D. replied matter-of-factly, "I'd locked all the profits of our first weeks of business in there... gold bars, gold coins, mostly... and important papers—though God knows what the fire's done to the insides of the thing. Getting to that money would help a lot, though."

"Meaning you wouldn't have to gamble or go into further debt with Ezra Kemp?"

He turned and gave her a measured look, as if weighing the advantages and disadvantages of taking her into his confidence. "It's bad enough Kemp's the only source of decent lumber," he said, "but having to pay nearly double for him to advance it to me on credit is worse, and... if I'm not soon able to pay as I go, he could ultimately end up my partner, which is something I'd like very much to avoid." He shook his head with an air of discouragement. "The biggest hurdle to getting this lot cleared is that there're just not enough workers available for this kind of back-breaking labor."

For a few moments, Amelia and J.D. silently scanned the charred, splintered boards and mounds of broken glass and crumbled concrete.

Finally, Amelia proposed quietly, "I can probably get workers to clear this out."

J.D. turned and stared.

"How?"

"A Chinese crew."

"Amelia, don't be absurd!"

"I think I know a man who can supply you as many workers as you need."

"Right, and every white laborer I've managed to bribe to work here will walk off the job."

"Not if we build a high fence around the property and the Chinese work from midnight until an hour before the deliveries arrive."

"So you've given this idea some thought?" he asked, regarding her closely.

"Yes, I have."

A look of skeptical hope filled his eyes. "And you say *you* can supply these men?"

"I believe so. At any rate, I can ask. Are you willing to take the chance?"

A voice inside Amelia's head called out... *and what kind of chances are* you *taking?* What would Julia Morgan say to this dangerous scheme, proposed without her knowledge or consent?

J.D. regarded his architect for a long moment. "I've discovered since you returned from Paris that you're a woman not to be underestimated, Amelia Bradshaw."

She ignored the feeling of pleasure that washed over her.

"It's a very risky proposition, Mr. Thayer." She wondered if she'd gone slightly mad even to suggest such a scheme. "Dangerous, in fact, for you, for me, and certainly for the Chinese workers. Angus would *definitely* think we're completely daft."

"Angus McClure can be a world-class fussbudget."

"And we must inform Miss Morgan, of course."

"No!" he said firmly. "She'd have to advise against it, and I don't want an argument over this."

"You do realize that I jeopardize my own position, don't you? I promised Miss Morgan to keep her informed about everything I do."

"Then why did you offer to supply Chinese workers when you know your employer would most likely disapprove?"

Amelia flashed him a faintly sheepish smile. "Because I would like nothing better than to see this hotel open on the anniversary of the quake—alongside the Fairmont. We need to rebuild the cistern so we can get our plumbing functional as soon as possible. And," she added with some vehemence, "I detest Ezra Kemp."

J.D. paused, his dark eyes revealing nothing. "Well, mostly I'd prefer to beat the Fairmont in this race. But you're right… hiring Chinese to work at night to clear out this mess appears to be about the only way I can see for both the Morgan firm and the Bay View Hotel to get out from under Kemp's thumb and finish this hotel on time."

Amelia remained silent for a moment. Kemp and his ilk were fast acquiring a stranglehold on the recovery of San Francisco. Just as with the cruel discrimination against the Chinese people, their domination of the building trades was increasing by the day. It just wasn't right!

"So you're willing to take this risk?" she asked.

"To get the money out of that safe, I'm willing to risk almost anything. But no one must know, Amelia. Not Kemp. Not Miss Morgan. Not the Committee of Fifty. And certainly not Dick Spitz and his men." He turned, seized her hand, and gave it a conspiratorial squeeze. "I give you my word, we'll succeed in this, and do it right under their noses!"

Well, now, she thought, enjoying the warmth of his touch, *I've just shaken hands with the devil.*

CHAPTER 17

A FEW EVENINGS FOLLOWING Amelia's late-night visitors outside her basement quarters at the Fairmont, she was again awakened by the muffled sound of the cistern being opened and the low, sing-song chatter of voices. Outside, wispy fog half-obscured the figures of Loy Chen, little Foo, and a third person—all gathered around the open well.

Amelia watched from the basement door as Loy inserted the hose into the cistern. Then he seized the other end and trailed the simple siphoning device down the slope to the huge jug positioned in the wheelbarrow that he used for transporting the water to his makeshift laundry establishment.

As the group wrestled with the unwieldy hose, Amelia realized that the newcomer was a young woman in her late teens with black hair cut in a chin-length bob and shiny as a patent leather shoe.

Amelia returned to her room and reached for her boots—now kept in her satchel at night to avoid their becoming nests for homeless rats. She donned the woolen coat acquired from donations at the Presidio's Red Cross shelter when she'd served as a nurse, and hurried outside.

"Here." She smiled at Foo who looked suddenly apprehensive. "Let me give you a hand. Your end of the hose seems to have a mind of its own." The young Chinese woman helping the child to keep the hose in place darted a fearful glance at her co-workers. "Hello, Loy," Amelia called softly. The enveloping fog invited whispers. "How's business?"

"Good!" he replied cheerfully, manning the hose at his end. "Everybody like clean clothes. You up early. How's hotels?"

"Good," she echoed. "Everybody wants them to open on time. The workers are doing their best to see that it happens."

When the enormous jug in the wheelbarrow was filled, the trio at the cistern pulled out the hose and jumped back to avoid getting splashed. Loy smiled. "Thank you, missy. You work hard too."

"And who is this?" She nodded in the direction of the young woman.

"Cousin. Family dead."

Even in the diffused light of near dawn, Amelia could see the girl lower her gaze. The skin on her right cheek was scarred, as was her right hand and, Amelia suspected, the arm shielded by her right sleeve.

"What is your name?" she asked gently. Barely out of childhood, the young woman looked up, wide-eyed, and cast a questioning glance at Loy. "Does she not speak any English?" Amelia said to Loy.

"Tell name," he directed his cohort.

"Shou Shou," the girl replied, barely above a whisper. She pointed at the laundryman. "Loy save me."

"From the fire?" Amelia asked, concerned by the scars disfiguring an otherwise lovely young woman.

Shou Shou nodded emphatically. "Locked in—"

"We go now," Loy interrupted. "Like missy say—need sleep to work." He bowed from the waist and herded his charges down the hill without a backward glance.

"Wait, Loy—"

But Loy kept walking down the slope, calling over his

shoulder, "I bring you dinner. Fish and rice. Seven o'clock. Workers gone then. Thank you, missy."

Amelia ran a few steps and caught his black silk sleeve.

"Please… I have something to ask you!" She lowered her voice a few notches. "Can you supply fifty men to clear rubble at the Bay View Hotel?"

A look of undisguised joy lit Loy's features. "Sure, Missy! When? Tonight?"

"No, not tonight," she replied hastily. "Call on Mr. J.D. Thayer tomorrow and he will discuss arrangements. The men will have to work at night—"

"Oh, Mr. Thayer very nice man! He friend of Ling Lee. She friend to Shou Shou and me. I *like* work for him. No one see us there, promise! Everything be fine, missy. I go tomorrow. See boss at Bay View."

Amelia was startled by the news this young man had known J.D.'s concubine, Ling Lee. Before she could say anything further, Loy Chen whirled on his soft slippers and in a twinkling, the three residents of Chinatown and their wheelbarrow full of water disappeared into the misty morn.

∽

J.D. inserted a finger between his neck and the freshly starched collar attached to his spanking new dress shirt. He noted with pleasure how good it felt to be wearing formal evening clothes again after so many months dressed in virtual rags. His new wardrobe was only the first of many improvements in his life, now that his father's banker friends on the Committee of Fifty had released the first funds of the loan they'd granted him for the reconstruction of the Bay View. The last of the money he'd had in his pockets the day of the earthquake now could be spent on a few luxuries, like some decent clothes.

A shipping carton containing the rest of his order from a New York haberdashery sat on the new brass bedstead, delivered earlier that day and set up in a room with only a raw wood floor and joists. He felt lucky, though. At least he and Barbary were no longer living like gophers in an underground burrow. Of course, the draft would continue to whistle through the plywood walls until the insulation and lathe and plaster were installed on the first floor level. But it was a damned sight better than a tent in the Presidio or a stone cold basement at the Fairmont.

Progress… he thought. *Progress.*

Amelia's brigade of Chinese workers were whittling down the mountain of debris behind the fence they'd built. His daytime crews had gone about their business, and if they'd noticed a change when they worked on the upper floors of the hotel and looked down at the land where the gambling club had stood or the lot next door he'd bought adjacent to his own land, no one said anything to him about it. J.D. had concluded that the chore of breaking up and hauling out the rubble was too lowly a task for Spitz's men and they just ignored it.

Lucky for him, Amelia had noted after climbing the scaffolding to the top floor that the head carpenter, Jake Kelly, had erred in the way his crew had installed the first roof joist. They had been forced to pull it apart and realign it properly. Dick Spitz hadn't been happy that the "lady architect" had caught the mistake, but *he* was.

Thinking of roof joists and climbing scaffolds inevitably drew his thoughts to the subject of Amelia herself—and that was forbidden territory. Even so, he couldn't stop reflecting on how calm and collected she'd been when she informed Spitz of the problem. Dressed in a clean shirtwaist and gored skirt and sturdy boots, she'd been a pretty sight debating with that uncouth lout. She was no classic beauty, to be sure, but with that figure; clear, smooth skin; and her mass of brunette hair piled atop her head, she was a *damned* appealing woman… even when she wore men's trousers beneath her skirt!

J.D. gazed into a shard of mirror that had started life in a gold frame and resolutely turned his thoughts to other subjects. He'd rescued the glass from the rubble and leaned it against one wall in his makeshift bedroom. For a long moment, he surveyed the handsome tweed suit, cambric shirts, starched wing collars, and two pairs of trousers hanging on nails he'd pounded into the wall studs. Knotting his tie, he began to consider various schemes to lure more capital to complete the rebuilding. To do that, a man couldn't look like some refugee, could he? Now, if the Chinese workers could hurry up and gain access to either the cistern or the walk-in safe still buried deep under the wreckage at the back of his property—or both—J.D. would consider himself a happy man.

Except for Ling Lee and Mother…

Funny how he'd begun to see the unfair treatment of these two women at the hands of men in their lives in a rather similar light.

Firmly putting all such errant thoughts aside, J.D. slammed his new hat onto his head and donned the stylish overcoat that would protect him from the evening chill. With a pat on Barbary's head and an order to "stay!" he headed outdoors for the Winton parked on Taylor Street, wishing that he didn't need to ask Kemp for yet another favor.

❧

J.D. parked the Winton near the wharves and strode up the gangway a few minutes before the Sausalito ferry pushed away from the dock. Soon the boat was heading north, cutting through the choppy water as it passed Alcatraz Island, a garrison where Confederate sympathizers and renegade U.S. soldiers had been held nearly half a century earlier. In 1901, the fortress's cannons had been dismantled and J.D. wondered what the desolate twelve acres in the middle of the bay was good for now.

Before long, the *Cazadero* nudged against the dock and J.D. disembarked for Sausalito's two-story terminal that let onto the commuter train platforms where standard-gauge electric cars would whisk him to Mill Valley in less than ten minutes. The quality transportation signaled that the territory across the Golden Gate straits was coming into its own as the locus of second homes for wealthy San Franciscans. Many city residents, in fact, had camped out in them since the quake. Marin County also served as a place where lumber-yards, shipbuilding, and dairy and vegetable farms thrived in support of the larger cities trying to rebuild across the bay.

J.D. climbed into the gold-lettered carriage and watched the verdant landscape slip past his window as the four-car train gathered speed along a stretch of seashore known as Richardson Bay.

No wonder Ezra Kemp liked Marin so much, J.D. thought with a glance at the giant redwood trees whizzing by. Kemp must feel right at home among his fellow ne'er-do-wells, grabbing up land for a song from distressed owners hit by the financial panic of the previous decade, then cutting down entire forests to sell uncured wood. These same envi-rons also attracted smugglers, rumrunners, off-track bookies, and a variety of other shady characters relying on the remote geography to provide cover for their questionable schemes.

I wonder where that puts me? J.D. mused, staring through the window at a half-mowed stand of redwoods marching up Mt. Tamalpais, its peak looming above Mill Valley. The mountain offered evidence of the clear-cutting that was providing San Francisco with the lumber necessary for the reconstruction. Amazingly, other than a few collapsed chimneys, hilly little Sausalito and the surrounding countryside showed few signs of damage from the quake, even though the area was located mere miles from the spot on the Mendocino Coast, where the newspapers reported the temblor had originated.

A few minutes later, the train pulled into the Mill Valley depot where, coat in hand, J.D. stepped onto the platform.

"Mr. Thayer, sir?"

"Yes, I'm Thayer."

"I'm to take you to Mr. Kemp's house."

Kemp had apparently sent his livery to transport him via the muddy streets of the little town that took its name from the first mill that straddled Fern Creek back in 1834.

The driver flicked the reins and guided the carriage out of the town center and into a glade encircled by a magnificent forest of mighty redwoods with branches so lofty they blocked any glimpse of the night sky. The conveyance passed a sign proclaiming that they were traveling on a bumpy road called Throckmorton Avenue.

Less than a quarter mile along an adjacent road that paralleled a rushing creek, he caught sight of winking lights tucked among the trunks of the thick-barked trees. Kemp's mansion built of river rock and redwood timbers was a fantasy construction that looked for all the world like a hunting lodge for Hapsburg royalty nestled deep in a parkland.

Terraced grounds rose in steps from the gurgling brook, etched by parterre hedges and dotted with camellia trees taller than J.D. himself. Stone turrets, capped with thick shingles coated with bright green moss, guarded the four corners of the massive house. A rolled roofline and ivy-covered walls added to the sense that even on a sun-filled day, the Kemp residence would be shrouded in darkness and mystery.

J.D. dismounted from the carriage, nodded to his silent driver, and watched the vehicle disappear around the side of the stone house into deep shadows. He inhaled air pungent with the rising damp and strode along the spongy ground until he reached a stone path, laden with the same tufts of furry moss that clung to the roof. The walkway led to a heavy oak door adorned with a wrought-iron knocker fashioned in the twisted countenance of a troll.

Despite the showy extravagance of his abode, Ezra Kemp largely kept silent about his family's origins. J.D. had made it his business, though, to learn that his former gambling partner was the son of one Klaus Kemp, a German immigrant who found work as a blacksmith repairing pickaxes in the mines of the Mother Lode. The bearded giant who was Ezra's sire had sought sexual satisfaction in the arms of a prostitute named Ellie Jenks—a slender young woman who had died giving birth to their ten-pound son. Ezra's large size and barrel chest bore the stamp of his hard-drinking father, long deceased. His lack of social niceties reflected the world of the mother he'd never known—and the stigma that her profession carried from beyond the grave.

Given such inauspicious beginnings, Kemp's innate intelligence nevertheless had taught him to seize opportunity when it knocked. He'd parlayed that and a certain mechanical ability into a highly successful lumber empire with saw mills scattered along Fern Creek and the Russian River in the heavily forested lands in regions of Marin and Sonoma counties to the north.

That spring's calamitous quake and fire had proven to be the most fortuitous event in Ezra Kemp's life. An entire city begged for the products he supplied: stately redwoods felled and hewn into usable lengths of lumber, along with the means to transport these goods to a city desperate for wood. After years of being shunned by the nobs of Nob Hill, he was suddenly asked to serve on the Committee of Fifty for the Reconstruction of San Francisco and had set his sights on making further inroads into the society that, ironically enough, J.D. Thayer had persistently spurned.

Thus, for J.D., the evening ahead provided an opportunity to demand better service and products from Kemp Lumber Company so that he might satisfy his ambition to be the first major hotel owner in San Francisco to open his doors before the first anniversary of the disaster of April 18. Once back in business, he could then pay his previous debts to Kemp for the destroyed gambling club and be free of the man he'd grown to heartily dislike.

"Ah... Thayer, welcome." Ezra himself had appeared at the front door to greet him while a manservant took his coat and hat. His host ushered him into a paneled study. "My daughter, Matilda, will join us for dinner, along with a school friend of hers visiting from back East. Emma Stivers is her name. The chit's a bit long in the tooth, if you ask me," he added sourly, "but they seem happy enough making pottery or whatever on God's earth they do in that studio of Matilda's at the bottom of the garden."

At twenty-seven, Matilda Kemp was—to be blunt—a bit long in the tooth herself, thought J.D., recalling the first and only time he'd laid eyes on the woman on the evening he'd come to this house to sign the purchase agreement for lumber to build the gambling club.

But then again, times were changing and many women no longer married by age eighteen. Unbidden, the image of Amelia floated through his mind. She seemed proud to admit she was thirty years old and focused on life as an architect—not as a wife and mother. Ling Lee had been another woman who had eschewed marriage and shown she was as capable as any businessman. Perhaps it was, indeed, a new age for women, he mused, accepting Kemp's offer of a drink.

"Cheers, Ezra." J.D. raised the glass of whiskey his host had poured from a crystal decanter. "I'm looking forward to a civilized meal with people who don't have to dust off their boots every time they take a step." He sank into a leather chair and offered another salute. "Let us drink to the opening of the Bay View before April eighteenth."

Kemp also raised his glass. "And may you beat that wretched Morgan woman and the Fairmont to the finish line."

"She bought her lumber elsewhere you say?" J.D. asked, biting back a smile.

"Yes, she did, the witch," Kemp replied with no sign of humor. "You know, I've often thought it might not be so difficult to arrange some unforeseen problem on the Fairmont site, if you catch my drift. What if, by chance, an entire section of her scaffolding mysteriously weakened and—"

"No need for anything that drastic," J.D. intervened, affecting a shrug. "We're proceeding nicely at the Bay View and should have no trouble opening our doors first."

He was beginning to see that Kemp was more than just an opportunistic, larcenous hardhead. Ezra's minions reported everything to him from key building sites around the city, intelligence he had then been known to pass on to the enforcers at City Hall. Kemp's bullyboys were perfectly capable of making a mishap on the scaffolding of a competitor appear an accident. As it was, it was dangerous for Amelia and Miss Morgan to be scampering around six stories in the air without Kemp's murderous musings.

Stay clear of this, J.D. Keep your focus where it belongs.

He swiftly assumed the air of a coconspirator in the push to open the Bay View before the Fairmont. "In fact, Ezra, you'll be pleased to hear that we're progressing at Taylor and Jackson with due speed—assuming I can encourage you to urge your people to deliver sound lumber in the correct length."

Kemp's genial manner toward his visitor underwent a swift change.

"My best wood goes to customers who pay their bills. Make good on the note due me for the *last* lumber you bought to build the original gambling club, J.D., and you will marvel at the efficiency of my employees."

J.D. carefully set his glass down on a small table to the right of his chair.

"You've known from the beginning that I can't give you the final payment on the old note until I open the doors to the new hotel," he replied matter-of-factly. "I can only use my insurance and loan monies on current construction. But rest assured, Ezra, you are the first creditor on my list. Thanks to funds from the Committee, you've certainly been paid handsomely for the lumber you are currently supplying me, so I think it's only fair, therefore, that you give my orders high priority for quality and an honest count. The sooner I complete the hotel and open it to paying customers, the sooner you'll be paid back on your original investment in the old club."

Kemp cast him a noncommittal look. Then, eyes narrowing,

he said, "You know, J.D., I'd be willing to forgo immediate payment of what you owe me from before the quake— which is my right to demand, by the way—if we could... uh... reach a certain understanding about something." He lowered his gaze to the rim of his whiskey glass as if deep in thought.

"And what understanding might that be?" J.D. asked warily. He could just imagine Kemp demanding a partnership deal in exchange for forgiveness on the money owed.

Kemp looked up from his drink. "That you begin to court my daughter."

"*What?*"

J.D. couldn't disguise his astonishment. He instantly regretted revealing his obvious dismay, but a man only had to behold Matilda Kemp in all her gangling awkwardness to understand his reaction.

"You heard me," snapped Kemp. "I have a daughter of marriageable age with no prospects in sight. You and she are near contemporaries, and despite your unhappy status with your family, I think an alliance of my wealth and your name could do wonders for us both."

"I have no intention ever to marry," J.D. declared bluntly. There was no point mincing words about such a preposterous proposal.

Not ever?

He immediately realized he'd taken a radical stance, considering the majority of women he'd known well had either been prostitutes or ninnies like Matilda Kemp. Even so, his experience in his own family showed all too clearly that a state of matrimony could create plenty of misery for everyone concerned.

Kemp, however, was doggedly sticking to the subject at

hand. "All the more reason such an alliance with Matilda would be of no personal consequence to you whatsoever. You'll live your life and she'll live hers."

J.D. was more amused than vexed at Kemp's outrageous proposal. "Have you discussed this idea with the lady in question?"

"I have hinted at your interest in getting to know her better," Kemp replied, straight-faced.

"I've met Matilda exactly once, Ezra, and exchanged a few inane pleasantries. How could you possibly convince her of my interest, for God's sake?"

"That is *your* task. Either that, or I will be forced to demand that you pay me the note for the gambling club in full. Immediately."

"You know all my funds are committed to rebuilding."

"A pity," Kemp replied. "Well, then, I expect I'll have to put a lien on the new hotel and have a word with the Committee of Fifty that you're in debt to me and it's my recommendation that the bankers not risk another loan since you're so deeply in arrears."

"So is half of San Francisco," scoffed J.D.

"Perhaps they'll see the wisdom of turning over the project to me, since I can guarantee its completion. After all, it's my wood, my foreman and carpenters you got through my good offices."

J.D. felt like reaching across the narrow space that separated their two chairs and slapping the smug look off his host's face. In Kemp's usual, grasping fashion, he'd done his best to wrest the Bay View away from him from the first, and by this time, J.D. was thoroughly fed up.

"Why are you suddenly so eager to marry off a daughter whose welfare you've ignored since her babyhood?"

"You know nothing of these matters."

"I know that the moment her mother died of pneumonia, you shipped Matilda east to boarding school and even after she returned, you have barely allowed her out of this house."

Kemp appeared nonplussed at the accuracy of J.D.'s observation. "What business is this of yours?"

"I make it my business to know with whom I'm dealing."

"She's twenty-seven years old. She should be married."

"She was twenty-six last year and you never showed a scintilla of concern."

"Let's just say marrying her off to you would benefit me in several ways, not the least of which is that I would be protecting my investment in the Bay View."

"You'll get your money. I'm a man of my word and I pay my debts."

"Perhaps I would prefer to own the hotel myself, rather than just the lumber *in* it."

J.D. regarded his host for a long moment. "Ah. I see. You couldn't win the Bay View gambling at cards, so now you're resorting to extortion. You've been hanging round Schmitz and Reuf too long, I fear."

"You were just damned lucky the night of the quake, and you know it. If you don't wish to revisit that event, J.D., or want problems on your building site, I suggest you lavish some attention on my daughter at dinner this evening."

J.D. couldn't believe that he'd been at Ezra Kemp's house for less than a half hour and could barely keep his temper under control. The man was infuriating. And dangerous.

J.D. set his drink down with a thud. "So... the charming host reverts to his bullyboy tactics from days of yore. Don't you realize, Kemp, that you can never worm your way into Nob Hill society—such as it is—behaving like a boor? You must at least make a show of civility, though God knows there are plenty of other thugs in evening clothes masquerading as pillars of society in this town. The only difference, my dear Ezra, is that they are better than you at covering their tracks—and their parentage."

A murderous look invaded Kemp's features. "Thayer, I'm warning you—"

"I like your daughter," J.D. interrupted, noting with satisfaction that he'd succeeded in goring Kemp's ox. After all, Big Jim Thayer taught him well in the art of deflating an opponent. He swiftly considered the various moves he could make in this treacherous game. He *had* to have a continuing supply of decent wood, since the hotel was covered in shingles and Kemp had bankrupted most of his fellow lumbermen. Even worse, J.D. needed Kemp's foreman, Dick Spitz, and his head carpenter, Jake Kelly—no matter how incompetent they were—to keep the unions from causing trouble and to continue their working full-bore on the Bay View to open on time.

And most importantly, he couldn't afford Kemp denigrating him to the Committee of Fifty at this crucial moment. Thanks to James Thayer Sr., his own standing with that body was not very high while he waited for the second payment of the loan that the bankers *said* they were willing to grant, but had not yet made good. A lien on the property right now by Kemp could prove disastrous. If only he could get into his damnable safe!

"You 'like' my daughter, you say," Kemp repeated, interrupting J.D.'s reverie. "Are you saying you'll agree to court Matilda publicly?"

J.D. decided in that instant that agreeing to this preposterous proposal might be the only way to buy time.

"I'm saying that I'll... consider it."

Oddly, his next thought was of Amelia after she offered to hire a crew of Chinese workers to clear the rubble littering the back of his property. What would the starchy Miss Bradshaw think of this "arrangement"?

It would disgust her... she would think you the cad that you are, on occasion...

"You'll have to do more than merely consider my proposal," Kemp snapped. "I want you to come here for dinner every Saturday. I'll be happy to serve as your chaperone."

"And if Matilda would prefer not to associate with a black sheep and known gambler?"

"She'll do what I tell her, or she can fend for herself."

"Mmmm... such fatherly affection."

"So you'll do it?"

J.D. retrieved his whiskey glass and took a sip, buying a moment's time to think.

"Understand this, Kemp. I'm not making any promise to marry Matilda. What I *am* willing to do is to better make her acquaintance and see if that might lead to something... acceptable."

Good grief! How did he find himself in such a ludicrous fix?

"So you'll agree to *begin* courting the chit?"

"If—and only if—you send me your best wood starting *tomorrow*. Agreed?"

"And *I'm* the mercenary, calculating one?"

"Do I get your best wood?"

Kemp regarded J.D. for a long moment and then said, "Agreed."

Even the lumber tycoon apparently understood there were limits to forcing reluctant parties to the altar.

"And Ezra," J.D. added, taking a last draw from his glass,

"if I receive one shoddy length of redwood, or if Dick Spitz or that so-called head carpenter you sent me make one tricky move at the work site, I have a few threats of my own I can make good on regarding a man's credentials for gaining admittance in to the world of Nob Hill. Understood?"

Kemp held J.D.'s gaze and then nodded. It was as if both men knew that they had pushed each other far enough and would have to wait to see who held the best cards in the next round of play.

Just then, a soft knock reverberated against the study door.

"Dinner is served, sir," ventured a manservant. "The ladies are waiting in the parlor."

"All right, Edward," Kemp snapped. "Just make sure, for once, the food is hot."

J.D. rose from his chair and turned to his host. "Is that capon I smell? First I've had in seven months."

Without replying, Kemp strode through the door, crossed the central hall of the grand house, and entered the parlor, leaving J.D. to make his own way into the drawing room where he imagined the gawky Miss Matilda and her visiting school chum awaited their arrival.

CHAPTER 18

"GOOD EVENING, FATHER," SAID a timorous female voice from inside the room.

"Mr. Thayer is apparently quite fond of capon, Matilda," Kemp said in a tone of forced joviality as J.D. followed in his wake, pausing at the door to the parlor. "What a fortunate choice you recommended to Cook, my dear."

Matilda Kemp stood in front of the fireplace's carved mantel in a room heavy with curved-backed velvet uphol-stered furniture, ornate gas table lamps, and bric-a-brac clut-tering every available surface. Apprehension emanated from her every pore.

She was inordinately tall, her height less than an inch shy of J.D.'s own six feet, and with bones as massive as a steve-dore's. An amateur sculptress, her paws were so huge she looked capable of throwing a clay pot large enough to encase the roots of a palm tree. Her face was long and broad, as was her nose. Her skin—by far her best feature—was clear, but she was unfortunately plagued with ears that flared at right angles to her head. Not even her elaborate hairstyle could disguise their fan-like shells.

"Good evening, Miss Kemp." J.D. made a stab at appearing the genial guest with the vision of unblemished lengths of redwood as his inspiration. "How nice to see you again."

To Matilda's right stood a woman as petite as her school

chum was gargantuan, and as pretty as her hostess was homely, with warm, hazel eyes; even features; trim figure; and auburn hair framed by the red-flocked wallpaper behind her.

"May I present Emma Stivers," Matilda ventured meekly. "We were friends back east in school and—" Matilda hesitated, incapable of finishing her sentence in a room filled with the heavy presence of her father, who divided his look of disapproval between his daughter and her friend.

Emma Stivers extended her hand and met J.D.'s gaze. "How do you do, Mr. Thayer?" she said in a calm, steady voice. "And how are the rebuilding efforts in San Francisco coming along? Matilda and I are absolutely starved for the latest gossip."

Surprised by the young woman's display of easy confidence, J.D. replied, "Very well, thank you. And welcome to California."

"Thank you," she smiled, dimples flashing. "I understand from Matilda that you are employing Mr. Kemp's lumber to build an exact replica of your hotel damaged in the quake. I must say, I feel fortunate to have been on the train somewhere in Nebraska, I believe, when that tumultuous event occurred."

"You *were* most fortunate, wasn't she?" J.D. smiled for the benefit of the poor, tongue-tied giantess standing beside him.

Emma linked her arm with her friend's. "Matilda has quite kindly asked me to stay on, despite the chaos that has reigned everywhere since the upheaval. She's made her home practically my own."

"Yes, yes, well come along," Ezra grumbled, clearly bored with Emma's niceties and his daughter's lack of social graces. "Soup's getting cold."

Their host barged ahead, leaving J.D. to escort a woman on each arm into the gloomy dining room, devoid of ornamentation save for a stuffed owl and a stag's head attached to dark paneled walls.

J.D. suppressed a sigh as he settled in for what no doubt would be a tedious seven-course meal. He had come to Mill Valley in hopes he would solved his building supply problems. Now he had an even bigger snarl to untangle—his supposed courting of Matilda Kemp. He'd bought some time, all right, but he wondered how much.

And at what cost?

And then the thought crossed his mind, for a second time: what would his architect think of this development?

❧

Amelia jumped down from the cable car as it glided to a stop at Mason and California streets, zigzagged over to Taylor Street, and briskly walked the four blocks to the Bay View. She hurried into an area in the unfinished lobby where J.D. had set up as his temporary office.

He looked up from the pile of papers spread out on a wide board held by two sawhorses that he used as a desk. Barbary also raised his head, recognized her, and settled back into his morning snooze.

"How did you find things at the dock?" J.D. asked.

"Bad news, I'm afraid, Mr. Thayer," she announced. "Your furniture shipments were not on board the *Enterprise* when she docked today. The harbor master thinks they're on the sister ship *Endeavor*, which arrives next week."

"Perhaps it's just as well," J.D. looked grim. "Your crew did not get to the safe last night as I expected. So until I can locate my gold bars, or receive the next loan payment from the Committee of Fifty, I'm stone broke."

Amelia stared at him, aghast.

"But then how will we pay the day workers this Friday, and—"

Their conversation was abruptly interrupted by Ezra Kemp marching across the lobby, his heavy footfalls echoing on the raw floorboards.

"Thayer!" He ignored Amelia completely. "You and I need to have a little conference. *Now!*" He looked briefly at Amelia. "Alone."

Barbary gave a low growl and followed Amelia, who headed down the hall off the lobby, addressing J.D. over her shoulder. "I'll be in the back room, recalculating some load factors on the bedroom chimneys so your workers might *possibly* understand how to do their jobs correctly this time." She left the door ajar so she could hear what had put such a bee in Kemp's bonnet.

Kemp sat down and glowered at J.D. across his makeshift desk. "City Hall is unhappy that you're employing Chinks," he said without preamble.

"And that affects me how?" replied J.D. calmly. For the last month, the newspapers had been full of stories about the nefarious "fixers" at City Hall.

"Thayer, I'm warning you—"

"The Chinese do the work that Caucasians won't."

"Dick Spitz and his men know what you're up to and they don't like it."

"Last I knew, Spitz and Jake Kelly work for *me*. If your men are willing to load chunks of concrete and wood into wheelbarrows and transfer the rubble onto wagons for disposal along the bay's shore for ten cents an hour, they should just speak up and offer their services. I'll be glad to hire them instead of the Chinese."

"There'll be trouble, J.D. The Chinese Exclusion Act—"

"My new hires are already in the country. And besides, why should you care? I hear Reuf and Mayor Schmitz will be indicted on fraud and corruption this week."

"It'll never stick, and your hiring the slant eyes could cause problems with the union hiring halls," Kemp countered, "and *that* will make waves with Reuf's people—which is trouble I don't need. I'm through waiting for you to cough up the money you owe for the shingles you've bought *this* time around. I don't want any more delays in payment."

"Sounds like you're pressed for funds," J.D. observed, wondering how Kemp would describe the mahogany complexion of his mother, Consuela Diaz-Reims Thayer. "Too many nights gambling on the Barbary Coast? Or perhaps you've overextended yourself investing with your cronies downtown in some of Chinatown's new whorehouses? I hear Donaldina Cameron is on the warpath again. Word is she's rebuilding the Mission Home on Sacramento Street and has the ear of some important folks on Nob Hill."

"Who?" Kemp demanded.

"Rudolph Spreckels comes to mind, and that Burns fellow who's on loan from the U.S. Treasury Department to look into corruption out here, plus the same crowd that's bringing down Reuf and Mayor Schmitz." J.D. smiled faintly. "Not that I involve myself in politics, but I would judge that it's not a good time to make a public fuss concerning these matters, Ezra, if you hope to maintain your status with the Committee of Fifty."

"I'm just protecting my investment in the Bay View, I'm going to have to ask you to pay what you still owe me right now, in full."

Kemp was playing his best hand, J.D. thought. He figured he'd win either by getting a chunk of money to pay off some pressing debts, or, failing that, he'd accuse J.D. of using illegal immigrants, obtain a lien on the hotel, and shore up his lowly status with the powerful construction bosses who would, in turn, steer business his way. The only thing holding Kemp back was his desire to boost his image with the nobs by marrying off his ugly duckling to a scion of one of San Francisco's supposed "First Families."

It was all such nonsense.

J.D. envisioned the pile of debris at the rear of his property that had been shrinking each night. In a few days' time, it should be gone and the upright safe and its contents of gold bars and coins would be his again.

"I shall bring you a bank draft for the complete amount outstanding before the next meeting of the Committee of Fifty," he offered pleasantly.

Kemp regarded him narrowly. "And what if I say that's not good enough?"

"And what if I say you'd better not push your luck as far as your membership in that august gathering?"

"You're bluffing, Thayer. Your father wouldn't raise a finger to help you."

"No? Would you care to test that theory?" He gestured toward a pile of paper on his desk. "Haven't you heard about blue blood versus plain old water? And now, you can see by these invoices I have a lot of things to attend to. See you at the next meeting."

❦

Amelia waited a decent interval before she approached J.D. to talk about the information she couldn't help but overhear.

"Loy's men may not be able to get to the safe in time to satisfy Kemp," she said, approaching J.D.'s desk and taking a seat. "They're working as fast as they can, but you've seen what it looks like down there. What do we do if you can't pay Kemp the money and he tries to ruin you?"

J.D. rolled his eyes. "I knew you were lurking back there, listening to every word."

"Well I'm *worried*, Mr. Thayer. I think the man is angling to gain total control of the Bay View and oust you by one nefarious means or another."

"He can't do that, because by Thursday, I'll expect Loy's men to have recovered my safe."

"I can't promise that," Amelia insisted. "Ezra Kemp's a dangerous, unscrupulous man, a man who left you and my father for dead the day of the quake."

"I'm touched that you don't regret I survived," he said with a faint smile.

Ignoring his levity, Amelia continued with increasing frustration. "Why don't you realize that he'll stop at nothing to get what he wants—even if we do, by some miracle, manage to excavate down to the safe? How do we even know that the valuables you say are in there aren't burnt to a crisp or melted beyond reclamation?"

Thayer continued to make notations on the papers on his desk, refusing to look up to meet her concerned gaze. "I've got everything quite under control, Miss Bradshaw," he replied, no longer in the mood to joke. "And I'd appreciate it if you kept your very pretty nose out of my business."

❦

It was dark by the time Amelia returned to her sleeping quarters at the Fairmont that night. Brooding about Kemp's unexpected appearance at the Bay View and J.D.'s dismissive attitude toward her very legitimate concerns, she locked the massive front door, made her way across the lobby and down the back stairs to the kitchen to have her evening meal.

She had just turned the corner after walking down a long, freshly painted corridor when she pulled up short. There, outlined by the open door to the pantry, Loy Chen was locked in an embrace with someone whose identity Amelia couldn't immediately determine, given that both figures were clad in black pajamas like those worn by everyone in Chinatown. At her sharp intake of breath, the pair sprang apart.

"Shou Shou!" Amelia gasped. "Loy! What in the world is going on, here?"

Shou Shou gave a mortified cry and buried her head in Loy's shoulder. The laundryman put his arm around her and looked defiantly at his benefactress.

"She not cousin to me."

"No? Well, that's a blessing, but you lied to me," she said sternly.

"I save her."

"I know that, Loy. From the fire."

"No. Well, yes, I do that. But I save her from bad Chinese too."

Still recovering from her shock, Amelia advanced toward the pair. "Is she one of those women kidnapped from China and brought here?"

Loy nodded emphatically. "She good family in China, but made bad lady here. Bad Chinese lock her up in house with iron bars. I *love* her."

Amelia's glance shifted from Loy's earnest face to Shou Shou's scarred one, now bathed in tears. "But, Loy, you told me you were engaged to a girl in your homeland."

"My uncle do that. I love Shou Shou. She from my village. I love her. I save her in fire. Many die in that house. Many die in other houses. Chinese not counted. Papers say five hundred die in quake and fire. Maybe five *thousand* Chinese die—and no one important count *us*!"

It was Loy's longest speech in Amelia's memory and his voice broke in the first show of emotion she'd ever seen him display.

"And so, since the earthquake, you've been hiding Shou Shou from the highbinders, am I right?" she asked softly. There were fifty Chinese men brought over to help build the railroads to every Chinese woman, and the kidnappers had long been guaranteed a profit when they abducted pretty young girls like Shou Shou and forced them to be sexual slaves—for a profit to their captors.

"Foo's mother die too. He Shou Shou's friend's little boy."

"Do the bad Chinese know Shou Shou's with you?"

"I kill them if they come!" Loy stated defiantly.

Amelia suddenly imagined that Loy Chen could be descended from a tribe of Asian warriors.

"They will come, Loy. The brothels are already beginning to open again and the highbinders are up to their old, bad ways. This is very dangerous for you. For both of you."

Loy tightened his arm around Shou Shou. "I know, missy. That's why I hide Shou Shou in basement, here."

"She's been sleeping at the *Fairmont*? Where?"

"Behind big, new furnace. Nice and warm for Shou Shou."

Amelia could only imagine what Julia would say if she discovered that her deputy had been providing safe haven for Chinese runaways fleeing from their unscrupulous owners. And what if the Law brothers found out that Chinese slaves were hiding here?

Amelia knew from the first she should have told her employer about her private "charity work," but feared

Julia might not feel the same burning sense of injustice that she did if it compromised the older architect's allegiance to her clients.

Julia's credo echoed in her head. *Above all things, Amelia, the client is king.*

"How long has Shou Shou been sleeping here?" she demanded, filled with a growing dread for the consequences that could result from her own rash behavior.

"When we meet you that night, I show her furnace room. Shou Shou very quiet girl," he said proudly. "I keep Foo with me at laundry. Pretend he my cousin too."

Good heavens, she thought. Shou Shou and Julia Morgan had slept under the same roof!

"Well, this won't do, Loy. My first duty is to Miss Morgan and the Law brothers. I'm not like Miss Donaldina Cameron. I can't simply—"

"You know Lo Mo?"

"Who?"

"Lo Mo," he said impatiently. "Missy Cameron. 'Little Mother.' She save Chinese girls like Shou Shou from bad owners. You *know* her?"

"I've met her," Amelia answered, equally impatiently, "but, Loy, you—"

"I look everywhere for her. She can help, but she not in Chinatown anymore."

"How can she help?"

"She get lawyer to help. She get minister to marry us. I be Christian now," he announced. "I help Missy Cameron find sad Chinese girls like Shou Shou. She come and save them. Climb down roof, sometimes, to get girls out. Make them Christian, like me."

"You helped her do that?" Amelia was dumbfounded.

"You helped her rescue girls who didn't want to be prostitutes anymore?"

"Some like Shou Shou *never* want that. Bad Chinese and white men make them do bad things. Lock them in rooms with bars," he added, pointing to Shou Shou's scars.

"And my lawyer helps Miss Cameron," Amelia murmured, remembering the kindness of John Damler. Miss Morgan knew Miss Cameron, and Miss Cameron knew lawyer Damler. *The Ladies All-Knowing Society,* she thought ruefully. And no one ever said a thing.

Amelia was fairly sure now that Julia would be sympathetic to Shou Shou and Foo's plight, though she doubted her employer would endorse the Fairmont Hotel becoming a stop on this newfangled Underground Railroad.

"I know where Miss Cameron is," Amelia said thoughtfully.

"Lo Mo? You *do*? Where?" Loy said excitedly. "I know she help us."

"She's moved everyone from San Anselmo over to East Oakland until the Mission Home is rebuilt. My friend, Dr. McClure, mentioned it a while back. There's a new Chinatown over there. Some of the Chinese will probably never come back to San Francisco."

"You take us?" Loy asked. "She get minister to marry us and then lawyer can help Shou Shou. Lo Mo not like girls living on own. And, good judges *like* Chinese girls to marry merchant like me. Brothel men leave her alone after marriage, see?"

"What about your fiancée in China?" Amelia reminded him of the girl who'd been plighted to him years before, when they both were youngsters.

"My family in America dead. Uncle far away. Shanghai. I not meet Uncle's friend's daughter—*ever*. I love Shou

Shou," he repeated defiantly, as if Amelia would take his uncle's part.

Even arranged Chinese marriages were in jeopardy in this new century, she thought, and couldn't help but approve. She turned to regard the slender young woman by Loy's side. If Shou Shou's owner caught her now, her scarred cheek and hands would condemn her to mortal drudgery in the bowels of some brothel. Loy loved her enough to risk his own life to save her not only from the fire, but also from a life of degradation.

"It will be my pleasure to take you to see Miss Cameron," she declared quietly. "I will call her by telephone. I can take you to her when I return to see my aunt in Oakland next week. In the meantime, you must be *very* careful, Loy, to keep her hidden from everyone. Even from the people who work here. You were very careless tonight. I could have been someone else coming upon you two like this."

"I know, missy. Nobody here like Chinese."

"That's not true, Loy. *I* do."

CHAPTER 19

Loy Chen and his bride were married the following week in a simple ceremony at 477 Eleventh Street in East Oakland at a home donated by one of Donaldina Cameron's Presbyterian supporters. Dr. Henry Sanborne, the pastor of the local church, performed the nuptials witnessed by Donaldina Cameron, John Damler, Angus McClure, Aunt Margaret, and Amelia, who was asked to serve as Shou Shou's only attendant. Lawyer Damler promised to file a petition in the San Francisco courts stating that Shou Shou had been kidnapped from China and was now married to a legal immigrant, laundry merchant Loy Chen. As required by law, Dr. McClure attested the couple was in good health.

Much to Amelia's astonishment, J.D. Thayer walked into the Oakland residence just as the ceremony concluded.

"Don't looked so surprised," he whispered. "After all, I employ the man."

He turned to greet Donaldina like a long lost friend, which only deepened the mystery.

Amelia judged the marriage celebration itself to be a touching mixture of tradition and "make-do." One of the women in Miss Cameron's charge had loaned the bride a magnificently embroidered Chinese silk wedding ensemble and little Foo stood beaming by Loy's side, holding the ring.

Afterward, a modest reception was cobbled together with donations of dried fruit, fruit punch, and delicate cookies that the younger children in Miss Cameron's care had helped to bake. Even Aunt Margaret contributed a splendid chocolate cake made from the first cocoa she could find since the quake.

"It looks just beautiful," Amelia murmured to her aunt as Donaldina set the cake on the large dining room table. "It was so nice of you to do this when you don't even know the couple."

"A wedding gives one hope, doesn't it?"

Margaret had shed at least twenty pounds since her brother's death and the food scarcity that immediately followed the quake. Amelia actually thought she looked healthier than she had in years. Her aunt's eyes were sparkling as she glanced at Angus and J.D. engaged in lively conversation with lawyer Damler. "What charming gentlemen you've come to know, Amelia," she added with a knowing smile.

Amelia frowned. There was no point in allowing her aunt to fantasize about anything. "I work for the gentleman on the left, and the other two are just friends."

"That's not what Dr. McClure leads me to think," she retorted with a smug little smile. "He told me just today that he wishes you'd get down off those scaffolds and enjoy life as a normal young woman should."

Ignoring her aunt's remark, Amelia moved into the large home's parlor to watch while Donaldina herded her charges into two lines. Soon the room was filled with the reverberation of Chinese songs that sounded high-pitched and exotic to her ear. Afterward, each child approached the impromptu visitor's reception line and was introduced by "Lo Mo" to the guests, as well as the bride and groom.

A dozen or so children had passed through when Miss Cameron said to Amelia, "May I present Wing Lee?" The Presbyterian missionary bent down to urge the tiny girl to make a proper bow, which she did, beaming broadly.

Amelia sensed that the attention of both J.D. and Angus was immediately drawn to the adorable creature whose shining black hair moved like a curtain when she inclined her head. Of mixed Chinese and Caucasian parentage, the child's brown eyes were more round than almond shaped, and her skin pale ivory rather than golden brown. Her little chin had a deep dimple that winked when she smiled at her elders.

"Does she understand English?" Amelia asked Miss Cameron.

"Quite well," Donaldina answered proudly.

J.D. knelt and placed his hands on the child's delicate shoulders.

"Wing Lee, I knew your mother," he told her gently. "She was a fine woman."

Startled, Amelia whispered to her hostess, "This is Ling Lee's child?"

"Why yes." Donaldina was clearly surprised by Amelia's knowledge of this private matter. "Yes, she is."

Wing Lee's dark eyes gazed solemnly at J.D. "My mother live with angels now."

J.D. rose while Angus placed his palm on the little girl's head. "Aye, lassie," he said gruffly, with a swift look at J.D., "Let's hope so."

J.D. reached into his jacket pocket and withdrew several silver pieces, handing them to Donaldina. "Here," he said. "Please take this to help care for the little ones."

"How kind, Mr. Thayer," she murmured. "Every penny helps. You have my deepest appreciation, especially since

I'm aware how difficult things have been for you since the quake."

J.D. dug into another pocket and pulled out a small rag doll the size of a piece of corncob with clothing that had been made from a discarded dishrag. Amelia noted Wing Lee's eyes widen as she gazed at the painted face and button eyes.

Angus looked over at J.D. and shook his head. "I dinna know where you managed to find such a toy, but I think she likes it, right, lassie?" he added as J.D. handed the doll to an ecstatic Wing Lee.

Amelia was dumbfounded by what she had just witnessed. Thayer was down to his last bean, yet he had given money to help Miss Cameron's charitable work.

And a doll to his illegitimate daughter...

Amelia was well aware that J.D. was no choirboy, certainly, but perhaps he possessed a far shadier past than she'd been willing to concede—fathering a child he'd committed into someone else's care, and continuing his unholy alliance with Ezra Kemp by employing men obviously loyal to the reprehensible lumberman.

Rather than remember the man's charm, it was far wiser to remember his sins, she reminded herself. The cold truth was, J.D. and Ling Lee had been lovers and he'd obviously abandoned this child to the Mission Home. To give the devil his due, Wing Lee was half Chinese and born out-of-wedlock and her mother was dead, so practically speaking, J.D. could hardly be expected to raise a child on his own...

Don't let him off so easily, demanded a voice in her head.

The man consorted with women of easy virtue, she reminded herself. When he and his paramour had a child together, they'd banished the little one to Miss Cameron's care. J.D. did today what men often do, she thought: offer money to assuage a prickle of conscience.

After the festivities, Amelia chose to stand at some distance from both Angus and J.D. during the cold ferry ride back to San Francisco.

∞

Work progressed at the Bay View the next day without further incident, with the principal advancement being wooden shingles hammered onto the immense roof. For Amelia, walking down Taylor Street from the Fairmont that morning, just the sight of the familiar turrets rising against the winter sky made her breath catch as she approached the site.

"Looks like the lass has done you proud, J.D.," said Angus, visiting his friend to see what headway had been made recently.

"We may just win this contest yet!" J.D. exclaimed with one of his rare displays of joviality.

Amelia could only imagine what Julia Morgan would say if she heard them comparing the effort required to build a small hotel versus the Herculean job of restoring a six story, 465-room edifice that had been consumed by white-hot fire and where the interior floors had fallen seven feet. Julia's ear infection had abated enough for her to resume making regular trips to the Fairmont site, though Ira Hoover often still stepped in as her second-in-command when other clients or her fragile health kept her in Oakland.

Amelia heard the sound of an engine coming around the corner, and turned to observe a motorcar none of them recognized pull up in behind the Winton that was parked in front of the building site.

"Hello, J.D.," hailed a man Amelia thought looked vaguely familiar. "I heard you were going to give it another go. Mind if I look around?" He pointed to his companion who was unloading photographic gear. "This is Eric Gabler. He takes the pictures. Hello Dr. McClure."

"Hello, Mr. Hopper."

The visitor turned back to address J.D. "How's it going? Looks like an exact replica of the old hotel."

"New and *improved*," J.D. emphasized. "Let me give you a tour."

"There's got to be a story about getting this thing up in such a short time."

"Now that the mayor's under indictment, what else have you got to write about these days?" Angus pointed out.

"Not much. Just a couple of murders on the waterfront and Donaldina Cameron fighting Chinese prostitution again. Did you read in our newspaper that somebody actually tried to dynamite her new mission building on Sacramento Street? She had come over from Oakland to inspect the construction and found the sticks on her front steps. She calmly walked over to the trash bin and dropped them in it."

"Oh good heavens!" exclaimed Amelia. Julia had designed Donaldina's new headquarters as a special favor to her crusading friend.

"Miss Cameron's an amazing woman," J.D. agreed.

Suddenly, Amelia knew who their visitor was: James Hopper, noted reporter for the *San Francisco Call*, the newspaper that had recently moved back from temporary headquarters in Oakland and had begun to be printed within the city limits again. Gabler was the photographer that had taken her picture at her farewell party the night before she'd departed for school in France.

"Is it true you've got a lady architect working for you?" Hopper asked, looking baldly at Amelia.

For her part, a grim sense of foreboding descended.

"Two, in fact," J.D. said, grinning. "May I introduce Amelia Bradshaw, deputy to Miss Julia Morgan, whose architectural firm I've hired. They're also doing the reconstruction on the Fairmont—which I intend shall open its doors *after* the Bay View greets its first guests before the anniversary of the quake."

Amelia felt Hopper's critical glance take in her smudged shirtwaist and skirt coated with limestone and fine particles of sand. She knew the cuffs of her father's worn tweed trousers peeped under the blue serge hem. Strands from her upswept hairstyle had escaped in an untidy tangle, and her palms were positively filthy. She nodded peremptorily to avoid offering him her hand.

"Didn't we meet once before?" he queried.

"Fleetingly. You did a very kind story about my grandfather and me a few years ago."

"That's right! Bradshaw! You're Charlie Hunter's granddaughter! The one who went to that fancy school in France. *Now* I remember… you wore a silver beaded dress to your going-away party!"

"What a memory you have, Mr. Hopper."

The reporter wagged his finger at her and laughed. "How could we forget, eh, Eric? Standing in that slinky ensemble with all your school chums bidding you bon voyage. What a mob scene." He pointed to the shingled walls. "Seriously, J.D. Do you really think you'll be ready to open before the eighteenth of April?"

"Amelia, explain to Mr. Hopper how the interiors will be finer than ever by the time we're finished. Tell him about the expensive furniture you've ordered on my account."

She knew from hard experience the way Julia would react if her deputy said one word to a reporter. "Mr. Thayer has become an equal expert in such matters, haven't you? *You* tell Mr. Hopper," she insisted.

J.D. looked at her as if he thought she was acting very strangely. "Don't be silly, Amelia. Show him the architectural plans."

Reluctantly, Amelia showed Hopper the initial drawings she'd made to recreate the original hotel, adding all the modern conveniences. The reporter remarked, "I'll bet you'll be excited when it's your turn to choose the colors for the walls—right, Miss Bradshaw?"

Amelia looked first at J.D. and then Angus, and all three stifled laughter.

"She *designed* the building, you nit-wit!" J.D. said, laughing.

Amelia tried to control the damage she knew was being inflicted on her relationship with Julia. "Julia Morgan's *firm*— for whom I work—is responsible for the designs, Mr. Hopper, and everything is supervised entirely by Miss Morgan. My work here is primarily structural. But Miss Morgan—"

"*Structural?*" Hopper gazed at her skeptically.

"I was trained at UC Berkeley in engineering."

Keep your mouth closed, Amelia!

Angus chimed in with a recitation of her credentials. Amelia intervened by reviewing Julia's stellar accomplishments as the first woman ever to gain a certificate in architecture from the famed French institution of architecture.

"Well, who *designed* the blasted building?" Hopper demanded.

"She did," chorused J.D. and Angus, pointing at Amelia.

"Oh... no, no, no! I was assigned the job of doing the

preliminary drawings. Ira Hoover, in our firm, and I helped with the architectural plans from which we work, but it's *Miss Morgan* who—"

"Based on Charlie Hunter's original concept," corrected J.D.

"But *everything* at Taylor and Jackson is under the direction of Miss Julia Morgan, herself," Amelia emphasized, growing desperate. She shot Angus and J.D. a pleading look. "*Everything!* Really, Mr. Hopper, I insist you speak to her before you write anything in your newspaper."

As soon as the words were out of her mouth, Amelia knew that Julia would be angry if she referred a reporter to her—and angry if she didn't. As Morgan's deputy on the project, she'd become a trapped rabbit, about to be shot and skinned.

"But you're the one on site, here, aren't you?" Hopper insisted, sounding irritated by the convoluted conversation they were having. "You're supervising the hotel you dreamed up, correct?"

Before she could answer, Angus preempted her reply. "Believe me, Hopper, *this* is the lassie who's responsible for just about everything you see here."

"No! Truly, Mr. Hopper." She was almost frantic with worry at the notion the reporter might put Angus's words into the newspaper. "Mr. Hoover and I work under the direct supervision of Julia Morgan. We didn't hire the construction crew… Mr. Thayer's responsible for that… but the design is a product of the *Julia Morgan* firm. It is her office, her vision for—"

"You're too modest, Miss Bradshaw. Typical of your sex," Hopper declared briskly. He opened his notebook and scrabbled a few lines.

J.D. nodded affirmatively. "And, she won the *Prix d'Or* while she was studying architecture in Paris."

"You did?" asked Angus with a look of admiration.

"So did Miss Morgan!" Amelia exclaimed "She was the first woman in the *world* to win a *Prix d'Or* and a *certificat* from the L'École des Beaux Arts."

"Will you show me around?" Hopper gestured toward the construction site.

Amelia shook her head firmly no. "Mr. Thayer is your best guide."

"Come now, Amelia," J.D. said. "I know practically nothing about the nuts and bolts of construction." He gave Hopper a rueful look. "If Jimmy boy is willing to give us a little ink in his newspaper after all the bad news his paper wrote about the old gambling club—and my initial troubles finding funds to rebuild—we should be exceedingly grateful, right, Hopper?"

"I write it as I see it," the reporter said with a shrug.

"Mr. Thayer knows more than enough about building his hotel to fill your pages." She tried to signal J.D. that he was doing her a disservice to foist her on Hopper, but he appeared oblivious to her discomfort.

"I insist, Amelia. You're in charge here, so be a good little architect and tell Mr. Hopper how absolutely wonderful this place will be from the moment we open our doors and start counting our guests' money."

He was teasing, of course, but Amelia knew he wanted her to dazzle Hopper with descriptions of the beautiful features the hotel would soon display.

"Mr. Hopper, I'll be happy to show you what we're planning here, if you promise me you'll explain to your readers that I merely work for Julia Morgan's firm. I want you to say that everything on this site is completely under her direction. Is that understood between us?"

"Sure, sure," he murmured, gazing at the scaffolding that

now reached three stories high. He looked over at J.D. "Can we climb up there?"

"How's your insurance policy at the paper, James my boy?"

Hopper looked skyward. "Fine, I guess. I don't suppose you fellas would show me what the view looks like from the top floor?"

"No, sir!" Angus shook his head. "You won't see *me* risking m'life creeping up there."

J.D. gestured toward Amelia. "As I've said, here's your guide, Hopper. Miss Bradshaw, will you do the honors?"

"You climb scaffolds?" Hopper asked incredulously.

"I have to," she replied shortly, and then regretted having said anything at all.

Hopper pointed at the rotund piece of equipment that tumbled sand, water, and the other ingredients necessary to make concrete for the sidewalks. "First, let's get a photograph of the three of you standing in front of this machine."

Amelia shook her head. "Absolutely not! I don't pose for pictures, Mr. Hopper, but feel free to take whatever photographs Mr. Thayer deems appropriate. I'll start up the scaffolding. Come up when you're ready."

She'd reached the second story by the time Hopper and J.D. began to follow her to the roof level. When the two men caught up, Hopper ushered her to the edge of the platform and pointed toward the bay. The bay's waters were sapphire and the surrounding hills golden brown.

"This is perfect," Hopper enthused. Then, gesturing to the area where Amelia and J.D. were standing, he called down to his photographer, "Hey, Eric! Quick! Get some good shots of *this*!"

❦

Amelia had lived in silent dread from the moment reporter James Hopper arrived at the Bay View building site. If she mentioned the occasion and nothing was written, Julia would still be cross. If he published something, she was bound to be reprimanded severely, so she concluded it was better to pray Hopper would dismiss the work of a bunch of women architects as not worth the expenditure of his time and ink, and leave well enough alone.

One late afternoon, a week after Hopper's visit, Amelia walked into the Morgan firm in its handsome new headquarters in the newly restored Merchant Exchange building on California Street in the burgeoning downtown section rising from the ashes near the San Francisco Ferry Building. There, laying open on a long library table in the middle of the drafting room, was the late edition of the *San Francisco Call* featuring a double spread by James Hopper and photographer Eric Gabler.

Fortunately, the central workroom was deserted this early evening hour. Amelia knew immediately by the look on the Julia's face that there was trouble ahead.

"No one in the Morgan firm ever gives interviews about our work," Julia declared angrily before Amelia could take her coat off. "Ever!"

"I didn't give an interview," Amelia replied hastily. "This Mr. Hopper suddenly arrived at the site a while back and started asking questions."

"You should have referred all questions to *me*."

"I did. I begged him to get in touch with you before he wrote anything. As it was, he spoke mostly to your client, whom he seemed to know fairly well. And every time a subject was raised, J.D.—I mean, Mr. Thayer—or Angus McClure, who was there, volunteered answers. I could hardly get a word in edgewise."

Julia pointed to several quotes by Amelia. "You appeared to manage quite well. And besides, you never said a word to me that you'd spoken with a reporter."

Amelia stared at the newspaper article and heaved a sigh. "I didn't mention it because I knew you'd most likely have this reaction and I hoped he wouldn't bother to write about two women architects." She glanced up at Julia, whose face was stone, and silently cursed J.D. and Angus for spouting responses to questions that Hopper had showered on her. The story's headline couldn't have been worse.

WOMAN ARCHITECT RECREATING
A FAMILIAR JEWEL ON NOB HILL

"Each chance I had, Julia, I told Mr. Hopper that both Ira and I worked under your direct supervision. That Mr. Thayer had hired the Julia Morgan *firm* and I was just the person you'd assigned to keep an eye on construction as the hotel neared completion."

"That is not at all the tenor of the article," snapped Julia.

"But that's what I *said*, when I said anything at all."

"And I am incensed that you hinted the Bay View will open before the Fairmont, pitting one of my clients against the other like that."

"I didn't say that! Mr. Thayer and Dr. McClure mentioned that possibility in jest. Julia, I can hardly be blamed if—"

"I find it very easy to blame you for shameless self-promotion and a lack of good sense in talking to a reporter *at all*." She gestured toward a photograph filmed from the ground level. It showed Amelia standing at the highest elevation of scaffolding, her manly trousers clearly visible beneath the hem of her skirt flapping in a gusty wind.

"But look," and Amelia pointed to a paragraph near the end of the story, "Mr. Hopper says right here that I'm an employee of the Julia Morgan firm and he goes on to note your many accolades and—"

"I don't wish to be mentioned in *any* article, as I told the man when he called," she retorted.

Amelia fell silent. So Hopper *had* heeded Amelia's plea and attempted to interview Julia, to no avail. There was nothing any underling of Julia's could say or do that would change the situation or erase the fact the article touted Amelia's own achievements much more than Julia's. On one level, Amelia could understand why her employer was upset. Even so, Julia had *refused* to speak to Hopper, and so the newsman wrote about what he'd learned at the building site from Angus and J.D., probably putting *their* words in *her* mouth, and added a few things on his own for good measure. Although Amelia knew she hadn't *caused* the problem, the entire situation was distressing beyond words.

She tried another tack. "Honestly, Julia, I can't see how this article will hurt us, can you? Perhaps Hopper's interest in women architects will actually do you and the firm a good turn, and may even attract additional clients. Please believe that I mentioned your name every time he asked a question," she pleaded.

"Well, that was a mistake, Amelia. You know perfectly well that I am a very private person. And in my profession, I prefer to emulate the anonymity of the medieval guilds. I don't want my office marginalized by being incorrectly known as a firm that hires only women, thus driving away male clients. It has been my strict policy to let our work speak for itself. Let the newspapers discuss what the architect builds *after* it's built—not the architect himself."

Amelia gestured to the article. "But the problem was that your client, Mr. Thayer, was delighted to have his new hotel described in such glowing terms."

"Undoubtedly, *you* are delighted also to be the subject of such compliments, but not *I*. And despite your family's former connection to the Bay View, the new building is purely a product of the Julia Morgan *firm* and—"

"I repeatedly told Mr. Hopper that," Amelia interrupted. Julia's attack had suddenly become personal and she'd had enough. "But, in truth and with all due respect, Julia, I *did* design this version of the Bay View."

Her employer's eyes flashed with irritation. "Amelia, you are beyond the pale."

Amelia stared at her clasped hands resting in her lap. "Surely you remember that, given my knowledge of the site and our time constraints, you'd assigned me the bulk of the initial design work. Ira helped calculating the load factors, but had trouble engineering the elevators. In the end, he turned the majority of the schematics over to me because he knew I had a degree in engineering and understood the challenges of that steep hill better than anyone in our office—except you, of course. What he showed you for your approval was principally *my* work. But in the spirit of a team effort, I made no mention of that—and I told him not to either—especially because Ira is a good friend and a hard worker. The poor man has been slaving fourteen hours a day for months now. You signed off on everything regarding the Bay View, and that was fine with me."

"Amelia—"

There was no mistaking Julia's warning tone, but Amelia couldn't stop the words from pouring out.

"I am convinced I will never achieve your greatness, Julia.

But in the case of the Bay View Hotel, it is my concept, my design, basically my plans, and I am overseeing its construction at your request. Even so, I couldn't give a *fig* if that information is included in any newspaper article or not, and I did everything humanly possible to give you all the credit for it—and that's the God's truth."

Amelia was nearly breathless by now.

"How can you expect me to believe that?" Julia stabbed an angry forefinger at the newspaper spread out on the table. "You were simply tooting your own trumpet and nothing you can say convinces me otherwise. This is insubordination of the worst kind."

Amelia struggled not to let tears edge into her voice. "I was *not* the person who volunteered the information to James Hopper *or* his photographer concerning the hotel. I even refused to pose for a photograph in front of the building. If you don't believe me, perhaps you should discuss this entire matter with Mr. Thayer."

"Whom you've no doubt deliberately beguiled, just as you have his friend, Dr. McClure."

Amelia stared across the table at her employer, grateful that everyone in the office had left for the day. Everyone, that was, except Lacy Fiske, who appeared oblivious to their heated discussion while she pounded her typewriting machine in the next room.

"I have not 'deliberately *beguiled*' anyone," Amelia protested, stung by Julia's characterizing her as some temptress employing her feminine wiles. "I am just trying to do the best job I can under exceedingly difficult circumstances."

Julia heaved a melancholy sigh. She appeared as genuinely distressed as her beleaguered employee. "Well," she said slowly, "I've warned you repeatedly about my position on dealing with the press, so in my judgment, this most recent development is totally unacceptable. My only recourse is to discharge you for a serious breach of professionalism. I'm assuming supervision of the final phase of the Bay View's construction."

Panic gripped Amelia as the reality of her financial obligations to Aunt Margaret, her mother, and her own future whirled through her mind. Before she could reply, however, Julia walked toward the door by way of dismissal.

"How distressing that it should take an incident like this to make you understand how I work in this office, Amelia. I'll expect you to submit your final design for the Bay View's back garden before you leave tonight."

This can't be happening…

Like a sleepwalker, Amelia took a seat at her slanted drafting table. Lacy had stopped typing and was preparing to accompany Miss Morgan on the evening ferry to Oakland. The dutiful secretary shot Amelia a discreet look of sympathy but said nothing. Once the two women donned their coats and left the building, the place grew eerily quiet.

CHAPTER 20

THE FOLLOWING MORNING, AMELIA arrived at the construction site at her usual time, rehearsing during the walk from her basement quarters in the Fairmont to the Bay View how she would inform Thayer that she'd been sacked.

She'd had virtually no sleep and was to some degree relieved that Morgan's client was nowhere to be seen. Her gloom was only heightened when Jake Kelly, in charge, today, of the crew hammering shingles on the walls framing the first floor exterior, challenged her every directive.

Kelly barely acknowledged Amelia's request to check the wooden slats for splits and cracks before they were affixed, turning his back and strolling away with a mumbled, "I've already given them a look-see."

Amelia followed in his wake. "Well, please check them *again*, Mr. Kelly. If yesterday was any gauge, we'll have rain pouring into the ballroom at the first storm."

Kelly had appeared ready to refuse outright, but Amelia stood her ground, hands on hips, and eventually he complied with her order. By mid-morning her head was throbbing and she felt like jumping into the bay.

Around noon, she heard the familiar sound of the Winton chugging up the steep incline on Jackson Street. J.D. brought the car to a halt near the cement-making operation, yet he remained in the driver's seat, hailing her with a shout. When she drew near, he ordered, "Amelia, please get in."

"You need to speak to Jake Kelly about the shingling—"

"It will have to wait. Tell Kelly he's in charge. Get in."

"But he's a surly lout, and besides, I'm furious with him today."

"No wonder Miss Morgan discharged you. You're willful and refuse to take orders, just like he does."

She stood, hand resting on the vehicle's door, staring at J.D.

"So Julia's already told you she's let me go?"

J.D. shrugged. "'Fraid so."

Amelia looked at her boot tops, willing herself to maintain her composure. Finally she murmured, "Well, I guess you might as well put Spitz and Kelly in charge, period."

"*You* are in charge." Silenced by this, she could only look dumbly at him sitting behind the wheel. "Get *in*," he repeated. "We're going to the Cliff House for lunch, Miss Full-fledged Architect."

❦

Through the Cliff House restaurant's windows, Amelia watched the surf pound against a cluster of rocks a hundred yards off shore. Now that Julia had officially terminated her employment, an avalanche of regrets and recriminations had come tumbling down and the notion of striking out on her own seemed utterly absurd.

"Amelia, look at it in this light," J.D. offered cheerfully. "You're beyond Miss Morgan's reach now. When she announced to me she'd sacked you, I explained that I'm happy with you as my principal designer and construction liaison and didn't want to make a change. She said I'd have to choose—her or you—so I did. You. You're rid of her and she's rid of you. You still have gainful employment, so everybody's happy."

"I'm *not* happy," Amelia retorted, then fell silent.

She was highly gratified to think a Julia Morgan client had enough confidence in her work to ask her to remain on the job. But far outweighing that was the plain fact that she felt sad and embarrassed that she was held in disgrace at Julia's firm.

Her mind churning, Amelia continued to gaze through the restaurant's large window. To her right stood the mammoth iron and glass building housing the tile-lined pools of the Sutro Public Baths. It was a sparkling, early autumn day, yet she now felt as gloomy as if the landscape were dripping with fog.

"Can't you see what's happened?" J.D. chided. "The apprentice has bested the master."

"I'll never best Julia Morgan!" Amelia replied vehemently. "She's a genius."

"Oh, come now. You're just as good."

"No, I'm *not*! She's on a par with any of the great men… Frank Lloyd Wright, David Burnham, Stanford White—in his good years," she amended. "And she runs a fine firm. Her clients are her primary focus and she cares passionately about the quality of the work done for them in her name." Amelia pushed her fork around her plate, toying with her uneaten filet of sole. "It's just lately, everything I did seemed wrong, seemed to make her angry with me. Actually, she's kind as can be to the support staff. She even paid for the schooling for the child of one of the men who works for her."

"And so, your sins were…?"

"She believed I overstepped. That I was a self-promoter. I honestly don't think I was, but Hopper's article in the *Call* was the last straw. Julia detests the press and is very strict, with very clear ideas how things should be run. I *agree* with that! How could it have come to this?" she pleaded, mortified that her eyes were suddenly brimming with tears.

"Regardless of what you might think, Julia Morgan is human," J.D. said matter-of-factly, "and I expect she's just the tiniest bit unsettled by how swiftly her junior associate has come into her own. The disasters in San Francisco tested everybody's mettle and you rose magnificently to the challenge. You're not sitting at her feet anymore, Amelia. You've earned the right to stand beside her and I think she finds that rather upsetting."

"She found everything upsetting," Amelia replied, anger colliding with her remorse. "She disapproved of practically anything I did."

"Like what?" he asked curiously.

"Such as my hiring Loy Chen to make me supper each night, or my having dinner occasionally with Angus McClure, or—"

"Did you tell her he'd proposed marriage?"

Amelia was aghast and must have appeared as shocked to J.D. as she felt the night when Angus finally lured her to dinner at Tadich's restaurant and then, out of the blue, brought up the subject of marriage.

"How do *you* know that?" she demanded.

"Angus told me," he said, shrugging. J.D. gave her a sly wink. "And he also told me you'd turned him down."

"Oh Lord!" Amelia said, hating that her cheeks felt hot.

Angus had only gotten so far as to say he thought that the time had come for them both to settle down before Amelia had made it clear as gently as she could that she would decline his or *any* offer of marriage. Angus had been a stalwart friend, and she cared greatly for his welfare, but like Etienne, he assumed she'd give up architecture once she became a wife—which told her that he understood her not one whit.

J.D. laughed. "I'm warning you, Amelia, he'll try to ask you again."

"Good heavens! Let's not get off the subject. Julia Morgan has just *discharged* me, and that's bound to be all over San Francisco in a day or two. And by the way, she was furious you'd egged on that reporter to gain publicity for the Bay View. Frankly, I think she disapproves of you nearly as much as she does of me!"

"Maybe that's because she knows I think you can do just as good a job as she can."

"You *didn't* say that to her?"

"I didn't reveal *all* my secrets," J.D. said, clearly enjoying this conversation.

"Oh for pity's sake, this is serious! The woman has given me the boot after all the struggles we've shared as fellow students and architects." She gazed at the pounding surf. "I feel absolutely wretched about it."

"Amelia, you did nothing wrong," he said gently. "It will all work out, I expect."

Amelia severely doubted that, but found it supremely ironic that it should be J.D. Thayer offering her solace in this situation. He speared a piece of shelled crab with his fork and paused before popping it into his mouth. "Actually, I think she likes you very much."

Amelia slowly looked up from her plate and asked warily, "Why do you say that? She's just sent me packing."

"She definitely admires your work or she wouldn't have given you the Bay View to design and eventually oversee, but I imagine she figured she'd have you under her control a good while longer."

"Control?" she said slowly. "Is that what you think this is about?"

"I do indeed, but if I've learned anything about you, Amelia, I would advise Miss Morgan that's quite out of the question. Now, eat your lunch and let's get back to work."

⁂

On the drive back from the Cliff House, Amelia attempted to relax against the back of the passenger seat while J.D. talked.

"Julia Morgan looked positively stricken when I said I preferred to keep you on this job as architect and site supervisor."

"Positively furious was more like it, I expect. And by the way, why *did* you tell her you wanted me to continue at the Bay View instead of her?"

"I've observed that you can do the job, and I'm fast running out of funds," J.D. said flashing a grin across the front seat. "That means that I can better afford your fees than Julia Morgan's."

So he didn't prefer her skills, just her price tag.

"Oh. I see. My difficulties with my employer have done your bank account a good turn, is that it?"

"Your *former* employer," J.D. reminded her. Looking pleased with himself he added, "But absolutely. I think I've got myself a bargain. You're *good*, don't you realize that yet? And if it soothes your spirits any, in my opinion, Miss Morgan overreacted to Hopper's article in the *Call*. I know your intentions were pure. I watched you try to credit her for everything, even though you did all of the work."

"Promise me you didn't voice that opinion to her!"

J.D. shook his head, his eyes alight with amusement. "I'd seen Hopper's piece in the newspaper and figured it would land you in hot water. I went down to her office this morning and explained exactly what happened during Hopper's visit to the site, but she was unbending about what she considers your insubordination. As far as I was concerned," he added, "her attitude annoyed me. I didn't like being forced to choose."

"Well then, given what you told her about how that reporter behaved, why would she still insist you pick either her or me?"

J.D. wheeled the Winton through the upper gate of the Presidio and drove the winding road through cool stands of trees before he answered. "Just like you, my dear Amelia, Julia Morgan likes to win and is willing to take risks to do that against all competitors. She figured she was Queen Bee. She looked utterly shocked when I said I would happily retain the services of the architect who had thus far done such a fine job."

"Oh good Lord," groaned Amelia. "What must Lacy and Ira think?"

"If they're your friends, none of this will matter much."

But Amelia doubted that. Perhaps their pleasant association couldn't withstand this break with Julia and she would lose three associates instead of one. Wouldn't Lacy automatically side with Julia?

Meanwhile, J.D. pointed to a package he'd placed on the floorboards when he'd entered the Winton. "You didn't eat your lunch, so I had the waiter pack it up for your supper."

"Thank you," she murmured.

"And I want you to move into the Bay View so we won't waste time or money housing you now that this break with Julia means you have to leave the Fairmont's basement. Your traveling back and forth to your aunt's in Oakland by ferry would eat up time." Amelia looked at him with alarm, but before she could respond, J.D. added, "And you've got to learn to drive the Winton. I'll need you to fetch supplies and be able to get to the docks in record time when goods and equipment arrive, instead of sending our workers who need to remain on site, or having you spend most of the day riding a cable car to and fro. We're on a tight schedule and a strict budget, my girl."

"I'm not your girl," Amelia said under her breath.

"What did you say?"

She wasn't anybody's "girl," not even Julia Morgan's. As of today, she was Amelia Bradshaw, architect—and single practitioner. She would show Julia someday she'd made a big mistake to discharge her so unfairly. She was on her own now, and she'd better toughen her hide and show all of them what she was capable of. She would do whatever it took until the reconstructed Bay View reopened its doors before the Fairmont Hotel could have its roof repaired!

"Look, Mr. Thayer," she said, eyeing him steadily. "We might as well deal with one particular subject right now. People will talk no matter what we do, but if I'm to live under your roof and we're to work together on this project as business partners, we both must agree we will maintain a strictly professional association in every regard."

For the second time that day, J.D. appeared mildly amused, which irritated her no end. "That sounds eminently sensible."

For some reason, she was even *more* irritated that he'd agreed so readily, but also relieved. She tapped her finger on the vehicle's window ledge and then realized it was something she'd seen Julia do many times while she was playing for time.

"Good," she said crisply. "That takes care of that problem. And how long will your funds last, if I may ask?" She could very well be unemployed again before long.

"The money will last until the wall shingles are in place. I'm due for a second loan to finish the interior and pay for the furniture we ordered C.O.D.," he added.

His money would last only two more weeks!

"But I'm actually not that worried, Amelia," he continued. "I'm betting Loy and his crew will dig the last few feet of rubble very soon and secure your grandfather's safe. Even if the gold bars melted, they're still legal tender."

The fellow was a high-stakes gambler for sure. J.D., her late father, and Ezra Kemp were probably different versions of the same kind of man. Into her head popped a vision of the partial poker hand she habitually kept in her skirt pocket.

She gazed at the dazzling blue-green bay as the Winton left the boundary of the Presidio and sped down Lombard Street. Amelia squinted against the water's glare. A deep sense of melancholy about the breach with Julia settled into her chest that the spectacular scenery could do nothing to assuage.

❧

It was mid-afternoon when they pulled up in front of the Bay View. All was quiet on the building site.

"That blackguard, Kelly!" Amelia exclaimed. "Look! His crew left this wall half shingled and they've gone home for the day!"

"Without you here, cracking the whip, I can see we're in serious trouble," J.D. replied, only half in jest. "Good thing I rehired you."

Just then, a tall, rotund figure suddenly stepped from the shadows at the hotel's entrance.

"However you two slice it, I think you're both in serious trouble." Ezra Kemp walked toward their car and glanced down at the passenger seat. "Heard you got sacked today, Miss Bradshaw."

"I've merely changed employers," she replied coolly. Her mind was whirling over how swiftly one of the workers, overhearing J.D.'s conversation with her at the curb, had reported events back to Kemp.

"Well, does your employer have the funds to pay you, or will you be recompensed some other way?"

Amelia stared at Kemp, outraged by his innuendo. Meanwhile, J.D. exited the Winton and strode toward their unwelcome visitor.

"To what do I owe the occasion, Ezra?"

"Same as before... I want the money you still owe me for the gambling club we built."

"And to emphasize your point, you told Spitz, Jake Kelly, and his men to depart early, am I correct? Well, you'll be pleased to learn the bank's approved my second loan and the paperwork is being drawn up as we speak."

Amelia knew for certain J.D. was bluffing. He'd just told her he was waiting for the loan to be approved, but she had to admire his cocksure attitude in the face of Kemp's attempt to intimidate him.

"I'm not waiting for *paperwork*, J.D." Kemp said, his eyes narrowing. "I want you to stop employing those Chinks and pay me what you owe me. *Now.*"

Amelia could feel her pulse racing. Had carpenter Kelly's oft-voiced suspicions about the Chinese night laborers been relayed to Kemp?

"Well, wait you must, I'm afraid," J.D. told Kemp pleasantly. "But not for long."

"I'm not waiting," Kemp declared. "And I expect you to appear for supper tonight, as we've agreed."

"Terribly sorry, Ezra, but I have an obligation that just came up. Perhaps next week, when I bring you that bank draft."

Kemp eyed Amelia speculatively. "I don't think you understand how it will affect your health if you don't meet your previous obligations, Thayer. But maybe there's a better way to make my point clear."

And without further comment, he strode down Jackson in the direction of Chinatown.

"He's out-and-out threatening you!" Amelia exclaimed when Kemp was out of earshot. "The man is outrageous! And now, half your construction crew are beholden to him and not you." Thayer didn't reply. Before she could exit the motorcar, J.D. resumed his place behind the steering wheel. "What are you doing?" she demanded as he put the vehicle in gear and pulled away from the curb.

"You, my dear Miss Bradshaw, are about to have your first driving lesson. We're both going to need speed and mobility if we're to outfox the nasty Mr. Kemp, not to mention saving money every time I send you to fetch supplies instead of one of our workers."

Twenty minutes later, the pair retraced the route to the Presidio and J.D. pulled the Winton to a stop on the parade grounds.

"This is madness!" Amelia exclaimed. "I have absolutely no idea how to operate this enormous machine."

"Would you like to learn?"

Amelia's gaze roved the length of the shining blue, open-aired motorcar that had been her grandfather's delight. The notion of being at the controls of such a powerful contraption overcame her trepidation at learning such a dangerous skill. Who cared who her instructor might be?

"In actual fact, I'd *love* to! But do you think I'm strong enough to control such a machine on these steeps hills?"

"Well you turned the crank just fine on your own on the day of the quake, remember? Driving it is the easy part."

"It *would* be wonderful to be able to go on needed errands when you were busy somewhere else... but—"

"We'll make this short and sweet." J.D. killed the engine, reached down to the floor of the vehicle, and retrieved the crank. "Step one. Remember how to start it?"

As they often did when something triggered a memory about the quake, frightening recollections of that day once again sprang to the surface. The smoke. The terror that the car might not start or that she'd break her arm trying, and then they would all burn to death. Amelia pushed these unwanted thoughts aside.

"Yes. Yes, of course I remember how to start this vehicle. Hand it to me, please."

She exited the car, inhaled deeply, inserted the crank into its narrow shaft, and gave it a few forceful twists, vastly relieved when the motor turned over, caught, and began running.

"It always starts up wonderfully well," J.D. said.

"Of course it does. My grandfather only bought the best," she replied tartly.

J.D. looked at her briefly and then put the car in gear. "I've brought you back to the Presidio because there are plenty of open spaces here, and no chance of mowing down any unsuspecting pedestrians."

The parade ground was deserted in the late afternoon, with only a few tent dwellers curious enough to stand on the sidelines.

"Right," J.D. announced. "Now we'll see how well you can shift the gears. Switch seats with me."

As the sun dipped over the bay, Amelia struggled under J.D.'s tutelage to coordinate the motions of her hands and feet and succeeded only in grinding the gears so badly she thought the metal parts would fall onto the parade ground.

"No, no, no, Amelia!" he chastised. "Gently! Smoothly! Don't attack it as if you were in a boxing ring."

"You'll have to get out of the car."

"What?"

"You're giving me fits, barking orders like I'm one of your carpenters. Get out of the car and let me see if I can do it on my own."

"All right, but—"

"If I don't get the hang of it this time, I'll quit. It's starting to get dark and I'm afraid I'm going to destroy this poor machine. That would even be worse than not learning to drive it."

J.D. exited on the passenger side and stood a few feet distant.

"Stand behind a tree, please."

"For heaven's sake, Amelia."

"I mean it. Over there. Behind that cypress."

J.D. disappeared behind the tree trunk while Amelia took another deep breath. With renewed determination, she put a gloved hand on the gearshift. She released the brake and the car began to roll down the slight incline. Slowly, she shifted the lever while moving her feet in a similarly smooth manner. The car traveled forward relatively smoothly.

"*I did it!*" she whispered. A buoyancy, like air in a boat's sail, filled her chest as she made a wide, arcing turn and started up the incline.

Her feeling of triumph was short lived when the

engine immediately began to strain. *Downshift… downshift sl—o—w—ly* she cautioned herself and felt a flush of victory when the gears meshed, caught, and gave the car a boost up the low hill. Giddy with glee, she promised herself that if she ever returned to Paris, she'd drive right down the Champs-Elysées, her hair pulling free of its pins and streaming behind her.

For the next fifteen minutes she piloted the car in slow circles, shifting the gears with reasonable skill and braking as required. At length, she made a final, slow turn at the north end of the open area and coasted downhill, intending to halt just shy of the cypress tree where J.D. was waiting with what she could only judge was the broad grin of a proud papa.

Ten feet away she shifted her feet, planning to glide to a perfect stop. Instead, she mistakenly put a foot on the accelerator and the motorcar lurched forward. At the last possible second, she swerved, missing the tree by inches. She finally managed to screech to a stop, though by this time, her entire body was shaking.

J.D. peered from behind the tree. "Perhaps you think you have good cause, but convince me, please, that you didn't intend to kill me."

Amelia's forehead rested against the steering wheel and her breath came in gasps.

"I did not… intend… to run you over," she said, her voice muffled by her sleeve. "But I nearly killed myself."

"Nonsense! You did wonderfully well!" J.D. walked to the driver's side and patted her on the sleeve. "You should have seen this car when *I* first started to drive. I had to have plenty of dents knocked out of it. All it takes is practice, but you did it. You can drive!"

Amelia raised her head to the scattered applause from a

few refugees standing on the edge of the field. She smiled weakly and waved at the motley crowd that had no other amusements than to watch her herky-jerky efforts to tame the horseless carriage.

She looked over at J.D., her feat beginning to dawn on her. "I can drive," she breathed. "I can actually *drive* this blasted machine."

"All right, all right… no resting on your laurels." J.D. climbed into the passenger seat. "Put us in gear, my dear Miss Bradshaw, and let's see if you can get us safely to Tadich's."

"Tadich's? With you? I can't do that," she blurted.

"Why not? You've gone there with Angus."

"Once. And he's not my employer. No, you're very kind, Mr. Thayer, but I'll just drive us back to the Fairmont, and you'll have your evening to yourself."

"You've lost your room there, remember?"

"Oh Lord…" she murmured.

"So Tadich's it is. You can sleep in one of the Bay View maid's rooms. It's a bit drafty, but at least it has a door that shuts." He pointed to her boot resting on the Winton's floorboards. "And easy on the accelerator, if you don't mind."

CHAPTER 21

Amelia's driving lesson concluded with an uneventful return to the heart of the city. Mercifully, she and J.D. arrived a block from Tadich's restaurant before dusk had become evening. She carefully downshifted and made a remarkably smooth stop next to the curb.

J.D. looked across at her from the passenger seat, a trace of the grin he'd displayed at the parade grounds pulling at the corners of his mouth.

"Well done, Miss Bradshaw. I believe you can call yourself an expert driver now. Your many talents continue to amaze me."

"Thank you," she said, just short of breathless.

"No one can deny that you certainly *are* a woman of the twentieth century."

"I like convenience as much as the next man."

J.D. put his head back and roared with laughter. Then he looked at her squarely, his admiration undisguised. "And you have a sense of humor, Miss Bradshaw. Who would have thought it?"

"And *you* like to laugh, though I don't think that you do it very often, Mr. Thayer."

They were both smiling broadly and she felt a subtle shift in the tenor of their banter. Before she was aware of what was happening, J.D. leaned across the car and gently seized her chin in his hand.

"But I must correct you on one thing. You don't, in the slightest, resemble a man. In fact, not at all."

It almost seemed to Amelia as if an arc of electricity connected them now, blue and pulsing. They locked glances and, like magnets, each leaned imperceptibly toward the other.

And then he kissed her. On the lips.

Surely he will soon pull away, she thought, and when he didn't, she closed her eyes and allowed herself to sink into his embrace, her mouth welcoming the first, astonishing contact with his lips.

A cable car trundling nearby clanged its bell a block away and Amelia's eyelids shot open. Good gracious! Here they were in broad daylight—well, dusk, she thought, glancing over his shoulder. How preposterous that two adversaries who had battled in a San Francisco courtroom less than a year previously were kissing in a motorcar parked in front of Tadich's Grill for all the world to see.

Amelia pulled back sharply and fumbled with the handle on the car door.

J.D. reached out and laid a hand on her sleeve. "Aren't you going to say thank you?"

She turned to stare at him, wide-eyed with embarrassment. Then she realized he was teasing her again.

"Yes, of course. Thank you for my driving lesson," she managed primly.

"That's all?"

She felt hot and flustered and thoroughly put out with herself as she made a determined effort to recover her dignity.

"For the many skills you undoubtedly have, Mr. Thayer, I commend you."

"To which skill are you referring, exactly?"

"You know which."

His glance was challenging, but she refused to take the bait. They waited in silence for a few moments longer before J.D. said, "Shall we go in to supper? I'm sure you'll have many times in the future when you can dazzle the world with your prowess... at the wheel."

He was deliberately provoking her and she cursed the flush of heat fanning her face. Rather than answer, she opened the car door and got out. What else was she supposed to say to him now, she wondered. That his first, brief kiss far outshone the fumbling attempts of a boy she knew at Berkeley? Or even the prowess of First Officer Etienne Lamballe, for that matter?

She may have seriously enjoyed their embrace a minute ago, but the fact was they were architect and client, a relationship she had an obligation to keep strictly professional. She had no business allowing J.D. to kiss her or making ridiculous comparisons with other men—given her rather limited experience in the ways of the world.

But you're not a total neophyte, are you, Amelia? If his kiss felt that marvelous, what would it be like if you and he...?

She turned to walk toward the entrance to the restaurant, deeply regretting she'd accepted an invitation to dine in public with her employer.

"Wait!" J.D. called after her.

When she turned to face him, his expression had grown serious.

"Amelia, before we go in, I need to talk to you about something you may hear soon from other sources..."

She had no desire to listen to any confessions concerning his relationship with the late Ling Lee. He'd kissed her just now— and she'd let him. Well, it was up to her to see that it wouldn't happen again. She held up a gloved hand to halt the discussion.

"There's absolutely no need to enlighten me about any aspect of your private life, Mr. Thayer," she said, keeping her voice steady. "What just happened was a mistake. My job is to help you complete the rebuilding of the Bay View on time and on budget. Nothing more, nothing less."

J.D. appeared to accept the sharp veer in their conversation. "And if all continues to go well," he replied, "we'll be open for business in March, *ahead* of Miss Morgan's Fairmont and the first anniversary of the quake."

Amelia felt a stab of guilt. Julia's efforts at the other hotel would, by necessity, take much longer because she was a stickler that every aspect of the reconstruction be done properly—unlike the work of the demoted site supervisor, Dick Spitz, and his crony, carpenter Kelly.

"Well, doesn't that rather depend on our making the masons rebuild the chimney properly so your guests will have heat in their rooms and the place won't burn down—again?" She flashed him a challenging smile. "Maybe I'll take a drive down to the docks tomorrow and see if that load of bricks has arrived or any of the furniture you ordered has made its way to San Francisco."

"I knew if you learned to drive you'd be dangerous."

She felt a sudden attack of melancholy, thinking about the beautiful furniture her grandfather had collected over the years that had gone up in smoke.

"You know, Mr. Thayer, on the outside, the Bay View may look the same, but it will never be quite like the hotel my grandfather built. That beautiful bank of gilded mirrors in the lobby… the plush red furniture…"

To her surprise, Thayer leaned toward her and seized her hand. "Whatever my sins, Amelia—and I am quite aware they are many—I do appreciate that it can't be easy for you to rebuild the hotel your grandfather created. I am vastly impressed by your skills, and I thank you for them." His touch was dangerously comforting and she wondered at the sudden change in his mood. He was speaking to her now as if she were an old friend. "Sometimes it's beyond bearing, trying to recover what's been lost, don't you think? There are days when I feel like climbing on board some ship and sailing off to Timbuktu—wherever that is."

"Paris, Mr. Thayer," she advised soberly, wondering that they had lingered so long in conversation on the sidewalk in front of Tadich's. "Head for Paris. A much more pleasant escape, I can assure you."

"I expect your time in France changed everything about you." His mood had shifted again and his lips faintly curved. "Now that you and I have shared a kiss, I think it wouldn't be amiss if you stopped calling me 'Mr. Thayer,' agreed?"

She dropped her gaze to stare at her gloved hand resting in his. "On the contrary, given the tasks that lay ahead, I'm afraid 'Mr. Thayer' it must remain."

Just then, a guest at Tadich's burst through the door onto the pavement. In a move that left her feeling mildly bereft, J.D. released her hand.

"When in doubt... flee to Paris," he murmured. "I'll remember your suggestion."

Walking separately into the restaurant, they spent the rest of the evening discussing supply budgets and labor schedules for the work yet to be done.

❧

After a very fine dinner at Tadich's, J.D. pointed the Winton up Vallejo Street, turning left onto Taylor Street. He glanced at the passenger next to him, tendrils of her brunette hair swept back by the breeze in the open-air motorcar.

He'd been impulsive tonight, something he prided himself on *not* being in most instances. Fortunately, Amelia Bradshaw had imminent good sense, along with her obvious talents as an architect, and during the rest of their meal they'd both exhibited admirable restraint.

His mind, however, had begun to travel in directions that had him worried. He certainly did not need any additional complications in his life. Before he could go any further with such thoughts, however, he noticed an ominous glow illuminating the night sky.

"Sweet Jesus!" exclaimed Amelia. "Look! Over there! The sky's orange."

Images of fire and littered streets and streams of refugees fleeing toward the Presidio played out in J.D.'s mind as if the quake and fire of only months ago were still tormenting the city.

"Oh God, not again," he groaned.

Amelia pointed at a team of horses straining to pull a brass fire engine down the street, their clanging bells renting the night air. "They're heading down Taylor Street," she said, her voice growing shrill. "It's the Bay View!" she half-sobbed as J.D. slammed his foot on the accelerator. "Dear God! The hotel's totally engulfed in flames!" They could hear another fire brigade clanging its way up a nearby street, heading for the corner of Taylor and Jackson. "The entire neighborhood might burn down again."

But all J.D. could think about was the hotel that he'd worked so hard to raise from it's charred foundation and for which he and Amelia had both absorbed so many body blows.

"What about Loy and Shou Shou and little Foo?" Amelia cried against the wind as the Winton screeched to a halt a block from a battery of fire engines gathered to battle the blaze. "What about the *workers*?"

"Nobody's there," he shouted across the passenger seat. "Except Barbary."

By the time they ran to the corner, the scene had taken on a surreal quality. He could hear the fire crackling and feel the heat. He ran up to one of the volunteer firefighters.

"I'm the hotel's owner, J.D. Thayer. For God's sake, what happened?"

"A big explosion happened, that's what!" The fireman was rapidly unwinding a length of hose from a large metal spindle. "Who might still be in there, sir?"

J.D. scanned the burning wreckage. "As far as I know, no one," he replied. *Except my dog...* He couldn't think about that now, for chaos reigned everywhere on the street.

The firefighter gave him a relieved look, seized the front end of the hose, and charged toward the burning inferno.

How could this be? J.D. demanded silently.

Everything had been in working order only hours earlier. Someone Dick Spitz had recruited supervised the installation of the boilers the day before. Only Providence had saved his Chinese workers, though. He'd had time to offer to teach Amelia to drive this night because Loy's men weren't scheduled to return until after the boilers had been inspected and they could once more attempt to clear the final debris near his buried walk-in safe.

Just then, a pair of shingles atop one of the Queen Anne turrets hissed and disintegrated, sending a shower of sparks into the fog clinging to the night sky. J.D. attempted to gather his wits, thinking, suddenly, that the disaster could well have been man-made. Kemp had been known to send his bullyboys to other sites where he was at odds with the owners. Why not dispatch an arsonist to finish the job? The scoundrel may have known there was no insurance on the building because the financially strapped owner hadn't the funds for such luxuries. With J.D. bankrupt, Kemp could claim the property in lieu of the money he was still owed by its owner—and rebuild on this choice piece of land at below cost.

Amelia had been very astute to suspect Kemp of wanting to take total control, he thought. *Why didn't I pay more attention to what she was saying…?*

J.D. bolted away from the fire engine, dodging members of the fire brigade as he rounded the corner to view the conflagration from the Jackson Street side of his property. With Amelia trailing a few steps behind, the first faces he recognized among the onlookers were those of Julia Morgan and Ira Hoover. Miss Morgan's hair was fashioned in a braid plaited down her back. She and her deputy had obviously dressed hastily at the Fairmont and run to his aid.

"Oh thank heavens you're both all right!" Julia exclaimed, her owlish eyes glistening with tears as she caught sight of them. "We were so *worried*." Before he or Amelia could react to her show of emotion, Miss Morgan added, "So fortunate you both weren't inside, Mr. Thayer. So *very* fortunate."

"Yes…" he replied faintly, the full, financial impact of the night's events beginning to dawn on him. He would have to pay many new fees to redraw rebuilding plans, as his originals were surely cinders by now.

"Who else might have been in there?" asked Ira, his gaze glued to the conflagration.

"No one, thank God." J.D. felt Amelia catch his eye and they exchanged a knowing glance. "The boiler installers finished their work, and Spitz's men had departed by the time we left for supper downtown."

His architect shot him a warning look.

"It's a blooming miracle the place was empty," Ira said, relieved.

"Yes, what an enormous blessing," agreed Julia Morgan. She closed her eyes and nodded, as if contemplating the burden of answering for the safety of the construction workers—even if the Morgan firm had not been the one to hire Thayer's crew.

"Barbary!" Amelia exclaimed. "Oh, J.D... what about the dog?"

The foursome stared as another section of the roof collapsed in a shower of sparks and intense heat. J.D. shook his head and looked away.

Julia gently seized his arm, saying "Come with us for a moment, will you?" she urged. "I want you to see what's happening further down on Jackson. It appears you've had some kind of explosion."

"That's what a fireman said," Thayer replied.

J.D. allowed himself to be led down the hill. A group from the brigades had been attacking the south side of the property with healthy doses of water, and successfully doused the section of the hotel where the original basement office was located.

"Where did you indicate the boilers should be installed?" Julia asked Amelia suddenly, her tone sharp. J.D. sensed Amelia's alarm as she turned to face her former employer.

"In the basement, next to the south wall, as you approved, Miss M."

J.D. added, "And I was the one who hired the men who installed them. The boilers were due to be inspected by the city later today."

How simple it would have been for Ezra Kemp to get his hands on some dynamite, thought J.D. Stores of the stuff remained from Army supplies used to create firebreaks during the great firestorm of a year ago and he suspected that Kemp could easily pay handsomely for access to contraband material whenever he wanted it.

Amelia pointed to the extensive wreckage toward the rear of the structure. "Did you have a look at the boilers, once the job was done?" she asked J.D.

"No," he murmured. "There was no time. I had my meeting with you this morning, Miss Morgan, and then a conference with Miss Bradshaw about her taking up the reins. Then there was her driving lesson… and later, we had dinner at Tadich's, and… well, here we are."

The group fell silent and the only sounds were of fire-fighters calling for more water to pour on the roaring blaze. J.D. looked down the hill toward Chinatown and considered how one's fate rested on small, seemingly insignificant daily decisions. If he hadn't decided Amelia should learn to drive, would he have then taken the time to have a look at the boilers instead? Would he have known what he was looking at, anyway? And as far as the city's inspection process, that was all a sham anyway. He'd been asked for a bribe by the city official due to inspect the boilers—and paid it. An inspector might never even have appeared.

By this time, Julia Morgan's expression was grim. "If the guts of the boilers were installed improperly, pressure may have built up and forced them to blow on a cold night like this," she said. "It's only one possibility, of course. Any number of mishaps could have occurred."

"It looks as if the whole place was dynamited," J.D. said, voicing his darkest speculations. "I don't think it was the boilers at all."

"Look over there," declared Ira. "The fire has diminished significantly now, thanks to the brigades."

And thanks to the weather gods, thought J.D. Fortunately, it was a windless, damp night. The volunteer firemen had arrived quickly and the near-empty lot behind the hotel had been a boon in preventing the fire's spread to neighboring structures.

"We heard three loud explosions," noted Ira.

"Well, a stick of dynamite under each boiler would do the trick, don't you think?" J.D. replied with a bitter tinge to his tone. He turned toward Amelia. "Or you were right all along, Miss Bradshaw. It could well be my own idiocy that's caused this. I hired Spitz and Kelly against your advice, and they hired workers on the cheap who most likely weren't up to the task of installing—"

He couldn't finish his sentence. The consequences of his desperate attempts to conserve his cash that subsequently led to tolerating shoddy workmanship during the construction felt like a huge boulder crushing the breath out of him.

"There can be tremendous force when natural gas is involved," Amelia intervened gently. "It can build up in the line and be ignited by a spark, or the pressure was incorrectly calibrated in the boilers themselves, which certainly isn't *your* fault. There might have been any number of problems you couldn't have foreseen. Or Kemp did, indeed, have his bully-boys blow it all up," she added with an edge of anger.

To J.D., her kind words about the catastrophe not being his fault were an appreciated antidote to the poisonous brew of guilt and self-incrimination. He felt Amelia's hand on his sleeve.

"Don't be too hard on yourself, J.D.," she said. "You've been required to cope as best you could during terribly trying times."

She'd called him by his first name in front of her former

employer. Her touch was tender, which steadied him some-what, but still, there was no escaping the obvious. He'd hired Kemp's people for expedience's sake and against Amelia's strong protests, and now was paying the price—either through their incompetence or their murderous intentions.

But before he could respond, Miss Morgan spoke up. "You'll both need a place to sleep tonight. May I offer you shelter at the Fairmont? I'm certain the Law brothers would want me to extend you their hospitality. Just come over to us when you are ready to leave here. Your rooms there are still available."

It was a generous offer from Morgan, who probably felt her fit of pique against Amelia had in a small, but perhaps significant, way contributed to this debacle.

"Thank you, Miss Morgan. That's very kind. Miss Bradshaw," he addressed Amelia, trying to preserve her already tattered reputation in front of her former employer, "why don't you go along to your old room at the Fairmont. I have no idea how long I'll need to stay here. The fire—"

His voice trailed off again as he stared at the mountain of burning embers where the rebuilt hotel had once stood. How could such catastrophe strike *twice*? His disjointed thoughts drifted to a memory of his last glimpse of Ling Lee. They'd found only bits of remains under the rubble after the earthquake and fire, so J.D. had long concluded that her spirit still lurked here somewhere.

Then there was poor Barbary, who had survived the first quake and fire only to perish in this disaster. And where was the spirit of Amelia Bradshaw's grandfather, Charlie Hunter, who had passed away in his bed in the hotel he'd loved and lost? Had he cursed this corner of Taylor and Jackson? Or had Ezra Kemp?

"Come, Ira… Amelia. We shall be on our way now,"

Miss Morgan announced. "Mr. Thayer, we'll have your old room in the basement ready, whatever the hour."

As Amelia prepared to follow Morgan she suddenly exclaimed, "Look, J.D! Over there! There's my grandfather's old safe! At least you've found that—finally. And when the embers cool, you'll be able to get access!"

J.D. peered in the direction she was pointing, mesmerized by the sight of the burning wreckage.

"That's the *safe*? Free and clear of debris?"

"Yes. Definitely," Amelia confirmed. "Can't you see? The explosion must have blown the last of the rubble away from it. It's still intact and it's supposed to be fireproof."

He could feel a foolish grin begin to spread across his face. His life was in shambles. His rebuilt hotel was ruined. His poor dog was dead. Until a moment ago, he thought he'd run out of cards to play against Kemp. But perhaps one had been up his sleeve all along.

Or two.

And another good thing...

I've kissed Amelia Hunter Bradshaw and she kissed me back.

And thanks to the contents of his newly uncovered safe, he had a goodly amount of gold—at least enough to start over again. Gold was gold—in bars or melted blobs of metal. Even better, he now had Amelia in his full employ and would elevate her officially to supreme site supervisor as well as architect, once he'd fired Dick Spitz and Jake Kelly.

His vow to beat the Fairmont and open the Bay View's doors before the April anniversary of the disaster was nigh impossible to keep now, he realized, his gaze fixed on the flames dancing around the iron safe fifty feet from where he stood.

But by some miracle, his luck had held.

Except for Barbary.

CHAPTER 22

Ezra Kemp's daughter sat behind a small desk outside her father's office at the Mill Valley lumberyard. Her large, blunt-fingered hands rested on her typewriting machine, her broad shoulders hunched as if she hoped her ungainly frame might melt through the floorboards.

"Good day, Matilda," J.D. said pleasantly, hoping to put her at ease. "Helping your father, I see. Is he here?"

She stole a glance at him and then stared uneasily at the blank piece of paper rolled into the black machine. "Oh! I-Is he expecting you?"

"He won't be surprised to see me," J.D. assured the flustered soul—which was a lie—then turned the doorknob and walked into the inner office unannounced.

Kemp was sitting at his desk reading from a pile of invoices, his wire-rimmed spectacles perched at the end of his bulbous nose.

J.D. handed him a bank draft for twenty thousand dollars. "As I promised."

Kemp reared back in his chair and removed his glasses, obviously startled to receive payment. "I heard your hotel just burned down."

"Your information is correct. Here's what I owe you for the wood that was in my late, lamented hotel. I'd like a receipt."

"Where'd you get the money?" Kemp demanded suspiciously.

"From my reserves."

"What reserves? You're probably deeper in debt than you ever were."

"I believe that is a better description of *your* financial situation," J.D. replied.

Despite his own cool demeanor, J.D. felt like grabbing Kemp by the throat and squeezing the life out of him, not only for sending mismatched or unusable lengths of wood upon occasion, but also for deliberately ordering the Bay View's boilers installed incorrectly—or perhaps even having them dynamited. J.D. was sure now, after closer examination, that one of those reasons was the cause of the explosion that destroyed his brand new hotel before its doors were even open.

The silence between the men lengthened, but J.D.'s gaze never wavered.

"All right," Kemp replied finally. He pulled the bank draft toward him to examine it, then reached for a pen and scribbled on a sheet of paper proof that his debtor no longer owed him money. "Found your safe, did you?"

Ignoring Kemp's question, J.D. tucked the receipt in his pocket. "I'm sure you also heard that there were tremendous explosions before the fire started. The boilers that Dick Spitz's team installed blew up their first day of operation."

"So I understand." Kemp had the good sense not to smile, but his pudgy fingers fiddled with the papers on his desk. "Bad luck. Especially since the word I hear is Fairmont's opening on April eighteenth, as scheduled."

"Needless to say, I won't be using your crew next time," J.D. said, turning to go.

"Next time?"

"I'm starting to rebuild immediately."

"What you'll do immediately is marry my daughter."

J.D. halted, his hand on the doorknob. "And why would I do that?" He slowly turned around to face Kemp. "I owe you nothing now."

"Unless you marry Matilda, I will blackball you among my friends in the building trades and City Hall and make sure no one else around here will sign your building permits, sell you lumber, or hire on to work for you. And I'm guessing you didn't find enough money in your safe to completely rebuild the Bay View, so I plan to have a word with my colleagues on the Committee of Fifty not to advance you any more loans."

Clearly Kemp had taken off the gloves, shedding all pretensions to civility.

"And why would the Committee listen to the words of a notorious thug?"

That insult was for you, Barbary…

Kemp didn't flinch. "You're obviously a very bad risk. Some even think you're cursed for employing those Chinks. Believe me, your own father is one of my allies."

"I wouldn't rely too much on my father's loyalty. And as for the Committee of Fifty, I should warn you that one is *born* to that circle, Ezra. You cannot simply sharp elbow your way in."

Kemp's shifting gaze told J.D. more than words ever could that some of his bellicose threats were pure bluff. However, the lumber baron undoubtedly possessed the ability to sow seeds of doubts and he couldn't allow Kemp to plant his poison. Much as it disgusted him to do it, he would throw this mean dog a bone. He walked across the office and pulled up a chair.

"Since I know perfectly well you are capable of making my life miserable, perhaps you and I can find a compromise—on one condition."

"I don't think you're in a position to name conditions, J.D."

Ignoring this remark for the bluster it was, he continued, "I will consider paying Matilda court when the hotel is finished and open—but *only* if she is truly willing."

Kemp smiled faintly. "Oh, she'll be willing."

"You can't physically force your daughter to the altar, Ezra."

"Indeed I can." Kemp placed his pen on the desk.

J.D. glanced at the open door, hoping that the poor, frightened creature hadn't been privy to this entire discussion. "We'll have to see, won't we?" Before Kemp could comment, J.D. added, "One more thing. I will be buying my goods from other suppliers with no interference from you. Understood?"

Kemp's smile was even broader. "That's your decision. As long as you do as I say and court Matilda, patronize whomever you wish."

"And I will hire whomever I wish to work on-site."

"Again, that's up to you, though I offer you this friendly warning: The construction workers from the hiring hall and my political associates will come after you if you keep hiring out of Chinatown. When's the hotel to be completed?"

"By the beginning of summer."

"Impossible!"

"Watch me—which is why I'll be too busy to hold a wedding any time soon."

Kemp rose from his chair. "June is a grand time for fancy nuptials."

"But, Ezra," J.D. said, his tone just shy of insulting, "don't you know better than anyone that one can never predict what can cause delays in construction. I doubt the wedding will be in June—maybe July is more likely."

By July, let us hope that those Washington investigators like Burns will have people like Kemp behind bars.

And with that, Thayer strode through the open office door. One look at Kemp's daughter convinced him that she had overheard their entire conversation. The unfortunate creature sitting behind her desk looked as if she were about to be guillotined.

"Good-bye, Matilda." He leaned over the desk and said, barely above a whisper, "You have far less to worry about than you think." Then, in a normal tone of voice he added, "Please give my warmest regards to your school chum, Emma Stivers," J.D. said, recalling Matilda's childhood friend who was as petite as Kemp's daughter was gargantuan. "Is Miss Stivers still visiting here? I so enjoyed meeting her that night at dinner at your papa's."

Matilda nodded affirmatively and replied in a low, strangled voice, "Yes… Emma's still here… thank heavens."

"I hope you both will pay a visit to the Bay View building site in a few weeks to see how we shall rise from the ashes after our latest misfortune. As I remember, Miss Stivers had a lively interest in life in our beleaguered city following the quake."

"Yes…" Matilda said with a gulp, her eyes filling with tears. "She's ever so much more curious and informed than I about what's *au courant*." And then she suddenly buried her face in her hands, shoulders heaving.

Rattled by this outburst of emotion, J.D. mumbled good-bye and retreated into the bustling lumberyard. Several men were loading a line of wagons with milled timber that would soon be transported by barge across the bay to scores of construction sites in the recovering metropolis.

This latest confrontation with Ezra Kemp had most likely shaken poor Matilda down to her shoe tops, but J.D. figured that at least he now knew most of the cards her father was holding in his hand.

∞

J.D.'s next task was to consult with Amelia about the plans to begin at once rebuilding the twice-charred hotel.

"I want to make this hotel virtually fireproof," he announced.

J.D. rose from a wooden box and immediately bumped his head against the top of the canvas tent that Angus had liberated from Army stores on the Presidio. He swiftly resumed his seat with a rueful shrug of his shoulders.

"I'm sure we can find a design that won't burn like shingled construction and will also be perfectly suited for this site," she declared reassuringly.

J.D. thought about the other equally claustrophobic tent set up next door that provided him a place to sleep and little else. Fortunately for Amelia, the morning after the Bay View fire, the civic-minded Law brothers insisted that she retain her nun's cell in the basement of the Fairmont, despite her recent breach with Miss Morgan—and Julia had made no protest.

Or perhaps everyone was conspiring to save what remained of the young woman's reputation. James Hopper had interviewed J.D. following the spectacular fire, and the next day, the *Call* had trumpeted Miss Morgan's "protégée" Amelia Bradshaw having been selected to build the newest rendition of the Bay View for the indefatigable hotelier.

As for Amelia, she couldn't care less where she slept, so long as her new employer liked her radical ideas for the latest version of the Bay View Hotel. And if Julia was upset by the newspaper article, well, it couldn't be helped.

If J.D. wanted a design that would resist fire, she'd be more than happy to accommodate. In fact, she'd been mulling over several concepts for the lot at Taylor and Jackson and had only been waiting for the right opportunity to propose them. She launched into a brief description of the plans that had kept her up at night.

"Reinforced concrete, with terra-cotta cladding?" J.D. mused after she'd finished her excited pitch for a revolutionary design. "What about your favorite turrets?"

"I've ideas of a slightly altered version. We can't make the Bay View impervious to fire, J.D., but we've learned a lot in the last year about making structures fire-resistant. Trust me, it'll be a huge advancement from what was there before."

"Precisely what will this hotel look like?" he asked in a skeptical tone.

In response, she unrolled a large piece of paper she'd hijacked from a discarded pile of plans at the Fairmont and on the back had drawn the outline of what she was proposing. J.D. had said "fireproof" and this might be her only opportunity to offer a scheme that would both meet his requirements and be esthetically pleasing for a corner in San Francisco she still considered her special providence. Pointing to her preliminary sketch, she tried to keep her voice even.

"My concept for rebuilding the hotel this time is to create it in the same general *beaux-arts* style as the Fairmont, only make it uniquely suited to the smaller, steeper site." A few minutes later, she was nearly breathless from explaining the rest of her ideas for a new incarnation of the hostelry.

J.D. murmured, "But isn't the Bay View renowned for its Queen Anne shingled style?"

"Well, as you've said, we certainly know that a wooden

structure like the old hotel easily catches fire. And these days, wood—and especially redwood—is in short supply and most of it is controlled by blackguards like Ezra Kemp. If we build with reinforced concrete, we'd solve two problems at the same time."

"A miniature Fairmont? Interesting…"

"No, not an imitation of your competition down the road. Rather, I'm thinking it will be more like San Francisco's version of *Le Petit Trianon* in France," she replied, wondering if he'd guess she was teasing. "Wonderful entablature…"

"What's that?"

"Graceful, carved or poured concrete moldings affixed over doors and windows that give the walls a sculptured look."

J.D.'s brow furrowed in thought. "But surely you wouldn't try to copy a building that's twice the size of the structure you intend to erect?"

"No, not at all," she replied, growing serious now. "In Paris, I know of the most beautiful small hotel whose basic design could easily serve as inspiration for your site. It would be its own, perfect version of *beaux-arts* style, and be harmonious with its neighbors, including the Fairmont, to create an integrated, architectural whole atop Nob Hill."

"I see," J.D. replied with a nod that signaled he understood her basic concept.

Encouraged, Amelia said, "The Fairmont and the Merchants Exchange Building and many other structures reflect the grander, classical designs that forward-thinking planners envision for the new San Francisco. Don't you think the new Bay View should be part of that movement, and yet make its own, distinct statement?"

"And does your former employer hold the same view?" J.D. asked with a mischievous wink.

"Needless to say, I haven't discussed these ideas with Julia. In fact, she's perfectly civil when our paths cross occasionally over at the Fairmont, but there's a distinct chill in the air, believe me, especially since Hopper's absurd characterization of two women architects competing with each other atop Nob Hill."

"Well, aren't you competing?" J.D. declared.

Amelia hesitated. "I suppose we are—now. And it's sad, really. I'd love to review these ideas with her. She's absolutely brilliant with this type of design, and totally conversant with reinforced concrete as a building material, which is why I thought of building a fire-resistant *beaux-arts* structure would be so perfect at Taylor and Jackson. I also thought this would offer us a wonderful opportunity to incorporate all those principals of coherent neighborhood planning that she and I learned at L'École."

J.D. regarded Amelia intently. "So are you telling me, Amelia, that you're ready to abandon Charlie Hunter's vision at Taylor and Jackson streets?"

"What my grandfather built was a jewel in its day. But he'd be the first to agree that it's a new century. San Francisco has a larger view of itself now, a view he fought for all his life. This newest incarnation of the Bay View offers us a chance to be part of this wonderful esthetic and—"

"Let's do it," he said, cutting her short. "That is, if I like the full-scale drawings you produce." A smile tugged at the corners of his mouth, indicating that he was either laughing at Amelia's unbridled enthusiasm or joining in with it.

Amelia hesitated and then asked the question she couldn't ignore.

"And your present funds are sufficient for this noble experiment?"

"I have the funds in hand to pay for first-rate renderings," he replied. "Shall we leave it at that?" His air of joviality disappeared at the mention of money. "And now I have a question for you."

"Yes?"

"If we use poured concrete instead of wood as our primary material, does it enhance—or negate—our chances of opening our doors on or before the anniversary of the disaster?"

Amelia heaved a sigh. "You are still obsessed about beating the Fairmont, aren't you?"

"Yes… I'm afraid I am."

She felt herself smiling. "Well, it might surprise you to learn… now, so am I!" She rose from her seat. "We have six months. Normally, I'd say it's impossible, but with the use of poured concrete as our principle building material, I'd say our chances are fifty-fifty, depending on unexpected events."

And they both knew that the unexpected was bound to come in the person of one Ezra Kemp.

❦

Amelia immediately got down to the business of creating full-scale drawings of her entirely new concept for the venerable Bay View Hotel.

Meanwhile, James Hopper and the *San Francisco Call* had a field day playing up the "horse race" between the two hotels both vying to open on the first anniversary of the quake and fire. Amelia could only imagine Julia's reaction when she read the most recent headline.

RIVAL FEMALE ARCHITECTS REBUILD CITY!

Even so, not an hour passed when Amelia didn't think of Julia Morgan and her staff working at the Merchant Exchange Building, five blocks down California Street. A few days after their conference in Thayer's tent, Amelia sent word to her client that she was ready to unveil for him her detailed sketches of her creation.

J.D. collected her and the rolled-up drawings stashed in her portmanteau in the Winton and they drove out to the Cliff House a second time for their afternoon conference about the Bay View's future.

"More tea, ma'am?" the waiter inquired.

"Yes, thank you," Amelia replied, patting the valise under the table with the toe of her shoe just to confirm its precious cargo was there. "It's delicious."

Her host sat across from her, his figure framed by the large window with potted palms at either side and overlooking the spectacular view. Violin and piano music wafted in the background, its lilting sound recalling for Amelia a sense of being in Paris. Reality told her, however, that she was sitting having tea with J.D. Thayer and was anxious to know whether he'd cobbled together enough funds to proceed with the new Bay View's construction.

That is, if he approved of the designs she'd brought to their meeting.

The lavish table was covered in snowy linen, heavy silver plate, and, she judged, nearly enough sweets to feed the remaining refugees at the U.S. Presidio. Her eye roved appreciatively around the elegant expanse of the room, taking in the beautiful paneled walls that gave the space its sense of grandeur. Thank God the fire never got this far west, she thought.

She took a sip from her delicate teacup and set it in its

saucer. "Isn't it wonderful to see visitors coming to San Francisco again?" she asked, indicating the packed room and wondering when they could get down to business.

"It will be even more wonderful when they check into the Bay View come April."

Amelia laughed and wondered if J.D. Thayer was a mind reader. He was as anxious about this new project as she was. "Well, we'd better get started building it, don't you think?"

"Exactly," J.D. said. He was staring at her with intense concentration. "Are you ready to unveil your masterpiece?"

She reached into her portmanteau and handed him a clutch of furled drawings about half the dimension of full-sized building plans.

J.D. nodded at a waiter to remove his teacup, saucer, and plate of sandwiches to one side, and her employer smoothed out the schematics she'd provided. For several long minutes he stared at the rendering of a classical facade. He peered at the elevations, and then the side views. Finally, he raised his gaze to meet hers and rendered his opinion.

"I love it."

"You do?" she said on the breath she'd been holding.

"This is absolutely beautiful, Amelia."

"*Really?*" she said, looking up from her scone with undisguised pleasure.

"You seem surprised."

"Relieved is more like it. I think I mentioned that there's a small hotel in Paris on the Rue Jacob that was my inspiration. *I* love it—but others might not share my passion."

Etienne had been too frugal to ever want to spend a night in that jewel of a place, but she'd vowed to herself she would lodge there on her next trip to France. That building was only three stories high, with a handsome carriage court entrance, complete with a magnificent wrought iron fence. Molded embellishments were affixed above the windows and entranceway. A fountain stood in the center and flower beds with stone cherubs peeking from the foliage bordered the field of slate paving stones that led to the porticoed entrance. She'd adored it at first sight.

"Well, looking at what you've created here certainly makes me want to visit Paris one day because *this* is one of the loveliest things I've ever seen." J.D. pointed to the detailed drawing of a front elevation flanked by Corinthian columns and anchored by a graceful fan of low stairs that led to the hotel's entry. "I'm excited to build this hotel."

"Really?" she repeated, staggered by his openly expressed enthusiasm. "Oh my Lord, that's wonderful! I love everything about it too."

"Well, you designed it," he said, his all-too-charming smile in evidence once more. Then he grew somber. "Are you certain we can obtain the supplies we'll need?"

"Sand, water, and gravel to make poured concrete are plentiful. And steel rods from suppliers I know of back east, who helped with the Fairmont, are a lot less likely to cause you misery than Ezra Kemp and his cronies supplying you lumber. The terra-cotta cladding on the upper two floors and the scrolled embellishments affixed above the windows and doors comes from a plant near Sacramento that's in full production. We can obtain the marble or granite for the stairways and floors—depending on price, of course—from New Hampshire."

"We'll need some lumber for the foundations and molds, won't we?"

"True, but it will be nothing like building an entire hotel out of wood."

"That's music to my ears."

"And, as promised, the structure will be relatively fire resistant, so your insurance premiums should be less."

"Even better."

"We'll install emergency water systems… hoses… all the things the old hotel lacked. How's your cistern?"

"A lot of burned rubble landed on the old one," J.D. answered resignedly, "but we'll get to it, and a while back I bought the lot behind me. It was available and it was cheap since there's so much rubble from the collapse of the house that was on it. I thought we could dig an additional cistern there as well."

"Where the old woman lived who buried her dog on the day of the quake?" An involuntary shudder skimmed down Amelia's spine as a host of disturbing memories assaulted her.

J.D. nodded. "That's the one. I don't remember very much after I located Angus at the Presidio and we came back to find you that day, but I vaguely recall your misadventure next door. Didn't she brandish a weapon at you or something?"

"She shot straight at me, but I ducked." She had a vision of the old woman screaming while waving the gun in her face, then saw in her mind's eye the dog's corpse, wrapped in a blanket, about to be laid into a traveling trunk. She could almost hear the incessant clamor of the fire brigades and smell the acrid scent of smoke that lingered for weeks. And could she ever forget the vacant stares of the damaged souls who never recovered their wits or the awful vision of Ling Lee's arm…

It seemed astonishing that she and J.D. Thayer could be sitting at the posh Cliff House, sipping tea, and recalling those ghastly events with such seeming casualness.

"J.D.?"

He set the drawing aside. "What?"

"Do you ever have… moments when thoughts about April eighteenth come back and—"

She fell silent, at a loss to describe the scenes of remembered horror that still lingered during her waking hours—and in her dreams.

"Yes."

"You *do*?"

"Yes, I do."

"Then I'm not mad when these unexpected bits of memory come crashing in and my palms perspire and I can't catch my breath?"

"If you are mad, then so am I and half of San Francisco too, I expect."

Relieved to see he understood, she ducked her head and hastened to change the topic. "With all that charred debris laying about, can you get to your own cistern?"

"I think so, and relatively soon. I had Loy's men clear much of that area at night this week. We can enlarge the old well without too much trouble, I believe, and connect it to the new cistern we'll build on the old lady's property, once we remove the rest of the rubble. Again."

"Then we should have all the water we need, plus the new back lot will provide for a lovely lower garden by the time we're finished." She pulled her father's watch from her pocket. "Goodness, look at the time! Can you give me a lift back? I must run if I'm going to get back to the Ferry Building and catch the boat. I'm seeing my Aunt Margaret in Oakland this weekend."

"By the way," he said, signaling to the waiter for the check, "I'll want my site supervisor to move to the Bay View as soon as we have a roof over our heads so there can always be someone on hand for deliveries. Also, I'd rather no one know my business at the Fairmont."

She was startled by his proposal, for she just assumed she'd continue living in her basement cell. When she hesitated, J.D. added, "I assure you that you'll have your own room. With a lock," he concluded pointedly. "I want it completely understood that *you* are to supervise every aspect of the construction. I want the building I see in these drawings and nothing less. Hartland Law told me how you handled those thugs sent by the mayor's office who attempted to extort more jobs for their cronies. I want that same, stalwart vigilance on my project."

"So you've checked me out with your competitor?"

"Of course I did. Who knows what trouble we might run into as we proceed? I needed to be sure you could handle unpleasant encounters with the likes of Spitz."

"And Ezra Kemp." It was a statement, not a question.

"Yes… him and any other of his cronies, including my father, who might prefer I not offer *them* any competition."

"You mean other new hotels are on the drawing boards?"

"This group always has plans afoot," he replied obliquely.

"And we thought the Fairmont was your chief rival," she said with a rueful smile.

"The Law brothers are gentlemen. We'll have a race to the finish, to be sure, but I don't think they'd blow up my building to win."

His gaze returned to the drawings, and he appeared to be drinking them in.

"Now that I've seen your designs, Amelia, I'm pleased you suggested reinforced concrete. It solves a host of difficulties. And the lines of the hotel are magnificent." He rolled up the sketches and rested them in his lap. "I think your work is first rate."

His bald, unequivocal compliment took her breath away.

"Why, thank you," she murmured.

He regarded her for a long moment. "Strange how things sometimes evolve in this life, isn't it, Amelia?"

She could only stare at him across the pristine linen, wondering what Grandfather Hunter would have thought about the bizarre sequence of events following his death.

Time seemed to freeze between them. The memory of J.D. kissing her after her driving lesson rose up and she tried, unsuccessfully, to push the thought from her mind.

"Yes, life can be very strange indeed," she answered finally. "I appreciate your kind words about my work. Building this won't be easy. There is such a dearth of qualified craftsmen, but I have an idea to go directly to Little Italy and recruit there, if you think that makes sense, Mr. Thayer."

"Amelia, if we're going to do this project together day in, day out, we might as well be on a first-name basis."

There was no way she could keep from smiling. "I admit that I've done my best to maintain decorum, but perhaps you've noticed we've been on a first-name basis—on and off—for quite awhile now."

She wondered if he ever thought of their driving lesson at the Presidio parade grounds, or their kissing in front of the restaurant? Most likely, a man like Thayer considered it merely an advantageous moment to...

J.D. flashed her a crooked grin. "Well, since we'll be working together in close quarters, I just thought it was a sensible idea to make this first name business official."

"Fine," she replied. "'J.D.' it is then."

Now all she had to do was build the building—and keep her door locked.

CHAPTER 23

ONCE AGAIN, LOY CHEN had provided the manpower—working nights only—to clear scorched rubble from the front of the property. As sections were freed of debris, Amelia had the day workers laying the foundations for the new hotel and soon the first batch of concrete was poured into the molds. Rows of square-shaped, spiral twisted steel bars, fourteen feet high, stood ready to be clad in still more concrete as the walls for the first floor rose swiftly along the same perimeter as the previous two hotels that had occupied the site.

Each workday, Amelia donned one of several pairs of her father's old trousers, worn beneath her blue serge skirt that Aunt Margaret had sent back with her from Oakland. To these she added a plain shirtwaist, warm jacket, and sturdy boots, arriving at Taylor and Jackson streets by five-thirty in the morning. Typically, the bay was socked in with fog until the late autumn sun burned it off around noon.

From Amelia's very first day on-site, her spirits began to rise. She felt back in her element, working in the out-of-doors, dealing with the crews of cement pourers, masons, carpenters, and suppliers. She and J.D. had recruited workers from Little Italy along Columbus Street who offered their skills and were willing to guarantee that from the plans she'd drawn, a beautiful, well-built structure would rise.

"This is marvelous," J.D. exclaimed when he and Angus McClure climbed out of the Winton one morning in early December on a mission to inspect the latest phase of construction. Large tubs of sand, limestone, water, and gravel were being mixed to make huge batches of concrete to construct the second and third floors.

Angus reached out and ran his palm over the rough surfaces, a wry smile on his face. "The walls are certainly going up fast, but I must say, Amelia, it looks a bit forbidding. Like a medieval fortress, wouldn't you say?"

Amelia dusted off the sand from her hands and laughed, relieved that Angus was behaving like his old self after that evening at Tadich's a few months before when—to her total astonishment—he'd hinted that he was considering another formal offering for her hand, and she'd gently refused him.

Since that night, Angus had not broached the topic again, which seemed to indicate that he'd also concluded that their relationship was better left as simple friendship.

Amelia pointed to a slab of concrete to their right. "Don't either of you judge anything about this building until we put on the terra-cotta cladding and apply the molded ornamentation," she cautioned good-naturedly, referring to pre-poured sections that resembled chiseled stonework and were virtually glued to the rougher concrete that formed the interior walls. "By the time I'm through, you'll think you've got yourself a Parisian villa."

"Terra-cotta cladding? What's it made of?" Angus asked.

"Gladding McBean, near Sacramento, has been making the stuff for years. They mix up huge sheets of clay, threaded with steel mesh for stability. Then they bake it in a gigantic kiln, like bread. They cool it, apply a glaze, and bake it again."

"Like making chinaware," J.D. mused.

"Exactly!" Amelia exclaimed, relieved J.D. grasped the process.

"Isn't it breakable?" asked Angus, brow furrowed.

"Yes, but they pack the sheets in padded crates and ship them to us by train, now that the rail system is working again. Once the masons plaster the sheets onto the concrete walls, you'll think they're blocks of stone. The ornamentation around the windows and doors is made of the same material and poured into molds to make the various entablature look like stone arches, acanthus leaves, or rosettes. Whatever you like."

"I think rosettes are a bit much, don't you, Angus?" J.D. observed dryly. "Leaves or simple arches will be just fine, thank you."

"My, you *have* studied those catalogues I gave you," Amelia teased.

❦

Amelia barely noticed when Christmas came and went. She found herself working daily at the Bay View and still sleeping each night once again in the basement of the Fairmont Hotel. The rains had set in and slowed their work on the top floor.

Despite their proximity, Amelia rarely ran into Julia Morgan, who was allowing Ira to attend to the daily oversight of the ongoing restoration of the larger hotel while the head of the Morgan firm forged ahead on the many other projects offered her in the post-quake building frenzy.

Amelia pitied poor J.D, still camping out on his property in an Army tent in dreadfully foul weather, but she knew he would soon have a roof over his head. Meanwhile, he preferred to save his funds for the tons of cement she had on order.

"Amelia, dear," Aunt Margaret complained when she

heard that her niece was soon to be housed at the same location as her male client, "I'm not at all happy with this arrangement of you working every day with nothing but men, let alone sleeping without a chaperon where your employer resides. I just hope that old busybody ferryman doesn't hear about this. You know what a gossip that Harold Jasper can be."

"Shou Shou can serve as my chaperon," Amelia replied.

"A former Chinese—" Margaret halted mid-sentence, and then added worriedly, "That certainly won't silence a man like Mr. Jasper."

"Well, everybody in San Francisco knows by this time that a natural disaster tends to create strange bedfellows," Amelia replied, thinking that, in her case, that was certainly true. And then corrected herself silently.

Housemates, Amelia… not bedfellows, surely!

❧

Loy Chen's men continued their stealthy routine of coming to work after sunset to dig a larger, deeper cistern behind the hotel where the house of the wealthy old woman who'd shot at Amelia had once stood. Soon the two cisterns would be joined, guaranteeing the Bay View had more than ample supply of water for its guests—and to fight fires.

By the end of January in the struggling metropolis, the basement levels and first floor of the new, *new* Bay View had their interior walls and ceilings plastered and were fit for marginal habitation. J.D. folded his tent and took up residence in the basement headquarters. He soon had set up his own temporary sleeping quarters and office now that the plaster had been applied and finally, thoroughly dried. Soon, Loy, Shou Shou, and little Foo followed suit, moving into various empty rooms and cooking for the owner, as well as providing clean laundry.

Amelia figured she'd make her move once the locks on the downstairs doors were installed. Given her own untrustworthy feelings when it came to her employer, such prudence seemed the only sensible plan.

❧

As for J.D., though he often found himself musing about the admirable Miss Bradshaw more often than was prudent, he dared not postpone paying a call on Matilda Kemp another day or risk antagonizing her father even more.

Thus, one surprisingly warm winter afternoon, he found himself at Ezra Kemp's front door in Mill Valley. Fortunately, he was greeted in the foyer by the exuberant Miss Emma Stivers. Her unpleasant host was apparently attending to business at the lumberyard.

"Would you like to see Matilda's studio at the bottom of the garden, Mr. Thayer?" asked Emma. "She's just finished a lovely piece of sculpture."

J.D. was relieved that this visit to Matilda's private domain would at least provide a diversion from the stuffy parlor in which they presently sipped tea and tried to ignore the long silences.

"Oh *no*, Emma." Matilda flushed with embarrassment and turned her head toward the fireplace. "Mr. Thayer cannot have any interest—"

"Oh, but your friend Miss Stivers is quite correct," J.D. interrupted. "I would enjoy seeing your work. Very much. And hers as well."

Anything to make the time pass faster.

"I merely dabble in watercolors to avoid feeling useless when Matilda attacks her clay," Emma protested good-naturedly. "Or I read a book. Life in Mill Valley is sublimely uneventful, it seems."

Emma Stivers's laughing glance put J.D. at his ease. Except for her charming banter, the weekly chore of "paying court" to Matilda Kemp had increasingly become a burden—but his efforts had, indeed, paid a decent dividend: Kemp and his cronies had kept their distance from the accelerated building project at Taylor and Jackson.

During these strange appointments, Kemp would return from his lumberyard in downtown Mill Valley to join in the tedious business of the dinner hour inside his stone-and-timber fortress. The host would then demand that J.D. stay the night in his guest quarters and J.D. would politely but firmly insist that he make his way back to San Francisco with a promise for a return visit the following week.

All this to keep Kemp from making my life miserable with the Committee of Fifty and his building supplier…

J.D. often found himself wondering during sham rendezvous like today's what his architect would think if she knew the onerous lengths he'd gone to see the Bay View open its doors first among the city's hotels.

Matilda was a nice enough woman, he mused, watching her big hands fidget nervously in her lap. The poor creature was mortally shy and terminally ungainly, and her apparent distress over her father's callous treatment elicited J.D.'s sympathy. Kemp's naked attempt to barter his daughter's welfare to gain a toehold in San Francisco society seemed as despicable as that of any Chinese highbinder.

Emma's voice interrupted his mental meandering. "Mr. Thayer? Shall we walk to the bottom of the garden now?"

"Ah, yes. The studio." He rose from the tea table and extended each lady an arm. "I'd be delighted."

Matilda's retreat lay beyond the terraced garden that descended toward the fast-running creek parallel to the road leading from Mill Valley proper. Like the main house, the one-room stone cottage featured windows framed by thick redwood casements. When the sun shone, leaded glass cast a rainbow of light on the Persian carpet. The shingle roof was covered with the ubiquitous moss spawned by the luxuriant damp of the steep-sided canyon. Stands of redwoods towered overhead, throwing long shadows across the surrounding banks of flowers and ferns. J.D. found the serene coolness of the place soothing.

"For most of the year, the large window here captures whatever afternoon sunlight there might be," said Emma, pointing to a wall made of floor-to-ceiling paned glass. A river rock fireplace in one corner glowed invitingly, alight with neatly cut wood.

In the center of the studio stood a potter's wheel. On it was a clay sculpture of a woman's head that J.D. recognized instantly as a likeness of Emma Stivers.

"Why, Matilda, this is a wonderfully true-to-life rendition." He turned toward the gawky twenty-seven-year-old and smiled. "I believe you're very talented."

Matilda blushed, and in that instant, her awkwardness grew ten-fold.

"Y-You're too kind," she murmured.

"She is *quite* good, isn't she, Mr. Thayer?" Emma said eagerly. She traced her forefinger along the bridge of the clay figure's nose. "She's caught my profile exactly."

"I should say so."

And a very comely profile it is too, J.D. thought.

He regarded Emma Stivers more closely. Clearly, she was her school friend's biggest booster and had remained in Mill

Valley much longer than he would have imagined such a lively, outgoing woman would find amusing. She was an attractive young person, with a trim waist; high, rounded bosom; and slender, graceful neck. Her clothes were of current fashion and high quality. He wondered about the circumstances of her life and family before she'd come west. Her cheery, though rather detached, demeanor intrigued him. Emma was quick to engage in friendly conversation with him whenever he visited the Kemp household, but she was no flirt and there was something about her he didn't quite fathom.

For no particular reason, J.D. again thought of Amelia Bradshaw and the spirited exchanges he'd had with her during the past few months. Emma and Amelia were rather alike in some ways—equally attractive and intelligent young women, yet Amelia was much more direct and *much* more to his taste and—

Now why am I making such absurd comparisons?

Both women, given the bizarre circumstances in his life currently, were definitely off limits to any random speculations about their individual charms.

Of course he hadn't felt that way in the Winton when Amelia had navigated the motorcar successfully from her driving lesson at the Presidio to the entrance to Tadich's. Kissing her that day *should* have been off limits, but he just couldn't help himself... and apparently, neither could she.

Just then, his self-censored thoughts were abruptly interrupted when Ezra Kemp appeared at the door of the studio.

"Thayer!" He ignored his daughter and her friend. "I want to see you in my study before dinner is served." He glanced at the two women and then at the piece of sculpture standing in the middle of the room. "I won't have that put in the garden, Matilda, so you'd better find some other place for it. A closet perhaps."

Matilda darted a mortified glance at her female guest and stammered, "B-But Clarence thought—"

"I pay Clarence to please *my* tastes on these grounds. A bust of your mother near the fern grotto is quite enough, thank you. You'll make the place look like a mausoleum." To J.D. he said, "Let's go."

Kemp made no offer of libation when they reached his paneled inner sanctum. Instead he sat behind his desk and glowered. "City Hall says get rid of those Chinks or they'll shut down your construction."

J.D. felt a stab of alarm. Loy and his crew had nearly cleared the old lady's lot the previous night and could continue digging the new cistern tonight. By tomorrow, or Friday at the latest, he'd be done with using Chinese labor for a while, which would reduce his exposure to prying eyes that might report him to the Committee of Fifty, his principle source of future funding. He couldn't wait until the day he could call a halt to sneaking Chinese onto his property, not to mention ending these tortuous visits to Mill Valley to "court" poor Matilda.

"The rubble will be gone in two days' time," he replied, affecting a shrug. "Tell them they have my word on that."

"Face it, J.D. Your fool cement bunker has already eaten up all the funds you found in your safe, hasn't it? You don't have a plug nickel right now and can't afford for me to raise questions about your illegal hiring practices with the Committee of Fifty."

So Kemp hadn't *yet* played this card with the Committee—or his father.

"You're right," J.D. agreed pleasantly. "But by now the point is moot. I'm virtually done with using Chinese labor at the site." He glanced at the watch dangling at his waist. Sears Roebuck's best. "I've so enjoyed my time with your daughter and Miss Stivers this afternoon, but I'm afraid I must depart before dinner."

"You may not be staying to dinner, but you're *marrying* Matilda, Thayer. Either that or, I warn you, there are many more ways I can think of to ruin your plans at Taylor and Jackson."

"Until next week?" J.D. said, smoothly ignoring this latest of Kemp's threats.

❧

A few hours before dawn, Amelia was abruptly awakened by someone pounding on the door to her small room in the Fairmont's basement. She was due to move over to the Bay View very soon and leapt out of bed at the thought that something terrible had happened at J.D.'s hotel— yet again.

"Missy! Missy, come! Bad men hurt boss man! Come! Come!"

"What?" Amelia was still too sleepy to be self-conscious about wearing her nightclothes in front of a Chinese laundryman who was whispering hoarsely at her from the door of her bedchamber.

"We need doctor! He very sick in Chinatown. Come quick!"

"*Who* is very sick, Loy?"

"Boss at Bay View!"

"Mr. Thayer?"

"Yes! He very, *very* bad."

"Good heavens!" she exclaimed. "Wait outside while I dress."

Fortunately, Julia wasn't there to hear all this commotion. She had taken the last ferry to Oakland and wasn't sleeping at the Fairmont this night.

Loy stood outside Amelia's door as she scrambled into her clothing. Her fingers were trembling as she buttoned the fastenings on her shirtwaist and donned her boots without bothering to find her stockings. Why in the world would J.D. be in Chinatown at this hour? Unflappable Loy had said he was "very, very bad," which could only mean something truly dreadful had happened.

"We get Dr. Angus?" Loy asked as they ran down Taylor Street toward the Bay View. Amelia could just make out the Winton parked in front of the entrance.

"Yes," she said breathlessly. "I'll drive to the Presidio to get him. Then we'll go to Chinatown."

In minutes she was trotting beside Loy, racing to the spot where the Winton was parked in front of the Bay View.

"What happened, Loy?" she said, panting from exertion. "Where, exactly, *is* Mr. Thayer?"

"Bad men came tonight and hit him. Hit Chinese too. Chinese all run away. Bad men took him in wagon to China Alley."

"Chinese men did this?"

"No. Round-eyes. They hurt Mr. J.D. very, very bad," he repeated.

So the Chinese called Caucasians unflattering names as well, she thought.

Fortunately, the Winton started right up when Loy turned the crank, hopped into the passenger seat, and Amelia sped away from the curb in a squeal of wheels. She didn't allow herself to focus on J.D.'s condition in some hellhole a few blocks away and, instead, allowed the sheer panic that had taken hold to force her to concentrate on piloting the vehicle down Lombard Street as if the Devil himself were chasing their tailpipe.

"Very, very bad" could mean the worst had already happened…

As they barreled through the night toward the Presidio and the possibility of recruiting medical help, Loy shouted through the wind, "We almost finish out back just as bad men come. Many others hurt too, missy."

Amelia felt wretched to think Loy's friends had come to grief on a job she'd secured for them.

"Do you know why they attacked Mr. Thayer?"

Perhaps J.D. had been gambling and neglected to pay his debts. Or maybe some old lover of Ling Lee's decided to even the score.

"Bad men no like Chinese working for Boss. Banged on heads with sticks…"

Sick at heart, Amelia focused her gaze on the road ahead and suddenly swerved just in time to avoid running over a dog that had wandered onto Lombard Street.

"Ahhhh…" Loy cried. "Missy bad driver!"

"I'm a *good* driver!"

"Hurry, but careful! Mr. Thayer maybe dead now. Doctor will know."

"You actually think he might be *dead*?" Loy's words echoed her own terrified thoughts. She pressed harder on the accelerator. Fear gripped her stomach and made her short of breath. What if he'd actually been killed?

Amelia fought a mental picture of J.D. lying dead in some dark alley a few blocks away. A lump rose in her throat. She couldn't deny she was close to tears over the possibility that the notorious James Diaz Thayer had been shanghaied—or worse. She strained to hear Loy's words buffeted by the wind whistling past the open-air car.

"I follow bad men down Jackson Street. To China Alley. Wait long time outside. Then, go see Mr. J.D. He not speak. So come find you. You bring doctor."

If he were still alive, would they be able to get help to him in time?

Amelia steeled herself as the Winton's tires screeched once again when she rounded a corner at high speed.

❧

Angus McClure was easily awoken, having spent his adult life being roused for such emergencies. Within fifteen minutes, Amelia had wheeled the motorcar to a halt on a steep incline on Jackson Street next to a narrow alleyway.

"You'll have to come inside with us," Angus directed. "It's not safe for anyone, especially a Caucasian woman, to be in this neighborhood in the wee hours. Stay close."

Loy led them down a narrow, steep-sided lane that smelled of urine and chickens and strange herbal scents that Amelia couldn't begin to identify. All the windows had iron bars designed to keep thieves out and the harlots in. Sad, silent faces peered out at them as the trio moved gingerly along the shadowy cobbled walkway in an alley that was half new construction, half burned out hulks.

Shou Shou and Ling Lee once lived near here…

Amelia could hardly bear to look at the poor creatures staring back at her, Asian women who were slaves in a country where some white women already had the vote! It was revolting. No wonder Donaldina Cameron had become their devoted advocate.

Loy pounded his fist repeatedly on a door at the end of

the alley. Finally, someone opened its little sliding window and peered out. After a lengthy, high-pitched exchange with much gesturing on Loy's part, the door itself swung open and Amelia caught a whiff of what she could only assume was opium smoke.

"Follow closely and don't say anything," Angus ordered.

"I'll try not to breathe either."

Amelia pulled her shawl more tightly around her head and shoulders and ducked her chin to her chest as they made their way through several foul-smelling corridors where tiny rooms branched off on both sides. Rough-hewn beds, cribs really, were built into the walls. Half naked women and effeminate young boys lolled beside glazed-eyed men snoring in drug-induced sleep. An odor of cooked cabbage nearly made Amelia gag, but she forced herself to swallow and keep up with Angus and Loy.

At length, they halted at a closet-sized room shaped like the others they'd seen. On the bed lay J.D., still and deathly pale, sprawled across a filthy mattress devoid of any covering beyond soiled ticking. An empty leather pouch used for carrying coins and nuggets lay at his side. For all intents and purposes, the man was nude, his trousers pulled down to his knees. His shirt—bloodied from a beating to his arms, ribs, and face—was wrapped around his shoulders and neck.

"Amelia, stand outside," Angus barked.

"Don't be absurd," Amelia exclaimed, advancing into the cramped quarters. "You and I dealt with far worse at the Presidio."

Angus leaned down and listened to J.D.'s chest.

"Robbed, beaten, and left for dead," he muttered, swiftly opening his medical bag. "Well, at least he's breathing."

"Oh thank God!" Relief swept through her, leaving

her almost giddy. "Do you think he's got another set of cracked ribs?"

"He's badly bruised, but I think his ribs withstood the pounding." He bent down and sniffed Thayer's hair. "Opium."

"Will it kill him?"

"I hope not."

Amelia thought she might be sick if they didn't immediately escape from this nightmarish hole. "Well, don't you think we should remove him at once?"

"Yes. Let's get him home." Angus pulled up J.D.'s trousers and together, the physician and Amelia, pulled down his shirt and put his jacket on his battered torso as gently as they could.

"Angus?"

J.D.'s voice was barely above a whisper.

"Yes, you idiot," Angus replied.

"What's she doing here?"

"More to the point, laddie, what are *you* doing here?"

"Kemp."

"Kemp did this?" Amelia said with a gasp. "*Why?*"

"Chinese workers…" he gasped.

"The man is such a patriot," Angus noted dryly.

"Would seem so. Sent bullyboys to warn me…"

"Or kill you," Angus countered.

Amelia couldn't believe what she was hearing. She knew Ezra Kemp was a rather boorish specimen, but she'd never known anyone who would shanghai his own associate!

She thought of the well-dressed, supposedly "respectable" white men she'd just glimpsed indulging their baser instincts in this opium-filled warren. She found it beyond shocking to learn just how sordid and depraved the underhanded dealings of the city's wealthier male citizens could be. Despite her view of herself as a sophisticated world traveler, she had never viewed the underbelly of society like this and it appalled her. Just as Julia had always warned her, it was a Man's World, all right, and she wanted no part of it.

Angus helped J.D. struggle to a sitting position. "Do you think you can walk to the motorcar outside?"

"Of course he can't walk!" Amelia exclaimed as J.D. closed his eyes and slumped against Angus.

His chest appeared as immobile as his ashen face. Could he have just died? Dumbly, she stared at him, a wall of emotion building inside.

Oh, J.D. No! No! NO…

Then she heard him groan and again, relief flooded through her so intensely, she realized in some distant corner of her mind that the world had titled on its axis just now as surely as it had on the day of the quake.

"Angus, let's *go!*" she pleaded. "We've got to get him out of here!"

"Loy, you take one side," Angus ordered, "and I'll take the other. Amelia, you get the doors."

Half carrying, half dragging J.D., they transported him to the vehicle parked in China Alley. With Amelia at the wheel, Angus and Loy looked after the patient stretched out in the Winton's backseat during the short ride from the brothel up the hill, to the Bay View Hotel. Together, the three ferried him to his room enclosed only with raw concrete and laid him on the brass bed Sears and Roebuck had recently delivered to the building site.

J.D.'s injuries amounted to several nasty bruises to his chest and arms, two blackened eyes, a gash on his forehead—adding to the scars he'd received in the quake—and a sprained wrist. The opium he had inhaled was apparently the cause of his semi-consciousness.

"You're not too bad, considering the fix you were in, laddie," Angus muttered. In a louder voice he asked, "What is your name?"

"You know my name, you fool," J.D. muttered, eyes closed.

From the foot of the bed Amelia asked loudly, "J.D., do you know where you are?"

"Hell," came the short answer.

CHAPTER 24

Hell was certainly the place J.D. Thayer appeared to have visited while in Chinatown. Amelia felt a surge of pity well up in her chest, revolted that human beings should continue to treat each other appallingly. Hadn't the earthquake and fire been cruel enough? Her heaviness of heart felt akin to the grief she carried for the loss of her father and grandfather.

Angus commanded Amelia as if she were still a nurse at the Presidio. "Here, get these filthy clothes off him. I'll set up my medical kit."

As she'd learned to do during the quake emergency, she efficiently divested J.D. of his garments, keeping her eyes glued to his face. Loy had fetched a bowl of warm water and two strips of cloth that she and Angus put to immediate use, washing J.D.'s bruised body from head to toe.

By silent, mutual consent, Amelia cleansed the grime from the patient's torso while the doctor dealt with regions below the waist and applied a liquid tincture to the patient's cuts.

"Like old times at the Presidio, eh, Amelia?" Angus said.

She nodded, gently scrubbing the filth from J.D.'s forehead where the scars from wounds made on the day of the quake reminded her of that terrible time the three of them had shared. The tanned flesh around Thayer's eyes was turning purple and was already puffy. The shell of one of his ears was red from the beating he'd taken, and Amelia felt a surge of outrage against men like Kemp and his ilk.

An impulse to cradle J.D.'s head against her chest and try to ease his pain suddenly came over her, feelings she quickly reined in with a glance at Angus, who fortunately appeared intent on the tasks at hand.

J.D.'s eyelids suddenly opened as she patted his cheeks and chin with the moistened cloth. "Thank you…" he murmured, and closed his eyes again. "Funny how you're the one who always does the rescuing…"

"Shhh…" She was buoyed by the conviction that his teasing words probably meant he would survive this terrible night. "Just sleep now."

"Here's a nightshirt," Angus announced. "I found it on a peg. Let's get it on 'im."

A few minutes later, Amelia made her way to the hotel's makeshift kitchen where Shou Shou had left a low fire burning in the stove and a tin of tea. Amelia brewed a pot, along with some bread that she lightly toasted on the hob. Heading back to the sickroom, she passed Angus in the hallway carrying the bowl of dirty water and a bundle of soiled clothes to give to Loy, who was waiting out back. She suddenly felt exhausted and longed for sleep.

"I'll just give him this cup and then shall I drive you back to the Presidio?"

"No… I'd better keep a watch on him till morning. See if he'll drink it. I'll be back in a few minutes."

When she reentered J.D.'s bedroom, an oil lamp turned low on a side table cast the corners in deep shadow. The patient was now propped against pillows and was staring vacantly into space.

Amelia set the teapot on a packing crate beside the bed

and poured a cup. "I thought you'd be fast asleep by now. Here, this might make you feel a bit better."

"Thank you, but I doubt it. The way I feel right now might well be terminal."

Amelia smiled at his attempt to joke and sat on the edge of the bed. "Well, at least those ruffians didn't beat your sense of humor out of you. Come, just have a sip." As she'd seen the Presidio nurses do, and had done countless times herself as a volunteer at the refugee sites, she put an arm around his shoulders and lifted the cup to his lips with her other hand. His own hands shook as he enveloped hers to hold on to the mug. "That's it... there you go," she murmured, and eased the rim to his lips.

He took a sip. "You made this?"

"Tea, coffee, and toast are the only things in a kitchen I know how to do. Is it drinkable?"

"It's wonderful. Thank you."

She broke off a bit of toast and fed it to him. "I'm happy to see they didn't kill you."

He arched an eyebrow. "You are? Are you sure?"

"J.D., for heavens sake!" She was uncommonly disturbed, somehow, that he might believe she took any pleasure in his most recent misfortune, despite their adversarial relationship before the quake. "Believe me, the one lesson I learned from April eighteenth is to value life over property. I was afraid tonight they'd left you for dead." She deliberately caught his glance and held it. "I've just driven you home from that hellhole. I washed the filth off your body, and I've made you some tea. What else should I do to convince you I'm really, truly glad you're still alive?"

He had the good grace to murmur, "Apologies, Amelia. I'd probably be dead if you hadn't fetched Angus from the Presidio."

"It was Loy who fetched *me* and then I fetched Angus. But there's something I want you to know."

She leaned forward to force him to look at her, amazed by her own forwardness. For some reason, she didn't care about propriety. J.D. was alive and had cheated death for a second time. Maybe the fact they'd both witnessed so much destruction made her reckless. The night's dramatic events had drawn her closer to this man, in spite of his unseemly life that embodied everything she wished to avoid in her own.

His eyes were clear now and staring into hers, and as she had felt when she found him in the rubble of the old Bay View, she had the eerie sense they were the last people on earth.

"What do you want me to know?" he asked quietly.

Before either of them knew what she was doing, she drew closer to brush her lips against his forehead. She could tell he was startled by her touch—and her candor—for he lowered his eyes to the coverlet that she'd pulled up chastely beneath his arms.

"It rather surprises me too, J.D.," she murmured against his skin, "to discover how very glad I am to see you're going to be all right."

"Ah… Amelia." She could see he was bone weary and slipping toward slumber again. "It would seem we make a habit of rescuing each other from the jaws of disaster."

"Or so it appears."

Amelia suddenly sensed someone was standing at the threshold to J.D.'s bedchamber.

"Well, well," said a voice from across the room.

Amelia turned around on the edge of J.D.'s bed to see Angus leaning against the doorway. How long he'd been there, she couldn't hazard a guess.

"Giving aid and comfort to the enemy?" Angus pushed

his shoulder off the doorjamb and advanced into the room. "You are a true humanitarian, Amelia."

Annoyed by his sarcasm, she removed the cup from J.D.'s hand, set it firmly on the table, and rose from the patient's bedside. She quickly assumed her Nurse Bradshaw demeanor.

"Now that you've returned, good Dr. McClure, I shall take my leave," she announced briskly. "I should think, Angus, that you'd be glad to see your two friends getting on so well for once."

She glanced at J.D., who by this time had closed his eyes and appeared to have dozed off again. Loy stood behind Angus in the doorway, peering in at the patient.

"Workers not come here now," he said with a worried look.

"Can you find new ones?" Angus asked.

Not easily after what happened last night, Amelia thought. Who knew better than she the labor difficulties J.D. was up against?

"Maybe find some more," Loy offered, but his face was the picture of doubt. "Mr. J.D. need pay more money, though. My friends afraid now."

"Tell them I'll stand guard while they work," Angus volunteered. He appeared to have reverted to his usual good humor where J.D. was concerned and patted the pistol tucked into his belt. "The brass at the Presidio owe me some leave. I can help out here for a few days until J.D. finally uncovers his cistern. The sooner you get this hotel up and running, the better for everyone."

Amelia reached for her shawl, musing that Angus and J.D. might be right—Kemp might very well prefer his former partner to disappear and somehow secure the hotel for himself. *Did J.D. still owe the man money*, she wondered. He'd paid off the original gambling club's construction costs, but there were probably still some unpaid bills for wood used in the first reconstruction of the Bay View.

You're just the architect, not the man's nursemaid or accountant...

"I'll leave you to sort this all out," she said. "Good night, everyone." She peered down at J.D. whose eyes were now at half-mast. "Feel better soon, Mr. Thayer," she added primly, reverting to his second name.

"I take back what I said to Angus about your driving," he murmured. "You didn't do badly on those hills."

"I'll consider that high praise then. Get some rest."

Angus declared. "I'll see you home."

"That's not necessary, Angus. Good night."

Amelia left Thayer's room, striding toward the front door of the lobby. The rough cement walls were so very different from the hotel her grandfather had built. Everything felt utterly foreign without the tall, ornate mirrors that hung on the first floor lobby in the old hotel.

And without grandfather...

Had she built a folly? Would anyone like what she'd done, even when it was finished? The new gas lighting fixtures were already installed, though not yet supplied with fuel. She cast an educated eye at the window casements facing Taylor Street, which fortunately appeared perfectly in plumb. The seams on the granite slabs that formed the front steps lined up perfectly. In all, the construction work was first rate, which cheered her on this gloomy night. She continued outdoors into the moisture-laden predawn, surprised to sense Angus suddenly at her heels.

"Amelia. Wait a minute."

By this time she was about to give the Winton's starting crank a spin. Angus strode to the front of the car and insisted on doing the honors. Amelia took the driver's seat and when the motor caught, he approached the vehicle's left side, apparently anxious to make amends for his sharp words earlier.

"Take care now, lassie," he offered, handing her the crank to stow on the floor of the passenger side. "I'd have you on my medical team anytime."

She smiled, relieved that the chill between them had evaporated. Angus was a good friend and someone she would always admire. He had leapt to his comrade's aid without question or qualm.

"Well, thank you, sir," she replied and winked. "May I properly be called an ambulance driver now?"

"I'd call you a battlefield veteran, to be sure," he murmured. Then, without warning, he bent forward to kiss her on the lips. Dumbfounded by this move, Amelia instinctively pulled back and stared into his pale blue eyes. "Surely," he said, "it's time for you to be in bed, lass. Let me escort you back to the Fairmont."

"Angus, I—"

His kiss had not been at all brotherly and that disturbed her. She shook her head emphatically. "And neglect your patient? I wouldn't hear of it." She wanted Angus for a *friend,* not a suitor. She enjoyed his company but felt not a flutter of physical attraction for him. It would be cruel to allow him to think of her in any other capacity than a good companion, especially since his friend J.D. had kissed her and—

That has nothing to do with this!

"Loy can mind Jamie for a bit while I see you home," Angus was saying. "I want to be sure you get back all right."

She made a show of pulling her driving gloves on more securely while she searched for an answer to fend him off.

"It's only four blocks, Angus. I've just driven thirty. I'll be fine." She put the car in gear and looked at him expectantly, willing him to take his foot off the running board. He did, with obvious reluctance, and she sped off into the night.

By the time she'd driven the short distance that separated the Bay View from the Fairmont, she felt bone-deep exhaustion. She came to a halt in the new garage at the back of the property where the construction shed was but a memory. Reflexively glancing into the shadows to be sure she was alone, she moved quickly over the terrain and inside the back door of the hotel. It had been a frightening, disturbing night and she locked the door securely, feeling as if some drugged predator from Chinatown might jump from the darkness to attack her.

Scolding herself for such silliness, she moved down the gloomy corridor and let herself into her small room off the kitchen, locking that door as well. She undressed, wondering if she'd be able to fall asleep before it would be time to drag herself out of bed and begin another long, arduous day.

It hardly seemed possible, but soon, the scaffolding would come down on this building and the owners of the Fairmont would host a gala anniversary reception. In contrast, the Bay View had yet to get its roof on and its second cistern completed, not to mention all the finishing yet to be done on the interior and exterior. This latest setback involving an attack on the Bay View's owner would only delay them further, not to mention having to recruit even more workers and pay them higher wages.

If J.D. had intended the Bay View Hotel to beat the Fairmont's scheduled opening by a week or more, as rumored, Kemp's hooligans had certainly left that plot in disarray.

❧

By noon the next day, J.D. felt well enough to rise from

his bed and totter over to a straight-back chair. He'd half hoped that his erstwhile nurse would pay a call to see how her patient was progressing, but when Amelia didn't appear, he assumed she was repulsed to have seen him at his absolute worst. It was positively uncanny how a woman who should be his permanent adversary had virtually saved his life—twice.

In the next instant, J.D. was roused from his musings by an unwelcome visitor who strode, unannounced, into the room.

"You're still alive, I see," Kemp said, eyeing the bruises on J.D.'s face.

J.D. offered only a brusque nod, fully suspecting that the lumberman was behind the violence of the previous night. What, then, was the bully doing here so soon after he'd ordered his thugs to attack?

J.D. might not have proof, but he was now convinced Kemp had masterminded all the recent assaults that could have killed him. Rather than reveal his hand, though, J.D. concentrated instead on controlling his breathing so his bruised ribs wouldn't send his chest wall into spasms.

"My laborers were frightened away by bullyboys some-body sent over here," J.D. said. "The aftermath of this vandalism will require my full attention this week."

"Pity. But I have more on my mind than a bunch of Chinks. I just heard that you had no insurance on the hotel that recently burned. How do you propose to pay me for the last batch of lumber that went into it?"

"You got your money I owed you from the destroyed gambling club and you'll get your money on the lumber I bought for the hotel that burned."

"When?" Kemp demanded.

"When the hotel opens for business. You'll get first dollar."

"I can't wait that long. I have no recourse but to file a

lien on the property this afternoon and inform your bankers of such."

"Oh for God's sake, Kemp," J.D. erupted, "quit playing this stupid hand over and over! If you don't stop these ham-handed attempts at extortion, I'll have my father and his cronies cut you so dead, you'll think your new home is the Presidio cemetery."

"The word I get is you're still not speaking to your father."

"Well, you heard incorrectly. As a matter of fact, I've been invited to visit my parents' house quite often lately. And if you noticed, Big Jim has never voted against me in the Committee of Fifty. He's as afraid of those government Treasury agents as you are."

Kemp was silenced for a moment, due, J.D. figured, to spies who reported on his regular visits to his parents' house on Octavia Street and his passing acquaintance with reformer Spreckels, the redoubtable Mr. Burns, and his investigators sent out from Washington, D.C.

Ezra pursed his lips in thought, and then said, "I'll hold off the lien if you propose marriage to Matilda tomorrow."

J.D. threw his head back and laughed, though he regretted it as a stab of pain sliced through his chest.

"So we're back to that, are we? A forced engagement? You're awfully behind the times, Ezra. Young people pick their own partners in the twentieth century."

Kemp shot him a peculiar look and then leaned toward the desk a fraction. "One day you might be thankful to hide behind Matilda's skirts."

"And that's because?"

Kemp smiled faintly and pulled out his pocket watch. "The ferry leaves for Sausalito in forty minutes. I'll tell Matilda to expect you on Saturday, as usual." He returned his watch to his waistcoat and stood up. "You really should get someone to attend to those bruises on your face. You look as if you ran into a Chinese highbinder." He narrowed his eyes. "Show up Saturday and it'll buy you some time to get the money from your father to pay me back."

Just then, Angus McClure appeared at the door. Kemp brushed past without a greeting.

"Jamie," Angus said in a low voice, watching over his shoulder until Kemp disappeared down the corridor, "Loy tells me it will take him some time to recruit new Chinese workers. As we feared, the old ones are scared to come back."

J.D. put his head back against his leather chair and closed his eyes. "Tell him I'll pay double. Just *get* them here as soon as you can. We've got to dig the rest of the cistern out back."

❧

Judging from Big Jim Thayer's expression when he looked up from his newspaper, J.D.'s father was surprised to see his son walk into his study after midnight.

"I had a bet with myself that you wouldn't keep your word," the elder Thayer said, pointing to the clock over the mantel.

James Thayer Sr., did not rise from his leather chair to greet J.D., but merely set his newspaper aside. The shades were drawn against the evening's chill, and a half consumed glass of after-dinner brandy sat on a table next to the bay window.

"I was about to call on you myself when I received your summons," J.D. said. "I told your messenger I would come, as requested, so here I am, Father. What's on your mind?"

"Would you please go over to my desk and open the top drawer? There's an envelope in there. Bring it to me."

J.D. did as instructed, reining in hopes for a requested

second loan payment from the Committee of Fifty. He handed over the large envelope. His father's hands trembled slightly as he withdrew the contents.

"What are those?" J.D. asked, noting his father held a clutch of photographs in his hand. Then, with a swift intake of breath, he scanned the pictures' sepia tones.

"Surely you recognize them," James Senior declared acidly.

J.D. took the photos and stared at several images of himself lying naked on a filthy bed, his limbs entwined with those of a slender Chinese boy. The photos were blurred, as if the photographer hadn't waited the requisite time for a proper exposure, but J.D.'s identity was unmistakable.

Good God! he thought with disgust. Amelia had been right. Kemp would stop at nothing to gain control of the Bay View.

"I was shanghaied, Father," he said quietly, unable to pull his eyes away from the lewd photos. "I was drugged and these pictures were staged. I suspect Ezra Kemp is behind this."

"And I suspect you are lying."

"I am *not* lying. A group of hooligans arrived in the dead of night, jumped me from behind, beat some of my workers bloody, and took me off to Chinatown, where they blew opium into my lungs. I awoke with bruises everywhere, a sprained wrist, two black eyes, and a headache I thought might kill me. I certainly didn't give myself this black eye, and I'll show you my purple rib cage, if you wish—or you can confer with Dr. Angus McClure, the physician who treated me."

"When you traffic with Chinese laborers, as Kemp tells me you have, what did you expect? They're the ones who probably shanghaied you, if what you say is true."

So his father and Kemp were getting cozier. J.D. wasn't

surprised. "The Chinese I employed were willing to work at night and for very little wages," he said, fighting to keep his temper. "They wouldn't bite the hand that feeds them, especially when no one else seems willing to hire Orientals." A cold fury was beginning to build in reaction to his father's disdain and Kemp's latest move. "I'm trying to reopen the Bay View, Father. The money I make from my guests can pay Kemp's bills for the hotel that burned and which, by the way, it's pretty clear he dynamited to oblivion."

"With no insurance against such calamity, I hear."

"It's nearly impossible to obtain, and besides, I couldn't afford it. And as for trafficking with the Chinese, I seem to remember you were quite involved with them at one point in your life. Perhaps you still are."

"I certainly didn't do nasty things with Chinese boys," his father retorted.

"Neither did I."

"You have the temerity to deny it? The proof's right here." He reached out and furiously slapped the photographs J.D. held in his hand. "The whole town knows that you kept Chinese whores on your payroll on Nob Hill. Why should I be surprised if you broadened your carnal tastes to include men?"

J.D. felt the blood pound in his temples and was sorely tempted to defend himself, but it would be foolish to show the last cards in his hand. He reinserted the photographs into the envelope to gain time to control his emotions. He made no judgments when it came to people's sexual preferences, but his father's accusations were born of the conflict that had festered for years just beneath the surface of their strained civility.

"We're now approaching some very dangerous territory, wouldn't you say, Father?" He strode to the small fire crackling on the hearth and tossed the envelope with its slanderous contents into the flames. Resting on his haunches, he watched as the paper darkened and curled into ashes. Ling Lee had described to him the degradation visited upon slender young men whom the Chinese brothel owners reserved for gentlemen with certain proclivities. Opium was as strong a weapon as a pistol.

"You can be sure glass plates of those pictures still exist somewhere," he heard his father say behind him. "You're ripe for blackmail at some future date, of course."

"By whom? You?"

"By the person who sent them to me."

J.D. rose and turned around. "And who might that be?"

It was Kemp, of course, thought J.D., and then another notion occurred to him. Perhaps his father was part of the scheme. Nothing would surprise him anymore.

The senior Thayer reached for the brandy snifter.

"I have no idea if Kemp was involved in obtaining those photographs," Thayer Sr., said, nodding toward the fireplace. "Some runner delivered them to the front door. Unmarked." He took a draught from his glass and swallowed. "Once again, I pose the question. Is there no end to your dishonoring this family?"

"I think we'd both have to agree that behaving dishonorably is pretty evenly distributed among the Thayers," J.D. replied, his voice low. "Let us not forget what happened to Grandfather Reims in the middle of San Francisco Bay, nor a few other black marks you've inflicted on our clan." He smiled bitterly, enjoying his father's discomfiture when he mentioned the rarely-spoken name of the elder Thayer's deceased father-in-law. He glanced at the fireplace, watching as the last of the blackened photographs fell into ashes on the hearth. "I gather I will not now have your vote for a second loan payment from your banker friends on the Committee?" J.D. asked, looking up from the flames at his frowning father.

"Your assumption is correct."

"Will you feel it your duty to tell them about these photographs?"

"What difference does that make? Whoever made them has copies."

"And will hold them as a trump card."

"As you've indicated, there seems no end to the disgrace, does there?" Jim Thayer's expression hardened but he said nothing more.

"Well, then… good night, Father. We'll just have to wait to see how everything plays out. And incidentally, I'll use the back entrance when I come next time. I plan to continue visiting Mother. I'm starting to see her in rather a new light."

Before his father could respond or forbid him to set foot in his house in future, J.D. strode across the room and closed the door to the study behind him, passing through the vestibule where the tall clock noted it was half past midnight.

Perhaps those seamy photographs had served a good cause, he thought as he shrugged on his coat. Whether his father had a hand in Kemp's scheme to ruin him or not, it was finally finished between them. As finished as these situations ever could be, given the terrible miscarriage of justice concerning J.D.'s deceased grandfather. Short of bars on the doors, Big Jim Thayer didn't dare prevent his son from visiting his mother from time-to-time.

Considering the worsening relationship between his sire and himself, he was convinced now that Connie Thayer would need his protection all the more.

CHAPTER 25

J.D. GLANCED AT A sliver of light shining beneath the door at the top of the landing. Despite Consuela's pills and sleeping potions, Signora Reims-Diaz Thayer was apparently having another fretful night. Above him he heard the landing creak. Then, Dr. George Ellers materialized in the gloom, clothed in a dressing gown, holding a glass of water and an amber vial.

"Ah," J.D. said in a low voice, advancing up the stairs, "the Angel of Death arrives with his nightly knock-out drops."

J.D. was in a foul mood, aggravated by the sight of the man he knew used medications instead of padlocks to keep his mother locked in her velvet-lined cell. That Ellers had also played a role in his grandfather's unhappy end only darkened his temper.

Ellers remained on the landing with an uncertain expression flickering across his face, as if contemplating whether to beat a hasty retreat without speaking to the son of his in-house patient. "I was just bringing your mother her medicine, but from the look of that black eye you're sporting, you could use some as well."

"So the doctor dispenses in his nightclothes, does he?" J.D. deliberately arched an eyebrow. "Of course, you're probably keeping her so sedated that by this hour, she doesn't even notice."

"Step aside, J.D.," Ellers demanded. "I'm only following your father's dictates."

"Oh, I'm sure you are," J.D. said softly, blocking his mother's bedroom door, "but if you don't want to find yourself sprawled at the bottom of these stairs, be a good doctor and return to your room. At once."

Ellers hesitated, then turned and disappeared into the gloom, his footsteps fading as he trudged toward the third floor. J.D. waited a moment longer and then gently rapped his knuckles against his mother's bedroom door. "Awake enough for a visitor?"

"George, is that you? Have you brought the tincture? I simply can't sleep and—"

"No mother," he murmured. "It's me. J.D."

He shut the door behind him and made his way across the shadowy room. Consuela was reclining on the chaise as she had been on his previous visit. A lamp glowed dimly on the table beside her. There were deep furrows between her eyebrows, and her lips quivered as if she were about to cry.

"Why, son—"

Her voice caught and J.D. could see that she was close to tears. Fortunately, the light was so low where he stood, she didn't notice the black and blue marks still streaking his face.

"It's long after midnight, Mother," he said gently. "Why aren't you in bed?"

"I was too tired to walk across the room, and yet I just can't seem to fall asleep. I'm so restless. George was supposed to bring my medicine earlier, but he never came."

She seemed fragile, defenseless, no longer the fiery woman he remembered from his earliest childhood when she was determined to erase all trace of her Spanish accent from her speech. Her inability to rest had pushed her to the edge of her ability to cope.

J.D. leaned down, his lips nearly brushing her ear. "Here, Mother. Put your arms around my neck."

"What?"

He scooped her up and carried her across the room, setting her carefully upon the large walnut four-poster bed that had been carved in Madrid by servants of her Spanish ancestors.

"In you get." He removed her slippers and tucked her legs beneath the bedcovers, smoothing the coverlet up to her chin. He sat on the edge of the bed and brushed a strand of her black hair, so like his own, off her forehead.

"What are you doing here at this hour?" she murmured.

"I came partly to see how you're getting along."

"Not well, James," she said with a sigh. "Your father says I'm too weak even to leave this room. And it's true… I'm very tired, but sleep just won't come. If only I had my medicine—"

"I've come with your medicine."

"You? What do you mean?"

He gently strafed the back of his fingers against her cheek. Her dark eyes were limpid pools. Her lids lowered as he continued to brush his fingertips along her golden skin. "That's right. Close your eyes and try to relax." He reached up and smoothed the palm of his hand from the crown of her head down the length of her shoulder-length black hair, repeating the soothing gesture that he wished would banish her need for George Ellers's potions and her underlying dread of being alone in the night.

"That feels so wonderful…" she murmured.

After a few more minutes while he stroked her hair, her eyes still closed, he turned down the lamp.

"Don't go," she said softly.

He could hear the panic underlying her plea.

"Not for a while," he murmured. "I'm right here." He remembered as a child she would sit beside his bed and caress his hair until he fell asleep. "That's right," he whispered in the darkness. "I'm here, Mother. I'm here. Just sleep."

A foghorn blew on the bay, a low, lulling sound.

"Cara, cara, Madre. Buenas Noches."

Twenty minutes later, Connie Thayer's son slipped down the stairs and silently let himself out the front door to his parents' house. Pulling his collar up against the damp, he walked to the Winton, turned the crank, and steered the motorcar in the direction of the bay.

A drive along the waterfront would clear his head. He would use the time to come up with another way to complete the Bay View's reconstruction without the support of his father, Kemp, or the Committee of Fifty. And he would think of a plan to pay off his uninsured losses from the fire and help his mother secure a safe haven for the years ahead.

If Consuela didn't have any fight left in her, any spirit remaining to push against her oppressors the way Ling Lee had, the way Amelia Bradshaw battled against forces who preferred her silent and demure, then he would find courage in his mother's name.

Somehow.

One thing was for certain, however. His remaining funds would last about two more weeks. His father wouldn't supply the capital necessary to complete the hotel or even help him secure a loan, and it would take him at least a month to explore some leads he had in New York. That meant there was no way he could open the Bay View ahead of Fairmont Hotel.

J.D. Thayer did not like to lose, but there was no help for that now. He slowed down the Winton to take the sweeping view of the tranquil bay. All he could do was forge ahead and hope that his mother, along with Amelia and the precious few people who mattered in his life, never saw those photographs.

∞

That same week, Amelia moved into a sparsely furnished room at the opposite end of J.D.'s basement quarters at the Bay View, to save time walking back and forth to the Fairmont and to be on hand for their constant decision-making. Another pressing duty her move accomplished was her ability to closely supervise the placement of the remaining roof joists and check over the hoped-for delivery of slate shingles for the roof.

Propriety be damned! she thought, brushing her hair her first morning in her new living quarters. If she were a man, she'd have been living on site from the project's beginning.

Ten minutes later, she was surprised when her employer greeted her in their makeshift kitchen on their first morning under the same roof. J.D. was in a cheerful mood and with a smile on his face nearly healed of its ugly bruises.

"Here." He handed her a mug of coffee he'd brewed on a secondhand iron stove purchased from a disenchanted resident decamping San Francisco for the eastern seaboard. Larger cooking equipment would soon arrive, C.O.D., replacing the rusty, secondhand antique, so the sixty-room hotel could feed one hundred guests a day, but for the moment, the dilapidated appliance suited their needs admirably.

"Thank you." She took an appreciative sip and set the cup on the kitchen table. "I'll reheat it when I get back."

"Where are you going?"

"Outside. Joe Kavanaugh and the carpenters left the site in a mess yesterday." Kavanaugh had turned up one day, claiming experience both as a carpenter and an expert in the art of building the wooden molds to frame the poured cement, but had proved to be nothing but a troublemaker. "I'm going to discharge him." She paused. "If that meets your approval, of course."

"Your reasons again?"

"Terminal laziness and rampant insubordination. I don't trust him for a second."

"Do you want me to tell him?"

Amelia paused. "No, but thank you. I think it's important for the other workers to know that I was the one who took this action—with your say-so, of course."

J.D. nodded. Amelia could detect a gleam in his eye reflecting either admiration or skepticism—she couldn't tell which.

"Good luck," he said. He pointed to the kitchen door leading to the hallway. "I'll just be in my office if you need me."

Amelia found Joe lounging on a low pile of lumber while the other workers were busy at their morning tasks.

"Mr. Kavanaugh," she said quietly, "may I see you a minute? Inside." Tall and muscular and with the appearance of a retired pugilist, the carpenter followed her into the kitchen. Amelia pointed to a chair. "Have a seat."

"I'll stand."

She regarded him for a moment and then reached into her pocket and extracted an envelope. "That's our problem in a nutshell, Mr. Kavanaugh."

"What is?" He leaned a shoulder against one wall, looking bored.

"You are not very good at following orders. I've just asked you to do a simple task—take a seat—and you somehow consider it a challenge to your manhood. From the very first

day, you have shown your disrespect by not doing the tasks
I've assigned to you, or doing them shoddily. I have explained
our ongoing situation to Mr. Thayer—that a carpenter and
chief pour man cannot demonstrate such insubordination in
front of his crew—and your employer concurs with what
I'm about to do. I've given you many chances to reform,
but you have made a choice not to work as a member of my
team." She indicated the envelope in her hand. "This is your
pay packet for your work to date. Please take whatever tools
you've brought to this site and leave the ones that belong to
us. Consider this your last day, effective immediately."

"W–What?" Joe said.

"In plain and simple language, Mr. Kavanaugh, you
are discharged."

The man looked outraged. "I want to talk to Thayer. He
won't cotton to some piece of fluff—"

"As I've already said," she interrupted in an even voice,
"Mr. Thayer has vested full authority in me and has already
agreed with my recommendation to ask you to leave
his employ."

Just then J.D. appeared at the hallway door.

Joe said, pointing a forefinger at Amelia, "She said you
wanted me out. That true? Or is she just actin' like some
high and mighty little—"

"If she says you're discharged, you're discharged. Good
day, sir."

Joe Kavanaugh narrowed his gaze and balled his fists by
his side.

"You can't do this, you two! I'll take everyone else
with me."

"Whoever wishes to leave this site is certainly free to go,"
Amelia said coolly, though her pulse had started to pound.

"I'll complain at the hiring hall."

"And I will submit affidavits of witnesses who saw the quality of your work on this project. Or more to the point, the lack thereof. I'm afraid you don't have many friends here at Taylor and Jackson, Mr. Kavanaugh."

The construction worker glared at Amelia and J.D. with an expression of impotence and barely contained fury. Amelia willed herself to keep her gaze steady. At length, Joe snatched the pay packet from her hand and stormed out the kitchen door.

"Quite the hard head you are, Amelia," J.D. said with an unmistakable look of admiration.

"I just hope it all doesn't come *down* on our heads," she replied soberly.

❦

By noon, J.D. and Amelia drove down the hill to Little Italy and discovered that her favorite workers released to date from the Fairmont project were already employed on other buildings downtown. Fortunately, the Fairmont' head carpenter, Lorenzo Pigati, had a brother, a concrete specialist named Franco Pigati, who was available. He would come to work on the Bay View Hotel project as the new pour man, bringing along several Pigati cousins as his crew, including Nico, Aldo, Dominic, and Roman, who knew the carpentry and plumbing trades.

"Problem solved," Amelia said gaily as she and J.D. drove back up the hill.

"You are… amazing," he said with a look of obvious relief.

"Now it's your turn," she replied as J.D. parked the Winton in front of the Bay View. "We have to pay their wages remember. What's your next move?"

"Ah… yes, the minor matter of money."

He didn't elaborate. Was he was considering another trip to a gambling parlor on the Barbary Coast as one of his "options"? Or did the strapped hotelier have other plans to cut costs until regular channels of additional finance materialized?

The following day, she was astonished when her employer joined Pigati's crew, serving as impromptu supervisor of building supplies.

"Saves one salary, right?" J.D. shrugged when she asked him what he thought he was doing. "If you can face down the likes of Jake Kelly and Joe Kavanaugh and climb scaffolding without a qualm, I can certainly act as courier to buy more nails or take delivery of lumber down at the docks."

"Are we down to pennies?" Amelia demanded.

"We're down to dimes. But don't worry. I'm waiting to hear from a banker I know in New York."

"Is there no chance your father would help now?" She was more than aware of the father-son estrangement, but as a prominent member of the powerful Committee of Fifty, the senior Thayer was on a first-name basis with every banker in San Francisco.

Amelia could see tension take hold around J.D.'s jaws. "My father and I haven't seen eye-to-eye since I was fifteen. He's probably the last person from whom I can expect help, Amelia."

"Well, what about your mother? Isn't she an heiress of some sort? Surely, after all your misfortune, she'd extend a helping hand to her son?"

"My mother has probably never paid for anything directly in her life. Her entire estate is managed by my father."

"Rather like the problem that faced my mother and me," she reminded him. She didn't wait for his reaction before she asked, "Well, what about your late grandfather?

He left you no bequest? My mother once told me that he was one of the wealthiest miners to emerge from the Comstock Lode."

J.D. pursed his lips and was slow to answer. Finally, he said, "Grandfather Reims drowned in the bay when I was a teenager."

Amelia was immediately contrite. "Oh, I'm so sorry, J.D. Did he die sailing? The bay can be so treacherous in a small craft."

"No. He fell from a ferry. Some say he jumped. Others wondered if he were pushed. I was underage when he died so his estate automatically went to my mother, which of course, meant that it was under my father's control—and still is."

"No wonder you have so few options," she murmured.

"*We* have so few options," he reminded her. "You signed on for this adventure, remember, so it would seem we're full partners in this folly, my dear Amelia."

In that instant of camaraderie, she wished they *could* be trustworthy allies instead of former adversaries, forced by necessity to cooperate. But of course, in truth, that's just what they were. J.D. Thayer might be a handsome specimen, and a very charming one—and Amelia frankly admitted to herself she found him devilishly attractive—but the Lord only knew what he had done to achieve his current tenure at the Bay View. She reminded herself that the only reasons she'd been thrown together with J.D. in such unlikely fashion were fate and circumstances.

Even so, as on the night she'd help rescue him from Chinatown, for the briefest moment, they both seemed utterly in tune with each other's thoughts. She locked gazes with J.D. across the kitchen table and it seemed to her that they perfectly understood the odds against their enterprise and their mutual commitment to do whatever was necessary to succeed. It made her wonder what kind of relationship might have developed had they met again as adults in Paris, or on an ocean liner, or on her transcontinental train ride across America—and not in the basement where her grandfather had once had his office.

Put the genie back in the bottle, Amelia, she admonished herself.

How could it be that one kiss and a look exchanged on top of a half-finished building—and now these recent moments of complete understanding—had uncorked such a potent force?

She turned toward the door. "I'll just be getting back to work," she said, and exited the office.

That evening, her employer was noticeably silent as Shou Shou served their evening meal on mismatched plates. Amelia caught J.D. gazing at her soberly.

For her part, she concentrated on the rice and fish. Two planks of wood resting upon sawhorses served as their communal dining table, and their seating consisted of mismatched chairs and wooden boxes they'd scavenged in the neighborhood. After dinner, J.D. assisted Amelia and Foo in the nightly chore of filling the kerosene lanterns used by the Chinese laborers to light the lot next door. Amelia touched a match to the wick of the first of twenty lanterns.

"I think we should leave the remaining piles of rubbish on the Pacific Street side where they are for now and employ Loy's men to finish digging the second cistern," she proposed. "I think it's prudent to get it operational as soon as possible. We can clean up the last of the trash at the end of the project when we're ready to landscape the terraced garden."

"That sounds fine," J.D. agreed, "because we definitely need to have plenty of water in case of fire. I believe I have finally learned *that* lesson."

Loy's latest crew would work all night, hopefully finishing this difficult job before daybreak. Exhausted by the long day she'd had, Amelia poured herself a cup of chamomile tea and sank into a kitchen chair.

"I take out lanterns too?" asked little Foo.

"Yes, please." The boy's grasp of English was improving each day, as was his confidence. Even though he was by far the youngest of her helpers, he eagerly took on any task she requested of him.

Amelia relaxed while J.D., Loy, Shou Shou, and Foo ferried the lanterns outside. She knew by the clatter and clang of shovels and picks that the night crew had arrived and immediately gotten down to work.

She must have dozed off, for she nearly jumped out of her chair when J.D. burst into the kitchen, followed by a group of Chinese laborers chattering in Cantonese while transporting an old chest as if it were a coffin.

"Look what we found!" J.D.'s customary sobriety was transformed into boyish glee. "Buried in the backyard of the old woman's place. The crew had barely begun to dig down beside the old well when they struck this." He pointed at the trunk that still had clods of dirt clinging to its sides. "I told them to bring it in here. God knows what that harridan was doing with it the day she took a shot at you."

"I know exactly what she was doing with it." Amelia ignored J.D.'s enthusiasm as she rose from her chair to address Loy. "If you've dug down that deep, your men need to continue at least ten more feet. Be sure to tell them to shore up the sides with the lumber stacked on the ground out there. We don't want any cave-ins." She reached for her shawl. "In fact, I should go out there and keep an eye on things."

"They're doing fine," J.D. assured her. He gestured

toward the battered trunk that now stood in the middle of the kitchen's concrete floor. "Let's see what we've got."

"A dead dog is what you've got," she said, as Loy and his group of workers trooped outside. "And it probably smells to high heaven."

J.D. paused, crowbar in hand. "A dog?"

"I saw the old woman burying it. The poor animal was killed in the big aftershock on the morning of the quake. Her Chinese manservant carried the creature around from the side of the house and they stashed it in the trunk. When I stepped forward to offer them a ride to the Presidio in your motorcar, that's when she pulled out the revolver and took aim. Don't you remember about all that?"

"Angus related your near miss, but I was out of my mind with pain from my cracked ribs when we came back to fetch you. But are you telling me you survived the earthquake and then nearly got shot by a crazed old lady burying her *dog*?" He turned to the trunk and added, "Well, let's see what else she was protecting. It's been a year. The dog is probably mummified by now."

"Mummy or not, I don't want to see it," Amelia declared, thinking, suddenly, about poor old Barbary, killed in the second fire. "I'm going to bed."

By this time, J.D. had pried the rusty fastenings open and was lifting the heavy cover. Sure enough, a bulky bundle wrapped in a blanket was obviously the dog. J.D. bent over the trunk and began to lift out the corpse.

"Good *night*," Amelia said firmly, turning to leave the kitchen. A second later, behind her, she hear J.D. swift intake of breath.

"Well, well…" he said, "will you take a look at *this*!"

CHAPTER 26

AMELIA TURNED AROUND AS J.D. placed the bundle on the floor. Heaps of ornamental silver and metal strong boxes peeped below the trunk's edge.

"Oh glory…" J.D. said gleefully.

She sped to J.D.'s side. "So Angus was right! *That's* why she shot at me. She thought I would try to steal her valuables!"

The newspapers had been filled with stories of home-owners returning to their burned residences and digging up the trunks they'd buried in advance of the fire sweeping up Nob Hill. For many San Franciscans, the collections of precious worldly goods they'd sequestered below ground had provided them with the means of starting over.

She peered into the trunk as J.D. lifted out a set of magnificent silver candlesticks and a large, polished wooden box filled with twenty-four place settings of sterling silver flatware. Then he glanced down at the dog's body wrapped in the blanket. "I'll just take this outside."

"An excellent idea."

A minute later J.D. appeared at the kitchen door. "I put the poor thing behind the construction shed and will ask Franco to have one of his men bury it in the morning."

"I thank you for that," Amelia said, wrinkling her nose.

"Don't worry. I think the fire took care of the odor. It just smelled musty. Open the jewelry cases," he directed, pointing to a stack of tooled leather boxes with TIFFANY and GUMPS stamped in gold.

Her fingers trembled as she flipped the catch on a flat box encased in burgundy leather. "J.D?" she said faintly. An array of gems winked at her from its velvet lining. "I think I've just found something that will pay the wages of Loy and his men, plus Franco Pigati and his entire crew for weeks. *Look!*"

Even in the diffused kerosene lamplight, the ruby and diamond necklace shone like stars in a night sky. The next box contained a diamond and emerald bracelet and matching pin. A black velvet pouch held five smaller leather boxes, each housing platinum rings with large diamonds, sapphires, and other precious stones in their settings. One velvet pouch contained a handful of unset gemstones, mostly emeralds and diamonds, whose value Amelia couldn't begin to estimate.

J.D. breathed a long whistle when she placed them in his hands. "Now, isn't *this* nice?"

Amelia snatched the lantern from the table and held it over the trunk. Lining the bottom were layers of gold and silver bars reaching half way up the sides.

"Hot damn…" she whispered, an echo of Henry Bradshaw's favorite exclamation when excited or upset. "That's more than you found in your safe, isn't it?"

"Much more. And how much do you suppose *this* will fetch?" J.D. assumed his full height and held a lady's pearl-handled revolver by one finger.

Amelia put a palm out. "Hand that over, thank you."

Laughing, J.D. shook his head. "Not so fast!"

"Absolutely!" she insisted. "Since the old woman nearly killed me with it, I'm the one who should keep it under my mattress for protection." She eyed the astonishing booty with growing excitement. "It certainly looks like I might need it."

"The gun's even got a velvet-lined box of its own, chocked full of ammunition."

"How ladylike." Then she broke into a smile. "Just think! We don't *need* bankers, J.D.! We don't need help from your family. And you certainly don't have to go gambling to raise money to pay for the building of this hotel, if that was your plan-of-last-resort."

"I'm not at all convinced I should let you have this gun," he teased. And instead of handing her the small weapon, he placed it on the makeshift kitchen table. Then, without warning, he enfolded her in a bear hug. "Can you believe this?" He kept hold of her and tilted his head back to smile at her. "Who could have imagined such luck?"

Meeting his glance, she replied gaily, "I'd say we've just been presented with a very large, very fortuitous way of paying for continuing construction." Before he could kiss her, as she sensed he clearly intended, she stepped out of the circle of his arms. An awful thought had just occurred to her. "Are you sure that you can claim all this as yours?"

"O ye of little faith!" He grabbed her around the shoulders for a second squeeze. "Of *course* this belongs to us! I own the lot back there, free and clear. The lawyer for the estate told me the old woman and her houseboy died in the fire and she had no heirs. The lot and everything on it—or under it—now belong to *me*, and it should just about cover the cost of making the Bay View the most elegant small hotel that San Francisco has ever seen! As far as opening our doors April eighteenth, we may not beat the Fairmont, but no one will hold a candle to us as far as our beautiful appointments."

"Yes, yes, *yes*!" Amelia cried, finally allowing herself to be caught up in his excitement. J.D. swung her around in his arms several times and then they broke apart and danced an impromptu jig in front of the rust-incrusted iron stove. She pointed to the treasure trove. "God knows how much all this is worth, J.D. Calm my racing heart, will you please, and let's put everything in Grandfather's safe, right *now*."

"Another excellent idea. We're just full of them tonight, aren't we?" and before she could draw away, he bussed her on the nose.

Amelia had never seen J.D. so lighthearted. His rather forbidding dark looks had been transformed by a wide grin and a continuing cackle as he surveyed his treasures.

"I'm serious," she insisted. "Let's get this booty into the safe this minute! But first, I'm putting the pistol and the ammunition under my mattress."

She swiftly stowed the weaponry in her bedroom and returned to the kitchen to pile the jewelry boxes in her arms. J.D. walked over to the sideboard. He removed two drinking glasses, and placed them inside a silver champagne bucket he'd pulled out of their neighbor's trunk. "Do you know what else I keep in that safe at the end of the hall?" he asked with a smirk.

"A lot of nothing, probably," she retorted, watching him drag the fusty trunk down the corridor that led to his basement office. "Until two seconds ago, you were practically out of jack, Jack! Don't bother denying it."

"Amelia, you are far too pessimistic for your young years," he said over his shoulder. "This should teach you to believe in Lady Luck. Now follow me, my dear, and step lively."

❦

J.D. placed the heavy silverware on the raw cement floor in his office and spun the new tumblers on his repaired strong-hold. When the combination clicked into place, he heaved open the heavy door. Inside, the walk-in safe was empty, save for an accordion file of legal papers, two small silver bars, and a bottle of champagne.

"You bought sparkling wine when you were nearly stone broke?" she marveled.

"You never know when you might need some bubbly for a celebration."

She hugged the stack of jewelry cases to her chest. "Well, these certainly are cause for one. It's an absolute miracle. No, it's *a trunk full* of miracles!"

"Hand them over, Miss Architect."

Smiling, she obeyed and watched with childish delight as he stored the slim leather boxes and velvet pouch plump with loose gemstones alongside the rest of the cache. Next he stacked the gold and silver bars to one side and put the polished wooden box with the sterling silver flatware on top, along with other pieces of household silver. Champagne bottle in hand, he slammed the door shut and spun the tumblers. He indicated she should take the chair facing his desk, then popped the cork and poured them each a glass of sparkling wine.

"To the Bay View," J.D. said, raising his glass and grinning.

"To the Bay View," Amelia echoed more somberly, wondering, suddenly, what her grandfather would think of toasting her family's hotel with the man who had managed to wrest it from her stewardship by means of an auspicious poker match. Nevertheless, she clinked glasses and drank in silence for a few minutes. Immediately, she felt a rush of warmth, taking it as a sign of how tired she was if only a few sips of champagne could have such an instant effect.

"J.D.?"

He took a draught of wine and looked at her expectantly. "What?"

"Why did you come back for my father and me in the Winton the day of the quake?"

J.D. took a drink from his glass and set in on the desk. Surprisingly, he didn't ask her reasons for bringing up the unexpected subject at this late hour. "I gave you my word I'd return with help."

"But you'd gotten safely to the Presidio and you were badly injured. Why didn't you just direct Angus to find us?"

"I might have burned in the fire if you hadn't helped me out of that place as you did. I figured if someone saves your life, you owe him. Or in this case—her. I wanted to be sure you escaped that inferno."

Amelia remembered Angus saying something similar about being indebted when he and J.D. fought in the Battle of San Juan Hill.

"But I'd said all those angry things to you on the day I got back from France," she persisted, "and you knew perfectly well that I blamed you for my father even being at the all-night poker games and also when the quake struck and—"

"You'd just been through a horrible ordeal yourself, making your way down nine stories in that ruined building, so I made some allowances for that. And besides, you'd offered to help me that terrible morning, even though I'd taken over your family's hotel and beaten you in court. You're a decent woman, Amelia. Not too many people like that in this world. I wanted to make certain you got to safety that day."

"Hmm…" She took another sip of her wine. Gazing at him over her glass, she said, "You know, I've kept those three cards that my father had in his hand when I found him in the rubble."

J.D. paused, his glass half way to his lips. "Really?"

"Yes. An ace, queen, and ten of diamonds. The ones he

said were part of the royal flush he claimed he drew just as the quake hit."

"Yes, I remember your telling me that at the Presidio. But you never found a jack or king of diamonds, did you?"

"No. I couldn't see any trace of them in all that wreckage."

"Hmm."

"Tell me again what you saw of his hand... just before the first jolt?"

He drew pensive. "At five-thirteen that morning, with the world turning upside down, I don't think I saw anything very clearly, Amelia."

"I expect not," she murmured.

He set down his glass. "All hell broke loose just as your father was playing his hand."

...All hell broke loose...

Those had been Henry Bradshaw's exact words describing the same instant. At least J.D. hadn't called her father an out-and-out liar, which *she* certainly had done to her father's face more than once in her life.

A few more moments of silence bloomed between them. Then J.D. said, "We'd better not let Loy and Shou Shou and the others see that dead dog."

"I don't want to see it either." She allowed him to pour her a second glass. "Makes me think of poor Barbary."

J.D. shot her an odd look. "It made me think of him too, poor fellow. He was a wonderful dog. Your grandfather raised him well." Then he added, "The Chinese are superstitious about exhuming the dead, you know. They'll only dig up remains if they're sending them to China for reburial. Ancestor worship and all that, plus I don't think we want word of buried treasure getting around. It's still a pretty unsafe place around here."

Amelia nodded, wondering if J.D. was also thinking about Ling Lee, buried in tons of rubble, her broken body never to be sent to her homeland for burial.

"Well, first thing tomorrow morning," she said, "when none of the workers are on the site, I suggest that *we* bury the unfortunate creature in the backyard with full military honors. The dog deserves that for guarding all that booty for a year."

J.D. smiled faintly. "A twenty-one-gun salute, at the very least."

"And I'm also going to dedicate a memorial rose garden in his honor—and to Barbary's."

J.D. leaned back in his chair, a melancholy cast to his gaze. "To placate the dogs' ancestors?"

"No, as a shrine of gratitude. It's only right. What we've found tonight gives the Bay View a new lease on life."

"You're right. I had exactly fifty-two dollars worth of silver left in that safe."

Amelia slowly shook her head. "James Diaz Thayer, you are a worse gambler than my father ever was."

"'Fraid not. I always do my gambling stone-cold sober."

"And that makes a difference?"

"Oh, yes indeed." J.D. reached across the desk and gently seized her chin between his fingers. "I believe you *will* create a shrine in honor of those dogs," he said, and then, before Amelia had any notion of his intentions, he leaned across the desk and kissed her.

It was a friendly kiss. Like his bear hug had been. Not like their first kiss in the Winton after her driving lesson.

Just friendly. At first.

Then, by mysterious mutual consent, his lips sought hers anew and despite a warning voice in her head, she leaned another few inches across the desk and responded in kind.

By the time he'd finished and settled back on his side of the desk, Amelia was in a combined state of shock and arousal.

"It's just the wine, J.D. That's all it is," she insisted loftily, settling back into her chair across from him. "I haven't had a glass in a year and a half. And this is champagne. It always has a curious effect on me."

"How lucky for me." He sought her left hand resting on his desk and held it, his callused thumb lightly grazing her palm. "Though I must beg to differ."

"About what?" She pursed her lips to keep from smiling idiotically. It had been a lovely kiss, really. Better even than Monsieur Lamballe at his most ardent.

"It's not just the wine," J.D. declared. "It's something else. What that is, I haven't quite determined." He smiled at her. "Old-fashioned lust, perhaps?"

Amelia burst out laughing. "You say that to all the girls." She marveled at how deliciously light-headed she was beginning to feel.

"No. I do not say that indiscriminately." He lifted the bottle from the desk and topped off both glasses.

"Any more of this champagne will get us into serious trouble," she insisted, and then found that she was giggling. "I lived in France, so I'm an expert on the subject."

"Really? How so?"

"Veuve Clicquot," she said solemnly, taking a delicious sip. "A lethal brand of champagne. One minute I was a declared spinster. Three glasses later, I was affianced to First Officer Etienne Lamballe of the *S.S. France*."

"That sounds rather romantic."

"Romantic? If I'd drunk anymore Veuve Clicquot that last month in Paris, my French husband would have gained control of my entire life and *that* would have been a disaster!"

"You are... *Madame* Lamballe?"

She laughed at his expression of consternation. "Almost. *Mais non... non!* I saved myself from the jaws of matrimony at the eleventh hour. You see, I didn't drink that last, fatal glass. I realized one night at dinner after we'd—well—after we'd lived together in Paris when Etienne had shore leave, that Monsieur Lamballe had only been *pretending* to support my desire to be an architect."

"Pretending? So he could...?"

"Exactly, the cad!" She held up her glass to gaze at the bubbles floating to the top of the rim. "Any fool knows that the quickest way to an architect's heart is to make believe you love her T square—and in Monsieur Lamballe's case, it worked."

J.D. exploded with laughter.

"Ah... I amuse you," she said, wagging her finger at him. "But luckily I was just sober enough to keep my wits. You see, that night," she continued, mesmerized by the golden liquid's bubbles rising to the surface of her glass, "Etienne drank the lion's share of the Veuve Clicquot and fortunately, it loosened his lips. His true ideas about women practicing architecture became only too clear, the mercenary little grubber."

"Perhaps he believed that marriage would spare you the kind of problems you've faced here with—"

"'Spare' me?" she scoffed. "He simply planned to *relieve* me of my inheritance when the time came!" She pushed her glass away from her. "Wouldn't he have gotten a surprise if we'd married and come back to San Francisco? What do you think he'd have said the morning after your poker game with my father when my family didn't own the hotel anymore? And just how do you think he'd have enjoyed our little earthquake?"

And then she dissolved into another uncontrollable burst of mirth.

J.D. pointed to their glasses. "Does this mean you don't want any more champagne?"

She shifted her eyes from the remains of her sparkling wine to the bottle he held in his hand. "Oh bother! You and I have done nothing but work for weeks on end and finding a trunk full of gold, silver, and jewels doesn't just happen every day, does it? I'm not engaged to *you,* so there's no danger, is there? *Alors, mon ami…* let's live a little!" she declared, polishing off what was left in her glass and demanding a fill-up.

"Good girl!"

She thought of Etienne's constant admonishments that all work and no play made Amelia a dull *mademoiselle*, indeed. Of course, Etienne's philosophy that first year at L'École had also been a devilish way of persuading her to join him in bed—and he'd succeeded, masterfully.

So what? She'd enjoyed that part… and his French letters had prevented pregnancy, just as he'd promised. She returned home with most of her pride intact, though not her virtue.

"Cheers," J.D. declared, gesturing with his glass. "I knew you had a spark of fun in you, despite those prim shirtwaists you're always wearing."

"Not like the dance hall girls, eh? You should see the wenches who do the can-can in Paris! Scandalously little clothing they wear." She narrowed her eyes and again wagged her finger at him. "And speaking of scandalous behavior—drunk or sober—you needn't go gambling anymore, Mr. Thayer. As of tonight, you've probably got all the money we need to finish this place, and so I'm expecting you to behave yourself, for once." She burst out laughing again, thinking that she was the most amusing person she knew.

"Amelia…" J.D.'s tone of voice brought her up short. "I give you fair warning. Drunk or sober, I have *no* intention of behaving myself tonight."

J.D. rose from his leather chair and came to stand by her side. Then, after a second's hesitation, he reached down and put one hand lightly on her shoulder.

"I can see your intentions all right," she murmured.

"And I can see yours."

Amelia remained very still in her chair, exquisitely conscious of his touch. The weight of his palm felt solid, yet his strong fingers kneaded the tired muscles in her back with strokes that were slow, rhythmic, and calculated to send her either flying from the room or sink deeper into her chair. After a full minute of silence while J.D. continued his wayward ministrations, she finally rose from her seat to her full height—which came only to J.D.'s shoulder—and set her champagne glass on the desk.

"No more wine," she said firmly. "I want to do this with a clear head."

She reached to cup his face between her hands, his black sideburns silky to the touch. With the pads of her fingers, she lightly traced the year-old scars that slanted across his forehead, raised white welts that cut into the darker skin around them. Then, slowly and with great deliberation, she stood on tiptoes to kiss him on the lips—knowing full well that she was definitely shaking hands with the devil once again.

She allowed herself the luxury of time, of sinking deeply into his embrace, imagining that J.D. found it startling for a woman in mannish shirtwaists and work boots to be so bold as to want a kiss to last forever.

Finally, murmuring against his lips, she said, "I wanted to do exactly that on the scaffolding that day. I always feel so free when I go up there, and there you were, climbing to the very top with me. I liked that." She leaned back in his arms and found herself staring into pools of darkness pulling her into the depths of the unknown.

"I wanted to kiss you too, that day."

"You did?" She felt as if she were a flirtatious stranger gazing provocatively at him through her eyelashes.

"You knew that I did." He leaned toward her, kissing her again, and now he wasn't teasing or flip. When, finally, he released her, he whispered close to her ear. "And did you have anything else in mind when we were at the top of the scaffold?"

She shook her head. "Certainly not! As I said, I haven't misbehaved like this since I lived in Paris." If he thought her a hussy because she'd already been with a man—so be it.

"No? Then why are you willing to misbehave tonight?"

"I haven't said I would."

"Oh yes… I think you have."

He pulled her closer so she could feel the strength of his arousal. She allowed the shock of it, the pure pleasure of it, to travel up her spine. "I suppose I'm rather tired of being such a paragon of virtue." She blinked gravely and announced, "And it isn't just the champagne. I very much enjoyed that kiss just now."

"As did I. And you're definitely *some* sort of paragon," he said, his playful tone underscored by nuzzling her neck in a fashion guaranteed to lead her into even deeper waters. "I'm delighted to hear you were a naughty girl in Paris. I would have been so disappointed to learn otherwise."

"Believe me, I'm no girl, and if I'm *not* a paragon of virtue," she replied with a deepening frown, "what kind of paragon do you suppose I *am*?"

"Perhaps you're a paragon of truth. You have no idea how rare that is." He bent down and kissed her on the forehead. "With your permission, I intend to discover who you truly are this evening, Miss Bradshaw."

"So, we're back to last names, are we, Mr. Thayer?"

"No, indeed." Smiling, he seized her hand and led her toward his sleeping quarters down the hallway from his office. "I rather doubt we'll use such formality this night."

CHAPTER 27

A T THE DOOR TO J.D.'s bedroom, Amelia hesitated, halting any forward progress past the threshold. "I've just had some dreadful second thoughts, J.D. *Think* about it! This is a terrible idea. One that we'll both regret in the morning."

"What if I guarantee you won't regret it one bit?"

He leaned down and kissed her so thoroughly, she knew right then he was a man to deliver on his promises. Of course, there were plenty of pressing reasons not to embark on an intimate relationship with James Diaz Thayer, but all she could think was what Julia Morgan would say if she knew her former employee was about to be seduced by Morgan's former client.

The next minute, she could hardly think at all because J.D. pulled her hard against the length of his body. He eased her back against the concrete hallway wall and pushed his pelvis gently against her hips. Soon, his thumb was strafing the tip of her breast through her shirtwaist, a reminder that their clothing was the only barrier between them.

"You're a woman who deals well with the facts, aren't you?" he whispered. "Well, what we're both feeling right now is *real*, wouldn't you agree?"

They stood entwined, surrounded by the rough, unfinished cement that she had helped to construct. She was mesmerized by his challenging stare and astonished by the raft of sensations radiating down her limbs.

"It's also foolhardy, reckless, and insane. The unvarnished truth is, I've never really trusted you, J.D. And I'm not sure I do even now."

"Never trusted me about what?" he murmured into her ear.

His breath was warm and soothing. All thoughts of her father's last poker game and the fate of women like poor Ling Lee flew out of her head. Amelia grasped for some shred of sanity while attempting unsuccessfully to ignore J.D.'s hand continuing to massage her right breast.

She heaved a small sigh and pushed her hips ever so gently against the swelling between his legs. "What we're doing right now is also appallingly unprofessional. But it's definitely real."

"And you're woman enough to admit it, aren't you, because we both know the pleasure that's in store."

Oh yes, indeed… *the pleasure*, Amelia thought, while little charges of electricity surged through her limbs. For several delicious minutes, she surrendered to the pure sensation of J.D. kissing her on each eyelid, her earlobes, and a spot at the base of her neck where the spurts of current shifted to bolts of lightning.

"Yes… oh yes, *please*," she sighed again as he began the task of freeing the top buttons on her shirtwaist. When his warm palm invaded her blouse and smoothed across her skin, she lost all sense of time or place, her heightened sensibilities blotting out everything except the astonishing feel of his hand cupping her flesh.

Finally, he stepped back and then led her through the doorway. Once inside his private rooms, he sat her on the bed, knelt, and slowly, deliberately removed her boots, stockings, and garters in turn. For a few moments, he massaged her calves and the soles of her feet.

Then he asked, "Stand for a moment, will you please?" He lifted her skirts and unfastened the button on the pair of man's trouser she habitually wore on site. "Now, this is a first," he said with a roguish smile as he pushed the cloth down the length of her slender legs. "Step out from them, please," he ordered.

"Oh Lord..." Amelia said with a sigh as J.D. began to pay rapt attention to the small, silk-covered buttons that marched down the front of her shirtwaist. As he unhooked each fastening, he pressed his lips on the patch of skin thereby uncovered.

"So warm..." he murmured.

In the way the memory of her first night with Etienne drifted through her mind, she was now wondering if J.D. thought at all of Ling Lee. In the next instant, all rational thoughts of the past were banished by the simple act of his fingers undoing the solitary button on the waist of her workday skirt.

"There," he said, the fabric falling to the floor. "That was easy."

"In Paris, I abandoned my corsets, so the next part's easy too."

J.D. chuckled. "Such a woman of the twentieth century you are." By this time, he had smoothed her petticoat over her hips and they both watched the garment pool at her feet next to her skirt and her father's trousers. "And such lovely architecture, Amelia," he whispered. His languid glance swept from her bare feet to her face. "So beautiful." He lightly settled a hand on each breast, still covered by her thin chemise.

She could have stilled his kneading fingers, but she realized with some surprise that she wouldn't dream of it. J.D. had been right a few minutes earlier. For better or for worse, she wanted exactly what he wanted and she watched him call forth sensations from her with a rising sense of anticipation and impatience. She helped him remove her remaining piece of clothing and then reached for his waistband.

"Here," she murmured. "Let me do that. And while we're on the subject of architecture, I'm longing to see…"

And then there were no more barriers of clothing or embarrassment or shyness, but merely a driving need to fall onto the mattress covering J.D.'s big brass bed. The room was chilly, as the hour approached midnight, but from somewhere, J.D. had secured a feather duvet that felt soft and welcoming when he gently eased her onto her back.

"The bed's just like the one you had before the second hotel blew up."

"Sears and Roebuck's best, darling," he said, bending forward to brush his lips against a sensitive spot below her breastbone. "When I like something, I never change my tastes."

A faint aroma of verbena teased her nostrils as J.D. lowered himself beside her on the duvet. The lemony tang mixed with his masculine scent and a whiff of sea air seeping through window frames scheduled to be caulked the following week.

Amelia reached her arms over her head and grabbed the headboard's bars, stretching contentedly, the champagne she'd consumed keeping her warm. "Remember the night of China Alley, when I sat next to you on the bed and gave you a cup of tea?"

"I don't remember the tea. I just remember you. Sitting on my bed."

How different tonight was from that time Angus and she had laid J.D.'s unclothed, beaten body on the bed. This night, she gazed boldly at his long, lean form, a man of thirty-six, in vibrant health—though his skin was scored by war and natural disaster. He lay beside her, hovering close with all his strength and power. She ran her fingertips along the scars on his rib cage and reached above his shoulders to touch the marks on his forehead for a second time. Then she allowed her right hand to drift downward, past his waist to his thigh where she found a patch of raised skin, the place a bullet entered his leg during the battle on San Juan Hill.

"You've lived a dangerous life, J.D. Thayer," she murmured, and slid down his body to kiss the wound.

She felt his hands lightly touch the back of her head and then press her firmly against him. The fire that had destroyed that other bed, that mattress, that hotel, was now forgotten in the urgency of a newly kindled flame. He allowed her the freedom to explore, to stoke the flames until a moment of near crisis, when he reached down and lifted her toward the pillows at their head so he could gaze into her eyes.

"Amelia... Amelia. Such a kind and generous lady..."

She only had time to gasp before his fingers gently slipped into the warmth between her legs. "Do they do this in Paris, I wonder?" he murmured into her neck.

Amelia, of course, was powerless to offer him an answer, for he'd begun to coax, to tease, to torment her into a state of rampant desire that had only dimmest echoes of Paris or anywhere else.

She had no doubt that what they were doing was utter folly, fraught with future complications she could not, in her present state of unbridled thirst, even imagine. But J.D. easily drove those last, sensible thoughts clear out of her head and smothered any reservations she might weakly summon at this late state by pressing the length of his body against her own.

The consummate gambler, tonight J.D. played card trick

after card trick in a high-stakes game calculated to provoke in her an avalanche of sensation as he marked every inch of her as his own. When, finally, he entered her with a sureness of his welcome and a dazzling display of skill, he repeatedly invoked her name, telling her of his unbounded pleasure and delight. In the end, she simply surrendered to the inevitability that she too had not changed her tastes for passion and risk-taking, nor would she decline this brazen invitation to feel fully and exquisitely human.

The earthquake and fire had nearly destroyed them, she thought, pulling him closer still, but fate obviously had another plan. Suddenly, Amelia couldn't care less what Julia Morgan or anyone else might think of her. She was *alive* when she could easily have been dead. She could touch and taste and smell and virtually see the very essence of this fellow survivor. She was in *this* bed, with *this* man. In this most precious place where, strangely, she sensed her grandfather's loving presence.

She luxuriated in the piercing feel of J.D. exhorting her to take the journey with him, and she knew, without a doubt, that the genie was well and truly out of the bottle—and might not ever be put back.

❧

The next day dawned with the kind of harsh reality that Amelia had fully anticipated the previous evening.

"Does your head hurt as much as mine?" J.D. inquired of the prone form that lay buried beneath the bedcovers. Amelia's unbound hair was completely covered by a pillow.

"It's my brain that's on a death march," replied a muffled voice. "Don't... even... whisper."

"Sorry, Amelia, but it's just come on daylight." He lifted

the pillow and gently pressed his lips against her shoulder blade. "If you don't want your reputation as a straw boss shattered forever, you'd best make your way back to your own room."

"Oh... *Lord*, J.D. We are such bad actors..."

Amelia painfully pulled herself into a sitting position and leaned her naked back against the headboard's cold brass bars. She struggled to tuck the rumpled sheet under her arms. J.D.'s sparsely furnished sleeping quarters, filled only with his bed and a few discarded packing crates serving for furniture, made it seem in the cold light of dawn as if they'd made love in a deserted warehouse.

"Not exactly in the pink, are we?"

"No. No, we are not," she mumbled. "And we are truly appalling people."

"We are not appalling."

"Well, reckless and foolhardy might be a more apt description... though I thoroughly enjoyed myself, Mr. Thayer."

"I'm mighty flattered to hear that, Miss Bradshaw. So did I. Although, now I'm a bit concerned that I didn't protect—"

"That's very considerate of you," intervened Amelia, "but in one regard, our timing was impeccable. I'm just about to have my—" She paused and vowed she would sound far more worldly than she felt. "There is no danger I'll conceive."

She swung her bare legs to the side of the bed and stared at the mound of clothing heaped in the middle of the cement floor as an avalanche of pleasurable moments with J.D. flashed through her mind. "Stay right where you are, will you, while I get dressed."

He reached out and firmly took hold of her arm. "No, *you* stay where you are for just a moment." He leaned over and lazily kissed her on the mouth. "That's just a little reminder of what got us into this fix."

For a few seconds, she allowed herself to luxuriate in the sheer masculinity of his naked chest pressed against her bare breasts. Then, reluctantly, she pushed against his shoulders and stood beside the bed. Aware of his avid scrutiny, she speedily donned her shift, tucked it and her wrinkled shirt-waist into her father's trousers, and fumbled with the fastenings up to her neck.

"I'm *so* thirsty," she said, and sank into a chair to hook the closures on her ankle boots.

"Sad to say, there's not a drop of champagne left," J.D. announced. He laid on his back, smiling broadly, hands behind his head, the sheet now chastely covering his mid-section.

Amelia's fingers stilled, her bootlaces ignored. She raised her glance to meet the gaze of a man whom she now knew intimately, yet not in the manner that really counted. She did not yet know much more than before of J.D. Thayer's true character—except that he was a skilled and generous lover—and amazingly enough, he hadn't asked another word about Etienne.

She'd realized long before last night that she'd thoroughly recovered from her love affair with the wily Frenchman, chalking it up to part of her education abroad. J.D., on the other hand, hadn't volunteered a single sentence about Ling Lee, a woman he had lived with for several years—or his feelings about five-year-old Wing. What could she assume except that he probably hadn't completely recovered from his loss?

Interrupting thoughts intent on their death spiral, she said, "Please don't purchase any more sparkling wine, J.D. We can't afford it, and besides… we can't afford it."

"Ah, remorse… remorse the morning after."

"I merely dread the complications of the 'morning after.'" She combed her hair with her fingers and then secured her topknot with two hairpins she retrieved from the floor, along with her gored skirt, which she draped over her arm. "It may surprise you to hear this, but I do not regret one instant of last evening—although it pains me to note it merely took two nights—sleeping under one roof—for this to happen."

J.D. shook his head with an amused expression.

"Well, the one thing I know for a certainty about you, Amelia, is that I never know what you'll say next."

"It's a new century, J.D. Women speak their minds, and besides, coyness never was my strong suit. But in the cold light of day we both know that we mustn't allow this to happen again while we both are still working to build this hotel."

"If we are discreet—"

She shook her head and then winced as her temple throbbed. "No. I know our brains are addled right now, but *think*! Liaisons like this always leak out. The workers won't respect me if they consider me some floozy whose principal occupation is warming your bed. We have an obligation to everyone, including ourselves, to get this hotel finished as quickly as possible." She paused. "And, of course, there's Angus to consider." They exchanged guilty looks.

"Even if he's still a bit sweet on you, darling, Angus is a big boy—"

Darling…

But that almost made it worse, she thought.

"He's been a wonderful friend to us both," she said, "and it just adds another layer to everything. I may not be working for Julia Morgan any longer, but if I were my own employer, *I'd* discharge me for allowing an intimate relationship to develop with a client. I might not regret one moment of what happened in this bedroom, J.D., but the possible repercussions could be lethal. It's the most unprofessional thing I could possibly do, and here I've gone and done it and—"

"Am *I* allowed to say why continuing this liaison, at this particular moment, is a foolhardy idea?"

Brought up short, Amelia put her hands on her hips. "Of course. Please do."

"I'm supposed to be courting Matilda Kemp."

"You're *what*?"

"Shhh!" He pointed toward the other end of the building. "Courting two women simultaneously, especially when one is Ezra Kemp's daughter, is extremely inadvisable, wouldn't you agree?"

Amelia could only stare at him, dumbfounded. Then with an arch look she said, "I don't think what you and I did last night could—in the wildest stretch of the imagination—be called 'courting.' I can't *believe* you're telling me this after… after…"

"Ah… I'm pleased to see that got your dander up. You've been sounding so cool and collected about everything." He rose from the bed and stood naked in front of her, trying unsuccessfully to grasp her hand. "I only told Kemp I'd *consider* courting the poor creature when he tried to blackmail me even after I'd paid my share of the cost of building the gambling club by demanding I pay past due lumber bills for the hotel that burned. When I confronted him about sending his bullyboys, he said his next step would be to get his union hall cronies to cut off supplies for the current hotel that we can't get elsewhere and prove we've been using Chinese labor right along. I have no doubt he could still attempt to make good on either of those threats, plus he also said he'd blackball me with the Committee of Fifty, including my father, so they'd call in the first loan. You must admit, the circumstances *were* rather dire."

"My, my…" Amelia murmured, avoiding everything but

J.D.'s dark eyes. "You know, in the heat of the moment, I'd really forgotten how convoluted your life is."

The chickens in J.D.'s rather sordid life were definitely coming home to roast, she thought glumly. Here was a man who partnered with Ezra Kemp in a gambling and wenching establishment, no doubt trading on the charms of Chinese women to fill their coffers. If that weren't enough, he'd consigned little Wing Lee to Donaldina Cameron's care even before her mother had died, and now he was acknowledging that he was courting a young woman he wasn't partial to as a means of paying past due bills for *lumber*!

She glanced down at his bare feet. Oh yes… James Diaz Thayer had certainly proved himself an exciting, inventive lover, but who *was* this man, really?

A cad and a cardsharp?

Possibly.

Yet, she had known this fact full well before she'd allowed him to take her to bed.

Have I lost my mind?

She remembered J.D. suggesting that plain, ordinary *lust* might be a factor in their unholy attraction. Lust and champagne and the excitement of finding a trunk full of treasure that would provide the funds to finish their dream hotel.

"Well, at least now you have funds to pay Kemp for the wood used in the hotel that burned. You won't have to court Matilda Kemp—unless you want to…"

"Want to? Have you had a *look* at the poor woman?" J.D. shook his head. "You were right, all along, Amelia. Ezra Kemp and his cronies haven't given up on attempting to wrest ownership of the Bay View from me."

But J.D. himself had been one of Kemp's cronies…

With a man like J.D. Thayer, a woman would be foolish, indeed, to assume she understood everything that was going on between the two men or to make more of the events of last night than were merited.

"Can he do that?" she asked, suddenly worried. "Get our sand and lime suppliers to refuse to sell to us? Most of them have never done business with Ezra Kemp."

J.D. reached for his trousers that lay in a heap on the floor. "Let's not concern ourselves with something that hasn't happened yet. What say I make the coffee?"

She quickly finished tying the laces on her boots. "I'll make the coffee. Take your time."

"Wait, Amelia." He buttoned his waist belt while she paused at the door. "Before you go, I'd just like to say—" Then he hesitated.

"Yes?"

She tried not to look at his bare chest or remember how the warm scent of him felt against her cheek. She wondered if she would now hear a full confession of his sins or a tardy acknowledgement of how much his late lover still meant to him. Amelia had the uneasy sensation that he was attempting to read her mood like an opponent's hand of cards.

"Last night," he began, "was... more than wonderful. But, now that I'm fully awake, I do agree with you that circumstances and that champagne bear part of the blame for what happened between us. Everything at the moment *is* rather complicated. The gold and jewels we've found will sort out things considerably, but I think you're right."

"About?"

"That we must be extremely careful not to let anyone else know you and I—"

"I absolutely agree," she cut in.

But I hate it…

"There are a number of dangerous forces lined up against us," he said.

"Against *us*? What forces?"

"Let's just say there are people who are not my champions—nor yours—and who'd prefer someone else be in control of the Bay View Hotel."

"Which people? Kemp? Who else?"

J.D. shook his head. "It would only be a guess on my part."

He knows, but he's not telling me…

"Well, as a first step, " she proposed, "let's agree—no more champagne."

He strode to the door, leaned forward, and kissed her on the cheek. "Sadly, Miss Bradshaw, no more champagne." Then, he kissed her again, although this time, the tip of his tongue invaded her lips just long enough to remind them both of the intoxicating night they'd spent together. At length, he pulled back and gave her a steady look. "And, unfortunately, I agree with you about something else." He placed a fingertip on her lips and she had to steel herself not to take it into her mouth. "No more of *these* delights. At least, until I can officially disengage from any association with the Kemps—father and daughter."

She gave him a brief nod of agreement and walked swiftly away from his bedroom toward the kitchen, hoping to discover that she was the first in the household to be up and dressed. Julia had been right to dismiss her, she thought. She was impulsive and willful and occasionally did not understand herself at all.

❧

Amelia forced herself to ignore all thoughts of the previous night and turned her complete attention to the difficult job of completing the roof. By midday, the Pigati cousins and their fellow workers swarmed over the top floor to cut to her specifications the last of the massive timbers and joists. Franco Pigati led the rest of the "Italian contingent" in the risky task of fastening the cross beams to the vertical concrete walls, open to the sky.

Meanwhile, Amelia sat at the table in the kitchen hunched over plans for the exterior landscaping. Further distracting her concentration and aggravating her persistent headache was the staccato sound of hammers hitting nails, although she took comfort that the steady din overhead meant progress was being made.

About forty minutes later, the site suddenly went quiet. J.D. had driven off on a mission to search for a source of wooden roof shingles since the slate ones they planned had never arrived by boat from Europe. She didn't ask where he planned to obtain this scarce commodity, as the less she was involved with the Kemps—the better.

He's courting Miss Kemp… how insane can this get?

Franco Pigati poked his head in through the doorway. "Miss Bradshaw?"

His worried expression hinted there was trouble.

"What is it?"

"A bunch of men are here to see Mr. Thayer. They say they're from the hiring hall."

A sense of alarm shot through her. "I'll speak with them."

Pigati looked at Amelia uncertainly, but then turned and led the way outside.

"Good morning, gentlemen, or is it nearly noon?" A cluster of four burly men in ill-fitting business suits and porkpie hats greeted her with nods. Across the street she recognized Dick

Spitz, Jake Kelly, and Joe Kavanaugh lounging against a tree. "What can I do for you?"

"You the missus?"

"No, I'm the architect and construction supervisor. And who might you be?"

"Mark Desso," replied the spokesman for the quartet, staring at her skeptically. "Down at the carpenters' hiring hall, we got a report you're using Chinks on this site."

She met Desso's malevolent gaze. "I can tell you without hesitation there are no Chinese laborers being employed as carpenters here." She pointed to Joe Kavanaugh, who immediately pushed away from the tree and slunk around the corner. "I think you should know, sir, that Mr. Kavanaugh was discharged recently for unacceptable work habits and insubordination. Kelly and Spitz were not rehired after a fire destroyed the rebuilding of this hotel due to their incompetence. If any of them brought this accusation regarding Chinese carpenters at this hotel, it is simply untrue and offered in spite." She gestured to the Pigatis. "You must know Franco Pigati? And his cousins, Nico, Aldo, Dominic, and Roman?" She pointed to the circle of men standing behind her, all of them wearing uneasy expressions.

"You work for her?" Mark Desso asked Franco.

"Her and Mr. Thayer. Yeah. They pay fair and on time, Mr. Desso. The only Chinese I've seen around here are the houseboy, his wife, and a little kid."

Franco Pigati was speaking the truth, as far as he knew it. Amelia was grateful that his crew had never laid eyes on the night shift. True, Loy Chen's men were not employed as *carpenters*, but she was just as glad the day workers had no idea there was a night crew being paid ten cents an hour to dig the cisterns and clear the remaining wreckage on the fenced-off back lot and cart it down to the landfill along the waterfront. She wasn't actually lying, she told herself. Just misleading a bunch of bullies.

"May I offer you men some refreshment?" Amelia volunteered. "Lemonade, perhaps?"

Mark Desso looked as if a beverage as mild as lemonade might poison him.

"Don't have time," he said gruffly. He turned to Franco Pigati. "Tell Mr. Thayer that if we hear he's violatin' the rules, here, he'll be brought to task, right and proper." He gazed belligerently at Amelia. "Never heard of no woman doin' this kinda work."

"Some of your members are working on the restoration of the Fairmont Hotel," she informed him coolly. "Julia Morgan is in charge there and I was formerly a member of her team."

"Last I heard, they had some fancy architect from New York on that job," Desso countered.

"Stanford White was shot dead by his mistress's husband," Amelia parried. She enjoyed the startled look on Desso's face in reaction to her blunt language. "Didn't you read about it in the paper?" she asked with an innocent air, of a man she was certain was illiterate. "The Morgan firm took over from McKim, Mead, & White and are doing the entire job now—on time and on budget. Now if you'll excuse me, my men aren't being paid to stand around."

She stared unblinkingly at the foursome until they retreated down the street. Suddenly, she doubted that the quartet had been the official representatives of San Francisco's carpenters at all.

CHAPTER 28

IT WAS AFTER TEN o'clock before J.D. returned to the Bay View that evening, following a day of wrestling with suppliers who were low on everything he needed to buy. By the time he walked into the basement kitchen, Shou Shou and Loy had already served dinner, washed up afterwards, and, with the help of little Foo, set the lanterns out in the back lot for the Chinese crew who were due to arrive soon to excavate the last foot of the cistern on the old lady's lot.

As for Amelia, she didn't trust either J.D. or herself to remain alone together without giving into temptation. She'd left a note for him in the kitchen with a cryptic description of Mark Desso's unwelcome visit and had already retired to her room. Then she swiftly blew out her kerosene lamp so no light would shine under her door to signal she was still awake. By the time she slipped into bed, she was more convinced than ever that the visit from the "carpenters representatives" earlier that day had, indeed, been prompted by the machinations of Ezra Kemp.

Exhausted after her hard day's work and a night of virtually no sleep in J.D.'s private quarters, she turned over in her narrow bed and ordered herself to relax. As she had all day, she stoically put aside all thoughts of the previous evening spent in J.D.'s big brass bed by mentally revisiting her multiplication tables. Before long, the fatigue of her efforts sucked her down in an undertow of dreamless sleep.

⊷

A child's voice cried out, the sound high and shrill. Other shouts and groans and violent noises pierced the silence of Amelia's bedroom. Her door suddenly slammed open, its inadequate lock broken, and the cries and screams burst upon her even more loudly, rousing her to instant wakefulness, her heart pounding.

A huge form loomed in the doorway. Shadowy light from a lamp in the kitchen outlined a man, but his silhouette was far too stout to belong to J.D. or Loy Chen.

Another figure appeared behind the first.

"Think this is her room?" queried a voice in a hoarse whisper.

Amelia tensed, drawing her knees closer to her chest. When the assault came, she jammed the soles of her feet, covered by the bed's blanket, into her attacker's lower midsection, aiming for his groin.

"Oompf! Owwww!" The man howled and stumbled backward, crashing into his confederate.

Amelia frantically felt beneath her mattress and pulled out the loaded pearl handled revolver that she had placed there only days earlier.

"If either of you takes one step closer I will shoot! Now, get out!"

"Ain't no pistol I ever seen around here," croaked a familiar voice.

"Kavanaugh, you're a dead man," shrieked Amelia, pulling the trigger without waiting to take aim. A blast of light flashed from the end of her gun.

"Christ Almighty!" roared the hulking figure that had led the way into Amelia's concrete boudoir.

"Are you hit, Joe?"

"I dunno. Are you? Hey Spitz, Kelly... where are you?"

The invaders scrambled to their feet and backed out of the chamber, taking off down the corridor in the direction from whence they'd come. Without considering the danger, or thinking coherently at all, Amelia dashed after them, fury coursing through her veins as she pursued them down the hallway and into the kitchen. She reached the threshold just as an iron skillet sailed by, landing with a thud in the chest of Joe Kavanaugh's companion, Jake Kelly.

"Uhhhhh!"

Loy Chen then tossed a second weapon from his arsenal of pots and pans, a missile that glanced off the right ear of Joe himself. Dick Spitz stood at the door, looking skinny and scared.

An avalanche of curses spilled from the victims' lips as they tumbled to the ground. Joe Kavanaugh was curled up on the floor, holding his head. Jake Kelly obviously had the wind knocked out of him and turned to stare dumbly at Amelia. She raised her revolver and squeezed the trigger a second time.

The weapon exploded with a bang.

Again, she missed. Kelly turned tail and ran.

"Jesus!" Dick Spitz grabbed Joe Kavanaugh by the shirt collar and dragged him to his feet. The two men bolted for the door and disappeared into the night just as J.D. thundered down the corridor and burst into the hotel kitchen. Meanwhile, the cries outside continued, a frightening sound of mortal combat.

"What's going on?" J.D. demanded. He was dressed, but his shirt collar was open, as if he'd been about to retire to bed. He stared at Amelia in her nightclothes, holding her pistol loosely in her hand while she attempted to control the trembling that shook her entire body. "Are you all right?" he asked, stepping to her side.

"Round-eyes come!" Loy said, practically shouting. He brandished another frying pan over his head. "Beat up Chinese. Very bad this time. Very bad!"

J.D. grabbed Amelia's revolver and charged the kitchen door.

"No, J.D.!" she cried. "There must be hordes of them!"

He ignored her and ran through the door to the outside, shooting the pistol once in the air. He raced across the rear of his property and dashed through the gate that led to the old woman's lot next door. Amelia and Loy armed themselves with kitchen knives and cautiously peered outside. By this time, only low moans could be heard coming from the direction of the unfinished cistern.

"Follow me, Loy," Amelia ordered.

Warily, they approached the back lot where the night crew had been at its tasks. Shadows from the kerosene lanterns cast macabre images of men rolling on the ground in pain, or sitting, dazed, on the edge of the open pit they'd been digging. Some of the injured leaned against the wooden fence that had been built to protect them from prying eyes. By this time, the hooligans had done their dirty work and disappeared into the night.

Amelia stood next to J.D., aghast at the carnage everywhere.

"Thugs. Here to intimidate and maim," he pronounced.

"Joe Kavanaugh, Dick Spitz, and Jake Kelly broke into my room just now," Amelia said. She tried to catch her breath and inhaled deep gulps of cold night air.

"Are you all right? You mean the fellows who worked on the first hotel?

"Yes... Kemp's men, and Kavanaugh must be one of them." Amelia felt J.D.'s steadying hand on her arm. "They tried... well, they tried to attack me, but I fought them off. I shot at them, but—"

"Christ Almighty, Amelia, you could have—I'll *kill* those sons-of-bitches!"

"Didn't you see my note?"

"What note?"

"*Jesú*, I should have stayed up to warn you! Warn these poor men," she cried. "Those same thugs came by with a man from the hiring hall… Mark Desso, he said he was. He said he'd gotten complaints we'd hired Chinese workers and if he ever had proof, he said he'd close us down. That's what I wrote in my note to you earlier."

Just then one of the injured men shrieked in pain.

"Good God," said J.D., "we've got to *do* something to help these poor people."

"Oh, J.D., this is all my fault! I should have—"

"It's *not* your doing. I went to Mill Valley today, among my other stops. I told Kemp this morning I wouldn't marry Matilda. This was his response. He's trying to show me who's boss."

A soft voice cried out. "Oh no! Oh NO!"

Shou Shou had run from the kitchen in her nightclothes and knelt nearby.

"Shou Shou, what is it?" J.D. asked, turning toward the sound of muffled crying.

"Foo! Little Foo."

Amelia and J.D. raced to her side where she cradled the small boy in her lap, rocking him gently.

"They hurt Foo!" Shou Shou wailed. "He just light lamps, not dig, like others. Why they *do* that? *Why?*"

"I'll help her get him inside and try to assist the others," J.D.'s voice was calm and steely. "Will you be all right driving to the Presidio to fetch Angus?"

A glance at little Foo's bruised face was all Amelia needed to fortify her resolve.

"I go with Missy," Loy declared fiercely. "I hold pistol for her. She safe with Loy Chen." He bowed politely, adding, "She very good driver."

Amelia didn't know whether to laugh or cry, so she retreated toward the back door of the hotel, calling over her shoulder, "I'll dress quickly, and we'll be off."

⌦

"One dead, five broken arms, a cracked pelvis, a skull fracture, and three sets of broken ribs," Angus reported, rolling down his sleeves as he appeared at the kitchen door. "Lots of cuts and abrasions, of course."

"And Foo?" Amelia asked. "He just lay there when I bathed him."

Angus's shoulders slumped with the fatigue of serving as a one-man infirmary for the previous four hours. "He's the skull fracture. You two will have to relieve Loy and Shou Shou in an hour or so, to let them get some sleep."

"Yes, of course," murmured Amelia.

"I'll see to the burial," J.D. said wearily.

"Better wait a bit. A few more may not make it."

Amelia felt another wave of guilt wash over her like a cold winter tide. If *only* she'd stayed awake to warn J.D. as soon as he returned last night instead of being such a ninny, worrying about propriety and her "moral weaknesses."

"I never dreamed something so horrible as this would happen—"

She yearned to throw herself into J.D.'s arms for comfort, but stiffened when it was Angus who squeezed her shoulders in sympathy.

"J.D.'s run-in with Kemp today must have triggered this, but it's nasty business, to be sure," Angus said. "It's bound to get out that you two employed Chinese laborers here at night. Then what will your day workers do?"

"Let's hope the Pigatis like the wages we pay them enough to stay on the job." J.D. turned to Amelia. "What do you think they'll do?"

"Let's just pray they *don't* hear about what happened." She blew the steam off her fourth cup of coffee. "I agree with you, J.D., that those men yesterday who came to the site couldn't be officials from the carpenter's hall. Even so, the Pigatis knew them—and feared them."

J.D. said, "They were probably just the advance troops, sent by Kemp to get the lay of the land. Joe Kavanaugh obviously came back with reinforcements."

"Maybe you'll get lucky and everything'll remain hush-hush," Angus said, rubbing his eyes. "If Kemp is behind this, he doesn't dare brag about what he's ordered done here."

"He won't stop at this little dust-up," J.D. predicted. He shook his head, admitting defeat. "This is bound to set us back recruiting workers and maybe even supplies. It's time we faced facts. There's no way we'll be ready for the April eighteenth anniversary." He reached for Amelia's hand. "At least you, Loy, and Shou Shou came through this in one piece."

Amelia gave J.D.'s hand a sympathetic squeeze. Angus regarded the pair for a moment and said, "Here's one scrap of good news. Loy Chen has already arranged for a Chinese benevolent society to house and nurse the men who've been hurt. A few of their members will come tonight, after dark, and move them, now that I've set the broken bones and stitched everyone up. You might get away with this if you don't let any of the day workers come near the ballroom where I've got 'em all laid out."

"Well, that *is* good news," J.D. said, staring off into space. "I couldn't even think that far ahead."

"And Loy also told me that Donaldina Cameron has organized her ladies to raise the necessary funds to help pay for their care," Angus added. "All on the q.t., of course." He pointed to the stove. "Do you think you could fry me an egg? I haven't eaten since midday, yesterday."

Amelia hardly heard his question. "When do you think little Foo will regain consciousness?"

Angus looked down at his coffee mug. "He might not. Shou Shou will tell us if there's any change." With a clatter, Amelia set her own mug down on the kitchen table. But before she could leave the room, the doctor warned her, "I'm afraid his chances of survival are slim, Amelia. Very slim, indeed."

She cast a stricken look at J.D. and removed her apron. "Can you fry Angus an egg? I'll just go and relieve Shou Shou."

❧

The seven-year-old lay on a pile of J.D.'s clothing that had been fashioned into a makeshift pallet. Raw sunlight shone through the ballroom's windows still devoid of the glass panes due to be installed within the week. Amelia shivered as a draft of chilly morning air brushed her cheeks.

She knelt beside Shou Shou, whose head was bowed. Soft Cantonese words tumbled from her lips. Amelia found herself praying as well, a disjointed plea to a God she didn't have much faith in to save an innocent child from the heartless cruelty inflicted upon him.

She opened her eyes and gazed down at Foo's immobile countenance. After a few seconds, she realized that Shou Shou had been whispering prayers for the dead.

❧

"I want you to get some rest, Amelia," Angus insisted. He took her by the hand and forcibly led to her room off the kitchen corridor. "Now."

"No!" she cried and could hear the shrillness in her voice. "There are a million and one things to do and I—"

When she allowed herself to think of the brutality that Kemp had undoubtedly unleashed, her anger nearly choked her. Keeping busy helped keep her fury at bay and also warded off thoughts of Foo. And besides, she had to see that every measure was taken to protect the surviving workers.

"J.D. will see to the removal of the Chinese tonight."

"But I worry that the day crew—"

"J.D. says they didn't suspect a thing. You were clever to have them spend the day unloading all that terra-cotta and stacking it out back. Loy stood guard to make sure no one came into the ballroom. He told everyone that there was a bad infestation of rats and that he would take care of it. No one ventured near the place. Now, just take off your skirt and shirtwaist and get into bed." He gently shoved her into her room and turned his back while she removed her clothes. "Under the bedclothes with you now."

"Yes," she murmured, a crushing fatigue already pulling her towards sleep.

"Good girl." To her surprise, Angus took a seat on the edge of her iron cot. He reached for her hand.

"Amelia—"

"Angus, thank you so much for all you've done for us." She was grateful for the non-stop medical care he'd dispensed during the last twenty-four hours, but she also desperately hoped to forestall any intimate conversation. "Now that I'm actually lying in bed, I'm suddenly totally exhausted. Good night. And thank you."

"I want you to think about something as you go to sleep." She obediently closed her eyes. His big hand squeezed hers. "I want you to seriously reconsider my offer of marriage."

Amelia's lids flew open. "Angus, this is not the time or place—"

"It's precisely the time and place," he countered. "Tonight proved it. We work well together as a team, and surely you must see now that you'll need protection if you are going to continue to work in the dangerous world of construction—especially in a rough-and-tumble city like San Francisco. I'm willing to provide you that protection—no questions asked—along with a home and all the freedom you require. I want you as my *wife*, Amelia, and I will shield you from dangers like this. Will you think about that as you drift off to sleep?"

Amelia could only gaze up at him as words refused to form in her head. Finally, she said, "You are a good and honest man, Angus, and I am honored by your offer, but I do not seek a shield. I seek—" She hesitated, not actually sure of what to say next.

"What, Amelia? *What* do you seek?" She could detect a note of annoyance that he was barely holding in check.

"I don't honestly know, Angus. I just know it's not a shield. It is not a man standing in my stead, doing what I should be doing for myself." And how could she tell him about her feelings for J.D. at a time like this, let alone the fact that she and J.D. had—

Angus abruptly interrupted her scattered thoughts. "There are important differences between men and women, Amelia," he said sharply. "And there are differences between dreamers like you and Jamie, and people like me, who deal with the ugly here-and-now. Jamie should know better, but perhaps you're too young or too ambitious, or too headstrong, to realize the risks you take every day. But you will."

He bent down and kissed her on top of her head in a gesture of resignation and mild irritation. Even in her over-wrought state, she knew Angus had seriously begun to doubt that he could ever win her heart—but that hadn't deterred him from wanting to make her his wife. But before she could offer a reply, he departed her narrow room without bidding her good night.

❦

Angus returned to the Presidio, the wounded were transferred to Chinatown, and Amelia plunged back into the work of readying the hotel for its opening day, which now, with any luck, would be the Fourth of July.

A few weeks after the terrible attack against the Chinese workers, she was startled to see a handsome woman with a wing of white hair under her hat walk up Jackson Street and step onto the hotel's property.

"Why, Miss Cameron!" Amelia exclaimed, striding past a pile of lumber to greet her. "How wonderful to see you! I intended to visit the Presbyterian Mission to thank you for all you did to help us after our workers… after all the trouble," she amended quickly, with a glance over her shoulder at the Pigati cousins. The men were fifty feet away, clustered around the wooden forms where several low cement walls would soon be built in the terraced garden. The hotel itself at last had its classic moldings and baseboards installed in all the rooms and painters were now swarming everywhere.

"It's good to see you too, my dear. I came to check on how Loy and Shou Shou are faring."

"It's been very hard for them, of course," Amelia confided. "We all miss little Foo terribly. He was such a loving spirit. You're so kind to come. Our new stove has been installed this week. Come into the kitchen and let me brew you a proper cup of tea."

When they entered the rear of the hotel, Amelia marveled at the effusive greeting that the normally reticent Shou Shou lavished on their visitor. The young woman indicated that Amelia should sit beside Donaldina and swiftly scurried around making tea. She set the pot and cups upon the spanking new worktable in the kitchen with all the pomp and ceremony due an Empress of China—which, in her eyes, Miss Cameron might as well have been.

"The injured men are recovering well," Donaldina reported soberly. Then she glanced at Amelia and said, "I do wish Mr. Thayer were also here. I wanted to thank him for his latest act of generosity. Please tell him Wing Lee and all the little girls her age in our care have new shoes and dresses, thanks to his recent kindness."

"Certainly I will. He had some sort of lunch to attend today," Amelia said, absorbing that fact that J.D. continued to support the child. In the weeks since the attack on their workers—and the solitary night they'd spent together—she often had no idea where he went, day or evening. "I'll be sure to give him a message."

"And something else." Donaldina paused, and then continued, "This concerns you also, my dear. I've been speaking regularly with Rudolph Spreckels, who, as you may know, is one of San Francisco's civic leaders trying to put a stop to the ills polluting our city." Anyone who read a newspaper knew that the California sugar baron had launched a public campaign to counter graft and corruption, as well as the countenancing—indeed, the encouragement—of forced prostitution by elected officials. "Mr. Spreckels has been very supportive of our fight to end the enslavement of women like Shou Shou, here," she added with a gentle look in the direction of the Chinese woman pouring tea.

"And my friend Ling Lee," Shou Shou murmured.

Amelia was startled to hear Shou Shou call Ling Lee her friend. Meanwhile, Miss Cameron said with a nod, "Yes, like Ling Lee, who was very brave to run away from the brothel, as she did."

"But she didn't stay with you at the Mission Home," Amelia ventured. "Why was that, Miss Cameron?"

"She had… a different view of life than we do at the home on Sacramento Street," Donaldina replied slowly. "But we fought the same injustice to women."

"You did?" Amelia replied, puzzled. "I thought she and Mr. Thayer… well… I thought that they simply continued the practice of—"

"You should probably speak with Mr. Thayer about those subjects."

Amelia sensed they both were uncomfortable with the direction of the conversation. She'd been fishing for information about Ling Lee, and that was none of her business, she chided herself. She and J.D. had been models of decorum in the melancholy days that followed Foo's death and had separately mourned the losses suffered that terrible night. She was ashamed of herself now, for even bringing up the subject of J.D.'s relationship with the Chinese woman who died in the quake. She should wait until he chose to tell her about their liaison—if he ever did. It was just that—

"You mentioned Mr. Spreckels?" Amelia said, bringing the conversation back to the crusader who had donated a hundred thousand dollars to the anti-corruption cause.

"Ah, yes. That's one of the reasons for my visit. He would like to speak with both you and Mr. Thayer to learn more about the disturbances you had on this property. Washington has finally sent us more Treasury men to help. They wish to know whom you suspect of perpetrating this dreadful evil on those defenseless workers."

Amelia felt uneasy. "I think Mr. Thayer would prefer to be discreet about the employment of Chinese on his project. I can certainly vouch that he paid them the agreed-upon wage, fed them each night, and provided sanitary facilities while they worked here. It's just with the frightening costs of trying to rebuild the hotel after losing it *twice*, he saw no alternative—"

"Both Mr. Spreckels and I understand that these have been trying and extraordinary times," Donaldina hastened to assure Amelia. "Loy Chen has always spoken highly of Mr. Thayer. In fact, we all respect him for protecting and providing for little Wing Lee, even after her mother died. But as for this latest attack, Mr. Spreckels needs *facts*, not hearsay, if he is to make headway with his reforms down at City Hall. Absolute anonymity will be respected, I assure you."

Amelia remained silent for a moment. "I cannot speak for Mr. Thayer," she said finally, "but I was an eyewitness to what was done by those hooligans and would be happy to tell Mr. Spreckels what I know—once the hotel is finished."

"And when might that be?" Donaldina appeared pleased with Amelia's response.

"After all these delays? Early July, I expect," she said.

"Well, no doubt we'll all be at the opening of the Fairmont

soon," Donaldina replied. "If I have the opportunity, I'll be sure to introduce you to Mr. Spreckels, and you can take it from there."

Amelia nodded, inhaled deeply, and tried to ignore the leaden feeling in her chest. The Law brothers had been decent enough to send them invitations for the gala evening. The Fairmont was schedule to debut first and thereby garner tremendous attention on the first anniversary of the quake and fire. She ached for J.D.'s disappointment. She smiled at Donaldina, though she could hardly disguise her sadness.

"It's hard to believe that it's been nearly a year since the quake and that the Fairmont Hotel opens in two weeks' time."

CHAPTER 29

O N THE EVENING OF April 18, 1907, Amelia stood in the lobby of the Fairmont Hotel atop Nob Hill amid a swirl of glittering finery. It seemed as if the entire city of San Francisco had come to commemorate the one-year anniversary of the 1906 earthquake and fire. Women in beaded gowns with feathers in their hair and men in starched shirt-fronts and black evening clothes filled the vast reception area. An army of tail-coated waiters bustled through the throng carrying silver trays bristling with a forest of champagne flutes.

The distinguished guests—many of whom had spent the better part of the year living in army tents—sipped the spar-kling wine to the dulcet sounds of a string quartet playing in the refurbished Laurel Court. The domed room buzzed in anticipation of the enormous repast being readied in the nearby grand ballroom. Afterwards, tables would be cleared, and the visitors would be welcome to dance until dawn.

Amelia marveled at how strange it felt to be standing on the Fairmont property without her sturdy work boots or cotton shirtwaist. Only yesterday she had been wearing a pair of her father's old tweed trousers underneath her sensible skirt while she inspected progress on the Bay View's roof joists in a driving wind. Truth was, she felt slightly out of place in the aqua beaded chiffon gown she'd bought two years earlier in Paris and retrieved from her aunt's house in

Oakland. The dress cost what was now a week's salary, and she was grateful she'd already owned something decent to wear on such a momentous occasion.

"Come, come, Amelia," Hartland Law said with a hearty wave. "You were certainly part of this effort at the outset. That's why my brother and I insisted you come to our opening," added the Fairmont's co-owner with a mischievous glance in Julia Morgan's direction. "Come stand in the reception line and help us smile at everyone."

Amelia looked over at Julia, somber in gray taffeta, standing near one of the soaring faux marble pillars. "Of course, Amelia," she said. "Do stand in line with us."

She and her former employer hadn't worked together for months, yet Julia didn't appear to display any acrimony this night. Next to her stood Ira Hoover, resplendent in white tie and tails, and to his right, Lacy Fiske, dressed in a conservative navy velvet outfit with lace collar and cuffs. She was beaming, apparently delighted to bathe in Julia's reflected glory.

"Ripping, absolutely ripping!" pronounced Rudolph Spreckels to the Law brothers. "You two have created an absolute triumph."

"Why, thank you, sir!" Hartland Law replied jovially. "Have some champagne!"

A photographer from the *Call*, poised to take a picture, shouted above the din at the illustrious group.

"Congratulations, everyone. Miss Morgan! Can we have you look this way, please?"

"Good heavens, *no!*"

"Oh, come now," Herbert Law chided her. "I know how you detest all this, Julia, but we should have a record of this marvelous night."

The reticent Miss Morgan, however, was adamantly opposed and stepped behind the looming pillar, making a show of talking with another well-wisher.

"Well then, come over here, Amelia," Hartland Law directed, pointing to a spot between his brother and himself. "You played an early part in our success, even though your *present* employer hopes to steal some of our trade," he added jovially. He motioned for several of his bankers to join in the lineup. "All right," he called to the photographer. "Snap your shutter, young man, and be quick about it."

Julia might be annoyed Amelia had allowed her picture to be taken, but Amelia figured she needed all the public recognition she could get. Once the Bay View opened, she'd be looking for employment.

After the pictures were taken, Hartland Law bent down and whispered in Amelia's ear. "You and Miss Morgan have fulfilled our faith in you, my dear. There were those who called us fools to engage you as our architects, but you've done your fellow damsels proud. I think your former employer has recovered from whatever it was that upset her a while back."

"Thank you… I hope so," murmured Amelia. Hartland Law was a keen observer and had to be one of the kindest men in San Francisco.

Her host glanced around the enormous lobby filled with music and merrymakers. "Just look at all this. An Act of God brought this city to its knees, but thanks to so much hard, dedicated work, she's risen from the ashes, looking better than ever."

"Let's just hope this crowd pays their room bills tonight," deadpanned Herbert Law.

Once the photographer drifted off, Amelia discreetly approached Donaldina Cameron, who introduced her to

Rudolph Spreckels. Both listened attentively while Amelia described events on the night Foo was fatally attacked.

"I greatly appreciate your candor, my dear," Spreckels said, "and rest assured, I will treat what you've told me with utmost confidentiality. President Roosevelt has sent Mr. Burns and his colleagues to help us stamp out this scourge of graft and intimidation."

Only mildly reassured that the likes of Ezra Kemp would be apprehended and punished at some point, Amelia turned to acknowledge a pack of silver-haired bankers and lawyers, as well as several officials from City Hall—those, at least, who were not currently incarcerated.

Back in March, His Honor the mayor had been arrested and was awaiting trial on serious charges of corruption. The greatest City Hall fixer of them all, Abe Reuf, had pleaded not guilty to accusations of graft and continued to live comfortably under house arrest in an impressive residence on Fillmore Street. The alleged offenses? Taking bribes in exchange for granting franchises for city telephone service and overhead trolleys, not to mention accepting "donations" for guaranteeing police protection for the illicit brothels and gambling enterprises. At least Spreckels and his good government squad had shown some muscle.

As far as this evening was concerned, none of the current political turmoil—not even the controversies over price gouging for lumber or the continued enslavement of female abductees in nearby Chinatown—could dull the festivities this night. It was clearly an occasion that marked the official rebirth of a city some had predicted—like Pompeii—would never rise again.

As Amelia surveyed the scene, she couldn't help but wish the Bay View had been able to open first and on the anniversary date. Still, she mused, each celebrant in tonight's gathering was a *survivor*, just as she was. The Fairmont's spectacular renaissance was proof positive that the new San Francisco would one day become everything Grandfather Hunter had predicted: a major seaport on the Pacific with grand architecture, vibrant commerce, and cultural institutions that would one day rival those of New York, London, or Paris. She was certain that if her grandfather were alive, he'd also be immensely proud of this latest incarnation of his hotel, rising from the rubble at Taylor and Jackson streets.

She glanced at the hordes still funneling through the Fairmont's grand entranceway and considered the fates of her father and grandfather, men so utterly different from one another and yet both part of the fabric of the city she loved.

Off to her right stood Aunt Margaret, put on the guest list at Julia's behest, Amelia surmised. Her older relative was decked out in a gown of ancient vintage and sat with a group of girlhood friends near the potted palms. Amelia felt a rush of affection for her. Thank God she had survived the cataclysmic events of 1906 and was here to celebrate San Francisco's astonishing triumph over adversity.

Out of the corner of her eye Amelia noted two gentlemen—a redhead and a brunette—chatting amiably with each other near the potted palms. Near them, Angus had suddenly appeared and was bending toward Amelia's friend and her grandfather's former caretaker, nurse Edith Pratt. With some relief, Amelia could see that the pair were deeply absorbed in conversation.

As Amelia continued to scan the throng, she wondered if the elder James Thayer and his wife would make an appearance this evening. And what of their son? Was the Fairmont's gala reopening too much salt in a wound? Now that the Fairmont was ready for business, she couldn't help but feel sympathy for J.D. and the difficulties they'd repeatedly encountered. Would he find the Fairmont's faux marble columns and triple alabaster domes arching over the Laurel Court an inspiration—or a bitter pill? There was no question, but that it would be awhile before paying guests would be filing into *his* hotel.

Is that why J.D. isn't here?

Amelia fought against her feelings of disappointment. As revelers inched through the receiving line, she perfunctorily nodded and murmured to people she knew until her eyes widened with surprise at the sight of two well-dressed women, one petite, the other gargantuan, following obediently behind Ezra Kemp.

Kemp abandoned them with a brief word, heading directly for the smoking lounge to hobnob with other city wigs puffing on their cigars.

Amelia watched the pair glance uncertainly around the vast lobby, looking lost. Unable to stem her burning curiosity about the woman J.D. had described to a tee and had been instructed to "court," she casually walked across the marble floors and said quietly, "Hello. I'm Amelia Bradshaw, Mr. Thayer's architect on the Bay View Hotel. I'm not sure he's attending the opening this evening so I thought I'd introduce myself. Have either of you had a cup of the punch?"

The slender young woman, half the size of the giantess standing beside her, swiftly extended her gloved hand.

"I'm Emma Stivers and this is Miss Matilda Kemp, the daughter of Ezra Kemp, Mr. Thayer's former business associate." She turned to her companion. "We're *delighted* to meet our first woman architect, aren't we Tilly? Mr. Thayer told us about your fine work, but we could certainly see it for ourselves as we drove down Taylor Street on our way here."

Amelia smiled and took the measure of Matilda Kemp. The lady in question had flushed scarlet during this exchange and was looking everywhere but at Amelia.

Meanwhile, Emma Stivers spoke up again. "You know, Miss Bradshaw, should we not have a chance to see Mr. Thayer this evening in this crush of people, please tell him we were looking for him tonight because we were unable to speak to him during his recent visit with Mr. Kemp in Mill Valley."

Amelia rapidly searched for a way to appear in the know about J.D.'s foray into enemy territory.

"Ah... yes. I believe Mr. Thayer was in search of another batch of cross beams for the Bay View's roof."

The two exchanged worried glances. "He did not order lumber," Matilda blurted.

"*Tilly*," Miss Stivers said in a tone that held an unmistakable warning.

"May I offer you a glass of lemonade?" Amelia volunteered, pointing to a long table with a large crystal punch bowl at one end.

The pretty half of the duo smiled at Amelia and widened her eyes, all fine manners and charm. "Lemonade sounds most refreshing, thank you, but in case we don't see Mr. Thayer," she repeated, "Miss Kemp and I merely wish him to know that, even though my friend here is perfectly amenable to Mr. Thayer's recent decision involving her, Mr. Thayer may still be hearing from Mr. Kemp *unexpectedly* once again and... well, we thought he'd like to *know* that, so as to be prepared for Mr. Kemp's possible visit."

Amelia felt as if the substance of the conversation had

been communicated in code. "Shall I tell Mr. Thayer to expect Miss Kemp's father soon?"

"Oh, Emma… I don't think we should…" Matilda's face was now the hue of a ripe tomato.

"Of course we should," Emma interrupted firmly, and then addressed Amelia. "Please tell Mr. Thayer exactly that. That Miss Kemp is perfectly fine with his recent decision concerning them *both*." She turned to address her companion. "That's right, Tilly, isn't it?"

Matilda nodded emphatically but didn't elaborate.

Emma smiled at Amelia. "The second part of the message to Mr. Thayer is that Mr. Kemp—or his representatives— may be calling at the Bay View very soon on another matter." Her manner grew grave, as if Ezra Kemp were sure to be a bearer of bad news.

"I'll be sure to tell Mr. Thayer that," replied Amelia, glancing toward the entrance door, "although, there he is… and you can tell him yourself."

"Emma!" Matilda cried, nearly screeching with anxiety. "What if Papa sees Mr. Thayer here? He was so displeased, there's no telling—" She clutched at Emma's arm, adding desperately, "Please… I think might faint!"

Emma Stivers caught Amelia's glance and inquired urgently. "Do you know where the women's restrooms are, by chance?"

J.D. had spotted their group but was waylaid by James Hopper, the reporter from the *Call* whose story about the Bay View had caused Amelia such grief.

"Over there," Amelia directed, pointing to the opposite end of the lobby. "Down the corridor to the left and then it's on the left."

"Come, Tilly, there's a girl," Emma said soothingly. "We'll

just have a good face splash, and you'll be right as rain." She smiled brightly at Amelia. "Good-bye, Miss Bradshaw. Thank you so much for your kindness, and be sure to deliver *both* messages, won't you?"

"Yes, of course," Amelia replied, amazed by how swiftly the pair decided to vacate the lobby.

Emma linked her arm with Matilda's and whisked her through the throng, disappearing among the swirling chiffon and dark-coated celebrants. Amelia didn't wait for them to turn the corner and disappear from view before beginning to fret over the news that Kemp could easily set his bullyboys on J.D. to beat him once again—or worse.

Her sudden fears were mollified somewhat by the recollection that—though Matilda Kemp may have worried about a contretemps between her father and J.D.—the object of J.D.'s "courting" didn't seem particularly overwrought concerning her supposed suitor's apparent decision to end their almost-engagement.

Suddenly her spirits rose. It would seem J.D. had unilaterally called a halt to his spurious courtship of Miss Kemp, a conclusion she found extremely gratifying.

Perhaps her employer was neither a cad nor a cardsharp.

What a lovely thought.

She and J.D. would certainly have to behave themselves until the Bay View Hotel was completed and had opened its doors. But after that, who knew what might evolve? Amelia's life had taken so many strange twists since she'd returned from Paris, she had given up trying to predict the future at all.

It was just a matter of being careful, that's all.

Amelia turned and beheld J.D. Thayer, roguishly handsome in full evening dress. He smiled warmly and extended his hand, which the architect shook primly.

His ebony hair was neatly trimmed, as were his mustache and sideburns. On his tanned face there was no trace of the beating he'd received weeks earlier. One would hardly suspect he was doing manual labor each day along side his construction crew.

"Turn around," he said. "Let me have a look at you." For a full five seconds, he took in her festive costume. "My, my," he said after another long pause. He eyed the modest ostrich feather she'd tucked in her hair. "May I say you look lovely this evening, Miss Bradshaw?" he added formally. "The picture of Parisian fashion, I might add."

She attempted to maintain her aplomb under the close scrutiny of several curious onlookers, including James Hopper. "How kind of you to say so, Mr. Thayer."

J.D. leaned still closer. "I was expecting to escort you here myself, but you ran out before I was dressed."

"I thought it advisable to arrive separately. I wasn't absolutely sure you'd turn up."

"Ah… I almost didn't, but then it would have been lovely to walk in here with you on my arm."

"J.D.!" she admonished. Then she asked in a low voice, "This celebration isn't too painful for you?"

"It smarts only slightly. I'm just relieved you and I are alive to enjoy it."

"My sentiments exactly." She inclined her head and whispered in his ear, "Miss Kemp and Miss Stivers said to expect another 'visit' from Ezra sometime soon, and that Miss Kemp is—in her friend Emma's words—perfectly amenable to your recent decision."

"I am sure that she is," J.D. replied cryptically. His glance swept the room, though he didn't elaborate any further.

"Kemp's in the smoking lounge," she informed him.

"You know, J.D., those two women were awfully nice, but they seemed frightened little mice, especially Matilda."

"They should be. Ezra Kemp doesn't give a damn about their well-being."

"How terrible for them."

J.D. gave her a somber look. "I expect that all of us must all watch out for trouble in the next little while. Meanwhile, my dear Miss Bradshaw, may I ask for this dance?"

"Is that wise?"

"Probably not, but let's anyway."

And so it was that on the first anniversary of the 1906 cataclysmic earthquake and fire, James Diaz Thayer and his architect, Amelia Hunter Bradshaw, entered the glittering ballroom and became the talk of the festivities as one of the handsomest couples to celebrate the opening of the Fairmont Hotel and the rebirth of San Francisco.

A few minutes before one a.m., J.D. walked Amelia home, kissed her soundly, and, once her bedroom door closed and its new lock secured, walked back to the all-night celebration continuing at the Fairmont.

❧

"So what'll it be, Thayer? The mutton or the veal?"

"Neither, Kemp. I want to talk to you." The hotel restaurant was full of noisy diners enjoying a full-course supper served all night "on the house."

"Really? What about? I heard your Chinks had their heads bashed a while back."

"And how did you hear that?"

"Oh, it gets around. You know what a small town San Francisco is."

"Ezra, your little game fools no one, especially me. I know

you sent those goons. They killed two people this time—including a defenseless child—and maimed scores of others, so this is no joke."

"You think anyone cares if there are two fewer Chinks in this town?"

J.D. abruptly stood up, ignoring the fact that his impulsive move might stir interest among their fellow diners.

"Sit down!" Kemp hissed. Lowering his voice even more, he muttered, "Thayer, I am giving you official notice that I will recommend that the board of directors of the Committee of Fifty call their initial loan for the first hotel you rebuilt on that property."

J.D. reclaimed his seat. If Kemp figured this was his principal card to play, J.D. was home free, for the bastard apparently had no idea of the money and gems he and Amelia had found in the buried trunk. Thayer had no need of the Committee's largesse any longer. He merely had to liquidate some of the found booty to get his hotel built, then open its doors and pay off his present expenses along with the earlier loans. The fees of paying guests would serve as a cushion and Kemp would no longer have any hold over him.

"And what makes you think that the board would vote with you on calling the old loan?" J.D. inquired calmly. "They can barely tolerate your uncouth presence as it is and will cut you dead as soon as they no longer need your lumber." He leaned forward and stared hard at Kemp. "Do you really think that board will vote your way just because you demand it? You have a lot to learn, Ezra, about the ways of the idle rich."

"They won't be pleased to learn you're violating the law and going against the hiring halls, employing Chinks who steal an honest man's wages."

"Honest men like Joe Kavanaugh, Dick Spitz, and Jake

Kelly who killed innocent people while working for *you*?" J.D. narrowed his eyes. "Why, I expect Burns and those government men would advise our local authorities that you could be held as an accessory to murder."

"As I said, nobody cares if a couple of Chinese are killed on a job."

"But you must know by now, men like my father despise attempts at unionizing working men and don't think labor laws apply to *them*. Trust me, sending Mark Desso from the hiring hall to do your bidding won't endear you to the likes of Big Jim Thayer."

"You can't prove my men were part of the… unpleasantness that night. I happen to know your buddy James Hopper and his photographer weren't there that night."

"That doesn't matter. I have plenty of proof."

"*What?*" Kemp scoffed.

Again, J.D. rose from his chair, this time determined to depart. "That's just the question you should be worried about, Kemp."

Ezra grabbed his sleeve. "Just a minute! It's that Bradshaw woman, isn't it? She told you she saw my men? Well, she's lying! No one will believe *her*!" He lowered his voice, spitting out his words. "I've heard it said you're paying that architect of yours for more services than just her building plans."

J.D. clapped his hand on Kemp's and removed it forcibly from his jacket. "I suggest that you inform Kelly, Spitz, and Kavanaugh that I have twenty-four-hour lookouts posted everywhere," he said under his breath. "If my men see anymore of your spies in the neighborhood, they have orders to shoot such trespassers on sight."

Then, J.D. turned his back on his host and strode past the Fairmont's busy maître d'.

The morning following the Fairmont's grand opening, work on the hotel proceeded uneventfully. Both J.D. and Amelia were swamped with pressing duties, leaving few moments for communication between them. Seven-year-old Foo's absence was painfully apparent, and there was little banter around their dining table. Loy kept to himself and Shou Shou's mournful expression was heartbreaking to behold. As for Amelia, she excused herself as soon as they finished eating supper and went to her chamber, turning the newly installed bolt on her door. The gesture was as much to keep herself from seeking comfort in J.D.'s arms as from any expectation J.D. would come knocking at her door after midnight.

The next day, after breakfast, Amelia stood by the entrance to J.D.'s downstairs office and rapped sharply on the half-open door.

"Two of the Pigati boys didn't show up," she announced from the threshold. "I just can't believe it. They've been so loyal up to now."

"They're still loyal. I've posted them on the third floor inside scaffolding."

"We're not ready to put the slate on, yet," Amelia protested.

As it had turned out, there were no wooden shingles to be had in all of San Francisco—other than those supplied by Kemp Lumber Company. However, miracle of miracles, the slate that had been ordered months before and assumed lost or stolen en route to the Port of San Francisco had just turned up at the docks. The roof would now be covered in the expensive material that was fire resistant and enhanced the *beaux-arts* motif of the overall design.

"Nico and Roman are on guard duty." J.D. rapidly moved the beads on his abacus and made notations on the sheet of paper in front of him. "There aren't any other lookouts to hire this week."

"And you didn't tell *me*?" Amelia demanded. "Their supervisor?"

"That's right." J.D. didn't look up from his papers.

"Don't you think you should explain why?"

His eyes remained focused on his desk. "I merely felt it a wise precaution."

Amelia was flabbergasted by J.D.'s cold, almost impersonal tone.

"Do you mind explaining *why* you think it's wise to keep your construction supervisor in the dark?" she demanded with rising irritation.

He set the abacus aside in frustration. "Because it just *is*! Now will you please allow me to get back to my work?"

Again taken aback by his testiness, Amelia advanced into J.D.'s office.

"No. I won't, O Mighty Hotel Owner! I want you to tell me right now what danger has prompted you to assign two of my best men to other duties without consulting me?"

"Because I pay their wages."

Amelia stared across the space that separated them and shook her head.

"J.D. Thayer, don't you *dare* do this," she said in a low, angry voice. She marched to the edge of his desk, snatched the papers he'd been making notes on, and crumpled them in her hand. "You may pay their wages, but their safety is *my* concern and they're under *my* direction, so I'll ask you not to patronize me, J.D. Not at this late stage. We may have—*briefly*—been lovers, but either you and I are working as full partners to build this hotel or you will find yourself building it by yourself."

J.D. regarded her for a long moment, appearing to mull something over in his mind. "Quite an Irish temper you've got there, miss."

"Scots-Irish," she corrected frostily.

He pointed to a straight-back chair. "Sit down." When she'd reluctantly complied, he said, "I've learned that Dick Spitz and Jake Kelly, from the first hotel, were always Kemp's spies on this site. I imagine, now, Kavanaugh is too and that he told Kemp every single thing that went on here, so Ezra could feel he had the upper hand. He's been furious ever since I announced that courting his daughter was no longer part of my building plans. Plainly, *his* plan from the beginning—just as you warned me—was to gain financial control of the Bay View by any means necessary. My guess is that he's assuming I haven't given into his strong-arm tactics to marry his daughter because—" J.D. paused, and then continued, "…because there might be another woman in my life. And now, I'm fairly sure, he thinks that woman is *you*."

"Oh." Chastened, Amelia bit her lower lip. "I see. Either Kavanaugh spied on us on the day I discharged him, which was also the day that you and I found the trunk and we— well, you know—and then the scoundrel tattled to—" She hesitated. "Or Kemp is just guessing that a man and a woman can't possibly work together in such close proximity without falling into—"

"You aren't finishing your sentences very well today, Amelia, but you're a very intelligent woman. And, as it happened, we *couldn't* work together in such close proximity without… well, could we?"

Amelia leaned forward to touch his hand that lay on the desk. "No, it seems we could not."

He gave her hand a squeeze while deftly withdrawing his own. "I had a rather nasty exchange with Kemp the night of the Fairmont's opening and I've decided to take his threats more seriously. Hence, Nico and Roman are now on the roof."

"That sounds like a sensible precaution, and thank you for telling me this, even at this late date, J.D. But honestly, don't try to shield me as if I'm a hothouse flower. I'll feel much safer if I know exactly what we're up against."

He nodded but didn't comment further.

She rose from her chair and turned to go. Then she paused and faced him again. "You know, if you and I are to… to find our way through all this, there must be no secrets. No private arrangements on the side. We must tell each other the unvarnished truth at all times."

J.D. looked down at his desk. "Ah… the 'unvarnished truth.' But what you must understand, Amelia, is that I've been a man on my own my entire life. I'm not in the habit of consulting anyone before I make decisions."

"As you may have noticed, I'm rather independent myself. But I very much appreciate being told what's happening where it concerns *me*. I'll do the same for you so there'll be no surprises on either side, all right? That way, we're each free to *choose* if we agree with the other person's decisions… and then make decisions on our own."

J.D. appeared to be mulling over her last words but all he said was, "Where are we on the roof?

Amelia paused. "The crossbeams are up and the wood slats on top of them were nailed down yesterday. When the tar paper gets here later today we'll be ready to roll it down. Perhaps those lookouts can also help us with that while keeping an eye out for intruders?"

J.D. leaned back in his chair, smiling faintly. "Always out to save a penny."

"When I can. Safely." Amelia shrugged and then disappeared down the hallway.

Once she left the room, J.D.'s expression grew somber. For his part, he was grateful that she wasn't aware of the most recent threatening note from Kemp, who was enraged to learn from his apparent spies that J.D. had secured slate for the roof and canceled the order for shingles from Kemp Lumber. This latest vicious warning had been delivered just that morning by the wagon driver who brought the last load of slate tiles to the site. If Amelia ever knew the "unvarnished truth" about what was contained in that ugly missive, J.D. would have to make damned sure that she left San Francisco for good.

In fact, he still might have to.

CHAPTER 30

MERCIFULLY, THE REST OF April and the month of May slipped by uneventfully. J.D. and Amelia kept busy in their own spheres, rarely exchanging anything more than pleasantries or information relating to their business, while Loy and Shou Shou somberly went about their daily routines never mentioning the loss of little Foo. Whenever Amelia felt a strange pang that J.D. made no move to see her privately, she sternly reminded herself this was just as it should be.

In the middle of June, Amelia looked up from an array of building plans spread across the table in her kitchen head-quarters when her foreman opened the back door.

"A Miss Julia Morgan is here to see you, Miss Bradshaw."

Startled, Amelia watched as Franco Pigati stepped aside, revealing Amelia's former employer standing alone in the doorway.

"Hello," said her visitor. "May I come in?"

"Julia! Please do." Amelia hastily stood up. "How... how grand to see you."

The petite figure appeared her usual trim self, dressed in a matching brown gabardine skirt and suit jacket, silk blouse with a mannish silk tie, and a small brown velvet hat perched at a jaunty angle. Her sturdy shoes were polished to a glistening shine.

"I'm sorry to interrupt."

"Oh no... it's—" Amelia was suddenly tongue-tied. Finally she said, "It's a pleasure." She pointed to a pot of tea that she always kept on the corner of the stove. "May I offer you a cup? I was just about to pour myself another."

"That would be lovely." Julia removed her gloves but not her hat. She gazed around the room and Amelia could tell her eyes were measuring the angles of the walls and the plumb of the windowsills. "Your work looks as if it's coming to fruition beautifully."

Amelia felt the knot in her stomach loosen slightly. "Truly? You think so?"

"Indeed."

"Do you think the front entrance is the proper scale for the building's height? Now that it's completed, I've been worrying a bit about that."

Julia smiled. "I think it's exactly right. And the mullions around the windows are especially apt. They conjure up the stern of a clipper ship, which is quite appropriate, considering one can view the bay from them."

"We have a number of difficulties still to overcome before our opening, but thank you for saying that. The construction is just about finished except for the roof and then there's the final landscaping still to do, of course. And thank heavens most of the furniture arrived in port today. It's rather a miracle, but I think we'll be ready by the Fourth of July—as Mr. Thayer announced yesterday."

"So I read," Julia said dryly.

"He doesn't seem to embrace your philosophy of never speaking to reporters."

"Well... we each look at these things in our own way."

Amelia realized that Julia's last statement was probably as

close to an apology as she was ever likely to receive. She smiled at her visitor. "I've come to believe that a balanced approach with our friends at the newspapers might be the best course for me," Amelia declared. "For instance, I won't give James Hopper an interview until the day *after* the hotel opens its doors—but there you are."

"I was terribly saddened to hear from Donaldina about the tragedy you had here with the Chinese laborers."

So, thought Amelia, Julia had heard from her old friend about the calamity at Taylor and Jackson. "You're so kind to ask about them," she replied. "My friends Loy Chen and Shou Shou, who work here now, are heartbroken, as we all are, but carry on, of course." She gazed somberly at her visitor as she handed her the hot beverage in a cream-colored teacup with the initials BVH etched in blue on its side. "You heard about little Foo?"

Julia nodded. "I saw Donaldina yesterday. She said he was such a dear boy."

"We're all still terribly sad." Amelia wondered if the stab of guilt that pierced her whenever she thought about what had happened to Foo would lessen with time.

"That's why I wanted to stop by and extend my condolences to all of you."

Amelia felt tears suddenly well in her eyes. "Thank you," she said, her eyes glued to her teacup. "That's really kind."

"And Mr. Thayer?" Julia asked. "How is he faring?"

Eyes still lowered, Amelia fingered the handle of her cup. "Very well, I should think." She reached for the teapot and carefully refilled Julia's cup, though it hardly needed topping off. "However, I believe he'll be extremely relieved when all this is finished and the workers and I are out of his hair. I also expect he's looking forward to being relieved of the burdens and expense of construction. Today, for instance, we learned that only half the furniture that had been unloaded at the dock was ever delivered here to the site. He's gone off to locate the rest and hire more teamsters to haul it to Nob Hill."

What she didn't mention to Julia was that J.D. told Franco—not her—about the waylaid furniture. It was just another instance of how he'd recently assumed an air of polite detachment, as if he really might be looking forward to the day construction was complete and their association officially concluded.

"And what are your plans, Amelia, after the Bay View opens? Professionally, I mean?"

It was a question Amelia had asked herself countless times, but coming from Julia, she hardly knew how to reply.

"I-I don't actually know." It was the absolute truth.

"No plans to marry?"

Amelia tried to disguise her amazement. "No, I have no plans in that regard. I'm just not sure of my next project."

She refused even to think about the implications of Julia's odd question. It had been more than a month and a half since the solitary night of "wild abandon" —as the novels of her youth would describe it—in J.D.'s private quarters had taken place. With each passing day, Amelia almost wondered if she'd dreamed she'd spent a night in J.D.'s brass bed.

"I thought perhaps your Dr. McClure…" Julia proposed delicately.

Amelia almost laughed at how off-the-mark her visitor was. "He's asked me to marry him. Twice," she divulged, meeting Julia's steady gaze. "I thanked him for the offer but respectfully declined."

"So did Donaldina," commented Julia with an arch of her eyebrow.

"He might still have a chance with our friend, Nurse Pratt," Amelia added, and they both smiled.

Amelia took a sip from her cup and added, "Angus McClure is a very wonderful man, but he and I simply don't see eye-to-eye on a number of things. He seems to think women architects need to be shielded from the world."

Now it was Julia's turn to stare into her teacup. "Many men are of the opinion women need to be protected from their own ambition." She reached for her kid gloves lying on the table. "Well, I mustn't keep you from your work. I merely wanted to stop by and pay my respects."

"It's wonderful to see you again." Amelia scrambled to her feet as Julie rose from her chair. "I truly appreciate your coming. I hope you'll attend our opening festivities."

Pulling on her gloves, Julia paused and suddenly smiled. "If I can, I certainly will. It was lovely to see you as well, Amelia. Please come by and say hello to everyone at California Street. Lacy and Ira, especially, wanted me to extend their regards—and, again, condolences regarding Foo."

"That's dear of both of them—and of you, Julia. I'd be delighted to pay everyone a visit sometime soon." A weight seemed to float off her shoulders. For the first time since their breach, she saw a glimmer of a chance that she and Julia might be amiable colleagues again, even if they didn't work together any longer.

"We'd all love to see you. And do keep me informed of your plans."

Her visitor departed as quickly as she'd arrived.

Amelia began to speculate whether Julia had paid this call in part to determine if her erstwhile employee might eventually be available for hire. The Morgan office was probably swamped with commissions and both of them knew how difficult it was to employ truly qualified people.

Amelia wondered if she'd enjoyed her freedom too much to go back to a working relationship with Julia that was bound to remain difficult, just because of the kind of forceful woman each of them was. And besides, she thought ruefully, Julia would never take her on again if her employee confessed about certain events that transpired the night J.D. discovered the trunk full of silver and jewels…

She gathered the tea things and deposited them in the kitchen sink, musing that she and Julia were just too different for there to be much hope that the two could find a middle path. It occurred to her suddenly that the fifteen months she'd been a practicing architect had certainly taught her that the role of a professional woman was fraught with complications. Sometimes, work and family and love—and lust—could not be as neatly compartmentalized as she had thought. Until her unexpected visitor had posed the question about her personal and professional plans, Amelia had only occasionally allowed herself to contemplate her future—post J.D. Thayer.

Now it yawned before her like a big black hole as dark as the bottom of the hotel's cistern out back.

⌘

On Sunday of the week in which the Bay View was to have its grand opening, J.D. left the hotel even before Amelia had emerged from her bedroom for a cup of morning coffee. She didn't see him later in the day either, for she took the ferry to Oakland for a much-postponed supper with Aunt Margaret. Amelia had been the sole support of her increasingly frail relative for months now, gifting her with enough cash so that the older woman's bills were paid and there was food in the larder—all with the excuse that Amelia stayed there on her infrequent days off and wanted to pay her share.

"Here, dear," Margaret said as soon as Amelia had hung up her coat. "This came the other day." She pointed to the frank. "See? Paris. You'll have to write your mother all about the new hotel. Perhaps simple curiosity to see what her own daughter has created will persuade her to come home."

"I tried that last month. I even sent a sketch."

Amelia sank onto a kitchen chair and opened her mother's latest missive. Two lines in, she reread the plaintive news that Victoria Bradshaw was, as Amelia had long suspected, nearly out of funds herself.

Paris is so hideously expensive that even Madame Hervé must ask for an increase in my room and board. I find, of late, that I seem to have reached some obstacles in my attempt to be a bona fide Artiste and have been humbled by the discovery of my creative limitations. That finding, along with the scarcity of friends and familiar faces, remind me of how very "foreign" one can feel when living abroad.

If nothing else, Amelia, Paris has shown me what difficulties you must have faced during your time at L'École des Beaux Arts and I do admire you for your perseverance. Perhaps I simply do not possess the temperament it requires if one is to be more than a dabbler in paint. I was especially reminded of this when I beheld your drawing of the "new" Bay View Hotel and then went to the Rue Jacob to view that cunning hostelry you told me was your inspiration. Your work is very fine, my dear, and I am full of approbation…

Amelia tucked her mother's sad, contemplative letter into her pocket. These days, her own daily routine seemed to comprise merely work and obligations—and very little pleasure. There wasn't much she could call her own except the satisfaction of looking at the Bay View and telling herself, *I built that.*

Amelia recalled the drawings that were spread on the long kitchen table in Nob Hill that plotted the Bay View's back garden. Once the shrubs and plants were installed, her official duties as architect and construction supervisor of the Bay View project were at an end.

Is the same true with my short-lived liaison with J.D.?

Just when she'd finally had the courage to admit to herself she had strong feelings for the man, he'd turned into a phantom, locked in his office most of the day, or out on the town until the wee hours at night. Even in private, he never reached for her hand or sent her a special look or touched her in any way. Amelia could no long avoid another truth: J.D. actually appeared to be avoiding her.

For a moment, she imagined herself packing her trunk once again and moving out of the hotel and back into her aunt's depressing little bungalow. But how could she give up the memory of her childhood home or the beautiful new one that rose in its place?

And where was J.D.?

A familiar sense of gloom invaded her soul, a lost, abandoned feeling she'd suffered whenever her father had disappeared into the bowels of the Barbary Coast for weeks at a time. A thought she'd successfully extinguished weeks ago now returned.

Had the gambler in J.D. been playing some clever cards in another sort of high-stakes game? A game to guarantee his ownership of the hotel they'd build together?

With unseeing eyes, she continued to gaze at the letter her mother had sent and felt utterly alone.

⁂

J.D.'s stated mission to find a part of the furniture shipment that stubbornly remained missing and have it hauled to Nob Hill took the greater part of Monday. During that time, Amelia continued to see nothing of him, thus robbing from her the opportunity to ask him outright what was going on between them.

Early that evening, after the workers had departed and Loy and Shou Shou returned from visiting friends in Chinatown, Amelia finally had a moment to herself to sit down, enjoy a cup of tea, and scan the *Call*.

The front pages were filled with accounts of the ongoing wrangles over the political fate of Mayor Schmitz and Abe Reuf, as well as the continuing efforts of Rudolph Spreckels and the men from the Treasury Department to bring them to justice.

Dismayed by several stories chronicling the pair's legal maneuvering to escape culpability for their sins, Amelia turned the page. For a long moment, she stared at a banner headline on the upper right portion of the society page.

MISS KEMP TO BE THE BRIDE
OF JAMES DIAZ THAYER

She blinked several times, wondering if she were hallucinating. The short article announced that the engaged couple planned to wed on the evening of July 4, 1907, "marking the triple celebration of their nuptials, the grand opening of Mr. Thayer's new establishment, the redesigned Bay View Hotel, and the nation's 131st birthday."

J.D.'s to marry Matilda Kemp in three days?

Before Amelia could recover from the shock of this announcement, a knock reverberated on the kitchen door, which she ignored. Her gaze was glued to the newspaper headline, her mind and body frozen.

The pounding intensified, eventually summoning Loy from his room. The young man cast Amelia a perplexed look as he opened the door.

"This is for Miss Bradshaw," barked a voice Amelia didn't recognize. "See that she gets it. Tell her it's very important."

Loy bowed politely, closed the door, and deposited a large envelope next to the newspaper, retreating to join Shou Shou in their room once again. Still stunned by the newspaper announcement, Amelia absently unfastened the envelope's flap and withdrew a raft of thickish paper. After peering at the first sepia-toned image, she looked away.

The night she and Angus had rescued J.D. from the brothel in China Alley surged back with a rush. She recognized that filthy bed. The torn bed sheet. J.D.'s clothing bunched around his ankles. She could almost smell the opium and cabbage and urine.

She realized instantly that these lewd photographs were meant to shock her—and they did, but not because of their content. She had already witnessed this scene of degradation. The photos were staged, of course, since J.D. had said he was certain it had been Kemp's men who had kidnapped, drugged, and beaten him that night. The pictures were also meant to disgust her—which they also did—but only because of the way they had been obtained and maliciously distributed into her hands. Perhaps the day's news of J.D.'s "betrothal" to Matilda Kemp was part of some larger scheme of Kemp's? The announced nuptials certainly would explain J.D.'s avoidance of her lately.

Amelia noticed a scrap of paper sandwiched between the photographs.

Copies for Miss Amelia Bradshaw:
    Study them well. You will be photographed the next time you take this scoundrel to your bed.

The note was unsigned.

Was it a potent threat from Ezra Kemp or merely a bluff? Could J.D. himself be the author, hoping to make it her choice to end their relationship, leaving him free of any claims she might make on the Bay View Hotel?

Both Kemp and J.D. were consummate poker players, she reminded herself. How could she possibly determine what was truly going on?

Amelia sat quietly for several minutes, absorbing the vicious warning and the fact that someone was trying to blackmail her into acceding to his wishes. If she filed a complaint with the authorities about this blatant attempt to intimidate her, her accusations would surely go unheeded—considering the rampant bribing of the San Francisco police force—and she would needlessly expose her private life to public scandal.

She rose from her chair and began to pace in front of the brand new, gleaming kitchen stove. Finally, she strode toward the newspaper she'd tossed aside and scooped it up, along with the envelope and its filthy contents, and threw the entire lot on to the fire in the hob. Random thoughts drifted through her mind while she watched the flames curl the edges and reduce it all to ashes.

One thing was certain: J.D. was no angel. She had long assumed there had been a seedy underbelly to his former life as a professional gambler and employer of comely Chinese women. Indeed, there was obviously some basis for his reputation as the black sheep of his family.

But this! Even assuming the photographs were phony and the engagement was forged under duress, all of San Francisco now knew J.D. and Matilda were engaged to marry.

And Amelia?

She had known nothing. Whatever was going on, J.D. hadn't been willing to share it with her or warn her before the news was printed in the paper. That spoke volumes as far as Amelia was concerned. Her sense of privacy—not to mention her pride—had been incinerated just as surely as the photographs she had burned.

Another wave of loneliness swept over her, as though she were standing on the headlands when a swift, summer fog descended on an otherwise sunny day. Turning her back on the fire burning brightly in the kitchen stove, she resolutely locked the hotel's doors, doused the lights, and abandoned the kitchen. Many facts were missing in this puzzle, but she was too disheartened to seek any answers tonight. In her small bedroom, she undressed in the dark, gaining comfort that the eminent Julia Morgan declared her erstwhile protégée's new hotel was beautiful. That was something at least.

Shivering, Amelia slipped beneath the chilly bedcovers.

The coldest winter I ever spent was the summer I lived in San Francisco…

Her thoughts drifted aimlessly as she drew her knees to her chest for warmth. Life seemed at that moment a rather solitary journey for so many that drew breath.

Each in our own narrow cot, she mused, despair settling on her like a shroud.

J.D. had not returned to the hotel nor had he prepared her in any way for the shocks she'd received this day. So, who was her true adversary, she wondered with a sudden, sharp stab of fear? Who had placed her in such grave, personal danger? The note alluded to her sexual liaison with her employer and threatened to ruin her in the public's eye. Whoever was trying to intimidate her obviously had the power and the knowledge to do exactly that.

She slipped her hand between the mattress and the bedsprings and felt for her revolver. Its cold metal gave her very little solace and for the first time since she was a child, she cried herself to sleep.

❧

J.D. stood at the door of the stone and timber estate and pounded the brass gargoyle doorknocker against the metal plate.

"Mr. Kemp is not at home," a manservant informed him. He rubbed his fingers on a napkin, obviously summoned from his supper. "He left this morning and is not expected back from inspecting his forest on the Russian River until tomorrow."

"And Miss Kemp?"

"She went down to her studio after dinner, sir," the house-keeper informed him. "Miss Stivers too. Working on a new sculpture, they tell me. Didn't want to be disturbed, they said."

What a stroke of luck, thought J.D., quickly adjusting his plan of action. "I'll just be on my way then. Please tell Mr. Kemp and the young ladies that I came to pay my respects before returning to San Francisco. Good night." It was best the manservant reported that J.D. had called at Kemp's house and returned directly to the city.

"Certainly, sir. And congratulations on your engagement."

Without responding, J.D. waited until the front door closed, then swiftly skirted the house and headed down the leafy path that led to the small stone building at the bottom of the garden. The tall redwood trees ringing the perimeter of Kemp's property cast the ferns and rock outcroppings into even deeper shadow under the evening sky. The only sound was of the rushing creek that added to the landscape's forest-like surroundings.

A leaded window at the front of the cottage was flung wide, and a glowing lamp provided J.D. with a clear view inside the studio. Low voices, barely intelligible, drifted toward him. He paused, transfixed by a startling sight framed by the window ledge. For a moment, it almost seemed as if he were staring at a portrait in an avant-garde gallery or atelier like those Amelia told him were everywhere in Paris.

In the middle of the room, on a stone pedestal, rested a torso made of clay, gray in color and slick with moisture. Not three feet from it, Emma Stivers knelt on a velvet-draped riser—her nude body a mirror of the statue.

Matilda Kemp was also kneeling, also nude, though her lanky hands and arms were dripping with liquid clay that she was reverently applying—not to the surface of her work of art—but to the alabaster skin of her school chum.

J.D. experienced a wave of deep embarrassment, an overwhelming sense that he was viewing something primitive, something private whose obscenity was not in the act itself, but in his watching it. Yet he couldn't pull his eyes from the scene.

Matilda's movements were full of poignant dignity as she scooped handfuls of moistened clay and lovingly stroked Emma's breasts, her arms, her neck.

"Oh yes…" moaned Emma Stivers. "Oh *yes*, my darling Tilly…"

J.D. determined to leave and shifted his weight in order to reverse his direction. His moving shadow must have caught Matilda's eye, for the woman suddenly looked up past Emma's naked shoulder and directly toward him, his white shirtfront a beacon in the gloom.

Her sharp cry of alarm positively unnerved him. Matilda sank on her haunches, covered her naked breasts with her arms and began to cry uncontrollably into hands coated with clay. Emma scrambled to her feet and ran behind a screen. For several seconds, J.D. remained rooted to the spot, then spun on his heel, and swiftly began to make his way in the opposite direction, his mind a blur.

"Mr. Thayer!" called a frantic voice behind him. "Mr. Thayer, please come back! *Please*, Mr. Thayer! Wait for me... I *must* talk to you!"

CHAPTER 31

J.D. HEARD RUNNING STEPS pursuing him in the darkness shrouding the path. He turned to see Emma, swathed now in a kind of kimono, her hair streaming behind her, a crescent moon shining above her shoulder. He halted and waited for her to catch up to him, totally mystified as to what to say.

"You mustn't marry Matilda!" she cried. "You *mustn't!*"

J.D. could think of nothing else to do but to put an arm around the woman's heaving shoulders and draw her close while she sobbed into his chest.

He patted Emma awkwardly on the back. "Shall we return to the studio and try to sort this out? I'm sure we can find some solution."

"Yes… *yes!*" Emma gasped. "There is so much you don't know."

It took a good five minutes before either woman could speak without becoming tearful again. J.D. decided the best thing to do was sit quietly while Emma and Matilda applied wet cloths to their clay-encrusted arms and necks to wash off the grime.

"Mr. Thayer said he would help us, Tilly!" Emma exclaimed, patting her arms with a towel. "Isn't that *wonderful?*"

Matilda turned her tear-streaked face toward J.D. with a look of bewilderment that swiftly turned to joy. "Truly,

Mr. Thayer? Oh thank God! Thank you *so* much! Oh… I think I'm going to faint."

Emma swiftly put an arm around her and gave her a comforting squeeze. "No, you're *not*! Mr. Thayer doesn't have time for any more of our hysterics." She addressed J.D. "Did Miss Bradshaw tell you Matilda was fine with your not wanting to marry her? Mr. Kemp, however, put that engagement announcement in the paper anyway. At the Fairmont we told your architect to warn you that Mr. Kemp plans more intimidation and who knows what else?" She gestured to Matilda that she should take a seat on a low footstool nearby.

"Yes," J.D. replied, "she gave me both your messages, including his latest threats, which I take seriously. In the last raid, several Chinese people were killed. One was a child of seven."

Matilda's face crumbled and she began to cry again.

Emma spoke up. "The newspaper announcement just goes to show that Tilly's father is now completely *fixated* on your marrying her. He sees it as a way of forcing you to share control of the Bay View Hotel. You'll be married to his daughter, over whom he maintains control, and if anything should happen to you…"

J.D. nodded that he understood Emma's implications.

"Does he realize, Matilda, that you'd… uh… prefer a woman to a man as your life's companion?" J.D. inquired politely. There was no point in voicing his outrage over the article in today's *Call* to these two hapless pawns in Kemp's game of chess.

"We pray he doesn't know about us!" Emma answered for her lover with a shudder. "The man has a violent temper, Mr. Thayer. Poor Tilly doesn't dare tell him anything about how she feels. And he's growing rather suspicious of me, I fear. We know he'll risk virtually anything to see her married to you, now that he's in such trouble with those men who keep calling here."

Matilda wiped her eyes on her sleeve. "Father's become dreadfully overextended financially. He paid too much for the forests he's purchased and made too many risky investments down in Chinatown following the disaster. The mayor and Mr. Reuf can't protect him as they once did—now that they're under arrest. My father's even been forced to go back to gambling to try to cover his IOUs. The men that visited here right after the Fairmont opened promised to *kill* Father if he doesn't pay his poker debts soon."

J.D. had heard the same rumors. Matilda's revelations confirmed what his informants had told him: that Kemp was a principal in several new brothels in Chinatown and had huge expenses paying the graft that such enterprises required.

All of this was music to J.D.'s ears.

"And he thinks that once you and I are married," Matilda continued tearfully, "short of disposing of you, he can force the sale of the Bay View to raise the needed funds to rid him of the creditors threatening to murder him."

"So the bully is being bullied," murmured J.D. He knew what Matilda and Emma didn't: that even if he paid off his debts to Kemp with cash raised from the gems he'd found in the trunk, the man still lusted after the respectability that came with owning one of the city's finest hotels.

Matilda's cheeks again were stained with tears as she told him woefully, "By my marrying you, he can get rid of me as well. He says I'm only an embarrassment to him and as ugly as my mother!" She pressed her handkerchief to both eyes.

"You have to understand something, Mr. Thayer."

Emma clutched her own handkerchief tightly. "Something quite… unpleasant. Tilly's grandmother was a… soiled dove up in the gold country. Poor Tilly never even knew who her grandfather was, other than he was an illiterate blacksmith. Her father is terribly ashamed of this, especially now that he frequents your world, Mr. Thayer. He's actually… quite mental about it all."

Matilda clutched Emma's newly washed arm. "Yes! He's positively *obsessed* by the notion of having me become 'one of the Thayers,' as he's always saying. Thinks that people like your father and the Stanfords and Huntingtons will count him one of their own and forget about his lowly origins. I feel rather sorry for him sometimes."

"Oh, Tilly, you poor darling, don't be ridiculous!" Emma exclaimed. "None of that excuses his dreadful behavior toward you and your mother!"

"But I suppose it does help explain it, doesn't it?" Matilda implored, wiping her eyes. "My mother once told me that his own father beat him unmercifully when he was a boy. She said we had to make allowances."

"No one *ever* deserves to be abused like that, Tilly," Emma scolded. She turned to address J.D. "Mr. Kemp is terribly cruel to Tilly, and he allowed his own wife to die because he couldn't be bothered to fetch a doctor in time. If he suspects that we—"

"I don't think he's overly fond of women, period," J.D. intervened, remembering tales Ling Lee had shared with him about her life in China Alley. "Dogs that have been kicked as pups often become vicious when full grown, you know."

"I know," Matilda murmured. "It's horrible. He's hurt so many people—"

"We're going to run away," Emma broke in, her voice

filled with determination. "Now that you know... everything... perhaps you'd help us?" she added hopefully.

J.D. was taken aback by the young woman's candor. "Where would you go?"

"Just away," Emma said defiantly. "We'll decide once we are safely gone from here." She reached over and tapped Matilda on the shoulder. "Tell Mr. Thayer what else you overheard."

"Father said just yesterday that he might do something terrible to that nice woman architect who works for you."

"Miss Bradshaw?"

J.D.'s entire body tensed, as if to absorb a blow. Kemp's threatening note hinting he suspected Amelia and he were lovers... and now his move to make this bogus engagement to Matilda public without J.D.'s even knowing—until he read it in the paper today—that her father put the announcement in the *Call*—all this news meant Ezra's actions constituted more than just another bluff.

"That horrid Jake Kelly and somebody named Kavanaugh were here recently. I heard the second man say that you're perhaps... well... fond of her, and if you are—my father thinks that by threatening her life, he'll force you to do what he wants—marry me to get the upper hand at the Bay View, using my share as your wife as leverage to take the hotel away from you."

Or have me killed and get it all...

"*Are* you... fond of Miss Bradshaw, Mr. Thayer?" Emma asked.

J.D. paused. "I have a great deal of respect for Amelia Bradshaw."

"That's not the thrust of my question, sir," Emma countered, eyeing him steadily.

"I wouldn't be a gentleman if I spoke in public of such personal matters, Miss Stivers." He was relieved when his cool reply prompted her to lower her gaze.

J.D.'s thoughts shifted to Kemp. A desperate man will play his last card if he thinks it will help him win the game—and the lord of this Mill Valley manor was clearly getting to the desperate stage. Given Kemp's previous actions, it wasn't far-fetched to think that his ultimate plan might, indeed, include arranging the tragic demise of his new son-in-law, thereby giving Kemp immediate, total control over the prized real estate at Taylor and Jackson. It had been known to happen before.

Matilda reached for J.D.'s hands and clutched them tightly. "Please, please, Mr. Thayer, help us! He has people watching me every time I walk off the property. This studio is the only place where he leaves us alone. It was my mother's sanctuary, and he couldn't *stand* her. Emma and I dream night and day how we can get away from here—"

"I wouldn't attempt to run away just now," J.D. intervened.

"But—"

"My advice is that you remain quiet and stay clear of him as much as you can. I promise you, I'll think of something."

Emma looked from her friend to J.D. Then she blurted, "What if you actually *married* Tilly?"

"What!" screeched Matilda.

"No! Hear me out," Emma said excitedly. "What if you, Mr. Thayer, wed Matilda on the Fourth of July, as the newspaper says you will, and then Tilly and I have a Boston Marriage—and *you'll* be free to do as you pleased."

"Pray tell me, Emma," J.D. asked with the first glimmer of amusement he'd experienced all evening, "what is a 'Boston Marriage'?"

"Two respectable women who love each other live together as 'friends' in the eyes of the world." Her pretty features were alight with excitement. "It's done all the time in Massachusetts. You, of course, as Tilly's supposed husband, could live your life as you wished—with Miss Bradshaw, if you wished—and Matilda and I could stay in your hotel, shielded from Mr. Kemp, and eventually we two could travel and—"

J.D. shook his head. "Ezra would still do his best to make my life miserable, and Miss Bradshaw would remain in danger as well."

Crestfallen, both women said, "Oh."

"But I will take it under advisement as a possible interim solution," J.D. said, turning an idea over in his mind. "Desperate times call for desperate measures."

He rose from his chair and made his farewells, his mind brimming with thoughts of the day's amazing turn of events. He had only a few cards of his own left to play and not much time to play them.

Marrying Matilda just might have to be one of them.

∽✵∾

The next morning, just after five-thirty, Amelia lay in her narrow bed and concentrated on her list of remaining chores scheduled that day. The newspaper headline announcing J.D.'s engagement and the photographs of him in China Alley clicked through her brain like pictures in a stereopticon.

Her plan was to simply take J.D. aside this morning and ask him about the newspaper article and demand to know what on God's green earth was going on. She would discover, once and for all, why he continually found himself in a tangled web of intrigue and conflict, a way of life that unnerved and repelled her.

A man with J.D.'s sordid history was not some rakish figure in a romantic novel, she reminded herself. She'd known that fact full well the night she'd allowed him to take her to bed. Until just recently, he'd seemed a trustworthy collaborator during the long, hard months they'd built the hotel together. Yet, in actual fact, *whose* word could be counted on—other than her own?

After all, he and Kemp had maneuvered her father into betting his supposed stake in the hotel. Before she'd seen the engagement announcement, she'd allowed the briefest fantasy to flit through her mind of a continuing association with J.D. in the management of a hotel they both prized unashamedly. She'd never daydreamed about marriage— given her unhappy experience with Etienne—but she'd gone so far as to imagine she and J.D. might truly become lovers and working partners.

But in reality, there had always been a part of the equation with J.D. Thayer she didn't understand. He'd told her quite directly he was not used to sharing his thoughts or decisions with anyone. What if he'd kept things from her that would make her detest him? What then?

The clanging of the first cable cars coming out of the restored brick barn lower on Jackson Street jolted Amelia into awareness that she mustn't tarry. Her mind was a black-board with a hundred conflicting calculations scrawled all over it. Even if J.D. didn't want to wed Matilda, the fact remained that Kemp's men had killed Foo and tried to rape Amelia in her bed—or worse. So why would a decent man have anything to do with such a repulsive sort of person as Ezra Kemp—let alone go into business with him in the first place or even *consider* marrying his daughter?

As Grandfather Hunter used to say, "Look at a man's

deeds, lass, not his stated intentions." But when it came to J.D., he'd neither stated his intentions toward her—honorable or otherwise—and rarely had his deeds revealed his true intentions.

Amelia leaned her head against the wall behind her bed and closed her eyes. The day had barely begun and she already felt exhausted from her mental gymnastics. She should just face facts, she told herself. Lust and too much champagne had been the potent combination that propelled J.D. Thayer to take her to bed that amazing night. She'd been sorely mistaken to think, even for an instant, that it meant much more.

Mistaken and a damnable fool.

She was no swooning female and she cursed herself on this cold, dank morning for acting like one. She was an architect who had made her way in a man's world and that was what mattered in the end.

Galvanized by the need to complete a few important details prior to the Bay View's grand opening Thursday, she rummaged in the trunk at the foot of her bed, looking for a clean pair of men's trousers. She dug down past several soiled garments until her hand rested on the pants Angus had returned to her in a bundle tied with string. More than once Amelia had avoided donning this particular pair among a collection she'd used as part of her work gear. The mere sight of the expensive black wool that her father had worn on the night of the quake raised too many painful memories.

Today, however—her last as the supervisor on the hotel site—it seemed almost fitting she should wear Henry Bradshaw's dress trousers in his honor. She swiftly buttoned the fastenings, used a belt to adjust the waist, and rolled each pant leg several times until her boot tips showed. As she often did lately, she didn't bother to wear a skirt over them, but strode into the chilly kitchen to make the coffee while everyone else still slept. Until J.D. rose for the day, the only thing she had immediate control over, she concluded, was work.

A mug of coffee warming her hand, she wandered outside into the characteristically cool July morn, strolling down the new slate path toward the gardens. It struck her that, by next week, she would be without her regular stipend from her current employer. Sooner, rather than later, she would have to set about getting another commission to keep up with her obligations. Perhaps Julia, in her current frame of mind, would be willing to refer some business her way for projects she didn't want or have the time to take on. Amelia clung to whatever shred of hope she could find this foggy morn.

At this early hour, more cable cars filed out of the car barn, their clanging bells a blatant signal along Jackson Street that the neighborhood would soon greet the day.

Amelia gazed at the new hotel that rose above her head, wrapped in a gauzy veil of mist bound to burn off by noon. Her eyes roved from window to window while she critically surveyed the series of arching terra-cotta mullions, graceful eyebrows that gave the three-story facade its elegance and solid appearance. The slate roof bestowed an even statelier mien on the building, as did the statuary that dotted the grounds. That week, a story in the *Call* with James Hopper's byline had blared:

A GRAND DESIGN BY A GRAND ARCHITECT

Already, people were describing the Bay View as a "mini Fairmont"—with luxury and elegance on a smaller, more intimate scale than the beautiful hostelry down the block. In just a few days, guests would begin to take up residence in the lovely new rooms with their silk drapery and gold faucets and their magnificent views of the water. The article had concluded:

And so, from the Fourth of July onwards, two luxurious hotels on Nob Hill will greet visitors from all over the world. Our recovering City will benefit mightily from this race to splendor in which San Francisco's only two women architects have been so ardently engaged.

Amelia had learned yesterday from Loy Chen that J.D. had already bestowed his belongings in the owner's apartments on the top floor. The hourglass had nearly run out of sand. Soon, Amelia's connection to the Bay View would be officially severed.

How she would have loved to live in the owner's apartments with J.D.—or even *alone*, she thought, with a flash of anger. If only she had five playing cards and the *truth*!

Increasingly disturbed by the unhappy realities confronting her, she wandered farther down the path toward the rear of the hotel's original property line to inspect a row of flower beds that had been prepared the previous day. Gamboling stone cherubs—ordered from France despite J.D.'s reservations—as well as a series of garden benches that the Pigati cousins had fashioned out of poured concrete were embedded in the earth at intervals along the path. Now that the cistern was operational, the rest of the grounds would be completed that very day in the area where the old woman's clapboard house had stood before the great fire had reduced it to cinders.

"Lucky Dog" had duly been buried under a newly planted pine tree, awaiting his stone marker and a second would be installed there too, commemorating her grandfather's dog Barbary who had taken such a shine to J.D.

Her mind filled with a jumble of memories, Amelia sipped her lukewarm coffee and gazed at a smallish pile of refuse that remained to be carted away from the Pacific Street side of the old gambling club site. The Pigatis and sundry daily workers were due to arrive momentarily to remove this eyesore, and then plant eighteen additional rose bushes in its place.

A gust of wind whipped Amelia's hair and sent a chill down her spine. Wishing she'd donned a coat before commencing her inspection tour, she clutched her mug in her left hand and sank the icy fingers of her right deep into the pocket of her trousers for warmth.

As she did, her fingers grazed something thin and papery. She halted in place, then slowly pulled two objects into the soft morning light. She stared down at her palm as shock and amazement turned into disbelief.

A pair of playing cards, stuck together at odd angles—one face up and one face down—lay cupped in her trembling hand. She made out the words "Bay View Hotel" etched on the top card, along with the initials "JDT."

"Oh… my… *God*," she whispered. After all this time, she finally knew for sure who'd won the notorious poker game on the night her world turned upside down.

Amelia sank onto a concrete bench and set her coffee cup aside. Slowly, delicately, she pulled the cards, one from another, and carefully placed them side-by-side on thighs covered by her father's twill trousers. There, outlined against the dark fabric, the jack and king of diamonds stared back at her.

Henry Bradshaw, notorious drunkard, perpetrator of lies, spinner of fantastic yarns made up of whole cloth, had been telling his daughter the truth.

Incredibly, Amelia knew without a doubt that—just as he'd

insisted—he'd drawn a rare royal flush in a hand of five-card stud in an all-night, winner-take-all poker game with J.D. Thayer and Ezra Kemp. He had *won back* Charlie Hunter's Bay View Hotel seconds before the cataclysm struck.

Even more incredibly, these two thin cards had been lodged for nearly fifteen months deep inside the pocket of her father's dress trousers, where he had attempted to stuff all five as the first shock hit. Amelia remembered gently dislodging the ace, queen, and ten of diamonds from the tips of Henry's crushed fingers. Then, at her father's insistence, she'd fruitlessly searched amid the rubble for the jack and king of diamonds that he'd managed to stuff in his trouser pocket—and that now peered up at her.

Her father had been sedated with laudanum until he'd died, and thus had no clear recollection of the immediate aftermath of the quake. He may not even have been aware that he'd succeeded in sequestering some of the playing cards in his pocket as he dove futilely for cover.

As for the trousers themselves, Amelia recalled her aunt sponging off the dust and grime with a cloth soaked in lemon water and baking soda. Obviously Margaret had been too upset by this painful chore to check the deep pockets for any personal items its late owner had left behind. Once the clothing had been cleaned, Amelia had stowed the trousers at the very bottom of her trunk, never having the heart to appropriate as part of her work uniform the last item of clothing her father had ever worn.

Until today.

It took her breath away.

She stared vacantly into space, a thousand images flitting through her mind. Horrible visions came back to haunt her—of her father's spats peeking from beneath the gaming table that had crushed his spine. Of J.D., slumped against the shattered doorway of the gambling club, bleeding from his forehead and half-dead. Of Barbary, whining softly by his side. Of the heat, smoke, fire, and death she'd witnessed that terrible morning, along with the infuriating image of Ezra Kemp pushing aside women and children to escape on board the ferry to save himself, while two hundred and fifty thousand wretched quake refugees scrambled for safety all over the city.

Despite the morning's chill, Amelia's shirtwaist clung to her back, soaked with perspiration. She trembled uncontrollably. Would these horrid apparitions never *cease,* grisly reminiscences that lurked just below the surface of her conscious thoughts?

In her mind's eye, she could picture the other three cards she'd stored in the top drawer of the chest at Aunt Margaret's. A small voice whispered that even though she now had in her possession all five diamonds in a royal flush, there once must have been at least three-dozen decks of engraved playing cards stored in the gambling club's cupboards on the day of the quake. Would the color of the ink, or perhaps J.D.'s initials on all five cards, help her establish the link between these two cards and the other three—and most importantly—prove that all five cards came from the *same* deck?

And even if she could confirm this, would anyone accept her evidence?

But what were the odds that the last two cards *missing* from Henry Bradshaw's royal flush would have surfaced in her father's dress pants pocket—the same garment he'd worn on the night of the temblor? Would either of the two surviving players in that infamous contest admit, now, to having seen her father spread the ace, king, queen, jack, and ten of diamonds on the gaming table in the wee hours of April 18, 1906?

If she showed J.D. these cards, whom would he declare—
a year later—to be the true and legal owner of the hotel
looming behind her?

And who had been lying to her all this time?

CHAPTER 32

A T THE OPPOSITE END of the Bay View property in a newly painted penthouse bedroom, J.D. dressed quickly, took the elevator to the mezzanine, and descended the stairs to the main floor, striding swiftly through the silent lobby. He glanced at the clock installed the day before in the oak paneling that surrounded the regal front desk. He had returned to the Bay View at 2 a.m. and now it was just under five hours later and he felt like hell. He hadn't even stopped in the kitchen for a cup of coffee after spending a sleepless night weighing the best course to take in the next twenty-four hours. By dawn's light, he had made up his mind.

He was certain that by now Amelia must have seen or been told about the engagement announcement in the *Call*, but he would have to deal with the repercussions of that later. His most important mission was to prevent Kemp from wreaking any more havoc in his or her life.

He stepped through the front entrance that opened onto Taylor Street and headed for the Winton, parked where he'd left it late the previous night. The motorcar started up without hesitation, and soon he was wheeling toward the Western Addition, the early morning air streaming past as he drove toward Russian Hill and Pacific Heights.

When the parlor maid opened the front door to his parents'

house on Octavia Street, the Thayer's servant appeared startled by the unusual hour of his call, but she politely ushered
her employer's son into the foyer.

"Your father's at his breakfast, sir," she said. "Shall I
announce you?"

"No, I'll just show myself in. Thank you, Sophia."

James Thayer was alone, seated at the head of a long,
mahogany dining table where remarkably few family meals
had ever been served. He looked up from his eggs and toast,
and immediately threw his morning paper aside in a gesture
of contempt.

"What are you doing here? If you seek my blessing for
this preposterous engagement of yours to Kemp's—"

"On the contrary, Father," J.D. interrupted, "I seek your
help extracting me from it." He sat in a dining chair to his
father's right.

"Oh, for God's sake, J.D.!" He pointed to the newspaper.
"The ink on the public announcement is barely dry and *now*
you come to your senses?"

"Kemp put it in the papers without my knowledge or
permission. I've spent the last few months telling him I
wouldn't marry his daughter."

"What? Why, the impertinence of that pushy,
overreaching—"

"He's far worse than that, Father. He's a murderer. He
hired a bunch of hooligans to attack my workers. Several are
dead, including a seven-year-old boy."

"We've had this sort of discussion before, J.D. When you
involve yourself with those filthy Chinese—"

"Wait a minute," J.D. interrupted for a second time, "let's
not forget your own involvement with a few Chinese in the
not-so-distant past."

Big Jim Thayer slammed both fists on the dining room table, rattling the chinaware so forcefully that a small bread plate flew off and crashed onto the hardwood floor.

"Will you get to the point and then get out?" he demanded furiously.

It was time now, after many years of waiting, to play the Ling Lee card. J.D. had wondered when the moment would come, and now it finally had.

"I merely employed Chinese women," J.D. said conversationally, taking a seat to Big Jim's right at the dining table and lifting his father's cup of coffee to his lips. "They worked for me as clerks, restaurant staff, and chambermaids and, in the case of Ling Lee, as an accountant." He leaned toward his father. "I paid them a salary. I didn't abuse them. I didn't force myself on them. Like you did."

His father's fork was midway to his mouth. He set it down with a clang.

"You're talking rubbish. You *lived* with the harlot. Everybody knows that."

J.D. removed a slice of toast from his father's plate, tore off a piece, and popped it into his mouth. Then he settled more comfortably into his chair and gazed across the table with an unblinking stare.

"Ling Lee was a very clever person, you know," J.D. said in a pleasant, unemotional voice. "Good with figures and with a memory that was truly astonishing."

"How do you have the unmitigated gall to speak in my presence of this person who caused such scandal to our family and—"

"You mean the woman you forced yourself on, Father? Or should I use the technical term? Raped."

James Thayer's brow furrowed. "I haven't the slightest

idea what you're talking about." He seized his fork and attacked a morsel of scrambled egg on his plate.

"Well, then, allow me to refresh your memory. Ling Lee is a woman you impregnated at a brothel off Jackson Street that specialized in virgins and young boys for the amusement of white gentlemen of means with peculiar tastes. I've since learned that silent investors in the enterprise on China Alley like you and Kemp apparently got *special* favors."

"How dare you talk to me like this. Get out!" The senior Thayer threw his linen napkin on the dining table in a characteristic display of rage and pushed back his chair to stand, glaring at his son.

J.D. also jumped to his feet, shouting now, unable to rein in his temper any longer.

"She was *fourteen years old*! You don't remember Ling Lee because all 'Chinks' look the same to you, don't they, Father? You don't remember her name or her face or that night in China Alley when you walked into a room dead drunk where they held her prisoner and she begged you not to take her. And several months later, when she saw you another night and pleaded with you to care for the child— *your* child—you treated her like just another slant-eye. Just another body."

"She was an extortionist," declared his father, spitting out the words. "She thought she would force me to acknowledge her half-breed when she had no proof whatsoever that *I* was the one who'd gotten the slut in the family way!"

"Ah, so you *do* remember the woman you raped."

"I didn't rape anybody," said Thayer. He heaved his girth into his chair once again and tucked his napkin in his shirt-front, affecting disinterest in their heated conversation. Then he picked up his fork and made a show of eating his eggs.

"I paid for the right to be in the room with that woman and do whatever the hell I pleased. My investment in China Alley bought the food you ate and this roof over your head and Ling—whatever her name was—merely tried to pry money out of me." He scowled at his son. "Now that you mention it, I *do* remember that."

J.D. grabbed his father by his shirtfront and pushed him and the back of the chair sharply against the dining room wall as tiny pillows of scrambled eggs spattered Big Jim's starched shirtfront. "Ling Lee was no extortionist!" His face was so close to his father's that he could make out the tiny red capillaries on his purplish nose. He released his hold and his father fell back into his chair, appearing stunned at his son's ferocity. "Fourteen years old and she'd never been with a man, and you hardly even *remember* the occasion! She was the mother of your child all right."

"I think it more likely *you* were the father," parried the elder Thayer. "*You* lived with the whore all that time." Big Jim lapsed into stony silence while J.D. reclaimed his seat and refilled his father's cup from the silver pot to give himself time to steady his nerves.

"Ling Lee escaped China Alley a few months after you'd taken her virginity and came begging to me in the dead of night, ill and afraid what her circumstances would do to her unborn child. She hoped that the Thayer son would take pity on her since the Thayer father had spurned her every plea. After she had your baby at the Mission Home, I supported them both for five years." J.D. leaned to within several inches of his father's face. "And yes, I loved her, Father. Like a brother loves a sister. I loved her for her courage. For the care and fierce protection she extended to her daughter. And I still support the child—my half *sister*—to this very day."

"That's rubbish! The bastard is your spawn, not mine."

"I didn't meet Ling Lee until she was five months pregnant. Her daughter—*your* daughter—is alive. Half Anglo. Half Chinese. A converted Christian, which was the price her Buddhist mother had to pay to keep her protected from the highbinders and so-called *Christian* people like you and Kemp. And by the way," he added, reaching out with his forefinger to jab at the hollow dimple on his father's face, "the poor child is cursed with the Thayer chin, just as you are—square with a cleft." He pointed to his own smooth chin. "I look myself in the mirror and thank God I was spared that mark at least."

"I've never considered you a real Thayer, and your relationship with that slut proves my judgment was sound."

J.D. gazed at his father with a murderous stare.

"Of course you never considered me a Thayer. Just like your little daughter, I've always been a *half*-breed in your eyes too, haven't I, because my mother was half Spanish? Consuela Diaz-Reims, the little brown enchilada you were willing to marry because her German father had struck it rich in the Comstock Lode and you were up to your muttonchops in debt. From the first *day*, you called her 'Connie Thayer' in front of your friends, didn't you? That is, when you spoke to her at all. You ordered her to make herself scarce and to stay out of the sun. You've treated her like dirt your entire life!"

"I'm warning you, J.D...."

"I'm warning *you*, old man," he said, seizing his father's shirtfront again in a powerful grip. "You used your Yankee lawyering and your double-dealing to hound your wife's own father to suicide."

"That's absolute balderdash!"

"*I* know what you did! I've had my own lawyers and

accountants trace the paperwork." He shoved his father back into his chair for a second time and wished he could shove him through the wall. "Your brothels needed an infusion of cash, so first, you embezzled Grandfather Reim's fortune and then made it look like he made idiotic business decisions. You deliberately broke the man, Father. You stole his money and covered it up. You had that quack Ellers prescribe medicines that brought his spirits low and then you made sure he was publicly humiliated so deeply that he jumped off the ferry, preferring to drown in San Francisco Bay than face the disgrace that he knew awaited him among the Thayers and their friends."

"You've lost a cog, boy," said Big Jim, but his glance slid away and he stared at his uneaten bacon. "Reims was an unstable man and Connie and you are just like him."

"You can lie to yourself, but you can't lie to me." J.D.'s voice was calm now, and he spoke in a monotone. "I was fifteen and I saw him jump."

"He was a self-pitying fool and a—"

"I'm putting you on notice, Father, and the same goes for your cronies who have invested in the Chinese brothels behind smokescreens and bribes to city officials. You'd all better move heaven and earth to put a stop to Ezra Kemp trying to extort me any further and from killing any more innocent people."

"Or you'll do what?" his father said with some of his old belligerence.

"Or I'll go directly to Rudolph Spreckels and those Secret Service people from Washington who are nosing around San Francisco these days. I'll let Jimmy Hopper of the *Call* in on the secret. I'll lay it out before all of them exactly how you and some of the so-called cream of San Francisco society rape

Chinese women without a care. How the 'San Francisco Thayers' really operate in this town. Where you invest your money. Where you bank your profits. I'll show them the ledger sheets proving how Abe Reuf and Mayor Schmitz are just the fronts for men like you and Kemp. And if I do that, old man, you can kill me if you like, but your precious name and reputation will be ruined in the eyes of the people who *really* count."

J.D. took satisfaction in seeing his father slump in his chair, silent and shaken by his son's furious assault. At length, Thayer senior waved a hand in the air and let it drop back onto the table.

"I'll take care of Kemp," he said wearily, as if all the fight had gone out of him. "He's been a thorn in the side of everyone on the Committee. He won't be missed."

"How? And how soon? My supposed wedding is three days from now."

"I have to talk to some people, make some arrangements, but I'll see to it in my own way—and *when* I wish it. Now, get out."

J.D. was tempted to force the issue of the timetable for retribution against Kemp, then thought better of it. If Ezra continued to think the wedding was going forward, he would be less dangerous to everyone concerned.

"Let me know if you'd ever like to meet my half sister," J.D. offered, smiling faintly. "Your little daughter will accompany Donaldina Cameron to the grand opening of my hotel on the Fourth of July."

"I won't be there."

To J.D.'s chagrin, Big Jim's expected refusal to attend the debut of his hotel—and all the other times he'd ridiculed his son's efforts to strike out on his own—still had a capacity to cut to the quick. In that moment, the younger James Thayer recognized that attempting to gain his father's attention and respect had been the primary engine that had driven his rebellious youth and his more recent desire to acquire trophy properties like the Bay View. He'd gambled everything he'd owned to get that particular possession, hoping with the pathos of an orphaned child that he'd win an even greater prize—his father's love, or at least his grudging admiration.

J.D.'s lust for the Bay View Hotel had begun the first time he gazed out Charlie Hunter's big bay windows and watched the serpentine fog slither through the Golden Gate straits. His aspirations to get his hands on it were rekindled the day he'd heard that the flinty old man had been stricken by a stroke amidst the palms in the lobby of his mirrored palace, and that his wastrel son-in-law was running—and ruining—that wonderful place.

J.D.'s insatiable hunger for Taylor and Jackson streets long predated his lust for the intriguing Miss Bradshaw, a woman whose existence he'd utterly disregarded until the day she slammed into his office, fresh from France.

By then, J.D. had wanted to own the Jewel of Nob Hill so badly, he'd sold everything he possessed and even went into business with a known drunkard and an outright extortionist to show his father that he could add up to something, after all. He'd had the arrogance to believe that the supremely clever Ling Lee, whom he'd grown to love like a sister and to respect for the capable businesswoman she was, would help him make enough money in the first year of the gambling club to pay off both Ezra Kemp and Amelia's father several times over. The place would be his alone and perhaps, at last, Big Jim Thayer might say, "Well done, son." Or at least reluctantly respect the wealth and property his son had acquired.

Nothing had turned out as he'd planned. Building the gambling club so swiftly had nearly broken him. In fact, to keep his financial juggling act going, he'd almost lost the prize several times in a few bizarre and foolhardy games of chance. It had been a wild ride, indeed, but now, he'd come nearly full circle. Lady Luck had favored him one last time on the morning of the quake. He'd retained control of the hotel and now would *never* sell, never risk losing it again, or let it fall into disrepair.

When he first met Amelia, she'd presented a major obstacle, for she was as devoted to the Bay View as he was. What a strange and unpredictable twist of fate that he should fall in love with the late Henry Bradshaw's daughter. Dear God, but it would be a hard price to pay if Amelia ever found out the truth about certain things—though he calculated that the odds were great she never would.

J.D. figured he was the kind of a man who never showed his entire hand. If he put his cards on the table and people like Kemp knew that his feelings for Amelia Bradshaw ran much deeper than an enjoyable night in a Sears and Roebuck brass bed, he put her life at risk. If he didn't tell *her* all the facts, and she found them out on her own, she'd probably walk out of his life for good.

Which she might do anyway, should he ultimately decide to reveal the "unvarnished truth," he reminded himself.

His one hope was that Big Jim could strong-arm Kemp into a corner so he could no longer threaten Amelia's life or shanghai him into marrying Matilda. If J.D.'s luck held at all, he'd later reveal Kemp's putting the engagement notice in the *Call* and his own successful counter-moves to stop the wedding. Then J.D. and Amelia could make a home in the place they both loved to distraction and share in its value, fifty-fifty. It was a calculated gamble, this decision to not tell her everything, but he'd risked far more in the past—and won.

And what of the poker game on the morning of the quake...?

J.D. concentrated instead on making a quick exit from the family dining room. With a brief farewell nod to his father, whose gaze remained fixed on a cold cup of coffee, the younger Thayer exited the dining room and mounted the stairs to his mother's apartments. He had a sudden compulsion to let his mother know that he understood everything now. Understood and forgave her—and himself—for their long separation as mother and son.

He'd finally grasped the root causes of her morbid shyness. He saw the reason, now, for her pills and potions. Her desperate search for a kind word, a friendly face. Anything to assuage the loneliness and fear that came from feeling like an outcast. He understood because he also knew how it felt to stand outside the charmed circle of social acceptance in a city like San Francisco.

Though Consuela didn't know it, she had unwittingly colluded with Big Jim Thayer in convincing their only child on some unspoken level that he didn't quite measure up to the almighty Thayers—and never would.

Because he was one quarter Spanish, with skin almost as tawny as his mother's, he'd been doomed from birth as an outcast too, in his father's eyes, and it was this deep-seated racism felt toward Big Jim's only son that had propelled J.D. out of his family home when he was just sixteen and taught him to fight for what he believed in and held dear.

Thayer reached the landing and knocked gently on a door to his right. When bidden to enter, he disappeared into Senora Consuela's private chamber.

❦

Blocks to the east of Octavia Street, Amelia stood in the hotel's doorway dressed in coat and a hat that sat on her head at a jaunty angle—and she was loaded for bear. Angus McClure was just coming up the front steps.

"Good morning, Amelia. Where are you going at such an early hour?" he asked. "I was just coming by to beg a bit of breakfast off you, now that your grand kitchen's been installed. I'm picking up medical supplies at the dock this morning and need to borrow the Winton to take them back to the Presidio, but I don't see the motorcar. Is J.D. here?"

"No."

Amelia had checked J.D.'s newly furnished bedroom in the penthouse when he failed to appear for breakfast. She had no idea if he'd even been home the previous night. No one had seen him anywhere all morning and the Winton was not parked on the street or in the commodious garage she'd built for it. She had been so angry a few minutes earlier, she'd almost thrown rocks at the lobby windows.

Angus regarded her for a long moment and then asked, "Is everything all right, lass? I trust the boilers are in fine fettle?" he added, with an amused lift of an eyebrow.

"I'm sure you're amazed to hear they're perfectly operational. I've just completed my final inspection. Basically, the project here is done. I'm sorry, Angus, but I have an appointment. Shou Shou will fix you whatever food you like."

"Amelia!" He placed his hand on her sleeve to restrain her from leaving. "I can see something's upset you. Tell me what's wrong. Has your work crew been giving you problems?" He reached toward her and grasped her chin between his fingers. "Look at those dark circles under your eyes! You look exhausted. All this rush-rush to make the opening date has put you under a terrible strain." He gave her cheek a little pat and seized her hand. "Come inside with me and relax a bit. I've been telling you right along that this kind of work puts too much of a burden on your shoulders. You ought to—"

"No!" Amelia yanked her hand away. "Please don't tell me what I 'ought'! I loved my work here. What I do not care for is your incessant badgering!"

She glared at him, anger coursing through her entire body. She'd had her fill of domineering men this morning. J.D. had made absolutely no attempt to contact her in two days or explain one word about his engagement announcement. Nor had she had a chance to confront *him* about the playing cards she now had in her possession. And here was Angus, berating her for merely trying to complete the bloody hotel on time!

Startled by her heated words, Angus could only stare. "Badgering you? What are you saying? I was merely observing that—"

"Well then, let me put it in *this* fashion. Many men of my acquaintance seem to think that it's perfectly all right to treat me as if I were blind, feebleminded, and thoroughly unable to discern my own intentions. Well, I'm *not*, and I have an appointment to keep, Angus. So if you will, excuse me, please."

"I'm just asking you to have breakfast with me, lass."

Amelia hardly heard him. "I don't know why so many men seem to believe that they can simply put shackles on a woman and take from her what they will, be it her trusting nature, her freedom, her ability to choose her own fate, or her money and inheritance!" she declared with an uncharacteristic vehemence. "To take everything from us because they think we're too *stupid* to look after ourselves!"

Before Angus could reply to this tirade, Amelia stormed

across Jackson Street and disappeared around the corner. By the time she reached California Street, she already felt contrite, knowing her fury was misplaced. The lion's share of the speech she had just flung at the good doctor more appropriately should have been addressed to his best friend.

❧

Amelia took a seat at her old drafting board that currently resided at the Morgan architectural firm in the Merchants Exchange building and swiftly penned her thanks to Franco Pigati and his entire crew *"for the splendid job you've done at the Bay View Hotel. I will forever be in your debt and hope we can work together again."*

On a second piece of paper she wrote:

Mr. Thayer:

The last of the rubble was cleared today.

This morning I signed off on everything but the flower beds at the very rear of the property, a section designated to honor "Lucky Dog" and Barbary, that should be planted by the time you read this.

Also: Mr. Pigati's crew should have placed the remaining uncrated hotel furniture as I've directed, but of course, you may see fit to make some changes, which I encourage you to do.

I have decided I could use an extended holiday so I am leaving immediately for France via train to New York. Please send the final payment of my fees, care of Miss Julia Morgan, Merchants Exchange Building, 465 California Street, San Francisco, California.

Sincerely,
Amelia Hunter Bradshaw, Architect

Her desire to avoid seeing J.D. until the July Fourth opening of the hotel had spontaneously given birth to a scheme whose success now depended on his believing that she would *not* be attending the hotel's grand opening a few days hence. And if he thought his marrying Matilda Kemp that night was devastating news to his architect, so much the better.

But you are *devastated...*

Amelia forced her thoughts back to matters at hand. Once J.D. got her letter, he'd readily assume that she'd found out about his engagement and had abruptly decamped for France in tears.

Amelia sealed the notes and addressed each one, placing them in envelopes with the name of the Julia Morgan firm printed in the upper left front corner. She gave both missives to Ira.

"You are a true friend, Ira Hoover."

He patted her awkwardly on her shoulder. "And you to me, Amelia Bradshaw."

"Everyone in the office has been wonderful," she added, battling a well of emotion that had risen in her chest.

"We're all glad to help," he replied affectionately. "I walked by the Bay View last week. It's magnificent. You are an absolute pistol, my girl."

"And not a word to anybody about my plan?" she pleaded. "I want everyone at the Bay View to believe I've already left for New York."

"Not a word to the contrary," Ira solemnly agreed.

Amelia expressed her appreciation, offered her farewells to Lacy and Julia, who'd promised to help her with the necessary arrangements to salvage what she could from this sorry mess, and marched out the office door.

She would, indeed, go to France, and there, along the grand boulevards, sidewalk cafés, and magnificent buildings, she would forget about J.D. Thayer and the treachery of men. She would revisit the Louvre and the Eiffel Tower and the Luxembourg Gardens and drive a motorcar down the Champs-Elysées with her hair unpinned, and revel in the fact that Julia Morgan believed she was an architect with true ability. She would stay at least one night at her favorite hotel on the Rue Jacob—alone.

She wondered briefly if she would ever run into Etienne Lamballe. She hoped her French was still good enough to tell him what she thought of *him*.

But before her departure from San Francisco, she would, by God, reclaim what legitimately belonged to her mother—and herself. And only *then* would she decide what direction to take for the rest of her life.

Chapter 33

S HE WAS SPITTIN' ANGRY when I saw her, lad, and she didn't say a word about leaving for France," Angus declared to J.D., who was sitting behind his new desk in the well-appointed Bay View basement-level office and holding a letter in his hand. "What have you done to the poor girl to make her flee like this?"

"Nothing... lately." J.D. was far more upset by Amelia's abruptly departing San Francisco than he was willing to admit to his loyal comrade-in-arms. He extended Amelia's letter toward Angus. "Read this if you don't believe me. It's all very matter-of-fact. She says she's leaving for Paris immediately—which I guess is today."

"She's gone? But I've asked the lass to marry me! Two or three times, in fact," Angus protested, "and, by the way, she never gave me a proper answer on my latest attempt."

J.D. was unsettled to realize that Amelia had disclosed to him Angus's first proposal—but not any subsequent ones.

"The first time I asked her," Angus continued with considerable agitation, "she talked about not wanting to change her life—or mine. She also said she didn't need any man to protect her or to do what she could do for herself."

"Well, *that* sounds typical for Amelia."

"The last time I proposed, I thought it wise to give her plenty of time to think it over. And then this morning, she prattled on about men putting shackles on women and controlling their inheritances and all sorts of other nonsense, before she stormed down the street. *You* must have said something to her, J.D., to make her go off like that."

"I haven't spoken to her today at all, or even yesterday, as a matter of fact."

J.D. knew full well, of course, at least one reason why Amelia might be furious. She must have read about his engagement to Matilda.

"You didn't see her at breakfast?" Angus demanded skeptically.

"No, I didn't. I had a very early appointment this morning and never saw a soul around here. I even left before the work crew arrived." He retrieved Amelia's letter from Angus and scrutinized it again. "By the time I returned and opened this, she was gone. She'd already directed Loy to send her belongings to Oakland and officially signed off on everything else here at the Bay View." He pointed to a sheaf of invoices spread across his desk as proof.

"Well, even if the hotel is finished," said Angus, scanning the letter addressed to J.D., "you'd think she'd at least say good-bye."

J.D. silently agreed and wondered, suddenly, if Kemp had made good on his threat to pass around copies of the photographs taken in China Alley. Surely, the man couldn't have sent such filth to a woman? And even if he had, Amelia wasn't faint of heart. She'd already *seen* for herself most of what the pictures portrayed.

No, what had probably prompted her abrupt departure was that she felt utterly betrayed by what she read in the newspaper. *And well she should,* he thought glumly. In more ways than she even knew.

J.D. glanced down once more at Amelia's letter, relieved in one sense that it guaranteed that Ezra could not make good on any of his not-so-veiled threats to do her bodily harm. If he tried to track her down, he and his henchmen would discover she'd taken a train for New York today and would soon be sailing to France.

By this time, Angus was pacing the office carpet. "I can't believe she'd miss the hotel's opening and even leave here before making sure everything was ready for its debut—unless she was mighty upset."

J.D. tried not to flinch under his friend's steady gaze. He needed a moment to think and, for the first time ever, wished Angus would make himself scarce. His presence was both a distraction and another reason to feel like a cad.

"She's done everything here that was expected of her," he said, affecting a shrug. "Her duties are at an end, so she appears to be taking a well-deserved holiday. We're ready to open ahead of schedule."

"And are you ready for your wedding, as well?" Angus said, eyes narrowing. "Certainly you haven't forgotten that event, have you, lad? You don't think perhaps that Amelia's seeing that engagement announcement in the newspaper triggered this? It certainly surprised and upset *me*! What in blazes possessed you to do such a ridiculous thing? You'll never get Kemp out of your life at this rate."

J.D. kept his gaze glued on the letter lying open on his desk and ignored Angus's probing question.

"I don't know if Amelia's even seen the newspaper. She's been pretty occupied this last little while. I think it's just as she said. Her job here is finished and so she's going to France. There's nothing mysterious in it at all."

"But do you have any reason to think that the surprise

wedding announcement would have shocked or distressed her?" Angus pressed. "You and she working so closely together as you have?"

J.D. looked up and regarded his friend for a long moment. At length he said quietly, "You know, don't you? Or at least you suspect?"

Angus peered down at his shoes. "I have to say that I've wondered at times if the two of you—"

He fell silent.

"Amelia and I... had become close associates over the months of building the hotel," J.D. admitted. "Or at least, I thought we had. The night we discovered the trunk buried next door with all the valuables, we celebrated with champagne and I... well, one thing led to another and—well... we're more than just colleagues."

Angus held both hands up as a clear indication he didn't wish J.D. to elaborate.

"I'm sorry, Angus. If it means anything to you, she'd already told me she'd declined your first offer of marriage."

His friend looked defeated. "She seems to think that if she married, she'd be turned into a domestic slave or something."

"It happens," J.D. said with a wry smile.

"Well, maybe this is all for the best. I don't want to wed a lass who regards marriage as a prison sentence." Angus declared. He regarded J.D. speculatively. "She probably turned you down too, didn't she? Figured you'd put shackles on her as well. And then you turned right around and asked Matilda for her hand, just to show her, and Amelia's pride is hurt. That's probably why she left."

"You're a far more honorable man than I, Dr. McClure. I haven't even had a *chance* to propose marriage to Amelia Bradshaw—or anything else. I've been far too busy fending off

Kemp and his hooligans and building this hotel. And besides, I'm supposed to be engaged to Matilda Kemp, remember?"

"*Why*, I ask again, have you done such a fool thing, Jamie? If you want my penny farthing on the matter—and I'm sure you don't—I think Amelia Bradshaw fell in love with you, and you with her, and now you've gone and made a terrible mess of everything by saying you'll marry Matilda to placate Kemp! Unless there's a part of this you haven't told me, it just doesn't make sense!"

Before J.D. could craft a response, both men heard the pounding of heavy footsteps and then a loud male voice booming down the hallway.

"You down here, Thayer?"

The two men inside the hotel office exchanged looks that signaled they both were relieved Ezra Kemp apparently hadn't heard the last of their conversation. When the man himself appeared at the threshold, he gestured toward Angus that he wanted the doctor to make himself scarce and leave the office.

J.D. said, "It seems Ezra here wishes to have a private word."

"If you need anything, laddie," Angus said, walking past Kemp, "I'll be in the back garden having a look at all the plantings Amelia ordered laid out. I was rather partial to roses when I lived in Scotland, but I never have had time for gardening 'til now." He shut the door behind him.

Kemp wasted no time in getting down to business. "I certainly hope, for your sake, Thayer, that Henry Bradshaw's scrawny little baggage isn't the root cause of the recent unpleasantness I've suffered at the hands of the Committee of Fifty."

He eased his bulk into the chair opposite J.D.

"What kind of unpleasantness, Ezra?" J.D. folded Amelia's note and slid it in a drawer.

"I've been removed from the Committee," he declared bitterly. "Your own father says Spreckels and the Secret Service want to talk to me. Apparently, you've gone and tattled to your daddy and now his friends say they don't want to buy lumber from me anymore unless I release you from your engagement and stop threatening to bash your head in if you don't marry Matilda." Kemp leaned against the edge of J.D.'s desk. "I said to your father, 'Fine... don't buy my lumber, but your son is still marrying my daughter.' I didn't tell him how I know this, but I'll tell *you*."

J.D. shook his head. "Matilda's marrying me will do you no good because you keep forgetting one thing, Ezra. I'm the prodigal son in the Thayer family. All those fancy folks you want to impress won't treat you a whit more cordially for linking your name to mine."

"Forget all that!" Kemp said. "When you marry my daughter, I'll be one step closer to taking back my stake in this place."

"And why would I allow that?" J.D. responded calmly. "And besides, you don't *have* a stake in the hotel. You've been paid back in full on your investment in a gambling club that doesn't even exist anymore. I've already delivered funds to repay you for all I owed for lumber supplies on the hotel your thugs arranged to have burned down. The main point is, though, that Matilda doesn't want to marry me and I don't want to marry her. You can't *will* it to happen. The wedding's off. And I would strongly suggest you stay out of the gambling halls and Chinese brothels, go back to Mill Valley, and keep your head down. Spreckels and those Secret Service men mean business."

"It *is* that Bradshaw slut, isn't it?" Kemp demanded, making no pretense of controlling his temper. "Joe

Kavanaugh says he thinks you definitely got into her knickers. You're such a fool! She probably wants from you what I want from you—this hotel. Who knows what her father said to her before he died?"

"You're wrong. She gave up any claims to the hotel long ago."

"You figure by cozying up to her, you can keep her from *making* any claims, should she act like her sex, change her mind later, and drag you back into court!"

"I paid Amelia Bradshaw a good salary to build this place and she's never, in all this time, challenged my right to reconstruct the Bay View."

"And she won't, damn her. Because if I even see you and her together—I'll know you double-crossed your old partner—and I'll make sure that the next ferry ride she takes will be her last." Kemp leaned forward again and poked a stubby finger at J.D.'s shirtfront. "You know I can make it happen, so you'd better marry Matilda on the Fourth of July. Don't forget, J.D, lots of people disappear on the bay. Remember what happened to your own grandfather."

"He wasn't pushed by the likes of you. He jumped."

J.D. stared down at his desktop while he attempted to keep his temper—not to mention a surge of fear—in check. Kemp was perfectly capable of what he was threatening to do to Amelia—and capable of covering it up. The question was, would he bother to send his minions all the way to Paris?

Kemp smiled faintly. "That Harold Jasper, the purser on the *Berkeley,* owes me a few favors," he said. "All I have to do is say the word and it'll look *as if* she jumped. 'All upset that Thayer diddled her and then planned to marry Kemp's daughter,' he'll tell everyone, including that reporter friend of yours."

Ezra heaved himself out of the chair and headed for the office door. From the threshold he added, "Like it or not, we're partners in this hotel again, J.D. And we'll seal the deal Thursday night at your wedding, won't we now?"

"How can you be sure you can make the bride do your bidding, Ezra?"

"The same way I can guarantee you will. She wouldn't want anything to happen to her good friend, Emma, just like you don't want Amelia Bradshaw to meet with an untimely accident."

"Jesus, Kemp!" J.D. said, banging a fist on the desk.

"I beat it out of Matilda what's been going on in that studio of hers," Kemp exclaimed, his face the hue of claret. "And, by the way—I know *you* know about it too, 'cause I beat *that* out of her as well. All the more reason for the nuptials to take place on the Fourth, as scheduled. I'll even give you those glass photographic plates for a wedding present. Once you two are married, there'll be no need for anyone else ever again to see those pictures of you in China Alley, and no one need ever know about my daughter's filthy little secret."

"Filthy?" J.D. laughed harshly. "Who's filthy? You're the one who invested in a brothel that supplies unwilling virgins and little boys to special customers—a legacy from your harlot mother, I suppose. Or was it that brute you called a father?"

"Shut up!"

"And where *is* Miss Stivers, may I ask?"

"Jake Kelly's keeping her company 'til Matilda's wedding day. The little strumpet'll be heading back east on the train July fifth—*after* she serves as bridal attendant for her dear friend. Everything will appear quite ordinary Thursday night. I've got the *Call*'s best reporters coming to write about 'the wedding of the year.' And I sent a telegram to *Collier's* to get Jack London down here from Sonoma. It's all happening, J.D. Get used to the idea of being a married man and my son-in-law, or something mighty unpleasant is going to happen to that lady architect."

"I see... but there's one more important fact you should know. You can call your dogs off Miss Bradshaw. She's completed everything here and left San Francisco this morning."

"Left? For where? Why should I believe you?"

J.D. reached into his desk drawer. The sight of Amelia's letter was reassuring. Should he use it? It was a risk, but the odds were in his favor that Kemp wouldn't try to hurt her if he knew she'd departed for France. And it would buy J.D. time to figure out what to do about getting his unwanted "partner" out of his life—permanently.

"Here, read her letter. She's probably already boarded her train for New York. Apparently she's taking a boat to France next week."

"Why would she do that?" he asked suspiciously.

"Her mother lives in Paris, remember? Miss Bradshaw's not even coming to the hotel's opening. That's what close *friends* we are. You're way off base about her, Ezra."

Kemp scanned Amelia's note to J.D. telling him where to send the final installment of her fee. He tossed the letter back on the desk.

"Glad to hear it, but I'm not calling off anyone."

"She's no threat to you. She's already gone."

"You could always be bluffing," declared Kemp. "As a matter of fact, I'll give Dick Spitz the job of watching all the ferries in and out of Oakland. If anybody sees her here before the wedding, I've got a special lumber barge christened with her name on the hull. So you'd better be playing it straight with me about her leaving the country if you don't want a tragedy to mar your wedding day."

Suddenly, it seemed to J.D. that, indeed, the safest course was for him to make his own brand of "Boston Marriage" with Matilda Elizabeth Kemp at the Bay View Hotel on the evening of the Fourth of July with bombs bursting in air.

Extreme circumstances called for extreme measures.

❧

Lacy Fiske's eyes were wide with admiration as she inspected the gown under Amelia's long black evening cloak.

"Trust me, Amelia. That dress will garner more attention than the new hotel."

Lacy, Julia, Amelia, and Aunt Margaret stood at the railing, waiting for the crew of the *Berkeley* to tie the ferry's lines to the pier on the San Francisco side of the bay.

"That's just what I said," Margaret scolded. "That dress is far too revealing for such a dignified occasion." Amelia's aunt was attired in her usual black bombazine.

"Julia brought back silk blouses from Paris," Amelia said by way of defending herself. "And of all the things I purchased in France, this dress is my favorite. Thank goodness I'd sent all my clothing from there to the bungalow in Oakland before the quake."

"Well, you look lovely," Lacy reassured her.

Amelia inhaled a gulp of sea air to calm her nerves and take her mind off the gown's dramatic décolletage. She had a very good reason for wearing a dress to her former lover's wedding that would halt traffic on Market Street.

J.D. had never seen her in it.

J.D. Thayer, you're going to behold me and weep...

She wondered if she had the grit to go through with her plan after all. Then she assured herself that she was just having an attack of the jitters. In Oakland, when the ferry had pulled away from the docks and headed across the bay to San Francisco, her heart nearly leapt from her chest when she'd caught a glimpse of the odious Dick Spitz. She saw him standing on the other side of the boat, his head bent toward Harold Jasper's as if they were conferring. When she peered around her clutch of friends to get a better look, the two men quickly turned and retreated to a lower deck. Thirty minutes later, she was positive she saw Spitz again, melting into the disembarking throng. The purser kept his distance from their group during the entire crossing, which also struck her as odd.

She patted her beaded handbag, glad she'd tucked her lady's revolver inside for any eventuality. J.D. had finally returned it to her after Foo died, though there never seemed time for him to drill her in shooting practice. Even so, after her previous violent confrontation with Kelly, Kavanaugh, and Spitz, she wasn't leaving anything to chance.

Again, she glanced down at the lemon-yellow silk chiffon evening dress purchased the week she gained her certificate from L'École. She had worn the gown in triumph to dinner at chic, romantic Lapérouse on the Quai Malaquais across from the Louvre, with Etienne Lamballe on her arm. It was the night she'd drunk nearly a bottle of Veuve Clicquot and he'd drunk *two,* and then declared he expected her to give up architecture when they wed.

How long ago that seemed.

"I fear tonight will be an awfully late evening, Amelia," her aunt said with a sigh, "and such a crush of people." She reached toward Amelia's cape. "Pull your cloak tightly around your shoulders, dear. It won't do for you to catch your death just before you take the train tomorrow night."

Amelia gave her aunt's shoulder's a little squeeze. "I feel fine, Aunt Margaret, and don't worry. We'll get plenty of sleep tonight so tomorrow we can have a lovely day together. What I have to do for the hotel's opening shouldn't take long."

Margaret Collins turned to address Julia and Lacy. "It's amazing, really. Amelia finally comes back to me in Oakland after more than a year in the city, and then, a day later, poof! She's off to Paris. You young people lead such a carefree life."

By this time, Amelia and her companions had made their way to the bottom of California Street where Edith Pratt waited for them in a staid gown of brown moiré.

"Thank you so much for coming," Amelia said to her old school chum who had nursed Grandfather Hunter during his last illness.

"I traded shifts at the Presidio hospital," Edith said. She murmured in Amelia's ear, "Did you know that Angus is serving as best man tonight?"

"No…" Amelia said under her breath, fighting against another wave of betrayal washing over her.

A cable car rumbled to a halt and the five women mounted the running board and settled onto the wooden benches. Slowly, the car began the steep ascent to Nob Hill. Amelia glanced at Lacy and Julia, both of whom had worn their smartest attire for the occasion.

"Thank you *all* so much for going to this with me tonight," she said in a rush. "If you weren't right here beside me, I'd probably take the next ferry back to Oakland."

"Donaldina will definitely be there with Wing Lee," Lacy volunteered, "so you'll have plenty of people to rally 'round during the hotel's dedication. I doubt any man would dare come near such a gaggle of females," she said with a laugh.

Julia nodded. "You're merely expected to greet the invited dignitaries and then you can discreetly take your leave before... well, before the other ceremony begins. We'll be right there with you."

And thus, I shall return to Oakland in the company of women.

That's what this path she'd chosen for herself undoubtedly meant, she thought with a deepening sense of melancholy. One could have success in the public sphere, but it certainly appeared to Amelia as if a woman who dedicated her life to architecture ruled out nearly everything else—everything except hard work and the company of a few female professionals who were forging this new trail beside her.

She'd made her choice, she told herself silently, and now she must follow through with it. She had provided to Julia and Lacy a sanitized version of events regarding J.D.'s withholding information about the outcome of the poker contest on the night of the quake. The Misses Morgan and Fiske had been awestruck when Amelia showed them the five cards now in her possession. To them it would seem that the evening's challenge was to stand stoically in a reception line in the presence of the man who was a gambler that had betrayed their friend's trust in order to gain title to Amelia's family legacy.

Aunt Margaret, on the other hand, assumed her niece was merely nervous to have the hotel reviewed by San Francisco's leading citizens. Edith Pratt had insisted on attending by Amelia's side when she heard from Angus about the threats Kemp had repeatedly made against J.D. and Amelia and felt it her duty to be there to help physically protect her friend from possibly being accosted by Kemp's bullyboys.

But even beyond any danger from Kemp, only Amelia knew the night represented much more than confronting J.D about the five playing cards tucked into her cloak's inside silk pocket.

She knew events this evening meant that she would never have a husband. She would never have a child. Her daydream of J.D. and her living as loving partners had been pure fantasy, and yet she couldn't imagine living with anyone else. She felt hollow inside. Bereft.

But there was no escaping plain facts. The day J.D. and she had sparred over his assigning the Pigati cousins to guard the hotel without informing her, she'd asked him to tell the unvarnished truth when it concerned her welfare—and he hadn't. It had obviously been a pattern, and who knew what other truths he'd neglected to reveal? He'd consistently put the hotel and his own welfare first. It was as simple as that. He clearly wasn't in love with his bride-to-be. He was marrying Matilda to save his stake in a *building*!

When it came to J.D. Thayer, cement had won over sentiment.

Well, she admitted to herself, when it got right down to it, there probably wasn't a man on the planet who could meet her standards, nor she theirs. She had married architecture, and that was the end of it. Yet there were times—like tonight—when her profession seemed a cold companion and she suddenly felt like turning toward Aunt Margaret standing to her right and sobbing like a child against her bombazine-clad shoulder.

Instead, Amelia slipped a gloved hand into the pocket of her cloak and fingered the five playing cards. They confirmed that her task this night entailed a greater gamble than anything her father had ever dared—and she intended to win.

CHAPTER 34

CARRIAGES, HACKNEYS, AND MOTORCARS jammed the courtyard entrance to the Bay View Hotel. Joseph, the elderly doorman, commanded an army of assistants in trim, brown uniforms stamped with the BVH monogram. In relays, they rushed forward to assist the elegantly dressed passengers onto the red carpet and usher them through the arched entrance.

The swarms of arriving guests walked past sculpted Cypress trees that flanked the portico. Nearby, stone statuary dotted the narrow flower beds that curved around Taylor Street and down Jackson, toward the grand gardens on the lower elevations of Nob Hill.

For Amelia, the opening of the Bay View Hotel symbolized that a degree of normalcy had finally returned to San Francisco. At this newest landmark of the fledgling twentieth century, she had replaced its flickering gasoliers with reliable electric lights. Elevators had augmented staircases, even in the service areas. Telephones were installed in every bedroom. Heaters and hot water boilers were fired with natural gas, not coal or wood. A fleet of motorcars garaged in the spacious underground parking area would soon be available to chauffeur guests wherever in the city they wished to go.

And as with the Fairmont, Amelia too had ordered extra fire hoses and on-site sources of water. All the materials she'd employed both inside and out gave the new building structural integrity and heat-resistance qualities that had been sorely lacking before the great quake and fire.

She stood at the grand entrance to the hotel, buffeted by the crowds pressing in from all sides, and did her best to concentrate on her accomplishments, not the yawning hole in her heart. From inside the Bay View, festive music wafted from a string quartet that played in a recess of the spacious, red-carpeted lobby. Flanking her were her companions and surrounding her were laughter and gaiety and a joyous sense of the city's continuing recovery, yet no matter how hard she tried, she couldn't put aside a sense of overweening sadness and apprehension.

"You all go in," she urged her companions. She needed a moment alone, and also a chance to say her good-byes.

"Are you sure?" Edith Pratt asked with a worried frown.

"Yes. I want to duck into the kitchen to see how the backstairs staff is holding up. I'll join you in the grand ballroom in just a few minutes."

Edith turned and hugged Amelia's shoulders while Julia Morgan's sharp eyes surveyed every detail of the terra-cotta-clad facade.

"Why, it's absolutely breathtaking, isn't it?" Edith exclaimed to the others.

"A petite Fairmont," Lacy said. She turned to her employer and now housemate. "Don't you feel like a proud mother hen, Julia?"

"Yes, I do a bit," Julia replied, and Amelia felt a rush of gratitude for Morgan's generosity of spirit.

Aunt Margaret at first appeared speechless as she gazed at the broad entrance of the glamorous hotel her niece had built. Then she turned and kissed her on the cheek. "I'm simply in awe of what you've created, my dear. Your grandfather would be too."

Her aunt could have said nothing more likely to bring moisture to Amelia's eyes. She swiftly ducked her head and fiddled with the tie at the throat of her velvet cloak.

"Go on, now, all of you," she urged. "I'll be with you in just a few minutes."

As soon as the four women disappeared into the crowd making its way through the front entrance, Amelia pulled the hood of her cloak over her head and sped down Jackson Street. She was relieved to see that the outdoor floodlights were bathing the side of the hotel in a soft glow that issued from the flower beds.

She entered from a rear door that led directly into the kitchen and paused at the threshold, pushing back the hood of her cloak to fall on her shoulders. A platoon of cooks, pastry chefs, servers, and wine stewards bustled in and out of the high-ceilinged room.

"Missy Bradshaw!" cried a voice. Suddenly, Amelia was surrounded by Loy Chen and Shou Shou and several other Chinese workers she recognized. They all had exchanged their laborers' clothing for the fancy brown livery denoting the dining staff.

The Bay View would be the first hotel in San Francisco to employ Asians in publicly prominent positions—as waiters in the elegant dining room—a gesture on J.D.'s part Amelia couldn't help but admire.

In an uncharacteristic display of emotion, Shou Shou threw her arms around Amelia and hugged her. "We thought you go to France!" she exclaimed.

"Soon," Amelia said, and put her finger to her lips. "Shhh… my being here is a surprise." When the hubbub died down, she asked, "Is Mr. Thayer in his office?"

"No, he go penthouse. Dress for wedding." Loy sounded

tentative. "Then he go to lobby… see to guests." He eyed Amelia grimly. "You know Miss Matilda?"

"I met her just once," she replied. To avoid any further questions, she smiled brightly and said, "I wanted to come down to thank you *all* for the wonderful job you've done and for… well, for the friendship you bestowed on me this past year." She extended her hand to Loy who looked as if he'd never before shaken hands Western fashion. "And especially you, Loy, and you, Shou Shou." She could feel the tears well up again. "I don't know how things will go for you now in the new hotel, but I just wanted to tell you how much I appreciate everything you've done to make this opening night possible." She paused and then went on. "I'm… I'm so grateful for the loyalty you've shown Mr. Thayer and myself. Thank you from the bottom of my heart."

Loy seized Amelia's hand and bowed his head over it. "You good friend to us, Missy. I do all hotel laundry now. You good friend to Chinese. Just like Lo Mo."

Equating her with Donaldina Cameron was the highest compliment Loy Chen could possibly bestow. Amelia wiped her eyes with the back of her kid gloves and produced a weak smile. "She'll be here tonight, I think. With Wing Lee."

"Wing Lee, guest of *honor*," Loy said, bowing proudly from the waist. "Stand next to Mr. Thayer in line, he say. And next to his mother, Missy Consuela."

"I'm glad," murmured Amelia, though she wondered how having J.D.'s child as part of the proceedings would sit with the bride, or with J.D.'s future father-in-law, for that matter. She was also surprised to learn Mrs. Thayer was attending the opening and supposed his mother must have finally made her peace with J.D. now that Ling Lee was dead.

"Well, I'd better go up," she said, nodding farewells around the kitchen.

"You take *back* elevator?" Loy asked with a disapproving frown as he escorted her down the hall along side her sweeping skirts. "Missy should take *front* elevator!"

"I'll get off on the mezzanine," she assured him, "and then come down the grand staircase, if that will make you happy. And besides, I want to see how the balustrade looks tonight."

"Yes, Missy." Loy nodded with a stoic expression. Apparently he remembered all too well the occasion when Amelia tore out a large section of the banister with a crowbar and then demanded Dominic Pigati reset it to her exact specifications.

"Good-bye, Loy. Be well."

"Good-bye, Missy. You good lady."

⌘

Amelia stood at the summit of the red-carpeted stairway that curved downward to a grand ballroom rivaling any in the courts of Europe. In one corner of the polished marble floor, the Bay View Hotel's string quartet played behind a forest of potted palms. Their music provided a gracious counterpoint to the noisy, excited chatter resounding off the mirrored walls.

This evening was a repetition of the opening of the Fairmont Hotel, only this time, she alone was responsible for the design and construction from the foundations to the roof. To Amelia's surprise, she had become amazingly calm while standing at the top of the stairs surveying the scene below. Her sweeping gaze absorbed the sight of enormous sprays of white floral arrangements dotting the ballroom.

J.D. is actually going through with this insane wedding!

Her rising anger was equal to the palpable sense of betrayal she was studiously ignoring. She retrieved her father's small pocket watch from her handbag and opened its case encrusted with tiny gold nuggets, stealing a glance at the hour and minute hands. Amazingly enough, the convex circle of cracked glass, shattered at 5:12 in the morning on April 18, 1906, shielded dials that had continued to function. She would keep it always as a reminder of that day... the day she found J.D. half-dead in the quake's rubble.

Twelve times nine... don't think about that... think about the playing cards... eleven times nine...

It was nearly eight p.m. Only minutes away from the bride's debut.

Hordes of celebrants milled at the foot of the staircase, the company attired in winged collars and starched linen shirts, swallowtail coats or beaded silk chiffon gowns. Several guests sported monocles and lorgnettes. A delicious aroma of roasted lamb sent down from the verdant farms of Marin County wafted from the adjacent dining room where guests would be served a midnight buffet after the festivities.

Slowly, unobtrusively, Amelia pulled a fan of tattered playing cards from inside her silk-lined cloak and held them by her side. In stark contrast to her spotless white kid gloves, three of the five cards remained splotched with dirt. All the cards she held had been used in a game of chance that must now seem almost dreamlike to the two surviving men who'd gambled in the bowels of the original Bay View Hotel—a lifetime ago.

Amelia noted that among those nibbling canapés and sipping bubbling wine were gentlemen whose economic muscle, back-room connections, and access to raw materials had helped to rebuild thousands of structures destroyed in the wake of the unparalleled disaster—a cataclysm that had leveled most of the city and still left more than fifty thousand residents without homes.

Like the reopening of the Fairmont, the evening's occasion had brought out a bevy of Stanfords, Crockers, Huntingtons, Hopkinses, and Spreckels, along with a new wave of politicians who not only wished to honor the newlyweds from two powerful families, but to celebrate another milestone in San Francisco's astonishing triumph over unprecedented adversity. And what better way to commemorate such a remarkable achievement than a wedding—an event pregnant with promise for the future.

How shocked these guests will be to learn the identity of the true owner of this legendary hotel site, Amelia thought defiantly. How embarrassed to hear the names of people in their midst who were responsible for unprecedented graft and the deaths of untold nameless women—women who had perished behind the iron bars of brothels, unwilling captives on the day the earth shuddered and the heavens burned. Women whose bodies had never been counted in the official death toll.

Surely, Amelia Hunter Bradshaw was the last person Ezra Kemp or J.D. Thayer expected to make an appearance on this occasion, for she now possessed the proof that could destroy at least one man's dreams, just as the quake and fire of '06 had shattered the hopes of so many others.

She noticed reporter James Hopper lounging in one corner of the ballroom talking to a handsome young man furiously writing in a notebook—and she quickly looked away. Then she returned her father's gold watch to her handbag and nestled the soiled remnants of that long forgotten poker contest next to the cherished timepiece—and her pearl-handled revolver. Next, she removed her velvet cloak and hung it neatly on the balustrade.

For a few more seconds she stood poised at the top of the stairs in her daring Paris finery and scanned the scene below. On the far side of the ballroom, behind a pillar, she spotted Jake Kelly and Joe Kavanaugh also surveying the crowd. Kemp's henchmen had squeezed into evening clothes and looked like matching, overstuffed sofas. With a start, she spied Dick Spitz posted near the ballroom's south entrance where gaggles of late-arriving guests joined the long queue for the reception line of civic dignitaries. He was obviously looking for someone.

Then she saw J.D.

He stood near the foot of the grand staircase, nodding and shaking hands with guests who were offering praise for his new hotel and congratulations about his pending marriage. A little Chinese girl stood shyly by his side. On his other side was a woman with a bronze complexion and shining black hair drawn sleekly into a chignon at the nape of her neck. J.D. frequently bent his head to speak to his mother and then leaned down and smiled encouragingly at the little girl.

Amelia steeled herself from thinking well of him for being so kind this night to members of his family that he had previously shunned. Better that her heart went out to the orphan child, she reminded herself, wondering how J.D. explained the identity of Wing Lee to the visitors filing by.

For a moment, Amelia caressed the polished walnut banister, an elegant symbol of a city that had literally risen from cinder and ash. Then, she slowly descended the crimson carpet. Soon a decision would be made and all secrets revealed.

But not yet.

♔

Reporters James Hopper and Jack London stood off to the side of the glittering throng, notebooks held loosely in one hand, champagne glasses in the other.

"What do you think the chances are that President Roosevelt will make a surprise appearance?" London asked.

"Zero," Hopper retorted with the vehemence of a City Room cynic. "The newspaper's had spotters at the train station all week. It was just that blowhard, Ezra Kemp, trying to drum up guests for his daughter's wedding."

"Well, it worked with my editors at *Collier's*," London noted, adding, "here I am, all the way from Sonoma."

"Is that bride not the ugliest creature you ever laid eyes on?" Hopper said pointing across the room to a massive collection of white tulle lurking at the ballroom's entrance.

London laughed. "And tell me, please. How are we supposed to describe her in print?"

"Blushing," Hopper said. "Always safe to call 'em blushing, no matter what they look like." He glanced in the other direction and noted an attractive woman, gowned in a stunning, low-cut yellow silk dress, pausing half way down the grand staircase. He took another sip of his champagne and gazed at her with admiration.

"Well, well… will you look over there, London." He gestured with his glass in Amelia Bradshaw's direction. "I happen to know that there's a woman whom I would refer to in print as a real looker—*and* a damn interesting one at that."

❦

Amelia hesitated on the final step, her eyes riveted on J.D. He was attired in starched white tie and tails, surrounded not only by his mother and Wing Lee, but by the reform mayor, Dr. Edward R. Taylor, and a host of city leaders, all of who were offering him their hearty felicitations. Dr. Angus McClure, serving as J.D.'s best man, stood to one side, appearing distinctly uncomfortable in his dress clothes. Shou Shou had just scooped up Wing Lee, undoubtedly on a mission to put the child to bed.

From Amelia's angle, a pained expression played across J.D.'s features as well-wishers approached, clapped him on the back and shoulders, and joyfully moved on toward the free wine offered, buffet style, on linen-draped tables positioned along the ballroom's side walls.

Amelia intently watched her erstwhile lover. The scars above his eyebrows had faded and now lent his tanned face character, as if the faint marks remained an outward symbol of the suffering all San Franciscans had endured. She thought of her own scars, which were camouflaged by the few strands of her hair not captured in her upswept Gibson. And then there were other wounds that couldn't be masked so easily...

She remained rooted to the spot, barely ten feet from J.D., willing him to turn and see her, and within seconds he did. They exchanged glances—his startled; hers, she hoped, expressionless. She threaded the rest of her way down the stairs, the space between them telescoping to less than a foot.

"You came," he murmured, his gaze never leaving her face. "You haven't left for France, yet."

Amelia extended no greeting but reached into her handbag and retrieved five playing cards. She displayed them inches from his starched white shirtfront. First she showed him the backs of the cards where his initials and the words *The Bay View Hotel* could clearly be read, despite the damaged edges. Then, she turned them over and fanned them across the palm of her kid glove.

"May I speak to you a moment, Mr. Thayer?"

J.D. glanced at the cards and stared at her wordlessly for a few moments. He looked at an astonished Angus McClure and then pointed to a private corner near a cluster of potted palms. "Over there," he directed.

Amelia didn't acknowledge any of the dignitaries in their midst; she merely followed the prospective groom to a secluded spot and prepared to deliver the speech that had been taking shape in her mind for several days.

"You may have seen these five cards before, but even if you haven't, the truth is my father played this royal flush in *this* hotel on the day of the quake and won back the Bay View property, fair and square."

J.D. gazed at the cards but made no response.

"Inspect them very carefully, J.D." She pointed to the ace, queen, and ten of diamonds. "As I told you twice before, these three were still in my father's hand when I found him pinned under the gaming table." She displayed the jack and king. "I found these two totally by accident, wedged into the right-side pocket of the dress trousers my father was wearing on the night of the quake when he played five-card stud at your gambling club."

"Why haven't you told me this before?"

"I only found the final two cards on the morning I left here." She pointed again to the ace, queen, and ten of diamonds. "As one might expect, these original three are rather worse for wear, having been in Father's hand when he fell to the ground in the quake. The other two that he'd managed to stuff into his pocket when the shaking started are in perfect condition, as you can see." She gazed directly into his dark eyes. "I wore the trousers for the first time the morning of my final inspection of the property. How else would I have this five-card sequence of diamonds with these distinctive marks and with the Bay View's name on the back—and your initials—if I weren't telling the truth?"

"I believe you."

Startled he didn't dispute her claim, she searched his face, his features now an expressionless mask.

"Good," she managed finally, taken off guard by his frank admission, "because what I'm presenting to you is the truth."

J.D. said, "I saw Henry Bradshaw lay down four sequential diamonds, and just as he was turning over the fifth card—as I told you before—the world turned upside down."

Amelia allowed her hand to fall by her side to keep him from seeing that it had started to tremble. "J.D., I don't know whether I believe your version of how much you saw or not. I don't even expect you to hand me the deed to the hotel."

"What *do* you want, then, Amelia?" he asked quietly.

"I want you to do the honorable thing and vest me as an equal, legal partner in this hotel we built together. I want you to pay my mother and me a commensurate, annual portion of your profits from this day forward. As I indicated in my note, I am leaving on the train for New York and thence on to Paris. However, I wish to know *now*—this very instant, before your marriage, and in writing—that both my mother and I may live in reasonable comfort for the rest of our lives, partaking of the profits earned by this hotel. Certainly, the gambler who was my father owes it to her, and I want that debt to be paid by *you*."

"And what will you do if I don't agree to this plan?"

Amelia gazed at his shuttered eyes, fully prepared for this moment.

"If you chose to fight me on this, I shall instruct my attorney, Mr. Damler, to sue you and put a lien on this hotel, asserting my *full* ownership by virtue of my inheriting through my late grandfather what my deceased father won back. I will compel Mr. Kemp to testify about that night. I shall also complain to Mr. Spreckels and to the Secret Service about the bribes you paid to get your gambling club built swiftly while I was in France, unable to defend my property, and how you continued to dispense graft with the result that the boilers in your second hotel blew up, endangering all of Nob Hill."

"And how do you suppose to prove that?"

Ignoring his question, she waved the cards in front of him once again.

"Furthermore, I shall insinuate you continued to bribe city officials through your ongoing relationship with Kemp, your future father-in-law," she said, feeling a ball of anger in the pit of her chest expand until she thought it might burst through the bodice of her low-cut gown. "Not only *that*," she added, swearing to herself should would not allow her voice to waver as tears threatened to well up, "I will grant an interview to Mr. Hopper and Mr. London, who are both here tonight, to tell the story of how you and Kemp attempted to cheat a family of poor, *defenseless* women out of their inheritance. It should make an especially interesting feature, given that everyone in San Francisco knows that *I* have designed and supervised the construction of your trophy."

"You? Defenseless?" A slow smile spread across J.D.'s face. "That's what I love about you, Amelia. You're just like me. You just don't give up."

"I am not at *all* like you, Mr. Thayer!"

"Oh yes, you are. You like to win."

Amelia was sorely tempted to slap the grin off J.D.'s face when Ezra Kemp suddenly elbowed his way through the crowd of curious onlookers. Following in his wake was a towering apparition clad in yards of white tulle and lace that did nothing to soften her athletic shoulders or bony hips. And trailing Matilda, dressed in a frothy pink silk evening gown, her devoted friend Emma Stivers appeared equally astounded to see the groom in a private *tête-à-tête* with a woman who was not the bride.

Kemp was livid, glaring first at J.D. and then at Amelia. "You said Amelia Bradshaw was on her way to France!" he bellowed, turning more heads.

"I thought she was," J.D. replied in a low, even voice. "She must enjoy weddings. Show him the royal flush, Amelia."

With her gloved fingertips, she again spread the cards into a fan.

"What about it, Kemp?" J.D. asked. "Want to provide Amelia the details how you tried to cheat her father *and* me that night?"

CHAPTER 35

J AKE? JOE?" KEMP CALLED over his shoulder, but the milling crowd slowed the progress of the two burly henchmen. Meanwhile J.D. began to speak to Kemp almost casually.

"You thought *you* would produce a hand that night that would make the Bay View yours, didn't you, Kemp? But around five a.m., Miss Bradshaw," he continued, his voice increasing in volume and now addressing Amelia and the surrounding throng, "I insisted on exchanging the stacked deck Mr. Kemp, here, had been using all night with one from my personal cupboard. See?" he said, seizing Amelia's gloved hand to turn the cards down, "here are my initials."

"That's preposterous!" Kemp thundered. "You had dozens of decks with "JDT" printed on them in the hotel. She has no proof that this hand came from the particular deck you unwrapped at five a.m."

"You must admit, Ezra, the earthquake and fire that destroyed the hotel that day improves her odds of being right."

"Prove it!" Kemp challenged her.

"No, *you* prove it," Amelia intervened, turning to glare directly at Kemp. "Produce just *one* other deck like this." She was so filled with fury she had to clasp her hands together to keep from reaching inside her handbag for her pistol.

"There've been *two* fires that swept this hotel, burning every-thing to a crisp, and one of them was probably engineered by you, Mr. Kemp. So, simply *show* me a surviving deck of cards that came from the old Bay View. I dare you!"

Kemp pointed a trembling finger at her. "She had the run of the place while you were building the first hotel, J.D. She probably found a cache of old playing cards in a safe, or someone from Oakland kept a deck as a souvenir, and now she's concocting this larcenous allegation—"

Amelia turned to confront the man who towered over her. "You *saw* my father's winning hand," she practically shouted at Kemp, waving the royal flush inches from his face. "He told me on his deathbed that you definitely knew that he had played these cards because you sat right *next* to him!"

"Then, why, missy, if you supposedly had these cards, didn't you tell anyone before tonight?"

"Because, Mr. Kemp," she said, narrowing her glance to look him straight in the eye, "until a few days ago, as I'd earlier told Mr. Thayer, I had only three cards—the ace, queen, and ten of diamonds. I'd retrieved them from my father's hand where he lay crushed in the rubble of the old hotel. He'd been abandoned by *you* when you fled the scene that terrible morning without offering anyone help—even including Mr. Thayer here, who was injured nearly as seri-ously as Henry Bradshaw!"

She separated out the jack and king of diamonds and held them up for the benefit of the crowd that pressed ever nearer.

"And then, through an astounding turn of events on Friday, last," she continued loudly, "I happened to put my hand into the pocket of the very trousers my father had been wearing on the night of the quake, and discovered *these* two cards from the same deck. He'd managed to stuff them into his clothing when he dove under the table that, seconds later, crushed his back when the ceiling caved in on top of it."

She shoved the cards under Kemp's nose.

"Take a good look, Mr. Kemp. My father *died* because of his injuries that night. These cards have returned to *haunt* you, sir." She fanned all five cards in her palm once again, displaying them for the rubbernecking throng. Aunt Margaret, Julia Morgan, and Amelia's other women friends, plus Donaldina Cameron, stood on the grand staircase, watching her in frozen silence.

"*A royal flush*," Amelia pronounced, enunciating each consonant for the benefit of reporters Hopper and London. "A rare event, by any standard. Drawn by my father, Henry Bradshaw, at Mr. Thayer's former gambling club on *this* site in a winner-take-all poker game at five-thirteen in the morning of April eighteenth, 1906!"

Amelia could hear the crowd murmur and J.D. begin to chuckle.

"Isn't it the perfect irony?" he said to Kemp, who appeared close to having a stroke. "Henry Bradshaw had us both beat, Ezra. Can you feature that? You have to admit it. Amelia here holds the cards that prove—"

Just then, Kemp roughly slapped the cards out of Amelia's hand. The roomful of people gasped as all five fluttered to the floor.

"Henry Bradshaw was a known drunkard and a liar. Now a *dead* liar, fortunately." Kemp jerked his head in the direction of Kelly, Kavanaugh, and Spitz, who, by this time, had burrowed their way to the first tier of people surrounding the principal players in the high drama.

Amelia heard her own involuntary gasp at the close proximity of the men who had rape or murder in mind when the midnight marauders attacked the Chinese laborers months before. The night seven-year-old Foo was beaten to death.

"Jake! Dick!" Kemp ordered. "Take her out of here. *Now!*"

Rigid with fury, Amelia reached into her handbag and withdrew her pearl-handled weapon. At the same moment, J.D. pulled back his arm and released a tremendous punch to Ezra Kemp's jaw, toppling him to the floor like a pile of lumber.

Just then, the sound of a gunshot ricocheted through the ballroom. Women screamed and men ducked for cover. The hulking figure of Jake Kelly lunging for Amelia halted in his tracks, unmarked by Amelia's shot that had lodged harmlessly in the beautifully polished parquet floor. Even so, a terrified Kelly spun in place and hurriedly melted into the crowd, followed by Dick Spitz and Joe Kavanaugh, running in zigzag courses to catch up with him.

In the middle of the uproar, J.D. leaned down and retrieved the five playing cards from the floor and then stood to his full height. Addressing the wide-eyed circle of dignitaries and wedding guests, he declared in stentorian tones.

"It's quite all right, everybody! No harm done. Fortunately, Miss Bradshaw here is a tad nearsighted and therefore a terrible shot, so no one got hurt." He gently seized Amelia's weapon from her trembling hand and stuck the small pistol into a pocket of his dress jacket. "In case anyone was wondering, though, this wedding is *canceled*. But, by all means, let the party continue!"

Stunned silence greeted this announcement. Meanwhile, J.D. smiled warmly at Matilda, who beamed back, an unmistakable expression of relief written across her angular features. Next to her, Emma Stivers whirled around and the two women embraced. He turned to reassure his mother, who appeared shaken but calm.

"Please, Mayor Taylor… everybody," J.D. loudly addressed the crowd, "stay and drink the champagne, eat the marvelous food prepared by our chefs, dance the night away. And *do* enjoy the view of the bay on the lovely moonlight this evening. The *genuine* fireworks should commence at around nine o'clock."

He nodded briskly at a couple of doormen who had rushed to the ballroom at the sound of gunshots. "Will the members of my staff please show Mr. Kemp to his room?" he requested, pointing to Ezra's prone, unconscious figure.

He paused, and the ballroom grew deathly silent. With a grin spreading across his features he declared in stentorian tones, "Amelia Hunter Bradshaw and James Diaz Thayer hereby declare the Bay View Hotel officially open for business!"

A rousing cheer went up as J.D. leaned toward the head bellman and said under his breath, "Tony, take Miss Bradshaw's weapon, along with the Winton, and get the other bellmen to help you. Escort Mr. Kemp to the next Sausalito ferry and see that he boards it. Remain on the wharf until the boat is at least halfway across the bay. Understood?"

Kemp was speedily conveyed from the ballroom and J.D. signaled for the musicians to take up their stringed instruments and attack Mozart once again. A low murmur among the astonished throng soon swelled into a cacophony of explosive chattering. Waiters began circulating with more champagne and hors' d'oeuvres, and within minutes, the party was once again in full swing. Meanwhile, Hopper and London stood to one side, scribbling furiously into their reporters' notebooks.

Amelia winced when J.D. grabbed her hand in an iron grip. "Come with me," he said. "I have a few things left to say to you."

"As do *I*!" Amelia retorted.

❦

J.D. and Amelia didn't exchange a word as they rode the elevator to the basement floor. Once inside J.D.'s office, he locked the door and gestured for her to take a seat. Amelia chose to remain standing, though, while J.D. sat in his leather chair.

"On the morning of the quake," he said, "here's what I saw. Your father began to put down a series of cards on the table, face up. I certainly was aware that he was on his way to a royal flush."

Amelia inhaled a deep breath and slowly took her seat. "What else did you see?"

"As you know, we were playing five-card stud. Drawing a royal flush is a one-in-a-million thing."

"But it happens."

"In all my years of gambling, I've seen only one."

"My father's."

"No. One other. I was barely eighteen."

She pointed to the five cards J.D. had put on the desk. "Well, now you've seen your second."

Without agreeing, he said, "As I told you, I saw your father begin to turn over the fifth card just as the first shock hit. I heard him shout 'Hot damn!' but I never clearly saw that last card." Amelia narrowed her gaze. "At least, that's what I've been telling myself for fifteen months."

She sank into the chair opposite J.D., silenced by the effect this equivocal revelation had on her. Finally, she replied, "Although what you've just said bolsters my case, I cannot tell you how disappointing it is that you knew much more about that night than you ever had the decency to tell me."

"I know," he said quietly. "And you have every right to feel betrayed. Why would your father have shouted 'Hot damn!' if his luck hadn't changed?"

"Exactly! Yet, the night you and I made love, J.D., I asked you if you'd seen the five cards. You said, 'I didn't see much of anything at that moment.'" She regarded him steadily across his desk. "You simply lied to me, J.D."

"You asked if I'd seen what your father held in his *hand*—and I hadn't. Not all five cards. Not clearly. I had only a second's glimpse of the four before he laid the last one on the table at the moment the rumbling began. As I said, the quake hit just as I heard him shout."

"That's splitting hairs, J.D. You gave no details of any of this on the night you shared my bed."

"It was *my* bed, if you'll recall. Sears and Roebuck's finest." When Amelia didn't smile, he continued somberly, "I know it sounds a very lame excuse at this juncture, but the night you and I became lovers, Amelia, I'd have said or done almost anything to keep you next to me."

Amelia pounded her gloved fist on his desk. "You prevaricated to get what you wanted! How will I ever know now, if you lied about this because you wanted *me*... or just my body... or you simply wanted to keep the hotel under your thumb?"

He paused. "I am an imperfect man, Amelia, as well as a man who loves you very much. Before I knew you, I fought and schemed and put up with your father's drinking and recklessness and Kemp's double-dealing for months. And when I survived that earthquake and escaped that fire and recovered from a punctured lung, I swore I would bring this hotel back to life one day. Your father's *possible* winning hand stood in the way in those chaotic days following the quake. Back then I wasn't really sure he'd actually drawn it and there was no proof of it anymore, so I pushed it out of my mind."

"You lied," she repeated softly. "You lied by omission. To *me*."

"I had just begun to fall in love with you and I didn't want the issue of who owned the hotel to stand between us. I was a very confused *hombre* the morning after we were together, believe me."

Amelia was torn between wanting to believe him and thinking about leopards never changing their spots. "But the hotel wasn't yours *or* my father's to play cards with in the first place," she reminded him. "It's always belonged to my mother and me. My lawsuit—which I lost because you secured a crooked judge to hear the case—made that very clear!"

"In the last months, I began to see all this from your point of view, but by then I'd invested every cent I had in this place. Fifteen months ago, though, I just didn't think of it in that light. And I didn't really know on the night we made love what I know now. I didn't really know *you*. I made love, but I didn't *know* love. Not like now."

"Oh please, J.D.!" she scoffed. "If I hadn't arrived toting a pistol just now, you'd be a married man. So much for loving me."

"We will get to that in a minute, but first I want to be clear on the ownership of the Bay View."

"Nothing will satisfy me but your admission that the hotel belonged to my mother and me when you played cards for it."

J.D. laughed harshly. "I admit that."

"You do?" she asked, the wind of fury taken out of her sails.

"Yes, I do. I see many things differently now."

"Such as?"

"Such as the importance of having at least one person in the world to whom I tell the unvarnished truth, as you call it."

It was Amelia's turn to laugh bitterly. "And now that you have—rather late in the game, I might add—it has not particularly endeared you to me, I'm afraid."

"Well, I've discovered that it will endear me to myself."

"Then tell me the truth about this. Why in the world did you and Kemp and my father ever go into business together to build the gambling club?"

J.D. clasped his hands on the desk and leaned toward her as if imparting a secret. Under his neatly trimmed black mustache his lips had a faint curve of amusement.

"I might as well confess that I've always lusted after this address."

Amelia set her lips in a hard line. He was obviously attempting to manipulate her with his charm.

"Why does that not surprise me?" Amelia said, but J.D. ignored her aside.

"When your grandfather became so ill, your father, for all intents and purposes, controlled the hotel. You were in Paris, and then your mother also decamped for France. Henry, of course, had no notion how to run the place successfully and was gambling away and drinking up his meager profits. I had limited funds, but the know-how to make the enterprise work. And I figured I could raise the needed funds through the kind of venture I knew best and save the place from complete ruination."

"By building a gambling club?"

"Yes, gambling. It had become my profession, like architecture is yours. Kemp could handily supply the lumber to build the annex at below cost. For about a half minute I thought, 'It's a match made in heaven.'"

"And then you three started goading each other into all those winner-take-all contests," Amelia said with disgust. "The first day I *met* you, you'd been playing cards for hours with the hotel as collateral."

"The trouble was," J.D. explained, "practically from the

first, each of us wanted to get rid of the other two and control the Bay View without partners. We were forever trying to snare each other in ridiculous all-night poker marathons."

"Did you, Kemp, or my father feel no remorse *whatsoever* for stealing the property you knew belonged to my mother and me?" she demanded.

J.D. paused and faintly shook his head. "Before I met you? No. I barely recalled I'd ever even known you, nor did I know about your close relationship with your grandfather. During his illness, your father stepped in to run the place, as tradition allowed. He challenged me to a game, betting the hotel in lieu of cash, and I won it. I'm ashamed to say, not one of us gave you or your mother a moment's thought."

"That's outrageous!"

J.D. nodded. "You've asked for the unvarnished truth, remember. But that was before I *knew* you, Amelia! Or thought about such inequities to women."

Ignoring this concession she demanded, "And what about the inequity of selling the sexual services of unwilling women in your club? How did you justify that?"

"We didn't sell their services."

"Oh please, J.D.!"

"We employed no prostitutes," he replied, his expression hardening.

"So much for telling one person the unvarnished truth," she snapped.

Just as she had, he slammed his fist on the desk. "But it's true! First of all, the women all worked for *me*, not for your father or Kemp. They were paid wages as housemaids and barmaids and nothing else."

"Well, what about Ling Lee?" she accused. "You never paid her—indirectly perhaps—for her 'services'?"

J.D. regarded her silently for a moment. Then he said, "You may consider me prejudiced against the women in your class, Amelia, but I think you should examine your own biases. I was Ling Lee's protector." For the next several minutes, he described Ling Lee's life as a woman kidnapped as a young girl in China and forced into prostitution. Amelia couldn't help but be skeptical.

"How did you even know her in the first place?"

"She came to me for help after she escaped the high-binders in China Alley, and I provided it."

"What about her little daughter? Isn't she yours?"

"No."

"No? Well, whose is she then?"

"Wing Lee is my father's child."

Amelia's mouth fell slightly ajar. "Your *father's*? But Wing Lee's mother was *your* lover!" Amelia scooped up the playing cards and her velvet purse from the desk. "Dear God, J.D., what else is there left to say?"

J.D.'s eyes narrowed and Amelia felt a pinprick of guilt, even though she believed *she* was clearly the injured party.

"Despite your prejudiced assumptions, Amelia, Ling Lee was *not* my lover," he said, "she was my *friend*. And the mother of my half sister. She was also the victim of my father's lust and the highbinders' greed. The only way I could protect her was to make the world think the worst of both of us."

"You were never…?"

"No. We were not intimate. Lovely as she was, it would have felt like incest to take my father's unwilling concubine to bed, especially when she had been dealt such great injustice by him."

Amelia felt like running from the room in shame and self-recrimination, but the sad, bitter expression on J.D.'s features kept her frozen in her seat. Fragments of past conversations flitted through her mind, statements by J.D. that carefully skirted the question of his purported romantic involvement with Ling Lee.

"Oh, J.D.," she murmured. "I am so, so sorry. Please forgive me. Why didn't I simply ask you outright about her, instead of imagining phantoms?"

"We both made some inaccurate assumptions, I think we could say," J.D. allowed.

"Poor, poor woman, to have been subjected to such a life. But then why did your mother join mine in supporting Miss Cameron's efforts to combat prostitution in Chinatown? Didn't she know her husband was one of the main perpetrators of those crimes against women?"

"No, she did not. My poor mother joined Donaldina Cameron's crusade solely at the *insistence* of my father. Big Jim figured her charitable work with Miss Cameron was the perfect foil while he invested behind-the-scenes in several lucrative brothels. He and Kemp earned much of their fortunes as silent partners in a number of bawdy houses in Chinatown. They did it quietly and anonymously while running other legitimate businesses. In the case of my father, his aboveboard enterprises, including his law firm, garnered him respect and admiration from the entire community."

"A member of the Committee of Fifty…" mused Amelia. "One of our revered City Fathers."

"As you may have deduced from your visit to China Alley that night, that brothel that he co-owned with a few fellow 'civic leaders' specializes in providing virgins and young boys to a certain clientele. It provided a lucrative opportunity, and my father—canny businessman that he is—seized it."

Amelia shook her head in amazement. "Who could

possibly dream that your father would be party to such a despicable thing?" Amelia wondered aloud. "*My* mother was always holding him up to Father as an example of a 'decent husband who provides for his family.'"

"In his younger years," J.D. continued, "this purportedly decent man had a certain, unquenchable taste for nubile, innocent girls, and how better to indulge in these proclivities than to secretly invest with their procurers? When Ling Lee realized she was going to have my father's baby, she begged Loy Chen, who was from her village in Canton, to help her escape from China Alley. Ling Lee's only hope was that I, as his son and with some small influence around San Francisco, would take pity on her—and I did. Loy and I took her to Donaldina Cameron's mission before her confinement."

"Then why did she come to live with you after she had her baby?"

"Because of religion."

"*What?* Unless I missed something, you're not a member of the faithful, J.D."

"Ling Lee had refused to become a Christian. She suddenly appeared at my door, extremely distraught. She felt she couldn't stay at Miss Cameron's Mission Home any longer and forsake her religion. She pleaded with me to take her in again. She said she wished to live as a Buddhist, in accordance with the teachings of her family, and respectably earn her way in the world."

"But why didn't she want her own child to live with her?"

"She had left Wing Lee at the Mission Home when she came to live under my protection because she knew it was the safest way to provide her some small education and to shield her from the slave merchants who might kidnap the little girl to recoup their investment in her escaped mother."

"Ah. Well, I can see why Miss Cameron might not completely understand the arrangement you two had."

"I'm sure she didn't. From then on, wherever I lived became Ling Lee's 'safe house,' a place where James Thayer and the Chinese brothel owners—whose property she was—couldn't get to her because they knew I wouldn't let them. My father guessed Ling Lee had told me the entire story of his raping her, so he simply shunned me as his wayward son."

"Didn't Kemp object to this charitable enterprise of yours?"

"Kemp never knew Ling Lee by sight during her China Alley days, so he assumed she was my concubine and never surmised the true situation between us. When he got drunk enough, he'd come in a secret door at the brothel, preferring to be entertained by young men rather than the women who worked there, so he never harassed Ling Lee, thank God. At the Bay View, all the Chinese workers dressed alike and *looked* alike to him."

"This is unbelievable!" Amelia exclaimed. "Did your father ever acknowledge Wing Lee as his child?"

"No. Even now, he tries to deny she's his daughter and says she's mine. He claims he couldn't identify the child's mother if she'd stood in front of him, and I believe him."

Amelia closed her eyes. "This is so ghastly. Poor little Wing."

"Wing's mother was a month shy of her seventeenth birthday by the time I took her in permanently," J.D. mused, as if to himself. "She taught me her skill on the abacus. She proposed that she earn her keep as my accountant." He gazed out the window with a faraway look. "Ling Lee had been abused by my father. I could only think of her and her daughter as my kin, and that's the way we lived."

"And so Wing Lee is your half sister by blood," repeated Amelia as the full impact of J.D.'s story began to sink in.

He pulled his gaze back from the window. "Ling visited her child often at the Mission Home. Until recently, Miss Cameron was deeply disappointed that her charge refused to convert to Christianity and held me somewhat responsible." J.D. laughed shortly. "Even more damning, Ling Lee lived under my roof without a chaperone."

"And the other Chinese women you hired?"

"They didn't seek Miss Cameron's help because, like Ling Lee, they wished to remain Buddhists. They merely wanted to earn their living honestly and send most of their money back to China where it was needed so badly, just for survival." J.D. had a ghost of a smile. "We ran our very own Buddhist underground railroad for a short time."

Amelia thought of Loy Chen hiding Shou Shou in the Fairmont's basement to keep the highbinders from finding her. He'd probably gotten the idea from his friends—Ling Lee and her protector.

"Why were you so noble when it came to these hapless souls?" Amelia heard the cynical note in her voice but couldn't hold anything back. "Why did you do all this if it only put you in danger and made you a pariah among your set?"

J.D. regarded her for a long time without speaking. Then he said, "Because I was a pariah myself. I know very well what it feels like to be an outcast."

Amelia looked at him sharply. "You? An outcast? You're a member of one of San Francisco's so-called First Families!"

"My mother has half Spanish blood—which means I'm a quarter Spanish. My father's bastard daughter is half Chinese. None of that is very acceptable among the lily-white Scots-Irish-Welsh establishment from around here, including my father. He wanted my mother's fortune but he didn't partic-ularly want *her*—or me." He scrutinized Amelia closely. "Be honest, Amelia. If you'd known all these sordid details I just told you, wouldn't you have found certain branches of my family tree slightly abhorrent?"

Amelia looked away and murmured, "Fifteen months ago? Yes, I believe I would have."

"And now?"

Silence filled the room. J.D. pointed at the tawny skin on his face. "Look carefully now, Amelia. How do you *truly* feel about aligning yourself with what my father so delicately calls 'a bunch of half-breeds'?"

Amelia slid her hand across the desk and touched the tips of his fingers with her own.

"I'll always remember the terrible sight of Ling Lee's arm poking out from the rubble," she said softly. "It haunts me to this day. And now that I know and love Loy and Shou Shou and still feel the loss of Foo, I… like you just said earlier… look at some things very differently now." She seized his hand and gave it a soft squeeze in what she prayed he'd take as a gesture of reconciliation. "After everything you and I have been through together, J.D., I'd be appalled if you'd abandoned that child."

She smiled at him faintly. "And now there's one more confession I think *I* should make."

Amelia was surprised to see the vulnerable expression that invaded J.D.'s eyes.

"And what confession might that be?" he asked.

CHAPTER 36

AMELIA LIGHTLY STROKED THE top of J.D.'s hand with her fingertips. "From the first day I saw you in Grandfather's old office, I admit it: I quite admired that tawny skin of yours. If that's thanks to your Spanish blood, I say 'Bravo'!"

J.D. remained silent, as if he were absorbing her last sentence, a word at a time. Then he said, "There's nothing like an earthquake to shake up a narrow view of the world, is there?"

"I suppose you're right," agreed Amelia. "But, there's something else I've never understood about your relationship with your family. I can see why you're estranged from your father, but why your mother? And also, why, then, was she here tonight?"

J.D. rose from his desk and poured them both a brandy from a decanter sitting on the sideboard. He handed her a snifter and then resumed his seat while he disclosed the chain of events in his childhood that led to his grandfather's suicide. He described his bitter feelings toward both parents, resentments that drove him to make his own way in the world as a virtual orphan, cutting himself off from any contact with his parents.

"Until lately, that is."

J.D. spoke briefly of his mother's virtual imprisonment

on Octavia Street and his determination to wean her from Dr. Ellers's medications and provide her a safe haven in his household. Tonight, he explained to Amelia, was his first attempt to show Consuela Reims-Diaz Thayer a world where she could become accepted for the person she truly was: a loving mother who needed no sedatives to dull her painful past.

"It has taken me a long time to begin to forgive Connie Thayer for standing silently by while her husband swindled her own father out of his last penny and made it appear to the old man that the loss of his money was his fault," said J.D. "I can never ride a ferry across San Francisco Bay without reliving the sight of my grandfather's body sinking slowly into the water, while all I could do was lean against the railing and watch him disappear."

"Oh, J.D...." Amelia felt a rush of tenderness, but before she could squeeze his hand again, he began to tap his fingers on the leather-topped desk.

"They didn't find him for weeks," he said quietly. "When the body finally washed up at the mouth of the Napa River, my father even refused to travel there to make an identification. My mother sent me with our livery driver to go claim it. Every time I think of it I—" His voice broke.

Amelia seized both his hands. "You were just a lad, J.D.! It must have been horrific."

He gazed at their entwined fingers as if he hardly saw them.

"My parents wore mourning clothes for months and pretended it was such an unexpected tragedy—and then the matter was never mentioned again. Mother knew perfectly well what her husband and Dr. Ellers had done to her own father," he said, looking away. "To this day, the sight of a black arm band makes me want to throttle the wearer. They were all such hypocrites!"

"I would imagine that your mother had few choices," she reminded him gently. "She was a woman without the support or training to do anything other than seek shelter and food from whomever would give it to her. The law of our land said it was perfectly acceptable for your father to take over managing her fortune. How could she have escaped his dominance? She had *you* to consider. In this country if a woman deserts her husband, the children of their marriage are then considered the property of their fathers." Amelia again folded her hands in her lap. "Rather like Mother and me when my father assumed control of Grandfather Hunter's estate without consulting either one of us."

J.D. caught her glance.

"I know this will infuriate you, my dear Amelia, but I've only just begun to understand the injustice of such traditions."

Abruptly changing the subject, he rose from behind the desk and opened the walk-in safe. "That brandy doesn't quite suit, do you think? Let us celebrate all this newfound wisdom with a glass of champagne, shall we?" he proposed, pulling out a plump wine bottle and an envelope that he slid into his inside jacket pocket.

"Veuve Clicquot?" she asked, her spirits beginning to rise for the first time in a week.

"Ah, *oui*," he replied in a terrible French accent. "Would you be so kind as to accompany me upstairs, mademoiselle?"

Amelia was torn between longing for J.D. to enfold her in his arms and wanting to ask him additional questions she needed answered before she succumbed to what she knew J.D. was planning. She remained rooted to the spot as she watched his back recede down the basement corridor, but at length she followed him from his office and caught with him at the elevator. Before he could press the button, she covered the brass plate with her hand.

"Not so fast, monsieur. We were speaking of women with few choices. What of poor Matilda Kemp now?"

"She and Emma want to move to Boston."

"Do they have the funds?"

"I have no idea. I hardly know the woman. Perhaps Emma has family money."

"That's rather cavalier of you, don't you think? Surely you can feel some sympathy for Matilda's public humiliation tonight—mostly caused by *you*?"

"Now, before you start flashing those accusing brown eyes at me, let me tell you that my assumed fiancée wasn't humiliated in the least by what happened tonight."

"Oh, come now—"

"As a matter of fact, she's very, very relieved that she and I are not to become husband and wife."

J.D. quickly recounted the relationship he unwittingly discovered between his intended bride and her school friend, Emma Stivers.

Amelia shook her head in disbelief. "You mean, they're…?"

"They are," J.D. replied with some amusement.

"Lovers?" Amelia blinked as she said the words aloud. Then she shook her head. "When I met Emma and Matilda at the Fairmont opening, I assumed they were just ordinary women friends, like Edith Pratt and me. Then, when I read the announcement that you were going to marry Miss Kemp… well, I was rather upset—"

"To put it mildly," J.D. interrupted, removing Amelia's hand from the elevator buttons and pushing the top one to summon the car. "You packed a pistol in that little handbag of yours, remember?"

Ignoring him, she continued, "When I read about your engagement, I thought Matilda a terrible snake-in-the-grass—and you as well!" Amelia paused. "The wrong assumption can certainly lead to the wrong conclusion, and ultimately, the wrong action."

"My, my, you *are* becoming wiser by the minute, Miss Bradshaw," he said with a chuckle. "Ah, here's the car. Let's first see how the party is progressing, shall we?"

Amelia nodded, grateful she could pursue a few more important questions that remained before inevitably heading to the penthouse.

"Thank you, George," J.D. said to the operator, and the three of them in the elevator traveled in silence until they reached the main floor.

The elevator doors parted, revealing the lobby packed with more guests than ever, drinking from champagne flutes and chatting in groups around the tables laden with trays of cheeses from the dairy farms north of the city and an elegant array of canapés. Amelia caught J.D.'s arm and pulled him slightly to one side near the protective fronds of several large pots of ferns and palm trees.

"What I still want to know, J.D., is *why* would you agree to this marriage if you knew neither you nor Matilda wanted to go through with it?"

"To protect you." He stashed the bottle of Veuve Clicquot in the nearest potted palm.

"There you go again!" she said, exasperated. "I've told Angus and I'll tell you, not every woman is asking for some hairy warrior to shield her from life's vagaries. I had finished the job here and told you in my letter that I was departing for France. You had no cause to 'protect' me. And you had a duty to tell me what was going on!"

"All right, Miss Woman Warrior, I *will* tell you what was going on. Kemp said that if he ever saw you and me together, he'd have you thrown overboard from the ferry on your way back to Oakland. Apparently, he thinks the purser—Harold Jasper, is it?—owes him a favor."

Amelia's eyes widened and she steadied herself on J.D.'s arm. "Oh my," she said in a small voice. She told him then of her glimpse of Dick Spitz on the ferry that very evening conferring with the purser. "Harold Jasper was Aunt Margaret's neighbor, for pity's sake! Kemp's tentacles reach everywhere."

"Good Christ, Amelia! Spitz was on the ferry *tonight*? The plan was to have you thrown from the boat and make it appear a suicide over your despair that I had married Kemp's daughter, leaving no strands that could be traced back to him."

"I thought it odd, seeing him on the *Berkeley*, but I suppose our group of four women on board made me unapproachable, thank goodness! Spitz vanished among the disembarking passengers and I didn't notice him again until I arrived in the ballroom."

"I'd learned from Kemp himself that Spitz, Kavanaugh, and Kelly have been assigned for a long time to keep an eye on you and, more recently, were ordered to do you harm."

"No wonder Joe Kavanaugh was furious when I discharged him."

Where were those rogues now, Amelia wondered, her apprehensive gaze darting around the crowded space. The small lobby orchestra had taken seats again and the leader raised his baton as dancers spontaneously began to sway to the lilting music, even though a larger ensemble was playing in the ballroom.

"As I told you when I posted the Pigatis on the roof,"

J.D. explained, "Kavanaugh figured that you and I—well, that we *might* be more than just client and architect. Kemp knew how my grandfather died and how I felt about it, so he figured that I'd take seriously his threats to have you thrown overboard—which I *did* take seriously, by the way," he added somberly. "So much was happening so quickly, I figured marrying Matilda was the best way to insure the safety of practically everyone involved—at least until I could get to France and explain to you what had happened."

"And bring Matilda with you as Mrs. Thayer?" she asked, incredulous. "I don't think I would have given you a very welcome reception, J.D."

"Matilda and I had already agreed that if we were forced to marry, we would, of course, never consummate it and would grant each other complete freedom."

"Perhaps so, but I still wouldn't have received you in Paris," Amelia insisted.

"Why ever not? Surely, you bluestockings don't hold with such outdated conventions as marriage, do you?"

"I don't hold with conventional marriages, no indeed."

"Ah… so are you referring, now, to shackles? Being ordered about by your lord-and-master? Things of that sort?"

"I don't know what you're talking about," she replied loftily, cocking her head to one side as if she were intently listening to the music.

"Angus said that's how you view matrimony. As a trap for hapless women. I figured that even if Matilda and I had to enter into this damnable alliance, a 'modern' woman like you wouldn't look particularly askance if I came calling in Paris—if, indeed, you wanted to see me again."

"Well, you miscalculated," declared Amelia, turning to meet his glance. "I have no wish to be shackled, but neither do I approve of marriage as a sham. I believe in an equal, *legal* union of hearts, if both parties respect each other—which is *rare*," she added pointedly.

"Well, that's a relief," he said, and Amelia could tell he was suppressing a smile. Then his expression grew grave. "Would you have wanted to see me again, even if your principles cautioned against it?"

She hesitated. This notorious gambler was clearly asking her to lay her cards on the table. *Well,* she thought, *in for a penny, in for a pound.* She was thoroughly tired of not speaking her mind.

"Yes," she admitted. "I would have wanted to see you again. Very much, actually."

"Ah ha!" J.D. said triumphantly.

"But before you count your chips, Señor Thayer, let me explain that I would probably have refused to see you, nevertheless."

"Why?" he demanded.

"Experience has shown me that most men feign approval of women working in the public sphere. Then, when it comes to the washing of socks and tending hearth and home, they do an about-face and wish their wives to be their servants."

"So I'm to be tarred by the brush of Monsieur Etienne Lamballe?"

Amelia shot him a sharp look.

"I think it's rather unfair of you to use what I told you about him against me," she said. "But no… not just him. Even dear, sweet Angus McClure is like that. I have no desire to be any man's servant. I wish to be a practicing architect. Someday, I might be willing to share my life with someone I love and have children with him, but only as an equal partner. And from what I've observed, the hallowed state of holy matrimony in our country—even in the twentieth century—generally rules that out."

"Well, now I have some questions for *you*," J.D. declared, leaning close enough for his breath to graze her cheek. "And the first one is… may I have this dance?"

He didn't wait for her answer before drawing her into his arms and gliding smoothly across the floor.

The two of them moved as easily as two riders on a tandem bicycle. "Didn't we dance together once in Cotillion?" she murmured.

J.D.'s expression reflected his amusement. "Why, I believe we did dance together at the Palace Hotel, wasn't it? Weren't you about nine-years-old, and I was fourteen? Our mothers' scheme, I would imagine."

The music swelled, and they easily wove their way through the crowded marble floor. Before Amelia realized it, however, J.D. had skillfully guided his partner in time to the music back in the direction of the bank of elevators, first pausing at the potted palm where he had sequestered his bottle of champagne. The next thing she knew, the doors in the middle opened and they glided into the brass car.

"Good evening again, George," J.D. said pleasantly, as if whisking his architect to his private suite was an everyday occurrence. "The penthouse, please."

CHAPTER 37

ONCE AGAIN THE THREE occupants in the Bay View elevator rode in silence, this time to the top of the hotel. Amelia and J.D. stood close to one another, but their arms didn't touch and it was all she could do to keep from reaching out to take J.D.'s hand.

"Evenin', sir, Miss Bradshaw," George said as they exited the car. "May I say congratulations to you both on the opening of the hotel. I know I speak for the entire staff when I say we're all quite happy the way things turned out."

Amelia felt her cheeks flood with color, but J.D. smiled broadly and replied, "Why thank you, George. I'm quite happy the way it turned out myself, aren't you, Amelia?"

But by this time, Amelia had propelled herself down the corridor and then froze in her tracks as she realized how quickly she'd been heading for the entrance to her former employer's private domain. She heard the elevator doors shut behind her and turned to face J. D., nearly running into his starched while shirtfront.

"Really, J.D.! Now my coming up here with you is going to be babbled about from the laundry room to the rooftop of this hotel! They'll never respect me now!"

"Of course they will! They already do. But my question to you is this: weren't we partners building this hotel? Didn't *I* treat you with respect?"

"On *this* hotel, yes. The building of it at least. But you showed me little respect when you didn't tell me the truth about what Kemp was up to these last few weeks."

J.D. pulled out his room key and opened the door to the owner's suite.

"It may be totally against your principles, but actually, I was being chivalrous," he replied, leading her by the hand into his inner sanctum where a few lamps around the well-appointed room glowed their welcome.

"I don't want chivalry," Amelia protested in exasperation, wondering whether she should sit on the love seat near the marble fireplace or remain standing. "I want always to be told the truth and I want equality."

J.D. set the champagne bottle on the mantel, shrugged off his dinner jacket, and folded it over a chair near a small desk positioned beneath a window that offered a sweeping view of the bay. Outside, the clear night sky sparkled with stars and moonlight illuminated the water all the way to Angel Island. "As I said before, I am an imperfect man, and perhaps a slow learner. I now stand corrected," he acknowledged. "Absolute truth and equality you shall have."

"It's not a commodity those of your gender find very easy to dispense," she replied.

"Oh, but I'm getting so much practice." He turned and pulled her close, smiling against her hair. "I'll tell you every single detail from now on. I'll happily marry you or *not* marry you—or be your permanent, adoring fiancé—whatever you like."

Amelia allowed his words to revolve in her mind. She had half a notion to seize his face in her hands and kiss him, but drew herself up short.

"Ah, so *half* ownership of the Bay View Hotel is better

than none, is that it?" she replied, tilting her head back to appraise him closely. "You admitted earlier that you've at least *considered* the possibility that my father won the place back, fair and square the morning of the quake. Now that I proved he did, you're making your best offer, is that it?"

J.D. released her from his embrace, drew a frustrated breath, and gripped the back of the chair where he'd laid his dinner jacket.

"Amelia... that card game was many moons ago. An earthquake and two fires ago. A *lifetime* ago. As I said before, I didn't even know who you really were until we began to work together. And you have to admit that we've *both* worked extraordinarily hard to build this hotel and the one Kemp's men blew up, wouldn't you say?"

"Yes," she admitted reluctantly, glad now they were alone where no one could overhear this prickly conversation.

"And I'd also ask you to remember that I borrowed and schemed and cadged the money required to rebuild on this land. I used my last gold bar to buy the lot from the old woman's estate. Then I spent every penny we found in the trunk on this place—I even agreed to buy those damned concrete cherubs from France you insisted upon! Don't you think I deserve to own half?"

A long silence grew between them. Finally, Amelia nodded slowly. "Yes. You deserve to own half. You earned it."

J.D. swiftly closed the gap between them and pulled her close again, a look of triumph gleaming in his dark eyes. "And what else do I deserve, since I love you madly, my dear?" he said with a chuckle.

She gazed up at him, playing for time. "I'm not sure."

He loves me...

And suddenly she knew now how much she'd grown to

love a man capable of change, capable of understanding the struggles that she too had endured in her three decades of life. But still there were questions…

Ignoring the comfort of his arms around her waist, she said, "I believe all the things you told me just now concerning the matters that have disturbed me from the time I'd returned from France, but it took you a very long time to reveal the truth of your side of things, J.D. How do I know you won't shade unpleasant realities in the future?"

"Because I won't," he said shortly, and she could tell he was torn between exasperation and feeling attacked. "Until a few minutes ago, you certainly weren't in any hurry to reveal to me that you possessed *all* the cards of your father's royal flush, or that you suspected that I'd abandoned a daughter to the Mission Home and slept with my father's concubine," he shot back. "I'd say much of your recent behavior constituted something close to fibbing—which is just what you're accusing me of doing."

Amelia had to admit to herself that she *had* fibbed—quite a lot, actually—saying she wouldn't be coming to the opening of the Bay View.

As if reading her mind, J.D. pressed her further. "And what about your letter summarily informing me that you were fleeing to France without a word to me in person, even when you'd planned to come here all along? Would you call that honest?"

Amelia felt a strong twinge of unadulterated guilt. "Well, it's not the most aboveboard thing I've ever done."

"Ah ha! There's no avoiding it, Amelia," J.D. said, chucking her playfully under the chin. "You also told several fibs by commission *and* omission. Which means that you're not perfect either."

Amelia took a few moments to mull over J.D.'s assertions.

"Yes," she replied finally, "I did exactly what you did. I shaded the truth for my own purposes and to protect my pride. And no. I'm not perfect either. Not by a long shot."

"Luckily I forgive you," he said, kissing her soundly on the nose. "And you, me?"

"Yes… but our agreement henceforth is to always put our cards on the table, yes?"

"Yes," he said solemnly.

"However, I do, truly, need to go to France to see my mother. I think she's lonely and sad and probably perilously close to penniless."

"Then I'll go with you," he proposed. "I'd love for you to show me Paris."

"And just who's going to run the Bay View?" she demanded, her glance sweeping the beautiful suite that had several duplicates throughout the hotel. "We've barely opened the doors. We have responsibilities, J.D.! And besides, what about Ezra Kemp? No one can afford to turn his back on *that* man for very long." She wagged a finger at him. "And by the way, I want my revolver returned to me, if you please. Who knows how long Kemp and those ruffians of his will pose a danger?"

"I'll give you back your gun only on the condition that you'll finally let me teach you how to aim it." Amelia gave him an annoyed look. "My bet is, Kemp'll have to lay low for a long while after tonight's display," J.D. predicted. "And besides, Spreckels's good government group is very interested in his involvement with prostitution, extortion, and God knows what else. The odds are very good he'll end up in jail."

"I don't know, J.D.…" she murmured doubtfully. "I certainly think it's wise if I avoid provoking Kemp by leaving immediately for France, but aren't you taking a big risk not to stay here, see to the hotel, and keep an eye on our nemesis?"

"Grady, Loy, and Shou Shou can run the back office. I'll put your friend Damler on the payroll to keep an eye on the legal side of matters, and we'll find someone to serve as a genial host for a few months."

Amelia looked around the room, feeling agitated by a keen sense of indecision.

"Ah… perhaps Miss Bradshaw isn't such a brazen hussy, after all," J.D. ventured slyly. "Perhaps she can't quite bring herself to travel openly with a man to whom she is not married or betrothed? Especially on a visit to her mother."

"That's not it!" snapped Amelia. "I'm thinking." And she began pacing in front of the fireplace.

"Has your reluctance to have me accompany you to Paris have anything to do with the dashing Monsieur Lamballe?" J.D. asked, surprising Amelia both by his question and the stern directness of his tone.

She felt a sudden, sweet compassion for this man who was so prepared to be slighted by the very people he cared for.

"Oh, J.D., no… *no*! If only you could have heard the speeches I have invented—in French—to let him know what I think of the man should I ever run into him again! I would dearly *love* to show you Paris… it's just that I'm worried that—"

She halted, mid-sentence, as J.D. reached into his inside jacket pocket and extracted an envelope.

"Well, then, if you're definitely going to France, there is no reason to delay. Here," he said, handing her the packet.

"What's this?" she asked, turning over the envelope in her hands. "I've seen those pictures of you in China Alley, if that's what's in here. Kemp was kind enough to send them to me a few days ago."

"Ah... so you *have* seen them."

"I saw the real thing, remember?

"You didn't see me photographed with the little boy..."

"It was obvious to me Kemp staged them."

"Go on then. Have a look at what's inside."

Puzzled, she unsealed the flap and withdrew a single sheet of paper. "What *is* it?" she asked, and then as she saw the envelope's contents, her hand began to tremble.

J.D. pointed to the paper she held in her hand. "Yes, it's the deed to the Bay View Hotel. Believe it or not, it survived the fire in a small iron box stashed inside your grandfather's big metal safe. Whether or not you'll do me the honor of taking me to Paris with you now, or marrying me, or living with me—or whatever the hell it is you prefer—I propose that *I* be the one to take a yearly percentage of the owner's net profits for the work I did building this place—and that *you* be the sole proprietor."

Amelia stared at J.D. and then at the document she held between her shaking fingers. He must have retrieved the deed when he went into the safe to get the bottle of champagne.

"Why are you doing this?" she asked quietly. "The place means as much to you now as it does to me."

J.D. gazed directly into her eyes and replied, "Because I want you to trust, for once in your life, that at least one man in your experience is capable of having your welfare at heart. I want you to trust *me*, and I need to prove to myself that I can trust *you*. It appears obvious that the only way we'll get beyond our past is if I give you this deed and we go into business together, so here it is."

Amelia's thumb rubbed against the raised, official seal on the yellowed document that contained her grandfather's familiar signature as the first owner of record.

"J.D., I'm… well, I'm stunned."

"And don't you dare ever say that I put shackles on women." He took a step closer, his arms at his sides.

"Never?"

"Never. Or that I like my women docile." He rested both his hands on her shoulders.

"I never said that."

"Well, then, prove it," he challenged. "Take the deed, agree to pay me a yearly percentage, and then ask me to make love to you tonight, Miss Bradshaw."

Amelia's eyes searched the fine, white scars above J.D.'s dark brows, wondering if she was risking the independence she'd worked so hard to achieve—or finally returning to the safe harbor that the Bay View Hotel had always represented in her life.

"*Well?*" he repeated.

Holding the deed in one hand and seizing one of his in her other, she led him past the wide doors and entered his bedroom, plush in its rich furnishings and bathed in soft lighting shed by amber-colored sconces on the wall.

"Why, Miss Bradshaw," J.D. said gesturing toward the bed, "you truly shock me."

"No I don't," she replied, pausing to shut the double doors. Turning toward him, she reverently set the deed on a nearby table and cupped his face in both her hands. For a few seconds, she ran the tips of her fingers over the raised scars on his forehead.

"James Diaz Thayer, you madman—I'll accept you *only* as a co-owner of this establishment—but I want you to put it in writing," she added with a smile that softened the seriousness of the moment.

"Yes, Amelia," J.D. replied with mock resignation.

"And will you do something else for me?" she asked sweetly, allowing her arms to fall to her side.

"What?" he replied warily.

"Please, *please*, open that bottle of champagne and then make love to me tonight."

Amelia could see the relief flooding his eyes now that all their cards were, indeed, finally on the table. It was his turn to raise his hands and frame her face as his lips brushed against hers.

"Your servant, *mademoiselle-signorina*," he murmured.

"No… my partner," she corrected in a whisper.

Before he could deepen their kiss, a sudden explosion of colored lights shone through the large windows facing the bay. Startled by the loud blasts, Amelia instinctively ducked her head beneath J.D.'s chin and felt his arms wrap protectively around her torso. They held on to each other, bracing for another blast.

"Oh good Lord!" she exclaimed.

"The fireworks!" they said simultaneously. They both inhaled a steadying breath and then melded together again, this time in a relieved embrace.

"For a second there, it sounded like that horrible dynamite the army used on the first day of the fire," Amelia murmured against his chest. "I'd totally forgotten that it's the Fourth of July."

She could only imagine the ohs and ahs bursting from the lips of their guests downstairs enjoying the pyrotechnics being launched from Fort Mason at the water's edge. They watched the breathtaking display until the last Roman candle burnt itself out and only the stars lit up the night sky.

J.D. put an arm around her shoulder and guided her toward the big brass bed on the far side of the room.

"My darling Miss Architect… now that we know we aren't being assaulted by explosions, quakes, or fire, may I have the pleasure of spending our second night together in Sears and Roebuck's finest?"

In answer, Amelia pressed herself against the full length of his tall frame. "Oh yes… but in future, can we not wait so long between such illicit assignations?"

"Illicit? Why, I intend to make an honest woman of you."

"Well, we'll see about that."

J.D. only smiled and swiftly began to divest her of her evening's finery, unfastening the tiny row of buttons marching down her back.

"Did you like my gown?" she asked, suddenly feeling bashful as the luxurious fabric fell away from her body.

"You wore this wickedly seductive dress on purpose, didn't you?" J.D. whispered into her ear, his breath hot against her skin as he began to pull pins from her upswept hairstyle. "You deliberately wanted me to know what I'd be missing if I married poor Matilda."

"What a mind reader you are," she marveled, luxuriating in the feeling of her long hair falling against her shoulders while a flood of confidence took hold at the thought of how she'd stood her ground until J.D. had satisfactorily explained his reasons for the planned nuptials that seemed a million years ago.

She slowly turned to face him clad in only her underclothes. J.D.'s gaze surveyed her from toes to forehead as he had that magical night in his makeshift living quarters in the basement.

"So beautiful, Miss Architect… so very lovely you are."

Then, without further comment, he leaned forward and kissed in turn the tops of each breast mounded above her corset's French lace trim.

"I thought you didn't wear these contraptions anymore?" he teased as his hands worked feverishly to free her from her laced stays.

"I don them only when I need to keep my guard up or my dress *on*—as I did tonight."

"Well, please observe, mademoiselle, how easily I have now breached your line of defense."

Amelia and J.D. both smiled as the last of her undergarments fell to the floor, joining her silk dress, shift, and petticoats in a frothy pile at their feet. J.D. had his dress shirt off in a trice.

"And now, Monsieur Thayer," she said, absorbing the sight of his beautiful bronze torso, "would you like me to show you what you *might* have missed?" she asked, boldly reaching for the button on his dress trousers.

"Yes, my dearest Amelia. Please do refresh my memory as to your wicked, wicked ways."

"And you'll do the same?" Amelia asked, smiling up at him.

"Of course," he replied. "Equality in all things, remember?"

CHAPTER 38

THE MANAGEMENT OF THE Bay View had provided complimentary hotel rooms for members of J.D.'s aborted wedding party, along with adjoining suites for Aunt Margaret, Miss Morgan, and Lacy, as well as Miss Cameron, Wing Lee, Connie Thayer, and Angus McClure. J.D. and Amelia were oblivious in their owner's suite to the merrymaking that lasted well into the wee hours before the guests finally repaired to their rooms.

The following morning, Loy Chen's crew whisked away the last remnants of the plentiful food and drink that had flowed throughout the celebration, while upstairs, J.D. and Amelia lazed in the big brass bed.

"I realize that I forgot to carry you over the threshold last night, but frankly, darling, I don't think I have the strength to do it this morning."

Yawning agreement, Amelia replied, "You'll have your chance to play the gallant when we stay on the Rue Jacob."

By lunchtime, the couple finally rose, dressed, and prepared to play host to their many guests.

"What will they think when I appear in this same gown," Amelia fretted as J.D. did up the buttons on her back.

"Here, put this to good use as a shawl," he offered, handing her a silk throw that had been spread upon a nearby chaise lounge.

Amelia's attire was utterly ignored when they appeared downstairs to find Matilda and Emma in a lather of anxiety in the private dining room where a late breakfast was being served.

"I didn't sleep a wink last night for thinking of what happened with my father last night," worried Matilda, who seemed on the verge of tears. She squeezed Emma's hand in an agitated grip. Loy and Shou Shou unobtrusively served cups of strong coffee while Matilda confided that the problems with her father were far less manageable than J.D. tended to portray them.

"You must *believe* me when I tell you that none of us is safe," she said. "My father has been humiliated in front of the very people whose high regard means everything to him."

"She's right," Emma chimed in. She turned to address Amelia who sat across from her at a table that had been polished to a dazzling sheen. "You probably know now, Miss Bradshaw, that Mr. Kemp threatened to have you killed if Mr. Thayer didn't do exactly as he wished. I don't want to frighten you, but that awful Jake Kelly said he meant it."

"And there's also Dick Spitz and that dreadful Joe Kavanaugh to consider," Matilda declared, "and who knows how many other ruffians my father employs? I know it sounds frightfully dramatic, but I tell you, he will stop at nothing to get even for this."

J.D. turned to Amelia. "All the more reason for you and me to go to France immediately and remove ourselves from harm's way for a while."

"What of poor Matilda and Emma?" Amelia demanded. "We can't just allow them to wander back to Mill Valley and take their chances that Kemp has come to his senses."

"You two can go to Boston, can't you, Emma?"

"My parents are saying now, they'll cut off my allowance

if I don't return to Massachusetts and live with them until I am married," she replied glumly.

"Well, then," J.D. said with a glance to Amelia as if to confirm her agreement, "you both can stay *here*." He smiled at Matilda. "You've kept your father's accounts. Why not keep ours and we'll find space somewhere in the hotel for you to use as a studio? And you, Emma. You're a lively young lady. How would you like to earn your keep by serving as one of the hotel's desk clerks, under the supervision of Grady, whom Amelia and I will promote to overall hotel manager?"

Emma and Matilda exchanged excited glances.

"What a splendid idea, J.D.!" Amelia exclaimed.

"And for everybody's safety, as of tomorrow, several Pigati cousins will serve as permanent security guards." Matilda and Emma exchanged relieved glances. "Loy and Shou Shou will be right here to help you two every step of the way, right, Loy?"

Loy smiled broadly, but before he could respond, a tremendous concussion resounded throughout the building.

Matilda emitted a high-pitched scream as the window on the far side of the room exploded, shattering glass in all directions.

"Can't be fireworks this time," muttered J.D. bolting in the direction of the deafening sounds.

Black smoke and debris immediately filled the air. Angus appeared at the dining room door, flanked by Aunt Margaret, the Misses Cameron, Morgan, Fiske, and Pratt, along with Wing Lee, who cried out in terror.

"Good God, what was *that*?" Angus shouted.

"It *can't* be the boilers again," cried Amelia, anguished. "I stood over the installer's shoulder for two entire days."

"It's not the boilers," yelled J.D., as a second explosion rent the air. "I think it's dynamite!"

"Holy Mother of God!" exclaimed Angus. "I believe you're right!" He ran to another of the shattered windows and peered through the smoke. "There's rubble all over the garden."

"You two come with me," J.D. directed the doctor and Edith, who was already dressed in her nurses uniform, ready to return to work at the Presidio hospital. "Loy, round up all the help you can get and order the staff to man the hoses down in the basement. Amelia, ring for the fire brigade and if you can't rouse them, run down to Powell Street."

"What about the guests?" Amelia asked, jumping to her feet and throwing her napkin into her chair. "Aunt Margaret, are you all right?"

"Yes, dear," her aunt said calmly. The older woman turned to J.D. "What can I do to help?" In a genuine crisis, Margaret Bradshaw Collins, survivor of Donner Pass, was unflappable.

"You, Miss Cameron, Miss Morgan, and Miss Fiske— would you all please station yourselves in the lobby and direct the guests safely out onto the Taylor Street side?" J.D. ordered. "I'm headed down Jackson."

"Certainly," Julia Morgan said, taking charge.

"J.D.!" Amelia cried. "Be careful! We don't know if all the dynamite's exploded."

Angus and J.D. dashed through the door that led to the kitchen, while Amelia herded the women toward the lobby.

"Emma and Matilda?"

"Y-yes?" they responded in unison.

Amelia figured it would be best to give the poor, frightened young women a task to keep them busy and their minds off the blast.

"Don't take the elevators, but go upstairs and knock on every single door on all three floors. Apologize for the inconvenience, but make sure everyone immediately leaves the hotel through the front entrance, away from the explosion. I'll telephone in the alarm."

Within minutes, Amelia was relieved to hear the clanging bells of the fire brigade coming up Jackson Street. She ran down the street's steep incline toward the rear of the hotel just as Angus and J.D. were struggling between them to drag a body away from the smoke and fire. Behind the trio followed Jake Kelly, leaning heavily on Edith's shoulder. The hulking figure stumbled through the smoke, howling in pain as blood spilled down his face. Dick Spitz trailing behind was in equally bad condition with burns on his face and forearms.

Amelia stood frozen in place, her hands on each side of her face, watching in horror as J.D. and Angus laid their disfigured victim in the street next to the fire engine.

Joe Kavanaugh no longer had any arms.

Nearby, the volunteers battled a small blaze in a storage area adjacent to J.D.'s office. A portion of one wall on the ground level had blown out, revealing sections of twisted steel and concrete, strong materials that had guaranteed that the rest of the building still stood solid as a rock.

Through the drifting haze, Amelia caught a glimpse of her grandfather's walk-in safe that appeared as impervious to natural and man-made disasters as ever. Beside the safe lay Ezra Kemp, a chunk of concrete the size of a wine barrel resting on his chest.

"Kemp's dead," announced J.D. "He must've been watching Kelly do the dirty work when a huge section of the wall blew out and fell on him."

"Oh my God," murmured Amelia, turning away from the carnage.

"The fools used dynamite as a weapon, but they didn't

know what they were doing," Angus declared with disgust. He swiftly removed his own shirt and ripped it in pieces to make tourniquets. Glaring at Spitz, he said, "You men are murderous idiots!"

He motioned for the wounded man to sit on the ground beside Jake Kelly while he and Edith attended to Kavanaugh, by far the more seriously wounded of the surviving trio. Joe's eyes were closed and his chest barely moved.

Meanwhile, the men of the local fire brigade hooked their equipment to the fire hydrants linked to the underground cistern that the Chinese workers had dug and soon doused what remained of the conflagration.

Trembling with relief that the flames had been handily extinguished, Amelia returned to Taylor Street to inform anxious friends and guests that the danger was past. She urged everyone to proceed to the main dining room where Shou Shou and the staff were quick to work up a luncheon buffet, dispensing plenty of coffee, tea, and reassurance that everything at the Bay View would soon return to normal.

When Matilda and Emma reappeared in the lobby, Amelia ushered them into a private suite off the front desk and had a tea tray brought in. J.D. soon joined them, his shirtfront stained with blood.

"I'm so sorry, Matilda," he said gravely, taking a seat next to the tall, ungainly young woman. "Your father was probably killed instantly when the dynamite went off. Joe Kavanaugh's wounds were severe and Dr. McClure couldn't stop the bleeding. He died ten minutes ago."

"And the others?" she said, barely above a whisper.

"Everyone at the hotel is fine," J.D. assured her. "Jake Kelly is missing most of his fingers and an ear, and Dick Spitz has burns all over his arms and chest. They both should survive, the doctor says, if gangrene doesn't set in. At any rate, I don't think we'll have much trouble from them anymore. Dr. McClure, Edith, and a policeman drove them to the Presidio in the Winton to be looked after at the army hospital, which is a lot more than they deserve. They'll both be under arrest before nightfall." He gave Matilda's shoulder a kindly squeeze. "The coroner's just come for your father. Amelia and I will help you see to final arrangements later."

Matilda began to sob quietly into her hands. "I'm just so thankful you all weren't *killed* and your beautiful hotel destroyed again!"

Amelia turned to enfold Matilda in her arms. "Well, thank heavens you and Miss Stivers are all right." She peered over Matilda's bowed head at Emma. "J.D. and I hope you both will remain here, starting today. Would you like to do that?"

"Most gratefully," replied Emma, wiping her eyes.

Julia, Lacy, Aunt Margaret, and Donaldina Cameron appeared at the door. Wing Lee clung to their skirts and gazed solemnly at Matilda, who continued to weep softly.

"Can we help in any way?" asked Julia with a look of concern.

Amelia rose from her chair and crossed to the door. "Yes, actually, you can. Would you kindly escort these poor dears into the dining room and let's all have some lunch."

Matilda and Emma were led out of the room. Amelia placed her hand lightly on Julia Morgan's tailored sleeve.

"Thank you, Julia. You are such a good friend."

"And you as well, my dear."

J.D. waited for everyone to leave and then shut the door behind them. Amelia hesitated and then held out her arms. He swiftly closed the distance between them and folded her in an embrace. His hair still smelled of smoke.

"I was afraid for a moment that the curse of Charlie

Hunter had struck again," he murmured against her neck, "and that *this* hotel too would come tumbling down."

Amelia held him to her for a long moment and then leaned back in his arms. How close she'd come in so many ways to losing him, this man she now knew as well as herself. Neither of them was perfect in this strange new world of men and women, working together for common goals. For a split second, she imagined them walking side-by-side along the broad stretch of sand that led toward the Golden Gate straits, each on a separate path, but close enough to hold hands.

"Oh no, darling" she protested with a broad smile. "Don't you realize that Charlie Hunter is your very own guardian angel?"

"How so?"

"Well, his granddaughter intends to reconfigure the dynamited area to add not only a sculpting studio for Matilda, but also a design studio off the basement where I can put my drafting board. Perhaps several drafting boards eventually— that is, if you agree."

An unmistakable look of triumph shone in J.D.'s eyes. "Oh, so it's definite? You and I are back in business together, are we? Does this also mean we're engaged now?"

"No." She smiled at him sweetly. "It means that, for a start, we're full partners. I propose that after we return from France, you run this hotel while I design the next one. We'll see how that suits us for a while. *Then*, perhaps, we could become engaged."

J.D. regarded her a moment. "Sounds perfectly reasonable. And one day, married?" He laughed and shook his head. "I never in my life thought I'd hear myself say something like this."

"Well, let's just say marriage is… within the realm of possibility."

"What about children?" J.D.'s bantering tone had vanished and Amelia detected wariness in his expression. "I want children with you, Amelia. I also never thought I'd say that to anyone, but I do. Are you willing?"

She met his unwavering glance. "Oh, I very much want to have children with you. It's the institution of marriage I find so—"

Before she could finish her sentence, he grasped her hand and held it against his chest. "It's all about building our confidence. What say you that we start with partnership—and advance from there? I'm betting that both of us might eventually come to appreciate the convention."

"Well, you were always a high-stakes gambler," she said, laughing.

What an incredible twenty-four hours this had been, Amelia mused, tilting her head for a brief kiss. She had thought last night she'd come to bid farewell to the Bay View forever, and here she was, walking along the plush carpeting of their beautiful, brand new building. Her mother would eventually come back from Paris and Aunt Margaret and Consuela would soon have hotel suites for themselves. The amazing turn of events had once again created a family-run hotel—just like the old Bay View.

Only better! a voice whispered in her ear.

Charlie Hunter would have been proud that she and J.D. had fulfilled his dream of helping to make San Francisco a port city that would vie with New York and New Orleans. She imagined that all the survivors of April 18, 1906, would always live in the shadow of what had happened here—and what could happen again. But in the strangest fashion, the disaster had also been a gift, showing at least two wounded hearts the crooked path to love and trust.

A few minutes later, Amelia and J.D. entered the dining room filled with paying guests sitting at tables covered in snowy linen and gleaming silverware. For a moment, they both stood at the door, absorbing the beauty and gaiety of the scene.

"We *did* it, J.D.," she murmured. "The Bay View has survived in a way neither of us could ever have imagined."

J.D. put an arm around her shoulder and drew her close. "And we did it together, my dear Amelia, even if we didn't win the race against the Fairmont. I think from here on out, the ghosts at our hotel will be friendly, don't you?"

She nodded and glanced around the elegant dining room. She could almost feel the spirits of her grandfather, her father, Ling Lee… and even dear Barbary. They'd never be alone here.

"May I tempt you with a bite of lunch?" she asked. "My spies tell me that the Bay View serves excellent cuisine, now that that hideous German chef is no more and Mrs. O'Neill permanently rules the kitchen."

"Your spies are correct—because *you* never rehired him," J.D. replied.

"That is true, and before I left on Tuesday, I begged Mrs. O'Neill never, *ever* to put sauerkraut on the menu again. I was delighted to learn that you'd already sent down the order. I *hate* the stuff!"

"Well, then, that does it!" J.D. said with a laugh. "We're obviously destined to marry one of these days. I cannot even abide the *smell* of sauerkraut!"

Amelia wanted to kiss him right then, but instead, gestured toward a north-facing window.

"Shall we take that table over there… the one with a view of the bay?"

Acknowledgments

Perhaps it's the result of my former life as a journalist, broadcast commentator, and observer of some extraordinary events in my own lifetime, but I have always been drawn to the notion of telling stories that take place on a "large stage" through the eyes of everyday witnesses and the documents they leave behind.

In *A Race to Splendor*, as in several of my historical novels, my fictional characters are distilled from the records of everyday people, struggling to survive epic trials and tribulations—and eventually triumphing.

That being said, the biggest thank you offered here in this Age of Digitalization is to the unsung librarians, archivists, cataloguers, and others who toil in the bowels of research libraries and historical societies around the globe.

In a work the length of *A Race to Splendor,* I specifically wish to pay tribute to the professionals who preserve documents, letters, diaries, photographs, architectural drawings, original images, and ephemera at such institutions as the Museum of the City of San Francisco and the San Francisco Main Library facility. I offer my undying gratitude for the existence of the Julia Morgan, Bernard Maybeck and other special collections at the Bancroft Library, in addition to the University's Environmental Design Archives—collections that form part of UC Berkeley's vast repository of research materials.

Thanks, too, are due the Julia Morgan and Sara Holmes

Boutelle collections at CalPoly in San Luis Obispo; the San Francisco Historical and California Historical societies; the Harriet Rochlin Collection of Material about Women Architects in the United States at the UCLA Library; and the special collections and newspaper archives both of publications in existence during the 1906-07 period of this historical novel, and the day-in-day-out archiving of current publications in paper files and now, on the Internet.

The Fairmont Hotel atop Nob Hill has an impressive collection of vintage photographs and historic material that they kindly shared with me during a meeting early in the writing of the book. The San Francisco-based firm of Page and Turnbull, specialists in architectural and conservation services for historic buildings, delved into Morgan's role in the 1906 restoration of the Fairmont during their work on the renovations of the hotel in the year 2000, and kindly recounted some of that adventure for me.

In preparing to write this novel, I read secondary sources too numerous to detail here, but the most noteworthy and readable for those wishing to learn more about Julia Morgan's body of work as well as events surrounding the cataclysmic 1906 San Francisco earthquake and fire include: *Julia Morgan: Architect of Beauty* by Mark Wilson (2007); *Julia Morgan, Architect* by Sara Holmes Boutelle (1988; paperback 1995); and *Julia Morgan, Architect of Dreams,* by Ginger Wadsworth (1990; part of a series of biographies for young readers).

Perhaps the most riveting nonfiction account of the early twentieth century catastrophe is to be found in Gladys C. Hansen's *Denial of Disaster: The Untold Story and Photographs of the San Francisco Earthquake of 1906* (1989). Born some twenty years after the temblor, Hansen became the City's expert on both the quake and the subsequent firestorm.

Even after her retirement as a City librarian, she made it her mission to account fully for the number of people killed, since a combination of bad record keeping and governmental cover-up had held the official figure at 478.

Not unlike the aftermath of Hurricane Katrina, the quake in Haiti, and the BP oil disaster, the "official" numbers surrounding the event continue to change. As of this writing, the confirmed death toll of the San Francisco catastrophe has passed five thousand and continues to rise. Numbers of Chinese killed were noted at about a dozen in the official reports of the day. Five hundred Chinese dead is the more likely number. The fires lasted three full days and destroyed 2,831 acres of the city. Thirty schools, eighty churches, and four hundred city blocks were consumed, leaving more than 250,000 of the city's 400,000 people homeless.

Thus it is that I wish to extend my profound thanks to Gladys Hansen and others who have produced some of these statistics by searching coroner's, medical, and Army records, church journals, city directories, old maps, and letters from mourning relatives about family members who were never heard from again after April 18, 1906. Each year on the anniversary of the shaker that hit at 5:12 that cloudless spring morning, we are given a more accurate assessment of the extent of this watershed event in American history.

On a personal note, many friends and members of my family supported what turned out to be my decade-long effort to research, write, and bring this book to publication. Local historian Daniel Bacon, his book *Walking San Francisco on the Barbary Coast Trail* (www.barbarycoasttrail.org), and his fabulous "live" walking tours of areas devastated in 1906 were invaluable resources. I deeply appreciate his encouragement and friendship to a relative newcomer to the City by the Bay. Authors Diana Dempsey, Michael Llewellyn, Mary Jo Putney, Gloria Dale Skinner, Bardet Wardell, and newsletter editor Diane Barr, along with cookbook author Diane Worthington and edible landscape expert (and my niece), Alison Harris, read various drafts and/or maintained over a long period both their enthusiasm and belief that this book would find a happy publishing home—and it did.

Part of the credit for this goes to editorial specialist Jennifer Jahner, who took pity on me at one difficult point in the writing of the manuscript and helped me find the correct spine of the story. My agent Celeste Fine of Folio Literary Management guided the project to CEO Dominique Raccah's Sourcebooks and all three women have my deepest gratitude.

A special debt of thanksgiving goes to my revered editor at Sourcebooks and its Landmark division, Deb Werksmen, and her fabulous colleagues, Dawn Pope, Greg Avila, Susie Benton, Sarah Ryan, Skye Agnew, and others on the Sourcebooks team. Deb's astute editorial judgment, her suggestions on the final draft, along with her inborn courtesy and kindness, make her the treasure she is, both as an acquiring editor and the person responsible for inspiring this author across the finish line.

Joy McCullough Ware not only merits one of the dedications in this book, but also a hearty sisterly hug for serving as a second set of eyes, scanning the typeset manuscript for "nonsensicals" and typos. Any remaining errors or omissions are clearly the author's.

Tony Cook, my husband of more than three decades—and a "recovering" journalist himself—extended his keen editorial sensibilities and sound judgment when it came navigating the publishing world.

My son, Jamie, and his wonderful new bride Teal, as well as friends on Facebook, were great sounding boards about cover design and "test marketing" among a younger generation of readers. A vintage photograph of the post quake, burnt-out hulk of the Fairmont Hotel, given me by Jamie one Christmas, sat by my computer for years as inspiration to tell this story.

As with every historical novel I've written, I keep asking the question: "What were the *women* doing in history?"

The person I must thank for originally posing this key query is a celebrated academic I once heard give a lecture at the Huntington Library in San Marino, California, where I've held a Readership in Eighteenth c. British-American History.

At one point in Professor Gerda Lerner's presentation, the author of *The Majority Finds Its Past: Placing Women in History* suddenly pounded the podium and—I'm paraphrasing some twenty years later—passionately declared to an audience of visiting and resident scholars, "Half of human history has yet to be written because the lives of women weren't properly chronicled by historians; and the half of human history that *has* been written is woefully *inaccurate* because the lives of women weren't properly chronicled…[she paused, and then added] …by (mostly) male historians."

I emerged from that lecture with my hair on fire! From that moment to this, tracking down "What were the *women* doing?" in any age became my quest.

In my six works of historical fiction—and certainly in *A Race to Splendor*—I have chosen to do some "chronicling" of my own.

So thank you, dear Dr. Lerner. And thanks to Michael Llewellyn and Tom Rotella for brainstorming with me to come up with the perfect title…

Ciji Ware
Sausalito, California

Ciji Ware enjoys hearing from readers at www.cijiware.com

Reading Group Guide

1. A number of recent natural disasters have taken place on or near America's shores: Hurricane Katrina in 2005, the BP oil spill in the Gulf of Mexico in 2010, and the massive earthquake in Haiti in 2010. Are these "regional" events, or do they impact the United States as a whole? In what ways did the 1906 San Francisco earthquake and firestorm impact the nation? What lessons did the country as a whole learn? What aspects were shunted aside?

2. How did California change as a result of the devastation of four hundred city blocks and some 250,000 people being made homeless in the space of less than forty-five seconds? What building practices and safety codes eventually resulted from this catastrophe? How prepared do you think your locality is in the event of a natural disaster?

3. What effects do such natural disasters as San Francisco's 1906 quake or events like the attacks on the World Trade Center in New York on September 11, 2001 have on the national psyche? Was the 1906 San Francisco earthquake a "first" for such a major event rattling the confidence of the entire nation?

4. The Chinese Exclusion Act was a United States federal law signed by President Chester A. Arthur on May 8, 1882. The measure allowed Congress subsequently to prevent any more Chinese immigrating to the United States. This ban against a specific nationality was intended to last ten years and wasn't repealed until 1943. In what ways was the treatment of the Chinese in the United States—and in San Francisco, particularly—similar to the Jim Crow laws and treatment of African-Americans in the South? In what ways was it different?

5. Chinese women were bought and sold in San Francisco as late as the early twentieth century. In the novel, Loy Chen has rescued Shou Shou from the "highbinders" who have forced her into prostitution in San Francisco's Chinatown. As a young girl, Amelia was forbidden to go near the district, and she later admits to her own prejudices against that race. How does the natural disaster affect her and other characters' perception of her Chinese neighbors? How aware were you that such Chinese slavery existed in the United States into the last century?

6. What does the novel reveal about the role played by some supposedly esteemed "city fathers" in the practices of gambling and prostitution? What conflicts and challenges face entrepreneurs, even today, who do not subscribe to such corrupt and illegal practices, yet, like J.D. Thayer, must operate within the stranglehold of local "power players?"

For additional reading group discussion questions, please visit www. sourcebooks.com/readingguides.

About the Author

Ciji Ware has been an Emmy-award winning television producer, reporter, writer, and radio host. A Harvard graduate, she has written numerous fiction and non-fiction books, including the award-winning *Island of the Swans*. When she's not writing, Ciji is a Scottish history and dancing aficionado. She and her husband live in the San Francisco Bay Area.

Island of the Swans
CIJI WARE

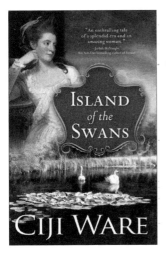

A passionate, flamboyant Duchess and a cruel twist of fate...

Jane Maxwell, the fourth Duchess of Gordon, was one of the most influential women of her time—a patroness of poet Robert Burns, advisor to King George and friend to Queen Charlotte, the mastermind behind her husband's political success, and a rival of Georgiana, Duchess of Devonshire. Spirited and charming, Jane captured the heart of her childhood sweetheart, Thomas Fraser, while her beauty caught the eye of his rival, Alexander, Duke of Gordon. Torn between duty and love, Jane is thrust into a lifelong love triangle that would threaten to destroy all that she holds dear...

"Ware's meticulous research and first class talent for invention reclaims a woman lost to history, a powerful and controversial figure in her day, all but unknown in ours." —*Publishers Weekly*

"An enthralling tale of a splendid era and an amazing woman." —Judith McNaught, *New York Times* bestselling author of *Paradise*

"A deep, complex novel exploring love, betrayal, healing, and renewal in the human heart." —*Affaire de Coeur*

$15.99 U.S./$18.99 CAN/£8.99 UK ~ 978-1-4022-2268-9

Wicked Company

CIJI WARE

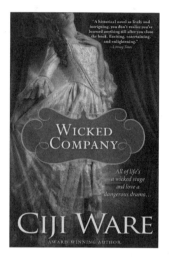

All of life's a wicked stage and love a dangerous drama...

In 18th-century London the glamorous Drury lane and Covent Garden theatres were all the rage, beckoning every young actor, actress, and playwright with the lure of fame and fortune. But competition and back-biting left aspiring playwrights with their work stolen, profits withheld, and reputations on the line. In this exciting and cutthroat world, Sophie McGann, a young woman with a talent for writing and an ambition to see her work performed, could rise to glory, or could lose all in the blink of an eye...

In Ciji Ware's signature style, real-life characters create the backdrop for a portrait of a glittering era, a love story, and a compelling glimpse into what life was like for an independent-minded woman in an emphatically man's world.

"A fascinating portrayal of London's theatrical milieu... Ware again proves she can intertwine fact and fiction to create an entertaining and harmonious whole." —*Publishers Weekly*

"So lively and intriguing, you don't realize you've learned anything till after you close the book. Exciting, entertaining, and enlightening." —*Literary Times*

$16.99 U.S./$19.99 CAN/£11.99 UK ~ 978-1-4022-2271-9